Jan lives in Orpington, Kent with her partner, Austin and her rescue dog, Fleur.

An avid reader, she has been inspired by a wide range of authors over the years and has now crafted her own novel. *The Girl Who Dressed Like a Boy* is to be the first of a trilogy.

For my daughter, Victoria and Austin, who always believed in me.

Jan Hale

THE GIRL WHO DRESSED LIKE A BOY

Maiden, Mother, Crone

AUSTIN MACAULEY PUBLISHERS™

LONDON * CAMBRIDGE * NEW YORK * SHARJAH

A CIP catalogue record for this title is available from the British Library.

ISBN 9781398486829 (Paperback)
ISBN 9781398486836 (Hardback)
ISBN 9781398486843 (ePub e-book)

www.austinmacauley.com

First Published 2023
Austin Macauley Publishers Ltd®
1 Canada Square
Canary Wharf
London
E14 5AA

To all the brilliant authors I have read over the years. My enduring thanks.

Table of Contents

Chapter 1
The End and the Beginning

How long the battle had raged, no one was sure, but the result was a disaster for the small East Anglian village. The grizzled old warrior stood panting, surveying what was left. He was a formidable sight, his face grim, his one good eye squinting through the smoke that rose from the burning homes of his friends. He was covered in blood, some his, but most Saxon. It had been a bad summer for East Anglia, the Saxon raids becoming more and more frequent and brutal. None of the chieftains from other villages could spare help for the weak.

Leith had seen many summers of combat but this was by far the worst he had encountered. There were no signs of life left in the village. He himself had been knocked unconscious and left for dead. A few dogs and chickens scurried amongst the carnage. There was nothing left here, the best he could do was to gather up what he could and leave to try and find a place in another village. His head ached and the glancing blow he had taken from the axe had ended in his shoulder, which meant his left arm was good for nothing.

He started checking the fallen to make sure that they were dead. Even in his sad state, he was unwilling to leave anyone alone and wounded in this dead village. As he entered one of the smouldering huts, he called out, "Anyone here?" Much to his surprise, he got an answer.

"Help me please!" a woman's voice begged. As Leith's eyes adjusted to the gloom, he could make out a fallen Saxon and pinned beneath him, he could just about make out some movement. He went forward and heaved the dead body off the girl below. The girl struggled to her feet.

"Kalea!" Leith cried in surprise as the girl flung herself at him. He hugged her with his good arm.

"Leith! I am so glad to see you." She sobbed with relief. The two of them helped each other out of the hut. Kalea sobbed again as she blinked against the bright light and then stood stunned at the sight of her ravaged home. Leith looked at her. Her gown was torn, her face dirty and she too was covered in blood, but not her own.

"We haven't got much time," he told her. He could not afford the luxury of allowing her to break down. "We need to be away from here." Kalea looked at him and nodded. "Gather what you can." She needed no more instructions and darted straight back inside the hut. Leith walked to another hut and salvaged a good blanket and some food. He went back to his own home and took out a clean shirt and his good heavy cloak. There was nothing else worth taking. When he came out, Kalea was waiting for him. She too held a pack.

"Now, which way to go?" Leith said quietly as he stood by her. Kalea brushed her long hair from her face.

"South," she said positively. "There are more towns to the south. Also, King Arthur is south and he needs to know what happened here and how his people are faring."

"What people?" Leith hissed sarcastically. "We're all that's left here."

"I know, Leith." Kalea sighed. "But I still think he should know. Besides, not so very far from here is a place where the horses go when they are left to graze alone. I am hoping that a few managed to escape and at least we can ride rather than walk."

Leith grunted. He was far to weary to argue. In fact, all he wanted to do was lie down and sleep. "Lead on," he said gruffly and then followed Kalea as she walked slowly away.

They had been walking for at least an hour when Kalea halted. Leith nearly walked into her. The effort of putting one foot in front of another was enough for him. He looked up hoping that he wouldn't have to fight again. He was lucky, Kalea had spotted some horses. Some of them had definitely belonged to the village, he recognised some of the ponies.

"Wait here," she instructed. Leith sunk to the ground with a groan of relief as Kalea walked quietly towards the horses. It seemed that she had not been gone a minute, although Leith knew that it would have taken her considerably longer. She returned leading four horses. Leith smiled at her, she was a strong one this one and had been clever enough to bring rope.

"Can you get on?" she asked bringing one mount close enough to him. Leith struggled to his feet and she did her best to help him and hold onto the horse that clearly didn't like the smell of gore on him. After a colossal effort, Leith was on board and Kalea passed him up his bundle. Then she lightly vaulted onto the back on another and taking the ropes led all three horses.

The sun was beginning to set when she finally stopped. Leith had been in half doze and immediately became alert. There in front of them was a rough shelter. A shepherds hut. He half slid and half fell from his mount. "I didn't know this was here," he said.

"Well, you wouldn't, would you," Kalea answered briskly. "You do warrior things." He grinned in return.

Kalea tied the horses to a tree and then grabbing her bundle, went in. Leith followed her. Kalea rooted around in the shelter and came up with a candle stub. Dipping in the pocket of her dress, she bought out a flint and soon had the flame going. Leith sank wearily on the make shift crib. Neither felt inclined to talk. Kalea gathered some kindling and soon had a fire going in the hearth. She ducked out of the low shelter and went to the horses. Soon, she had watered them from the nearby stream and hobbled them with ropes she had used as halters. Once more she returned to the hut. On entering, she saw that Leith was asleep. Slumped on his side.

By the light of the candle, she found an old cooking pot which had been left by previous occupants and went down to the stream to fill it with water. Once she put it on the fire, she opened her bundle and took out a rough sliver of soap and the only other dress she owned and went to wash in the stream. The water was cold but she sat in it and washed herself thoroughly and struggled to get into her clean dress. She had nothing to dry herself on and the cloth kept sticking to her. On her way back, she gathered more firewood.

Once back inside, she poured some warm water into a beaker and tearing some off some of the cleaner material of her spoiled dress, she went to Leith. Very gently, she washed the blood from his face. Leith shot awake and after much protesting, was persuaded to strip to the waist so she could clean and minister to him. She grimaced when she saw the wound on his shoulder. Quickly, she went back to her bundle and picked out a small bag. In it were numerous healing herbs and she sprinkled some onto the wound and using more of the same clean cloth, made a bandage and tied it firmly on.

"There's a clean shirt in my pack, girl," Leith said gruffly. Kalea fetched it for him and with help, he managed to get it on. "I'm not being much help to you, am I?" he muttered. Kalea met his eye.

"You're alive. I couldn't have done this alone." She left him for a moment and returned with a beaker of clear water to which she added some herbs before giving it to him.

"What's that?" he asked.

"It will help you feel better," she said. He downed it in one and shuddered. Kalea grinned. "You made more fuss over that than you did with that shoulder." Even Leith had to grin sheepishly at that. Kalea then handed him some bread and cheese. The sun was down and darkness stole around the hut. "Do you think we will be safe here?" she asked between mouthfuls.

Leith shrugged. "I guess. Safe as anywhere. I doubt the Saxons will be back this way just yet. They had everything there was to be had from the village. They'll likely move on to the next one." Kalea shuddered.

Leith looked at the girl in the firelight. She was one of the prettiest girls in the village. Daughter of another old warrior. One that had died in this battle. She was holding together well. Her father had been a dear friend. He had lost two sons and his wife to the Saxon raiders. Kalea was his youngest and only daughter and he had doted on her, but often said she should have been born a boy. She had always been headstrong and could see no reason why she should not do as her brothers did. And yet curiously she was very feminine to look at. Her hair was long and glossy. A rich red-brown and her eyes were as dark as night. She was slim and lithe limbed and her father had been hoping for a good match for her. There was no shortage of interest from the young bloods in the village. The raiders had put a hold on that. Once his sons were dead, the old man was reluctant to let go of his last living child. He wondered how old she was. She could be anywhere between 15 and 18 summers. Kalea looked up and caught him watching her.

"What are you thinking?" she asked.

"I was wondering how old you are."

Kalea shrugged. "Old enough I guess."

Leith smiled. "And how did you manage to survive the raid?"

"Luck. Pure luck." She sighed. "I didn't see much of the raid and had picked up the skinning knife when this huge hulk of a Saxon burst in and tried to rape me. In the struggle, I stabbed him. The only problem was that he fell on top of me. I fell back and must have hit my head. The next thing I know is I'm alone, everything's quiet and I just couldn't get out. I'm glad you found me. I could still be there. How about you?"

Leith thought. "Well, the blow from the axe felled me. I guess they thought I was dead. At least, I managed to take a few with me," he added bitterly. "Kalea, you father fought well."

"I know he did. He always would." And with that she began to weep.

"Come over here child," Leith spoke softly. "I may be an old man, but I still have one good arm to comfort you." She came and he held her as she sobbed against his chest. He made soothing noises and stroked her as you would a child but said nothing further. Grief was better released than harboured. It was a long time before she stopped crying and looking at her face, he could see she was exhausted.

"Let's try and get some sleep," he said. "Tomorrow, we will ride for Arthur's stronghold. At least there, we will be safe." *I hope*, he added to himself. She nodded and took a blanket from her pack and much to his surprise lay down on the cot next to him. Leith understood. He was her last living link with the village and she wanted to be close to him. He threw a blanket over himself and lay down close to her. They were both too weary to stay awake long.

Leith woke first the next morning. He eased himself free from Kalea. He was surprised how well he felt. After all, the battle had been a tough one and aside from the throbbing pain in his shoulder and a stiffness that he knew was from the exertion of wielding a sword, he felt not too bad at all. Kalea woke with a start.

"There, there child," Leith spoke softly. "We are still safe." Her face was white and her eyes were wide as remembrance of the past day came back. She shook herself.

"I had hoped it was a dream," she said quietly. She rose allowing Leith room to swing himself upright too. "Let me look at that shoulder of yours," she said firmly. Leith wasn't about to argue that it could wait. It would be quicker to let her have her way than to argue. With some help, he stripped off his shirt and she quickly unbound the bandage. "It looks better than it did yesterday." She studied it closely. Once again, she got the bag of herbs and this time took a pot from it. Wiping the old herbs from the wound, which made him wince, she applied the cream to it and rebandaged it. "You really need a wise woman to look at that."

"It will do." Leith shrugged himself back into his shirt. She handed him some leaves. "And what am I supposed to do with these?"

"Chew them," she said with a grin. "They may not taste that pleasant but they will help you with the pain." Leith stuffed them in his mouth and began to chew, almost at once, his face showed his disgust. "Don't you dare spit those out. It took me ages to find the good ones."

"I wish you hadn't," Leith said grumpily still chewing as instructed. Kalea left the hut and returned with the cooking pot full of water. She handed him a beaker and he was grateful to wash the awful taste out of his mouth. They shared some more bread and then busied themselves for leaving. With Kalea's help, Leith managed to rig up some kind of saddlebag and once this was completed, they loaded up the horses. Kalea had insisted on taking the cooking pot and the beakers from the hut. The shelter had yielded a wealth of goodies, items that under other circumstances would be considered useless. Twine, stubs of candles, a couple of old mats and a skinning knife. When at last, they were ready to set off. Kalea turned in the direction of the village.

"Kalea. There is nothing for us back there," Leith said sternly.

"I wasn't thinking of going home," she replied. "I was going back to see if I could find some more horse. They might have gathered there."

"What do we want with more horses?" he demanded. "We've got more than we can ride here."

Kalea was not to be swayed. "Well, I don't know about you, but I have no money and we can use them to buy what we need." Leith lifted his eyebrows. There was a good head on this girl's shoulders.

"Sound judgement girl. Lead on."

The journey did yield results. Quite a few of the horses had escaped the raiders and returned to the glade they knew so well. Even better, was that two of them were warhorses and were still kitted out with bridles and saddles. The horses were easy to catch, in fact they seemed quite relieved to see them. It certainly made life easier, riding with a proper saddle and bridle. Kalea had only wanted these two, but the others seemed to want to come too. They burst out laughing when they turned and found they had a whole herd following them.

They journeyed on. Not pressing too hard. Neither of them had anything to hurry for. That night they made camp in the open. The bread was getting hard but they were hungry enough to eat it. Kalea had managed to pick up some apples and they reckoned they had had a feast when they laid down to sleep.

It was about midday when they finally reached the next village. The warriors who were armed and ready for battle, met them in force. The chieftain recognised Leith and hailed him.

"Welcome Leith. How fares your village?"

"We are our village," came Leith's grim-faced reply.

The chieftain, Simon, face registered horror and shock. "You are most welcome here," Simon managed to say after he recovered from the shock. "Leave the horses, they will be seen too."

"We have need of a wise woman too," Kalea stated in loud voice. All the men turned to look at Leith's companion. She sat firm and resolute.

"Hush woman," Leith growled. "It's no more than a scratch."

"It looked more than a scratch to me!" she answered sullenly.

Simon grinned. "Have no fear young lady. We shall get you both fed and while you are eating, I will send for the wise woman."

"My thanks," said Kalea as she slid from the saddle. Leith joined her and they relinquished their small bundle of possessions and followed Simon into the main hall. Inside all was welcoming. A fire blazed cheerily in the hearth and the place was clean and tidy. Simon motioned for them to be seated and beckoned for the serving women to fetch food and drink. They both sank gratefully on the benches.

"So, my friend," Simon spoke gently, "we meet under less than pleasant circumstances. We ourselves were attacked yesterday. I lost few men though. We were ready for them." His face was grim. "Tell me what became of your village."

"We were attacked at dawn. The second time in as many days. We did not have time to regroup before the next attack came. We lost many a good soul in the first attack and the rest fell the second day."

"How did you and your young companion here, come to survive?" asked one of Simon's warriors, who had come to join them. Leith took the offered cup of mead and took a long draught. Then he began by introducing Kalea. "This young woman here is Kalea, daughter of Ren." Ren need no introductions. Those who had not fought by his side, had heard of this warrior. "I found her in her home. It seems that some lug of a Saxon had decided to rape her and she had skewered him through the heart with a skinning knife." The men now looked at Kalea in a new light. "Unfortunately for her, he fell on her. He was such a big ox that he knocked her out and the pair were left for dead. I, myself, was in the heat of battle when I took a blow from an axe, it knocked me out cold. So, I too, was left for dead." A murmur of conversation broke out. "When I came to, the raiders had gone and nothing was left bar a few ponies that had fled the village."

Simon sighed. "Hard times old friend. You are most welcome to make your home with us. Kalea, if you go with the women, they will see to your needs." Kalea rose but stopped when an older woman entered.

"You sent for me," she stated.

"Ah, yes, Sara," Simon said getting to his feet. "This is our wise woman Leith. Sara, Leith has need of your services."

Leith looked at Kalea who was watching him expectantly. He sighed heavily. "I fear you are wasting your time. It is no more than a scratch but my young friend here says I must see you." Sara turned to look at Kalea who gave a nervous smile.

"Let me be the judge of that." The tone of her voice left no doubt that she expected him to do as he was told. "Now where is it you are hurting?" With an apologetic smile at the men round him, Leith tried to struggle out of his shirt and failed. Kalea came forward and eased it over his head. Sara motioned her clear and removed the bandage. She peered closely at the wound. "Who has treated this wound before me?" she asked as Leith winced at her touch.

"Young Kalea," he hissed between gritted teeth as her probing went deeper. Once again, Sara turned her attention to Kalea. "You have done well child."

"Thank you, Mother," Kalea said respectfully.

"You have knowledge of the healing ways?" she asked turning her attention back to Leith's shoulder.

"Only a little that our wise woman taught me. I used to help her gather her herbs. Not enough to be of great use though."

"Come closer child and watch." Kalea moved closer and watched as Sara delved her fingers into the wound to see how deep and what damage there was. Finally, she got out a clean cloth and wiped her hands to show Kalea what she held. "Tis always wise to check in a wound of this type. He was lucky that the blow did not land squarely, as it is, it took this chip out his collar bone." She showed Kalea a sliver of bone. "When you feel, go gently, you do not want to do more harm than good." Kalea nodded. A bowl of hot water had been bought in and Sara then bathed the wound. Then getting another small bowl from her pack, mashed some leaves into a powerful smelling paste and plastered it on the huge gash. Leith by now, had gone quite grey with pain. Sara then used fresh bandages. Another bottle appeared from her pack and sprinkled it in his mead. "Now drink this. It will steal the pain."

"It's not like those bloody leaves that Kalea got me to chew, is it?" Leith muttered taking the goblet.

Sara smiled. "I would guess it is something similar. Now drink up." Leith downed it in one, shuddered then passed out. The men rushed to pick him up. Sara turned to Simon. "He will be fine. If the wound has not been infected, I will stitch it tomorrow. The girl was right. If that had not been seen to correctly, it would have killed him eventually." She turned back to Kalea. "Come child. Let us see to your needs now. I will bring you back to your protector later." With one last look at Leith, Kalea meekly followed Sara out.

Kalea returned to the drinking hall later with Sara. She had bathed and been given a potion to make her feel stronger. She had spent the remainder of the afternoon talking with the wise woman about herbs. The hall wasn't as full as it could have been. Kalea guessed that many of the men stood guard, looking for early warning signs of raiders. Leith looked up, caught her eye and smiled. He certainly looked a lot better. He too, had washed and smartened up and his colour was a lot better. Simon motioned them over and both Sara and Kalea sat next to Leith. Food and drink were offered round and the conversation naturally fell to the Saxons.

"Leith, will you stay with us?" Simon asked. Sara joined in. "If you stay, I would like to have Kalea as an apprentice." Leith didn't need to look at Kalea to know his decision would be final.

"Your offer is most welcome. However, we intend to travel to see Arthur and give news of the raiders personally."

"Would you consider selling the woman?" one of the young warriors asked earnestly.

Leith was stunned. His first instinct was to get up and give the young puppy a good thrashing. "No, I would not," he answered in a tone that brooked no argument. "She is a free woman. She is not mine to sell. And young man, if you had thoughts of winning her, a remark like that would scupper any plans you had." The young man looked sheepishly into his cup and refused to meet anyone's eye. Leith glanced at Kalea and patted her knee. She grinned at him.

"Do you know Leith? I think we make a pretty fair team."

He nodded laughing. "Yeah. Mayhap you're right. Your brains and my brawn."

The evening passed without event after that. As it got late, Sara got up to leave. "Do you wish to join me, Kalea?" she asked.

Before she could answer, Leith cut in firmly. "No offence my lady, by Kalea stays with me."

"I understand Leith," Sara responded. "No offence taken. You are family now." And with that she bade them goodnight.

Leith bent close to her ear. "If you want to rest, take the guest bed behind me. There I will be close should you need me and I shall join you later." Kalea nodded and excused herself. The heat of the fire and the noise of the men and women soothed her and she snuggled down on the skins and was soon fast asleep.

The next morning the women cleaning and tidying from the previous night, woke them. They were offered breakfast which they gratefully accepted. They had not finished when Sara came in. Leith looked at her warily and Kalea laughed.

"Come on Lieth, be brave. You have faced hordes of Saxons and don't flinch and in comes one wise woman and you look ready to run."

"Yeah, but the last time she touched me, I ended up flat on my back," Leith grumbled.

Both women laughed. Between the pair of them, they wiggled him out of his shirt and then Sara inspected the wound.

"That is healing quite nicely." She peered at the wound. "Now, I'll just stitch it up." Kalea watched closely as Sara neatly stitched the wound.

"There's something not quite right about the way you're looking at that, woman," Leith hissed through gritted teeth.

"Would you prefer me to swoon?"

Leith shook his head and grinned. "I'd probably pass out with shock myself, if you did."

"You'll do," Sara said packing up her kit. "I suppose it would be a waste of time telling you to rest until it is fully healed."

Leith grinned. "Sara, you are indeed a wise woman. I thank you for your kindness but Kalea and I must push on."

Sara shook her head. "Kalea, I bought you a gift." She added, "Come with me."

Leith looked at her puzzled. Kalea shrugged and followed Sara out. Leith had little time to ponder further as Simon came in and began to help Leith ready for leaving. "Are you sure, I cannot persuade you to stay Leith? I could always use a good warrior."

Leith smiled and slapped him on the back. "Simon, you have been overly kind to us and I am flattered that you would want me to stay. But I'm one eyed and currently one-armed old man, I wouldn't be that much use to you."

"Even with one eye, old man, you make a better warrior than some I've got," Simon retorted.

"Thanks," Leith replied gruffly. He was touched by Simon's sincerity. Kalea entered the hall.

"Excuse me my lord." She made a half bow. "Leith, I am ready when you are."

Leith who had been buckling on his sword looked up and his bottom jaw dropped in amazement. "You're wearing trousers," he commented stupidly.

Kalea laughed. "Yes. I am. If I am riding, I want to be comfortable."

Leith blinked. "Your father said you should have been born a boy and now I know why." He grinned broadly.

Kalea approached Simon. "Thank you for your kindness."

"You are most welcome." Simon grinned. It was hard to keep his eyes on her face when they were trying to wander over the long legs that were shown off so well by the trousers. "You of course, can return whenever you want."

Leith shook Simon's hand. "Thanks again Simon. And good luck with the raiders."

They left the hall and mounted up amongst the small crowd that had gathered to see their guests off. They waved and left.

Outside the village, Leith howled with laughter. Tears ran from his good eye but he was unable to control his mirth.

"What?" Kalea demanded.

Still braying and in between guffaws he almost squeaked. "You could have knocked me down with a feather when you came in wearing trousers. Did you see Simon's face?" he snorted trying without much luck to stop his laughter. Kalea grinned back. When at last he had at last managed to subdue himself, although, somewhere, giggles were lurking, he wiped his eyes. "What have you been up to in my absence? We have fewer horses and the rest seem well loaded."

"I traded up some of our hangers on," she explained. Watching as Leith's shoulders continued to shake with suppressed mirth. "We have food, proper saddlebags and water bags. Some skins and new blankets."

"I shan't ask. I am sure that you got a bargain."

Kalea was flattered that he trusted her to barter. "Perhaps it's just as well you don't know," she replied with a wicked grin.

That set Leith off again and his laughter was hearty.

It was another two days before they came to the next village. During that time, they had become closer than before. Leith had become her father figure and she the daughter he had never had. His shoulder had much improved and he was beginning to get some movement back in it. They had come a far way in land and the evidence of Saxon raids lessoned. As a result, the next village wasn't half as well protected.

Leith spoke to the leader while Kalea went about restocking their supplies. They drew some very curious glances. The one-eyed old warrior, with a pretty girl who dressed as a boy. They were made welcome and stayed the night before moving on. Leith was almost glad to leave. His newfound fondness of Kalea made him very protective and it made him uncomfortable to see the way men looked at her.

Kalea had another surprise for him. The following evening when they camped and after they had eaten, she suddenly produced a sword. Leith raised his eyebrows. "Now where did you get that tooth pick from?" he asked with amusement.

"I traded for it," Kalea announced proudly.

Leith roared with laughter. "Then child, you were robbed. It's a boy's sword."

Anger swept across her face. "Well, I am not a man, am I?" she spat angrily.

Leith did his best not to laugh but was unable to wipe the grin from his face. "This had not escaped my attention. And what do you propose to do with that sword?"

"I want you to teach me how to use it properly," she stated bluntly.

Looking down at his feet, Leith attempted to hide his merriment. He hoped that she did not notice his shoulders shaking. Regaining some composure, he met her eye. "I know your father said you should have been a boy, but sword play?"

"Come on Leith," she wheedled. "What does it matter? It's only a tooth pick, isn't it?"

Shaking his head and still grinning he rose. "I'll indulge you child. Now." He came up behind and putting both arms round her, he corrected her stance and moved her hands. "This is how you hold a sword. You might want to try it with one hand once you've mastered two."

Kalea looked doubtful, even the boys' sword was heavy.

"Now don't think we are going to launch into combat straight away," Leith went on calmly. "Because it doesn't work like that. First you do exercises to strengthen your wrists and become more flexible. Only when you have done that, can you go on to fighting. Remember, it is a sword and not a chopper." With that he stepped back and drew his own blade. It was so long ago that he had been taught, that he had to think for a moment about the training for holding a sword two handed. Then he began to move. Kalea watched in awe. "Right girl. Off you go." Kalea did her best to copy him. Every now and then he stepped into correct her. "Remember, balance is everything. Stand planted. Legs apart. Feel the weight of the blade. Now look! You've over balanced."

"But you said stand planted." Kalea glowered crossly.

Leith grinned. "Yes, I did. But it's not going to help you if you go over backwards. You have to be aware and have your weight placed to counter act the weight of the blade. You can be planted and still move." Kalea tried again and it was better. Leith watched her and nodded. "That's more like it."

The sword whistled through the air. Kalea liked the way it felt. The sweat poured off her as she practised the exercises that Leith had given her. Leith went and sat by the fire grinning at the determination on her face. Every now and then he called out instruction or encouragement. Kalea kept at it for ages before at last the tip of the blade sank to the ground and she stood panting for breath.

"Don't kill yourself girl," Leith called. "Rest now. You have plenty of time."

Kalea dragged herself to the fire and sat down with a sigh. "You make it look so easy."

"That's because I have been doing it since I was half your age." He grinned. "You are going to hurt tomorrow. Get some rest."

Kalea wrapped herself in her blanket and was asleep before she knew it.

Leith was right. Kalea groaned as she turned over. She did hurt. In fact, she could not find a piece of her that didn't. It was an effort to get up and light the fire for breakfast. Leith sat up and grinned as she sat down with another moan, to hand over the eggs and bread.

"Different muscles."

She grimaced. "I didn't know I had so many muscles," she complained. They broke camp and headed off out.

That evening, the same went on again. This time, Leith added some more moves, this time trying to encourage her to use one hand. Kalea was an eager pupil. Leith was surprised at the amount of effort she put into it. He also felt a certain pride in her. By the time she collapsed into her blanket, she was progressing well. Still two handed, her wrists not strong enough yet to manage one. Not combat ready, but proficient enough to hold the sword competently and make a few more strokes.

"Tomorrow, if you're good, we can start using a tree," Leith said as he watched her eyelids drooping.

"A tree?" she queried more asleep than awake. "It's a sword not a chopper." Lieth grinned and turned over to go to sleep.

Leith was happier than he had been for some time and it surprised him. They had lost so much and yet the bond that had grown between them seemed to more than compensate for it. He doubted that even in the village, he had felt this content. Of course, they had known one another long before. After all, Ren had been his best friend, but he had very little to do with Kalea although they spoke. His place had been with the warriors and hers...Well, hers had been whatever young women do. Leith had never married. Had plenty of women, but never felt the need for commitment and now it was as if he had been given a gift of a fully-grown girl child.

Because Leith wanted to encourage Kalea with her sword skills, they no longer stayed in villages. They bought their provisions and left. Leith was impressed. Kalea had advanced well. Perhaps not enough to be a warrior, but enough to be able to defend herself. Which perhaps, was all she wanted after all. Kalea was feeling fitter than she had ever done. Her body was growing accustomed to wielding the sword. Her movements were now fluid rather than having to consciously make the decision about which way to move. Leith now attacked her, very gently of course, but she was learning to block a blade and more importantly, use it to protect herself. Leith was very proud.

Perhaps because of this, they made slow progress. But travelling was not a safe business at the best of times and this was hardly that. A couple of times they had nearly run into danger. Brigands on the road and on one occasion a Saxon scouting party. This came as a surprise: Leith had thought them too far south to worry about Saxons. The brigands they had found and rode through, not with ease it has to be said, but Kalea did manage to bloody her boys' sword. The Saxons however, they fled from. The Saxons pursued them and sent them many miles out of the way before they managed to lose them.

Leith was impressed with her perception. Out on the road, they had an even relationship, neither one being treated as senior. The moment another person, or village came into sight, Kalea became respectful and mindful of all he said, trusting his judgement on if a situation was safe and ready to act at his slightest sign.

Chapter 2
The Centre

It was late afternoon when they came to a watchtower. They were immediately challenged. Leith explained he was here to request an audience with Arthur.

"Is that it?" Kalea was surprised that they had not been questioned more thoroughly.

Leith grinned at her innocence. "The moment we were spotted on the road, someone would have been sent to warn Arthur. They will know that we are two strangers alone and as such, provide no threat."

Kalea shrugged. They passed a wide river. "That looks like a good place to swim."

"And safe," Leith added. "Between the watchtower and the castle."

Soon they came in sight of a high wooden palisade. Entering through the gate, Kalea saw the biggest village she had ever seen. Her jaw dropped open at its size and amount of people rushing around doing their business.

Leith laughed. "It's a town." He realised that Kalea hadn't been outside the village and was overwhelmed.

"It's so big!" she was awestruck and then drawing her gaze away from the hive of activity, the castle stood imposingly impressive. "Oh!"

Still grinning, Leith led her to the castle gates negotiating the thronging crowd. It hadn't escaped his notice, that Kalea had edged her mount closer to his.

They were met not by Arthur but by Lud, one of Arthur's most trusted warriors. Lud was an old friend of Leith. He too was older, more grizzled and had lost an arm in battle. When he saw Leith, his face split into a huge grin, making him look at least a little more approachable. Leith slid from the saddle and the two men embraced in a huge bear hug that would have broken the ribs of lesser men. Kalea smiled.

"Leith! You old wolf, what are you doing here? It pleases my heart to see you."

"Lud, my old friend, it is good to see you too." There was a lot of backslapping going on and a few of the villagers stopped to see who warranted such a warm welcome from Lud.

"Leave your horse to the boy and come and see Arthur." Lud was turning Leith in the direction of the drinking hall.

Leith turned and smiled at Kalea who raised a quizzical eyebrow at him. "Lud, this is no boy. This is Ren's daughter, Kalea."

Lud stopped dead in his tracks and turned back to the 'boy' on horseback. Once he had a good look, he could see it wasn't a boy, it was in fact a lovely young woman.

"My apologies Kalea." He made a small bow. "I was so taken with seeing my old friend again, I didn't pay enough attention."

Kalea slid from the saddle and went forward extending her hand for shaking, which Lud did with as much aplomb as he could manage. The girl's handshake was firm and strong. Ren had taught his daughter well. He looked down into the dark smiling eyes and thought she had the look of her mother about her. Turning he called a young boy to take the horses and then led the two visitors to the drinking hall. The two men were chatting together and Kalea trailed along at the rear, not wishing to intrude on the reunion. They entered the castle gates and approached an impressive looking drinking hall and Lud led them up the steps and through the door.

Inside, Arthur was playing a game of wager with his childhood friend Kai. Kai was the adopted son of Lud and they had played together since they were tiny. Arthur was as dark as Kai was blonde and they made a striking pair. Both tall, lean and well built. Perfect fighting men. They looked up as the visitors entered. They exchanged surprised glances. Seldom had they seen Lud look so happy.

"Arthur, Kai, this is my old friend Leith," he said as Leith bowed low and murmured, "my liege." At a glance, they recognised the old warrior and as one, rose to greet him.

"Leith! My old friend. How are you?" Arthur asked with a broad smile and they clasped arms. "You remember Kai?" Kai stepped forward to be included in the handshaking and backslapping.

At last, Leith managed to say, "Arthur, I bring grim news from the east."

The smiles immediately vanished.

"First you must rest and eat. You must be tired."

For a moment, Kalea thought she had been forgotten. Then Lud firmly propelled her forward so that she stood shoulder to shoulder with Leith. "And this," said Lud waiting to see the look on Arthur and Kai's faces "is Kalea, daughter of Ren and Leith's companion."

Both men turned their attention to the slim woman who seemed have suddenly appeared from mid-air. They were stunned and Leith and Lud exchanged a conspiratorial smile. They hadn't realised that it was a girl and now they both took a moment to study her. Kalea fidgeted, aware that she hardly looked her best. Arthur and Kai barely noticed that. They were too busy looking at the long trouser clad legs and the beautiful, cherry red hair, her clear skin and her striking dark almond eyes. Kai swallowed hard and Arthur cleared his throat and stepped forward.

"I apologise, my lady. I had not noticed you there. I am Arthur and my companion here, is Kai." Kalea did her best to look composed and gave a small bow.

Kai nodded to her and then to everyone's surprise laughed.

"Excuse me, Kalea," he chortled, "my father," he nodded to Lud "has caught us wrong footed which he delights in. I am not laughing at you, but at us. You must think us most uncouth staring at you like a fish." And he made the appropriate movement with his mouth. Kalea grinned.

"Please be seated," Arthur said taking her gently by the arm and steering her to the best possible place by the fire. Lud and Leith grinned at each over.

"I'll organise some food and drink." Lud marched out still smiling.

"I've ridden too far." Leith sank into a chair gratefully and wasn't surprised to see that Arthur had seated her where he could watch her. He was even less surprised, when Kai went and sat as close to her as he dared. He smiled to himself. Oh, to be young again. Lud soon returned and sat next to Leith. A serving woman wasn't far behind and began to hand out mugs of mead. Kalea took hers and drank thirstily. She was extremely conscious of Kai's thigh, which was perhaps, accidently touching hers. She was frightened to move in case she offended this young friend of Arthur's although she could feel a strange warmth stealing though her. Lud noticed her discomfiture and commented. "Kai! Give the girl some room." Kai grinned ruefully and moved no more than an inch over. Kalea however, was grateful for that.

"So, what news do you bring us?" Arthur asked. His attention divided between Leith and Kalea.

Leith looked at Kalea and began. "Our village is no more. We are all that remains."

Arthur, Kai and Lud looked stunned.

"Saxon raiders?" Lud asked. Leith nodded and taking a draft of mead, told the tale that he had told so many times over the last few weeks. While he was talking, food arrived and Kalea ate hungrily. She had heard this so many times, it hardly seemed real any more. She also had begun to get embarrassed when Leith told of how she had escaped being raped by a Saxon warrior. He told it with such relish as if he was proud of her. She sighed. Although it was early, a full stomach and the warmth of the fire made her weary. Kai lent close to her ear. His breath tickling. "Are you alright?" he asked softly.

She smiled and nodded and responded quietly "I'm fine thank you. Just tired." Leith was just getting to Kalea's story and she wished she could just shrink. She was conscious of the fact that all eyes were turned on her, re-appraising this slim young woman. She looked down at her empty mead cup and hoped that this would be the last time she heard it. The moment passed and Leith finished his story.

Arthur spoke drawing her attention, "You do bring grave news. There are grim times, Leith. Mark of Cornwall is pressing me from the south and the Welsh are still not quiet."

Lud broke in. "We have just quelled the Welsh rebellion, Arthur. Is there nothing we can do for the people of East Anglia?"

Arthur looked grave and sighed. "My war band is only so big Leith. I have had to split them in two. One to stave off Cornwall and the other has just returned with me from Wales. I will send messengers to the Lords of Anglia and get them to meet with me and will discuss our options."

Leith nodded. "The only problem with that my Lord, is that they will be reluctant to leave their homes when they are hard pressed to protect them."

Arthur nodded. "In that case, I will have to go to them."

"But Arthur!" Lud interjected horrified.

"Lud. What alternative do we have? We cannot leave them alone. I will go with Kai and Leith and you will stay here. We will split the warband again." Lud hissed in disgust. Leith watched the exchange with interest. Arthur was a good leader given the chance but he was pressed on all sides at the moment. "Leith,"

Arthur continued. "I will not be able to leave for at least four days. My men are tired and I will not push them too far." Leith nodded. It would have to do. He was surprised that he had not received an out and out refusal. The lad would go far.

"So, for the time being we will rest." Arthur's face was thoughtful. "Leith, I would like to offer you a place with my warband. Not just for the journey east but for good. I would like to offer you a home in village. I understand if you wish to go back to your own people in the East, but you and of course, Kalea, are most welcome to stay here." Leith glanced at Kalea. She looked tired but gave an almost imperceptible nod.

"You are most generous Arthur." Leith was gruff with emotion. "We would be honoured to accept your offer."

"Oh no!" Kai sighed dramatically. "Now we've got two old men in the warband."

"Both of whom could whip you puppies with one arm tied behind their backs." Lud came back. They all laughed.

"Well at least that's one thing settled," Arthur stated positively. "I will make sure a home is made ready for you. Whilst that is being done, you may stay with me in the drinking hall. Kalea, of course, you can join the women—" He didn't get to finish.

"Kalea stays with me," Leith interrupted firmly.

Arthur looked at the man closely, gauging his motives and then nodded. "If that is your wish Leith, by all means. I just thought she would not want to share a room with so many men."

"She'll manage," Leith returned bluntly. "Now if you don't mind, we would like to freshen up."

Arthur and Kai were used to Lud's gruff behaviour and Leith came to Kalea's side to help her up. "Come on young 'un," he said kindly, "a dip in the river should soon wake you up." Kalea grinned and bowed to Arthur and followed Leith out.

"Now, what do you make of that?" Arthur commented thoughtfully.

"Lovely," Kai murmured his eyes still on the retreating pair.

Arthur cuffed him. "No, you dope. They are very close. Lovers?"

"Never," Lud said firmly. The two men smiled at each other. "And you can pack that in for a start. You will have to go through Leith first and he may be one eyed but he is a mean warrior." They all laughed.

Having retrieved two of their bundles, Kalea and Leith made their way down to the river. "So, Kalea, what do you think?"

Kalea shrugged. "What do I know of warriors? They seem alright. The village is large and I think we will be safe here."

"That's a very guarded answer," Leith said gruffly.

Kalea smiled. "Don't worry Leith. We will see how we like it. If we do not, we can always become travellers."

"That's all very well in the summer. But I need somewhere to keep these old bones dry."

She laughed. "You poor old man you. There's plenty of life in you yet."

Leith grinned. "You're good for the heart young 'un."

They had reached the river and Kalea had begun to strip off. Leith turned his back to the water and sat down.

"I see you're going first again," he grumbled. Kalea said nothing, but he heard a splash in the water.

"You're going to like this," she yelled. "It's very nearly warm."

"I know what your warm is like young lady. I expect to have frost bite when I come out."

It wasn't long before he heard her clamber out. She wrapped herself in some cloth and began to dry off. Leith began to strip off. "Aren't you going to turn your back?" he queried.

She giggled. "Such modesty. Leith, I had two brothers. I do know what a man looks like without clothes on."

"Not this one you don't," he said turning his back on her. She giggled again and did turn her back while combing her hair.

"Did I smell as bad as you?" she asked. "I guess I did. It's a wonder they let us into the hall. You smell like an old pig," she added.

"I'll have you be more respectful." Leith soaped himself off. "And I have no doubt you did because I thought you smelt alright."

Kalea laughed heartily. "Leith, what do you think of Arthur?"

The joy of feeling clean was making Leith quite mellow. "I think he is a good man and a strong leader. He may be young but he's got his head screwed on all right that one. He may not always get it right, but for the best part her tries."

Still combing her hair, Kalea nodded and went on. "What of Lud and Kai? Kai said Lud was his father but they look nothing alike."

Leith grinned to himself, "Lud is an old friend of mine. He was married and had a son, both killed by Saxon raiders. Lud raised a war band, I was among them and we drove them from our shores. When we went to loot the Saxon camp, Lud found a lad, no more than three summers old. He was little and afraid, so Lud took him as his own. He lost one son and found another."

"So, Kai's a Saxon."

"No, lass, he is no more a Saxon than you or me. He hates the Saxons and is one of the bravest fighters Arthur has." Leith strode out of the water and grabbed a cloth to dry with. Kalea raised her eyebrows although Leith couldn't see. "Come on Kalea," he added as he finished dressing. Kalea stood up and Leith smiled. She had her dress on and she looked beautiful now that all the grime had been washed off. "I'd almost forgotten that you were a girl," Leith teased. "So, which one of these two fine young men do you think you are going to marry?"

Blushing furiously, Kalea looked thoughtful. "Well, I'm not altogether sure. Which one would you favour?"

Leith's eye twinkled and he rubbed his chin as if considering a grave question. "Arthur would be the one to catch. But he is a leader and his time is very rarely his own. Kai on the other hand might be better. He would have more time and he is no doubt, a stout warrior."

"Kai it is then." They both laughed. "I could marry you," she said seriously.

Leith looked horrified. "I'm old enough to be your father, girl. What good would an old man like me be to a woman like you?"

It was Kalea's turn to tease, eyes twinkling, she sidled up to him and slid her arm through his. "We get on well, don't we?"

Leith laughed. "We get on well enough, that's true. Now, stop teasing an old man and pick your gear up." Kalea grinned and as she bent to pick up her bundle, Leith gave her a resounding slap on the rear. Kalea shrieked with indignation picked up her bundle and fled down the path laughing as she did so. Leith was aware, as he lumbered after her, that he had a silly grin on his face. But did he care? Not one bit.

Kalea was still giggling as she ran into the village. In fact, she was laughing so hard that she wasn't looking where she was going and barged straight into Arthur, who had been trying to sort out a new home for her and Leith. Neither one had been paying much attention and Kalea nearly managed to take Arthur off his feet. His breath exploded out of him and he reached out and grabbed her as much to steady him as her. Kai who had been looking in another direction, looked totally nonplussed as Arthur let out a great whoosh of breath and was as surprised as Arthur, to see Kalea hastily trying to pull herself together.

"I do beg your pardon," Kalea panted. "I wasn't watching where I was going." Now she was well and truly flustered, however she met Arthur's eye boldly. She was flushed from running and breathing heavily. She was also aware that she was dangerously close to hysterical giggles. Leith came panting up behind her and as he approached, he called.

"You hussy woman! What are you doing throwing yourself at the two most eligible men in the village?" That did it. Kalea dissolved into gales of laughter. Arthur and Kai looked at her in amazement. Then they looked at each other. Neither of them seeing the joke. Kalea was trying to say something but every time she opened her mouth she laughed more. The more she laughed, the more embarrassed she got and the more embarrassed she got the more she laughed. She was now bent over double holding her ribs. Lieth came panting up, still laughing himself. The two young men began to smile broadly. It was hard to remain serious when someone was beside himself or herself with laughter.

"Would someone like to explain what's going on?" Arthur asked still smiling broadly. "Kalea nearly knocks me off my feet and then falls about laughing. What is so funny?"

Still bent double with tears in her eyes, Kalea was in no position to answer so Leith stepped in. "I apologise for my young charge Arthur. It really was my fault. I was teasing her down by the river and have chased her all the way back. Pull yourself together girl!" he said gruffly, but was still grinning.

"I do apologise, Arthur." Her voice was still quaking with the laughter she was desperately trying hold in check. He grinned back at her.

"I don't mind women throwing themselves at me," he spoke with some merriment, "but it would be nice to know that they are coming."

Kalea clapped her hand over her mouth in an effort to suppress a new fit of giggles.

Leith seized her by the arm. "Come on woman. Let's get out of here before you cause yourself more trouble." He grinned at Arthur and towed her away. They hadn't gone ten feet, when they both started howling with laughter again.

"What was that all about?" Arthur asked Kai.

With a bemused smile, Kai answered, "I don't know. But it looked like fun."

When Leith and Kalea entered the drinking hall, they were surprised to see that one corner had screens of hanging blankets placed round one of the cots.

"It would seem that you are going to sleep there tonight." Leith was impressed at Arthur's consideration. Kalea looked at him and said with chagrin, "And to think, I almost knocked him on his backside."

Leith smiled. "I don't think he'd mind you knocking him on his backside in certain situations." Kalea's response was a thump. "Watch it! That's my bad arm." Leith gave it a rub.

That night the hall was full of noise and people. Kalea was seated between Arthur and Kai with Lud and Leith opposite them. Kalea felt awkward. Even in her own village she had not been treated so honourably. The only time she had been allowed into the hall, was a feast times, and that had been to serve at the tables. Generally, she would stay at home while her father and brothers caroused with their chief. Food and drink were plentiful and she realised after their scant provisions on the road, she was very hungry. However, she was not comfortable being seated with the warriors. She couldn't think of a single sensible thing to say and therefore was quiet. Arthur turned to her. He was aware that she was uncomfortable under his scrutiny, but couldn't help but stare. She smelt of meadow flowers, her hair was so glossy and her skin soft and smooth.

"So, how did you find it on the road?" he asked trying to draw her into conversation.

Kalea was not shy and met his dark eyes with her own. "It wasn't so bad. I had good company." She nodded in Leith's direction. He was deep in conversation with Lud. Their heads, close together and a smile lurking on their lips.

"But it must have been tough," Arthur continued, trying not to let a silence fall. Kalea understood what he was trying to do and was grateful. She rewarded him with a smile.

"It would have been a lot worse if it hadn't been summer. It doesn't help when you have such an old cross patch with you." She grinned in Leith's direction. "His old bones like sleeping in nice warm beds rather than on the hard ground."

Leith who had overheard joined in. "I didn't complain that much."

"No, not that much," teased Kalea. "The grounds too hard, the waters too cold…"

"Alright, alright!" Leith grinned. "Don't you listen to half the things this girl says Arthur. She doesn't know the half of it."

The smile on Kalea's face said it all.

Smiling back at Kalea, Arthur asked. "Did you know Leith well in your village?"

"No. I didn't. Of course, I knew Leith. He was a good friend to my father and he sometimes shared a meal at our fire. But he rarely spoke to me. He was too busy talking to my father and brothers about warrior type things."

Arthur grinned. He supposed it must be boring for a young woman. Kalea grinned back. He really was very good looking.

"So, you have only become close since the raiders…" He broke off aware that he was bringing up a very unpleasant matter for her.

Kalea was grateful for his kindness. "Yes. That's right. I suppose we formed some bond seeing as we were the only ones left."

Arthur looked concerned. "I am sorry. I didn't mean to remind you of such a," he searched for the right words. "Ghastly event."

"My lord you are a kind man. But do not concern yourself. Over the last few years, I like many have lost a lot. However, I am alive and happy to be so. There is little profit to be made turning over the stones of the past. I have at least, learned that much."

"Madam, you are an extraordinary woman." Arthur was impressed.

Kalea answered with a wry smile. "Not at all. No different to many others and a lot less special than some."

"You sell yourself short," Arthur commented with feeling.

"Well, thank you. I will not disillusion you." And hid her embarrassment in her beaker. "Thank you for the screens," she added quietly.

"Screens?" Arthur turned to see where Kalea was looking. "Oh those," he said with a sheepish grin. "Unfortunately, I can't say in truth that it was me. It was Kai."

Kalea turned to look at Kai, who at the same time turned to her having heard his name. "What have I done now?" he asked with a grin. Kalea smiled back.

"You made me some screens. I was just thanking Arthur, but he tells me it was you. So, thank you very much."

Kai's smile brightened even more. "You are more than welcome. I didn't think you would appreciate Arthur ogling you whilst you slept."

Kalea laughed. "That was very thoughtful. I am very grateful." Kai nodded and she sensed he was quite embarrassed by her thanks.

"So," he said changing the subject. "What do you think of the food?"

"You are talking to a woman who has spent the last week eating stale bread and cheese. I think it's wonderful."

Kai threw back his head and gave a hearty chuckle. For some reason, it made her shiver. She watched him curiously. Sensing her interest, he returned her gaze. The dark eyes drew him in and she smelt curiously sweet, like honey. Kai took a big swallow and Kalea blushed lowering her gaze to her cup.

"Would you like a refill?" his voice was husky and low. She nodded and held out her beaker. "I'm glad you decided to stay." His voice was quiet and meant only for her ears. Kalea looked up into his bright blue eyes. He cleared his throat. "Do you think you will like it here?"

To his surprise, she sighed. "I don't know," she answered truthfully.

Kai was concerned. "Arthur and I have found you a house at the edge of the village. It is old and needs some work but we have arranged for it to be fixed and it will quicker than having a new one built."

Kalea rewarded him with a smile. "Kai, it's not that. I must sound so ungrateful, and I didn't mean to be. You have been kinder than we have a right to deserve. It's just that…" She paused desperately seeking the right words then met his eye. "You will have to forgive me. I have only lived in one place. Until, now, I had not left my village. I suppose, I am frightened of starting anew," she finished in a flurry.

Kai reached out and took her hand. It was warm and smooth. "Don't be frightened. I understand, it will be strange for you but you have Leith. And I will be here, that's of course, if you want me too." He was fishing. She was so beautiful, he decided without conscious thought that he wanted her rather badly.

Kalea looked down at his hand. For some reason, she wanted the contact and hoped he wouldn't let go too soon. She looked up and met his eye. "I would like that very much." Her heart gave a flutter. This was a new feeling for her and she felt quite breathless. "I have a confession." His gaze didn't waver. "You see, I have always been a bit of a wild child. And I don't always do what young women are expected to do." She grinned sheepishly. "In the village, people were used to my wild ways but I think it might be frowned upon here." Kai's face expressed disbelief and Kalea added, "You don't believe me? Ask Leith."

"What must he ask me?" Leith looked up instantly took in Kai's hold on Kalea's hand and his obvious reluctance to let it go.

"Kalea tells me she is a 'wild child'." Kai grinned at Leith. "That she does things that many disapprove of."

Leith laughed. "You could say that. Ren said she should have been a boy and a fine warrior she would have made." Kai looked at Kalea who had her eyes downcast and was blushing. "Ride a pony? This one can ride better than most men. She can get a horse to do things that most couldn't. She has never been worried about what people think of her behaviour and at times it is far from maidenly."

Kalea looked up incensed. "Leith, you needn't have been quite so truthful." Arthur and Lud who had been listening to the exchange, laughed as did Kai. "They might change their mind and not let us stay."

"Have no fear of that." Arthur laughed and then noticed that Kai was still holding her hand. He frowned and Kai grinned and entwined his fingers with Kalea, which made her look at him and give a shy smile.

Leith was now in his stride. He had had a few cups of mead too many and was eager to extol Kalea's virtues as he saw it. He realised young women were not meant to do these things, but to him, it made her all the more special. "Even before her poor mother died, she preferred to run with the boy cubs rather than stay at home."

"I had two brothers; they were a bad influence on me," Kalea countered in her defence which caused much hilarity. "It's true!" she exclaimed hotly. "They teased me for being a girl, so I tried to become more boyish." This bought fresh laughter and Kalea gave a dramatic sigh of resignation.

Leith could not be stopped. "Spoilt that's what she was." Leith grinned. "After her mother's death, her father let her take over the home. Even taught her to use a dagger."

"I could use some more mead myself," Kalea muttered. Kai leaned over and got the jug and filled her cup grinning broadly. Kalea nodded her thanks and took a long draught.

"Slit your throat in a trice," Leith continued. Kalea groaned causing more laughter.

"It stood me in good stead," Kalea retorted.

"Aye, that it did girl." Leith swigged some more mead. "Spitted that Saxon a treat." Kalea covered her face with her hand now hugely embarrassed. "It will take a brave man to take you on." She wished she was anywhere else but here. Leith looked up and realised he had gone too far. "Now girl, it's no good taking on so. You are what you are. There is no disgrace in it and if people don't like it, it's their bad luck. For all your faults, and by the gods, you've got some." More laughter greeted this, "You are a beautiful and clever woman. The man who gets you as a wife is going to be lucky." And then perhaps realising that he was getting sentimental added. "And he certainly won't be bored." Even Kalea laughed at that. "That's if, I can ever bear to be parted with you me self." Kalea grinned at him. Leith returned it with interest and was pleased he had redeemed himself. "Drink up lass. I want to see if you can drink me under the table."

"I have no wish to end up under the table thanks," she said swigging down some more mead.

"Leith is so like my father. They seem to take great delight in teasing."

Kalea nodded to Kai in agreement. "Same generation. I expect they will be here a long-time swapping battle stories."

And so, it was. The hall emptied and the five of them were left. Kalea was sleepy. The mead, good food, the buzz of conversation and the warmth of the hall had combined to relax her. Her eye lids were drooping and it was a real effort to keep them open. Without realising it, she leant against Kai, who at first was surprised and then shifted his weight so that he could put an arm around her and support her. Kalea was too far gone to realise and with seconds was asleep her head nestled against Kai's chest. Kai grinned feeling very pleased with his self.

"Leith," he called softly. Leith looked up from his conversation. "Kalea's burnt herself out."

Leith was surprised to see Kalea nestled close to Kai but could see she was worn out. Kai looked so chuffed with himself that Leith had no doubt that he found the situation most satisfying. "Too much mead. I'll take her to her cot."

"There's no need," Kai said hastily. "She seems quite comfortable and it doesn't bother me."

"It wouldn't would it." Lud grinned. Arthur frowned. So, Kai had seized a lead on him. They had been rivals for women before. Arthur wasn't going to step aside.

A while later, Lud rose. "Come on Kai. You can't cuddle her all night."

"I could." Kai grinned but was clearly disappointed. Leith bent over Kalea. He was surprised by the old warrior's gentleness with her.

"Kalea," Leith said softly giving her a shake.

She came too groggily. "Was I snoring?" she asked.

Leith grinned and shook his head. "Time for bed." She allowed him to help her to her feet. "Goodnight," she said politely to the young men who answered her and with that she disappeared behind the screens and all was quiet. Leith took off his boots and lay down. He fell to sleep listening to the young warriors talking.

The next morning when Kalea woke, she couldn't remember going to bed at all. Nor could she remember undressing, which was a little worrying. She scrubbed her face with her hands. Then got dressed and stepped out from behind the screens. Leith was still snoring peacefully. As she came out, Arthur called to her in a soft voice. Looking round she saw him seated at the table eating breakfast.

"Come join me."

"Have you been here all night?" she asked with a smile that he returned.

"No. Did you sleep well?"

"Like a baby," Kalea said helping herself to some bread and honey. "I see Leith's still sleeping off the mead."

Arthur lent towards her conspiratorially, "Does he always snore this loudly? It's a wonder anyone got any sleep last night."

Kalea suppressed a giggle. "Only when he's been drinking. We would have got murdered on the road if he had made that racket." They finished breakfast and Leith was still asleep.

"Would you like to come for a walk?" Arthur asked.

Unsure, Kalea glanced at Leith. He was still snoring peacefully. "Alright." Together they left the hall. The bright sunshine made Kalea blink hard. "What a beautiful day," she murmured as much to herself as Arthur.

Arthur looked up at the clear blue summer sky. "Yes, it is," he confirmed. "Come on," he added, gently taking her by the arm. He led her down through the village greeting everyone as he did so. Kalea was impressed how approachable Arthur was. Leith was right, he was obviously a good leader and a person, who liked people. They left the village and came to the edge of a wood. "Come on," he urged. "I've got something to show you."

"Am I safe with you? And is it something I want to see?" half flirtatiously.

Arthur laughed. "You are quite safe with me," he said with mock seriousness. "Unless you don't want to be?"

"Least said, sooner mended," Kalea muttered allowing Arthur to take her hand and lead her forward. He led her deep into the wood and just when Kalea was about to ask what on earth they were doing, he motioned her to be quiet. Used to this sort of sign from Leith, Kalea again began to follow him moving very quietly. They came to the edge of a pool and Arthur motioned her to sit on a fallen log. She did so without question but raised an eyebrow at him quizzically. He held a finger to his lips then pointed to the pool then sat next to her. From their vantage point, they could see the pool and she had no doubt that if they went to the other side, no one would know they were there. Kalea was just about to fidget, when Arthur nudged her and pointed. She peered across the pool to where he was pointing. The bushes were moving and a magnificent stag stepped out into the clearing. Kalea's breath caught in her throat. She was totally entranced. The stag scented the air and then looked back through the trees. A moment later, a doe and a young fawn stepped out. Kalea held her breath, frightened to breathe in case she startled them. Arthur was no longer looking at the deer. While she was entranced, he took the opportunity to study her. She really was quite lovely. A slow smile played round the edge of her lips as she watched the deer come down to drink. Not long after that, the deer left, melting quietly back into the woodland as if they had never been there.

Arthur lent over to her and spoke quietly in her ear. "They're gone now and won't be back. Come on." His breath tickled her ear but she nodded and allowed him to help her up and lead her back the way they had come.

"They were beautiful." Her voice was low even though they were away from the pool.

Arthur nodded in agreement. "I often come and watch them when I am here. It is peaceful."

"Don't they fear the hunters?"

Arthur shrugged. "They don't seem to be. Perhaps they are protected by the old god of Herne the Hunter."

"Perhaps he is Herne." Kalea drew abreast with him. "Thank you for sharing them with me."

"You are most welcome." He smiled as he saw that she had pieces of twig and leaf in her hair. He lent forward to pluck out a twig. "You seem to be growing a tree in your hair."

"I'm not at all surprised. In fact, I wouldn't be surprised if I found a bird nesting in there."

Arthur laughed. "Come here my little wood sprite. I'd better tidy you up or they will wonder what we have been up to." She stepped forward and he began to pluck pieces of foliage out of her hair. Kalea was quite still; she was thinking about the deer.

"Arthur," she said raising her face to him. The question she had been about to ask died in her throat; he was looking at her in a very strange way. It made her feel odd. Suddenly he bent and kissed her taking her into his arms and pulling her close. Kalea was shocked. She had never been kissed by a man like this before. It made her feel strangely unsettled and she was sure they shouldn't be doing it. It was however, very nice and Kalea didn't resist although it frightened her.

A lesser man, would have pushed his advantage and taken this forward to its natural conclusion. But Arthur was not a lesser man; he was honourable although it was becoming harder by the minute. He sensed her innocence in her kiss and knew that was not experienced in these things and while he knew he had awakened her desire with his kiss, he also knew, that he could not take her with a clear conscience. He ended the kiss and could feel her tremble against him. Despite the fact that it had meant to be a gentle kiss, his body throbbed with desire. At last, he spoke, his voice gruff with passion, "Kalea, I...we must stop before I can't."

Kalea was confused. Her body wanted to explore further, but her mind shouted loudly, enough! No more! "That's alright. Let's go." She was aware that her voice sounded a little shaky. It was pride that saved her more than anything else. She knew that if they didn't leave now, she would reach for him and she didn't want to do that. They began to walk back through the trees. The silence was only slightly awkward which surprised Arthur. Kalea was not quiet because she was angry, but because she wasn't really sure how she felt.

In the end, Arthur broke the silence. "Kalea, I'm sorry. I didn't mean to; it just seemed the right thing to do."

"Don't be sorry Arthur. It was just a kiss." Kalea smiled brightly, *or was it?* she thought.

Arthur was a little shaken; he had not expected her to be so composed. He was sure that he was not mistaken, she was an innocent. Her response to his kiss had taken him aback. God, he wanted her. They had come to the river.

"I'm just going to wash my face and hands," she said startling him out of his reverie.

"I could do with that myself," he answered with a wry smile. Together they went down to the riverbank and stooped to wash. Arthur watched her closely. She felt his gaze and turned to him.

"I'm alright, really." He nodded in response and then added, "I'm not sure I am." She laughed and splashed him with water.

"Come on, don't be so serious." She then sprinted up the bank with Arthur in pursuit. The moment was gone and both of them felt an element of relief as they strolled back to the village.

Leith woke up and his head hurt. He groaned and rubbed his face with his hands. Too much mead and ale. He was getting too old for hard drinking. Sitting up, he looked round. The hall was deserted. He coughed and stretched. Pulling himself together, he pulled back the screens of Kalea's cot. It was empty. He looked round again to make sure he had not missed her. No, he was definitely alone. Arthur wasn't here either. Had the girl gone gallivanting off with Arthur? Well, there was no use worrying about it. The table had been laid with breakfast thinks. There was a jug of milk, bread, honey and oatcakes. Leith seated himself and poured a mug of milk and grimaced as he drunk it down. Knowing you would feel better once you ate and drank wasn't as convincing as your stomach, which said you would be better off in bed. He pulled off a crust of bed and began to chew.

A few moments later, Kai came bounding through the door. The young warrior greeted Leith with a smile. "Got a head ache old man?" he asked. Leith grunted in reply.

"Want some food?" he asked Kai.

Kai shook his head. "Where's Kalea?"

Leith appraised him with a good eye. "That's what I would like to know," he grumbled.

Kai's smile faded. "Where's Arthur?"

"Don't know," Growled Leith.

Kai scowled. "Are they together?"

"Don't know," Leith spat impatiently. "Look lad. I woke up and they were gone. Your guess is as good as mine. Now sit down or go away. Either way stop asking me damn silly questions."

Kai sat down. He had been looking forward to seeing Kalea and now he was in a bad mood. In fact, he was boiling. What was Arthur up too? Kai knew him too well. He knew that he would seize the opportunity to win Kalea over.

Leith watched him and despite his massive hangover, he had to smile. It didn't take a mind reader to know what was going on in Kai's mind. His jaw had taken on a set look and an angry tick in the corner. Leith liked the boy and didn't like to see him get all fired up, over what could be nothing. "Come on Kai lad, cheer up. Your face is so sour it will turn the milk."

Kai said nothing but stared at him with irrational anger. The moment was broken when they heard Kalea and Arthur coming up the steps of the hall. They were chatting happily. As they came through the door, Leith spoke first, eager to prevent Kai from saying something he may regret later.

"And where have you two been?"

Arthur and Kalea froze mid step before Kalea replied, "Arthur took me to show me the deer. Leith, you should have seen them they were beautiful." Kai looked malignantly at Arthur who came and joined him at the table.

"Well, girlie, don't you think you should have told me where you were going?" Kalea was about to protest when Leith turned on Arthur. "And you, you young pup, don't you go taking any woman in my charge without asking first." Kalea was shocked that he would talk to Arthur so.

Arthur however, was not. Leith was right. "Of course, Leith you are right. I am sorry that I did not ask and I will not do it again." Kalea stood gaping like a fish. Kai was beginning to feel slightly better but not much.

Leith looked Arthur straight in the eye. "Make sure you don't. Kalea, get your trousers on, we're going riding. And bring that toothpick with you," he barked.

When Leith was in this sort of mood, it was best not to argue. Kalea scuttled off to do as she was told. Arthur mouthed at Kai "Toothpick?" Kai shrugged and shook his head. It wasn't long before she was back, wearing a man's shirt and trousers and carrying a long thing parcel. "Get the horses ready," Leith growled and off she went as meek as a lamb. Kai and Arthur had sat silent, sensing the old man's mood but as he rose to leave, Kai said respectfully. "May I ride with you?"

"No, you may not," Leith answered in a tone that brooked no argument and with that he strode out.

"Someone woke up in a bad mood," commented Arthur. Kai looked at him with disgust and went to walk out. "It's alright Kai, nothing happened. We watched deer, that's all." Kai gave him a withering glance and walked out. Arthur shrugged and smiled he had no time to worry about Kai; he was too busy thinking of Kalea.

By the time Leith arrived at the paddock, the horses were saddled and ready to go. Kalea looked very nervous; she had rarely seen him in such a bad mood.

He came over and boosted her into the saddle. At the same time, he breathed deeply of her scent. He wanted to know what had happened and whatever her lips would say, her scent would not lie to him. There was a slight muskiness to her, different from her normal smell but to his relief, she did not smell sexed. Without realising it, he breathed a sigh of relief as he mounted his own horse. He led off out of the village with Kalea keeping abreast. It wasn't until that they were well clear of the village, that Leith spoke.

"And what was that all about?" he asked. Kalea was already defensive.

"We went and watched the deer that's all."

"Is it?"

Kalea blushed but met his eye. "Alright!" she gushed. "So, he kissed me. But that's all."

"I knew it," Leith hissed. "I'm not going to have to give you a lecture on the birds and bees, am I?" he growled.

Kalea couldn't help herself and laughed. "God no! I have seen animals' mate. I have even watched my brothers with their women."

"You what?" Leith was aghast. "You spied on your brothers?"

Kalea giggled. "Of course. I had to know what was going on and what a man did to a woman."

"Have you no shame woman?" he asked.

Kalea didn't answer at first and just smiled. Then eager to defend herself she stated. "Come on Leith. Don't be so shocked. There are women in the village younger than me and they are married with children."

"And there you have it!" Leith crowed with delight. "You have said it yourself; they are **married!** Not maidens. I don't want to see you with a bastard child. A woman with a child and no husband is only good for one thing and you are better than that girl." Kalea was stunned. She had no idea that Leith's view on thing like this was so strong. Leith continued. "A woman like that has no friends, the men use her, the women hate her for taking their husbands and sons and she is shamed." Kalea's grin faded from her face. She had not expected him to be so blunt. Leith saw her worried look and sighed. "Kalea, I have no wish to be so hard on you but you are not wise in the way of men and women. You were too busy being one of the lads when you were small and your father, bless him, did not wish to see you go when your mother died. Any young bloods showing an interest, were warned off. He was wrong to do it. You should have been out courting, not keeping house for an old man. And you never showed any interest in the company of other woman in the village. Most girls learn much of what they know from each other. As a result, you know nothing of keeping men at arm's length until they marry you, and I have no idea how to teach you."

"So, what do I do?" Kalea panicked.

"The best you can," Leith said with a grimace. "And I know with you, it will be enough. Your problem is that both Arthur and Kai want you. When two men want a woman, there is bound to be trouble. You know what it is like when two stallions want the same mare. They fight."

"But they're best friends." Kalea was horrified.

"They may be, but this will not end until one or the other has the prize," Leith growled grimly.

"I don't want trouble!"

"No. I know you don't. The problem is that trouble is what you've got and nothing you could have done would have prevented it. They wanted you almost from the moment they saw you. You are an unknown from the outside the village and therefore more mysterious and alluring than other women." He looked at Kalea's worried face. "So, my girl, it falls to you to be sensible. There is no way you can have both. You have to choose between the two. Make your choice clean and make sure the other is aware of your choice. Then stick by that choice and give the other a wide berth. If you don't, there will be trouble."

"How do I know which one to choose?" Kalea asked.

"There is no easy answer to that question. You and you alone must choose. Let your heart lead you. Your head is not always right in matters of love."

"What if I choose the wrong one?" she sounded even more panicked.

"Then that is something you must live with."

For a while she was silent, pondering the logic of it. Finally, she spoke. "What if I pick neither?"

"Then you risk the chance of spending your life alone like me. Possibly, with a stroppy young woman who gives you more trouble than she's worth," Leith said with a big grin.

Kalea smiled back. "So, you are telling me, there is no easy solution and whatever I do, someone gets hurt?" Leith nodded. "Well, thanks very much old man. It's nice to know what I've got to face."

Leith laughed. Eager to break the tension between them, he spoke, "Now get down off that horse and let's see what you can do with that toothpick of yours."

For the next hour, Kalea released her aggression and frustration at Leith with her boy's sword. Leith for his part was impressed. The complications of her life had seemed to hone her skills and a couple of times he had to work hard to stop her breaking through his defence. After an hour or so, Kalea was panting hard. So was Leith, but he was loath to show it. Kalea bent double leant on her sword. When finally, she got her breath back, she spoke, "Have I earned a swim?"

"You can't be serious?" Leith was aghast. "You only washed yesterday. You'll wash yourself away."

"Water never hurt anyone. You old fussbudget. I'm hot and sweaty and I really need a good wash off."

"Don't ask me to join you," Leith grumbled with a grin. "You can't go. You haven't got anything to dry with."

"Leith. It's hot. I'll dress wet. I'll be dry be the time we get back."

"Go on then girl." Resignation filled Leith's voice and he sat down with his back to the water. Kalea stripped off and threw herself in.

"Leith, this is wonderful," she called. "It's deeper here and I can swim."

"Lovely," Leith growled his voice dripping with sarcasm. Kalea laughed and swam away.

Kai had left the village on horseback to check the watchtowers at the perimeter of the village. He couldn't bear to be with Arthur, his anger still hot. Purposely, he had set off in the other direction from Leith and Kalea. He had no wish to upset the old warrior any more than he already was. He had completed most of his circuit when he heard voices and decided to check out what all the commotion was about. As he rounded a bend in the path, he caught sight of Leith sitting with his back to the river. Hastily, he scanned round to see where Kalea was. Splashing alerted him to her location. A large lump seemed to get wedged in his throat as he watched her naked lithe body skim through the water. He gave himself a mental shake. It was only a matter of time before he was spotted, so he rode forward boldly, hailing Leith as he did so. Leith was on his feet with his hand on the hilt of his sword in a trice whilst Kalea swam to the deeper water.

"Kai!" called Leith. "What the hell are you doing here?"

Kai rode towards him smiling broadly. "Well, as you wouldn't let me go riding with you, I decided to check the watch towers. I've one more to go and then I have checked the whole village." Then pretending he hadn't seen he continued. "Where's Kalea?"

Leith threw his head back and gestured towards the water. This gave Kai the excuse he needed to look towards Kalea. She stood with just her head and shoulders above the water and she smiled sheepishly.

"That fish looks familiar," Kai said with a grin.

Leith laughed. "That's a water nymph, that's what that is Son. I told you she wasn't conventional and you just can't keep that one out of the water."

"At least I don't smell bad," Kalea retorted. Kai had now reached Leith and dismounted still watching Kalea as he did so. Kalea made sure that she was well hidden by the water.

"It's definitely a strange looking fish," Kai continued.

"Come on girl," Leith called. "You've been in there long enough. Kai, sit down here next to me and let her get out."

Kai raised an eyebrow at Kalea and then did as he was told and sat with his back to the water. It wasn't long before he heard splashing and knew that Kalea had emerged from the water. "So, how long have you had webbed feet Kalea?" Kai asked without turning. He heard her giggle.

"From a baby," she answered. Leith shook his head in despair. Kai laughed.

"I'm dressed," Kalea stated. Both men got to their feet and turned round. Leith laughed and Kai stood with a silly grin on his face, purely amazed. "What?" Kalea asked unaware how provocative she was. The shirt clung to her wet body, emphasising her round breasts and hard nipples. Her wet hair clung to her shoulders wetting the shirt and not improving matters at all.

"Told you Kai." Leith laughed as much as Kai's stunned look as at Kalea. "She really doesn't understand what she looks like and this isn't exactly maidenly behaviour." Kalea looked down at herself and could see nothing wrong.

"I can't see what all the fuss is about," she grumbled causing both men to laugh. "And anyway," she said defensively. "I didn't know that we would have company. I thought I would be well dry by the time we met anyone." The men laughed.

"Come on girl, get aboard. I best get you back before you get into serious trouble." Leith chortled. Kalea collected her sword and wrapped it in a blanket.

"What have you got there?" Kai asked. Before Kalea could answer and dig herself a fresh hole, Leith answered.

"I've been teaching her some self-defence. What with all these men mooning around after her. I thought I'd better, so beware!"

"Can I see?" With great reluctance, Kalea unwrapped the sword and handed it to Kai.

Leith grinned as Kai examined it. Give the lad his due, he did it seriously. "That," Lieth explained "is toothpick."

Kai returned it to Kalea. "Well, I for one, wouldn't want to be on the end of it." Kalea smiled gratefully at him. She wrapped it up and Kai followed her to her horse. "Allow me," he said offering to boost her into the saddle.

"Thank you." She landed lightly in the saddle.

"Next time, you want to practise, let me know." Kai swung lightly onto his own horse. "I could teach you how to defend yourself from an axe."

Leith gave a half smile; the lad was eager to impress. "Best watch out lad, you could end up with your head off. She has some wild moves." They laughed and made their way back to the village. When they reached the paddock, Leith slid down and threw the reigns to Kalea. "You can sort out the horses' girl, I'm parched."

"As you command oh lord and master," called Kalea to his retreating back. All she got was a wave in response. "The rotten old turn coat," she grumbled to Kai as she slid from the saddle. "One minute he's moaning about me running off alone with a 'young blood' and then he wanders off and leaves me alone with another one."

Kai laughed as he undid the girth of his horse and pulled the saddle clear. "He knows when you are in safe hands." He pulled the bridle off his horse and slapped it lightly on the rump.

"Am I?" Kalea asked as she loaded her saddle on the fence and went to relieve Leith's mount of his.

"Are you what?" Kai countered. He had been too busy watching her and had lost the thread.

"Am I in safe hands?"

Kai gave her his brightest grin. "The safest."

"Well, I'm glad to hear that." Kai picked up her saddle as well as his own and Kalea followed him into the barn where the tack was stored. Kalea took Kai's bridle from him and went to wash the bits while Kai stacked the saddles away.

"You like horses, don't you?" he commented reaching up to put them on the waiting pegs.

"Very much so. They're so much less complicated than people."

Kai rounded so fast that he nearly took her off her feet. Reaching out, he steadied her. "Sorry," he said. "I didn't know you were so close." He realised that he was in no hurry to release her.

"I didn't know I was that close either." She grinned sheepishly. For a moment in the gloom of the barn, they stood grinning foolishly and then Kai kissed her. Kalea was more than ready. She had been acutely aware of him since he had turned up at the river. Aware of how close he had come lifting her onto her horse, how he smelt and the way he looked at her. His arms went round her and pulled her close, she did not resist and came willingly. Kalea's senses reeled. Kai's kiss was so very different to Arthur's. It was gentle, questing becoming more insistent and wonderful. Kalea could feel a warmth spread through her body and her arms went round him. As his tongue slid over her lips, her body seemed to ignite. Every inch of skin seemed to tingle and his hands felt hot and hard on her body. She felt more alive than she had ever done and pressed close to his body, unaware of the effect she was having on Kai. Her heart beat raced and she felt that she must be glowing with the heat her body was giving off. Finally, they parted. Lips still touching, Kalea breathed into Kai's mouth.

"Kai, no. I mustn't."

Kai forever the gentleman was struggling hard to regain his composure. He had guessed that she would be sweet, but not how sweet. "It's alright Kalea. I know we mustn't." But he was reluctant to let her go. She smelled so good.

Kalea lowered her head and spoke against his chest. "This is so confusing. Leith says that I am not wise in the way of men and women, I should have been with the other girls learning how to court and keep a man at arm's length."

Kai gave a quiet laugh. He was slowly regaining his composure. "This is a woman's art," Kai answered quietly.

"But how?" she asked looking up at him. He fought the urge to kiss her again. Instead, he grinned.

"You have asked the wrong man. I have been on the receiving end, but I can't say how the game works."

Kalea gave a big sigh and pulled away from him. "Leith says a woman should be wedded before she's bedded."

"Quite right too." Kai beamed happily.

"So, why is it, that when you kissed me, the last thing I wanted was to be wedded, just bedded?"

Kai laughed aloud and put an arm round her, wanting to keep her close. "An honest woman! Now, there's a rare thing!" he smiled down at her. "Kalea, Leith is right, your education is sorely lacking. Everyone feels like this. The difference is not everyone is so honest."

She looked at him in amazement. "Honest?"

"Honest," he confirmed.

"Would I feel like that, if any man kissed me?" she asked innocently. Kai couldn't resist probing. He wanted to know if she felt as strongly as he did.

"I don't know. How did you feel?" he asked realising he wasn't being totally fair with her and yet unable to resist the temptation. Kalea looked at him thoughtfully. She like him a lot. The warmth of his arm round her shoulders was reassuring and her heart began to race again. He seemed honest and kind, although somehow, she felt she shouldn't be discussing this with him, it seemed the right thing to do.

"Well," she spoke quietly trying to phrase it without seeming too forward. "Sort of warm and wonderful."

That would do. That was all he needed to know. "Kalea, I suppose it would be different with each man. But you only feel like that with someone you like a lot. And it felt the same for me too." She looked at him. He met her gaze and once again they came close to kissing. Kai cleared his throat. This was uncharted territory to him. "I don't know if I should be the one you talk to about this."

Kalea laughed releasing the tension between them. "No one wants to talk about it with me. I suppose I should consult a wise woman." Kai laughed too. Together they left the barn. Kai removed his arm not wishing to get in trouble with Leith and they walked towards the drinking hall.

"What Leith is trying to say," Kai pondered, "is that you mustn't get carried away in the heat of the moment." He watched Kalea as she met his eye. "It's easy to do, as you know. He means, you should take your time. Learn about your partner and see if you like them as a man as well as a lover."

A slow smile lit Kalea's face. "I see. That was easy enough to understand. Why didn't Leith just say so?"

Kai laughed. He was aware he did a lot of laughing when he was with her. "Because he is an old man who has never married and he didn't have the words to explain."

"But you managed."

"I'm not sure I did it that well. A woman worth marrying, is worth taking the time to get to know. The 'act'," Kalea knew exactly what he meant, "is easy enough, but it is far harder to make a commitment. Leith likes you, he believes, and so do I, that you are a worthy woman. He wants to see you courted, married and then bedded. And if that's what he wants, that is what I shall give him."

Kalea glanced at him shyly. His face was serious and it made her heart thump loudly. So loudly, that she was sure he would hear it. "Bold words Kai," she murmured quietly.

"They are not spoken lightly." He returned meeting her shy smile. "In fact, I intend to ask his permission to court you straight away. I feel the need to steal another kiss. You may not be wise in the way of men and women, Kalea," he added. "But whether you like it or not, I am bewitched." It gave him strange pleasure to see her blush.

"Well, my Kai," he liked the sound of that, "we will have to see what my guardian says about that." And she gave him a warning glance which made them both laugh.

Leith and Arthur were talking and looked up they heard their approach. The came in both with broad grins and were aware of the scrutiny they were under.

"Where have you two been?" Leith asked gruffly, looking at Kalea with a meaningful glare.

"Where do you think?" she countered. "Cleaning tack."

"You were gone so long, I thought you were making it," he responded.

"Well, if you had stayed and cleaned you own, it wouldn't have taken so long." Kalea was smarting under his scrutiny. Leith grinned but still looked for evidence of straw in her hair.

"I thought you were having a romp in the hay," he growled semi seriously.

Kai looked horrified. "What and risk being stuck by her 'toothpick'? It would take a braver man than me."

Arthur until this point had said nothing just observing the pair but his curiosity got the better of him. "Toothpick?"

Kai and Leith grinned at one another. "Leith has been teaching Kalea the finer points of sword play," Kai answered. They all laughed except for Kalea who pretended to be fierce.

"I hope you don't share your women, the way you share my secrets!" she pronounced indignantly giving Kai a friendly push.

"No, we do not!" Kai and Arthur said as one. This time Kalea laughed.

"Come and eat girl before you get yourself into trouble. Bad enough they know you can wield a sword." Kalea propped her boy's sword against the table and sat down. Arthur looked at her as she poured herself some water.

"May I?" he indicated the sword.

Kalea met his eye. "Go on then. You might as well have a laugh at my expense. Leith quite enjoys it."

Leith grinned and tore off some more bread. "I told you the girl had spirit," he mumbled in between mouthfuls. Arthur picked up the sword and unwrapped it. Kalea was so embarrassed, she looked down at her plate and waited for the caustic comments. Arthur and Kai grinned at each other and turned to an already smiling Leith. Arthur did his best to be sombre but didn't quite pull it off. Kalea looked up at him and grinned. "Go on Arthur. Good try but I'm not going to be offended. I think Leith has given me all the insults there are to be had."

Arthur's face split into a broad grin. "Well, young Kalea, this is quite some toothpick!" his comment was greeted by much laughter. He wielded it a few times. "And it's not so sad for a boy's sword."

"I told her she was robbed," Leith said doing his best to hide his smiles. Kalea shot him a harsh look.

"It's alright for you," she countered between mouthfuls. "You're big tough men. I'm not. I doubt if I could lift your swords, let alone do any damage with them."

"You'll not do too much harm with that either," Leith added. Kalea groaned.

"If you gentlemen will excuse me. I am going to find a wise woman and see if she needs and apprentice." She rose and swept out.

"Kalea!" called Kai. "We are joking."

"Leave her lad. She's a proud one another fault." They all laughed.

Kalea made an effort for the evening meal. With the help of the lovely wise woman, Ellen, she had purchased a second-hand new dress from the market stall. Ellen had helped her launder it and Kalea was pleased with it. She put it on and brushed her hair until it shone. Even Leith was surprised to see her so neatly groomed and the two younger men couldn't take their eyes off her. Not surprisingly, Kalea was seated between Kai and Arthur. Aware of their interest, she was amused. She had never been aware of her feminine powers until that day and now she found the whole thing, fascinating. Kai's thigh rested lightly against hers and she could almost feel the heat coming off him. Even when she was talking to Leith and Lud, she could feel their eyes on her and it made her a little breathless. *Leith was right,* she thought, *I know little of this art.* The meal was soon over and the men sat comfortably drinking and talking.

"Did you find a wise woman Kalea?" Arthur asked.

"Yes, thank you. I met Lud on the way out and he took me to Ellen. She was very kind." And she thought, *a lot younger than most wise women.*

"I'd like to know what you lot were thinking," Lud cut in. "New to the village, and not one of you louts could be bothered to show her the way."

Both of them looked chastened. "Sorry Lud," Kai answered. Then took a deep breath. "Leith. I would like to ask permission to court Kalea." Conversation at the table died. Leith looked at Lud who shrugged. Arthur stopped mid-sentence and was like a fish out of water. Leith met Kai's eye.

"Firstly, we must ask the girl if she is willing." He turned a questioning gaze to Kalea who was so shocked, she just nodded.

Lud laughed. "There you go Kai, there's the easiest hurdle over. Now, you just have to get past Leith." Leith grinned and once again met Kai's eye.

"The girl is in my charge you know," he stated.

"I know." Kai's voice held a level of respect and caution.

"If anything were to happen to her in your care, I would strap you within an inch of your life."

"I understand," Kai answered levelly.

Leith's stare didn't waiver. "Now young Kai, are your intentions honourable? I want no babies born the wrong side of the blanket." Even without looking, he knew that Kalea was blushing furiously and suppressed the urge to grin.

Kai however, was deadly serious. "I promise you that Kalea will bear no child of mine on the wrong side of the blanket." For what seemed to be an age the two men locked eyes.

Leith finally broke the contact. "Best not, or I'll see you gelded." He paused. "Well then lad, I give you, my permission." He lent across the table and clasped Kai's hand and the pair shook rigorously. Kai' face split into a broad beam like the cat that had got the cream. "Good luck to you Son." Leith smiled back. Kalea released a breath that she had not been aware she was holding and beamed back at Kai who was beside himself with relief.

Lud laughed. "And now the real fun starts."

"Kai's not lacking in courage Lud, I'll give you that." Leith smiled. "He'll need all he can with Kalea."

"That's hardly fair," Kalea countered. The men all laughed except for Arthur who was strangely quiet.

"I've never seen Kai look so nervous," Lud snorted in between gust of giggles. "I think he would rather face a band of Saxons than face you." This caused much merriment. Kai though smiling, looked sheepish.

The atmosphere at once became more relaxed. Kalea was girlishly happy and smiled at everyone and became aware that Arthur seemed distracted. She bent towards him.

"Are you alright?" she asked with concern. Arthur pulled himself out of his reveries and turned to her with a cold light in his eye that made her draw back.

"I am fine, thank you," he answered coolly. Inwardly, he was seething. Kai had pre-empted him. He had been waiting for Kai and Lud to leave so that he could ask Leith precisely what Kai had done. Despite the fact that Kalea hadn't known this, he was annoyed with her. He had thought that there could be something special between them. What had changed her mind? He turned his attention to Leith, who was deep in discussion with Lud and then to Kai who was listening with a faint smile playing at the edge of his mouth. After a while, he turned his attention to Kalea who was watching him cautiously. Meeting her eye wasn't easy, what he wanted to do was to ask her why she had chosen Kai but he couldn't in front of the others. He sighed deeply and Kalea placed her hand upon his arm.

"What troubles you, Arthur?" she asked.

Arthur sharply pulled his arm away. "You," he said quietly, careful that the others did not hear. Kalea knew that now was not the time to confront him and sat for a while feeling quite miserable. Leith had warned of this and she had fallen into the trap despite his warnings.

"Are you alright?" Leith asked catching the look.

"I could do with some air," she answered casting her eyes down.

"Then allow me," Kai leaped in. Looking at Leith for approval. Leith nodded. He took her hand and led her out. Once away from Arthur, Kalea felt her spirits lift. As they stepped from the hall into the cool night air, Kai remarked. "Well, I think that went quite well."

Kalea couldn't help but grin. "Which bit? The one where he said he would strap you within an inch of your life? Or the threat of being gelded?"

Kai threw back his head and roared with laughter. "Lud was right. Give me a band of Saxons any day."

"Still, it could have been worse."

"Could it?" Kai queried.

"Oh yes. If it had been my father, you would have most probably got a tongue lashing and still got no for an answer."

Kai put his arm round her and drew her close and felt her slip her arm round his waist. Together they walked through the village. It was late and mostly empty. Most had already gone to their beds. They walked down to the paddock where they could see the shadowy shapes of the horses moving around in the dark. The night was clear and the stars were bright in the sky.

"Isn't it beautiful?" Kalea threw her head back to look at the ink dark sky.

"Yes, you are," Kai said beside her. He had no wish to look at stars.

Kalea cuffed him. "The stars, silly."

Kai looked up at the bright sparks in the sky and then down at Kalea who was watching him closely. "The only stars I see, are in your eyes." He bent and gathered her into his arms. His kiss was met eagerly and Kai felt her body tremble against him. Kalea was once again overwhelmed with desire. It was exciting but at the same time frightening. The world seemed to condense into her body and the way his hands and lips felt on them. She trembled with the force of it and her body was afire, wanting only to be touched and kissed. What she wanted to do was melt into him. Kai was awash in his own emotions. Something welled within him. Something that was linked to his sexual desire, but wasn't quite. He wanted to make love to her, yes, that was definitely true, but also, he wanted to somehow squash her inside of him, so that she would always be there. It was a fierce feeling, a mixture of wanting to protect, consume and nurture. The kiss ended but his lips still brushed her. Her breath was quick and he could feel her heart pounding against his chest. Before he could kiss her again, Kalea spoke, her voice soft, her breath sweet against his mouth.

"Kai, I could lose myself in your arms." He smiled against her lips. "Please tell me. Are you serious about this?"

Kai's lips were still against hers as her whispered. "Deadly serious. I would have asked Lieth if I could wed you tonight, if I had thought he would let me." And he kissed her again. She melted against him. When they eventually came up for air, Kai cleared his throat and said gruffly. "Enough kissing for now. I'm in danger of ending up gelded or at the very least strapped."

Kalea laughed and still entwined in each other's arms they made their way back to the drinking hall. They were surprised to find that the others had already retired. Although Leith sat up on his couch when they entered.

Kai nodded to him and then lent down to whisper in Kalea's ear. "Goodnight lovely. Sleep well."

"You too," she responded and he gave her the lightest of kisses and left. Kalea looked at Leith who gave her a grin and settled down. She went behind the screens and undressed. Sleep wasn't easy to find. Her mind whirled with images of Kai and Arthur and her body was hot.

Kalea woke early the next morning. Her sleep had been unsettled. She scrubbed her face with hands trying to remove the sleep from her eyes. Having dressed, she came out from behind the screens and found that Arthur was already up and sitting eating breakfast. She drew in a deep breath and approached him.

"May I speak to you?" she asked in a conciliatory tone.

Arthur's dark eyes were hard. "There is nothing to say," he spoke bluntly.

"I think there is. Will you hear me out?" nothing but respect in her voice. Arthur shrugged and motioned her to sit. Kalea sat meekly and met his hard eyes. "I am sorry that I have angered you. That was never my intention." Arthur said nothing. "I know I must look very bad to you. Kissing you in the morning and courting Kai by sunset." Arthur pulled off some bread and began to chew giving no sign that he was listening. Kalea sighed. "I didn't mean it to happen, it just did. I am not well versed in the ways of men and women. You are the first man to have ever kissed me and I liked it. But afterwards," she paused. "You gave me no sign and," she looked down at her hands, "I wasn't sure if I hadn't dreamt it. Then Leith told me that both you and Kai liked me and there would be trouble if I didn't choose one and stick by my decision." She glanced up at him but his face was unforgiving and she hastily looked back down. "Then I was talking to Kai at the stable and we seemed to get on well and…" she was not about to confess to the kiss, she was in enough trouble "when he asked if he could ask Leith if he could court me, I just said yes." She sighed again. "I am sorry Arthur. It wasn't Kai's fault; he didn't know about you kissing me and…" Once again, she paused, wondering how to continue. "I don't want to cause trouble between you and Kai," she finished lamely.

Arthur looked at her bowed head and softened. He sighed as heavily as she had. "Kalea," he said wearily "I was going to ask Leith too." She looked up and met his eye. "I can't say I understand why and what Kai said to persuade you, but he must have put a reasonable case. Did you think that the kiss meant nothing?" he asked.

Kalea met his eye levelly. "I didn't know what it meant. I can tell you what if meant to me. A handsome, God like king was kissing me and it was wonderful. I didn't want you to stop." She gave him a shy smile. "But I haven't had a lad court me, let alone a king and I…Didn't know what to think. Then Leith gave you such a hard time and you seemed to withdraw and I wonder if I was so inexperienced, that you had lost interest in me. I didn't know what it meant to you." Arthur went to speak but she rushed on not wishing to hear. "And now, I don't want to. If I made a mistake with you, I am so, so sorry. But I will not make another mistake and hurt Kai. He doesn't deserve it."

Arthur nodded. "I see. It's alright. I don't pretend that I like it, but it's alright."

Leith had been lying awake for some time listening to this conversation. He felt very proud of Kalea. She had seized the bull by the horns and confronted a nasty situation and hadn't handled it too badly either. To warn them he was waking, he began to stir and cough. Through a squinted eye, he saw them turn to look, so he sat up and rubbed his face blearily, as if he had only just woken. Seeing them both there, he grinned. Hauling himself up, he lumbered to the table.

"And what are you two chattering about?" he asked.

Arthur stepped in. He was aware that Kalea didn't lie and suspected that when she did, she did badly. "This and that and nothing much at all. Kalea has only just arrived herself. She hasn't even begun to eat yet." As if suddenly aware that what Arthur said was correct, she poured Leith and her a beaker of milk and tore some bread off. Leith began to talk to Arthur about the Saxon threat and as if overhearing, Kai came bounding through the door. The big beam on his face told them all, that he thought this would be a good day and could be getting better by the minute. Kalea had to smile back; his mood was infectious.

"Good morning to you all," he said joining them. "Are you still eating? I would have thought you would have been long finished."

"You must have a guilty conscience if you can't sleep," Leith grumbled.

"Well, I confess, I have got a lot on my mind." Kai grinned.

"Take no notice Kai, he's always grumpy in the morning."

"I am not," protested Leith. Even Arthur smiled at this.

"Leith, I was wondering if I might take Kalea and her toothpick and teach her defence against the axe."

"I've heard it called some things before."

"Leith!" Kalea cried indignantly.

"Now, don't you come the modest maiden with me young lady. I know better," Leith teased causing her to blush. "Don't you have any work to do lad?"

"I got up early and did it. I've got a round of the watchtowers, but I thought Kalea might be allowed to come with me," Kai added hopefully. Leith looked from one to other.

"Alright Kai, take her away. And watch that toothpick of hers, she's got some wild moves." Kalea got up to get her sword. "Now young lady, before you go scurrying off, no bathing you hear?"

"But..."

"But nothing girl. You do as you're told."

Kai stepped in risking much, but willing to do so for her. "She will be quite safe with me, Leith. I shan't look and I have no need of being gelded."

"Easy to say sitting here lad. Harder to do in the situation. Have her by the river by noon and I shall meet you there."

Kai looked a bit crestfallen, but nodded. Kalea on the other hand, kissed Leith on the forehead and added. "As you command." She tried to scoot away but Leith was still fast and gave her a hard swat on the backside. "You be good Kalea, if you know how." Kalea was back with her sword in an instant and the pair made their way outside. They couldn't have got down the steps when they could be heard laughing.

Leith looked at Arthur, his face was calm. Suddenly he exploded out of his seat and kicked the bench over. "DAMN IT ALL!" he cursed storming round the table. Leith didn't flinch.

"Calm yourself Arthur. What's done is done."

"How much did you hear old man?" Arthur demanded.

"Enough," Leith responded evenly. Arthur picked up the chair and slumped dejectedly on it. "Don't be too hard on yourself or them. A mistake is a mistake. We all make them."

Arthur met his eye. "I should have..."

"But you didn't and it can't be undone. Hindsight is good to no one," Leith interrupted.

"She can't be that innocent," Arthur protested.

"Ah, but she is. And perhaps, that's the saddest part. She is a girl in a woman's body. Kalea was no more than a baby herself when her mother died and her father let her run wild. When she was old enough, she cooked and cleaned and kept home but he left her to run with her brothers. He meant well did Ren, but letting a girl run free is a dangerous thing. Fair enough when she looks like a little girl, but not when the girl becomes a woman, it is dangerous. I can remember her riding like the wind through the village, skirts flapping and legs showing. Not the sort of thing young women is supposed to do. The women of the village tried to take her in hand, but she always sneaked off and they soon gave up. There were plenty of young bloods that would have liked to take Kalea for a tumble, but they feared Ren and his sons and if one was even caught looking at her, they were warned off. Ren did her no favours, he wanted to keep her for himself. He did not remarry, he kept Kalea as a housekeeper. She is not like most women who chatter like magpies with other women. The only woman she had time for was the wise woman and then she talked herbs. Because her brothers gave chattering women a wide berth, so did she and women learn a lot from gossip."

"Why are you telling me this?" Arthur asked.

"Because I would not have you think ill of her. She is a good woman."

"You're very fond of her, aren't you?"

Leith gave a wry smile. "Only since we left the village. You learn a lot when you are forced into another's company whether you like it or not. The girl is strong, resourceful, quick and clever. She is not lacking in courage that one. In fact, she's braver than some lads I know. Her biggest fault, is she thinks of herself as too much of a lad." They both laughed.

"Alright Leith point taken. If I had spoken when I had the chance, it would be me out there with Kalea."

"Perhaps, you would rather face the Saxons than a one-eyed war dog too?"

"Perhaps, Leith, you are right."

Kai and Kalea got outside the hall before Kai said "Lead me to the Saxons!" they both laughed. "He doesn't get any easier, does he?" he stated.

"Scary!" Kalea giggled. "Race you to the paddock." And she took off at a run. For a second, Kai was too surprised to follow, this was not what he had expected. Then he ran after her, he could have caught her but he was laughing too much and he wanted her to win anyway.

She stood panting at the paddock. "Well! You're not very fleet of foot. I can see I am going to have to slow down if I want to be caught."

"You cheeky wench!" Kai grabbed her round the waist and hoisted her over his shoulder. She let out and indignant shriek and laughed as he carried her inside the barn and deposited her on a pile of straw. Her face was flushed with laughter and being hung upside down, she looked delightful. Helping her to her feet he pulled her close and looked down into her up turned face which was offered for kissing. It took no further persuasion, and they kissed in the gloom of the barn. "Come on," Kai said eventually, "we'll never get anywhere if we carry on like this and Leith will be waiting by the river ready to run me through." Smiling happily, they were soon on the road. It was a glorious sunny day. The sky was blue and the birds were singing and Kai thought it must be the best day in the world. Checking the watchtowers was an easy task. All he had to do, was check that each one was manned, that the watcher wasn't snoozing on the job and if they had seen anything unusual. It was a good opportunity to chat and introduce Kalea to some of the other men from the village. They in turn, were intrigued by this leggy young woman who had turned up out of the blue. Kai was surprised that she didn't say a lot, just smiling shyly. At last, they had checked everyone and Kai led them down to the river.

"This will do," he said dismounting.

Kalea slid from the saddle and slid her sword clear of its wrapping. Kai much to her amazement started to strip off. "Are you going swimming?" she asked nervously as he shrugged off his gilet and shirt.

"No. I wouldn't dare. It's warm and it's easier to move. Also, it will help you to see what I'm talking about."

Kalea smiled and took in his broad well-muscled chest. "But what are we going to talk about?" she asked flirtatiously unable to take her eyes from him.

"You're not trying to lead me astray, are you Kalea?" Kai asked removing his axe from his horse. Kalea was aware that she was staring. She had seen both her brothers naked but they had not inspired the feelings that Kai stirred in her. Watching the muscles ripple on his smooth back, all she wanted to do was touch him. Heat flooded her body and she felt herself blushing. "Kalea?" Kai looked over his shoulder and saw her embarrassment.

Giving herself a mental shake, she flirted. "Would I do such a thing?"

"I will put my shirt back on if you prefer." Kai was enjoying the effect he was having on her.

"Don't be silly. I've grown up with two brothers. I've seen much more than a naked chest believe me."

Kai grinned showing off his even white teeth. Swinging his axe to warm his muscles, he made a fine sight. The axe whistled as it cleaved the air.

"Right," he said seriously, "down to business. Fighting a man armed with an axe requires different moves that a man with a sword." Kalea held her sword at the ready. "A glancing blow from the axe does a lot more damage that a sword. You saw that with Leith. If that blow had landed true, Leith would have been dead." He watched Kalea carefully. She was listening closely. "Although the axe is deadly, it takes skill from the axe man to remain protected." He made several swings with the axe. "As you see, when I take the blade back to put my weight behind it, it leaves my chest unprotected. The same goes if I slice sideways." He demonstrated. "The weight of the axe as it passes through leaves the side of my body free."

"So, how do you protect yourself?" she asked.

"Aha! You will see that as you try and attack. Now go on. Have a go." Kalea looked at him doubtfully. "Come on Kalea, I won't let you hurt me."

Kalea shook her head dubiously but readied herself to attack. He nodded in encouragement. She flew at him with good deal more speed than he expected. Her blade was true and it took more effort than expected to deflect her blow.

"Not bad at all," he said as her sword flew from her and hand and left her defenceless.

"What do you mean not bad?" She sulked and waved her hands at him. "These aren't going to stop you chopping my head off."

Kai smiled. "No, maybe not. But you saw and opening and went for it and you were brave enough to face a swinging axe." Picking up her sword, Kalea turned to him.

"Only because you had no intention of causing me any harm." She readied herself again. At least, she did not lack courage. "What now?"

"Let's see if you can find a way through a swinging axe." Kai began to swing the axe in a defensive arc in front of him. Kalea stood watching, waiting for a chance. Kai was beginning to become aware that this wasn't going to be as easy as he had thought it would be. The combination of not hurting her but at the same time not making it too easy, was a difficult line to draw. She would know at once if he was letting her through and it was obvious, she did not want that. Suddenly, without warning, she moved, blade low and coming in behind the axe as it swung passed his body. Kai was as skilled at he could be and managed to stop the axe mid flow and bring it back to block the blade causing a tremendous vibration up

61

the sword. In an effort to keep the blade in her hand, Kalea was off balance and the gentlest shove from Kai sent her sprawling on her face. She rolled over looking indignant and Kai laughed offering his hand to help her up. She scowled at him.

"Your timing was a bit out there," he said as she stood shaking her wrist, which was still aching. "But nevertheless, I have seen young warriors with worse timing than that. You got the stroke right. Coming in after the axe was moving in one direction but you were slightly late. If you come in, just as the axe begins it forward arc, it is harder for the axe man to get his weight behind it in time to stop."

"How do remember all this in battle?" she asked still rubbing her wrist.

"Because you do it so often, that it becomes instinct. You must remember, that boys start learning these war skills from a very early age. Even as small children, they play at warriors and by the time they are your age they have been learning it for years. Don't think that you will never learn, but you cannot expect to learn in a day what others have taken years to learn," he said kindly.

"Let's do it again," Kalea said.

For nearly an hour, the two of them practised. Even Kai had worked up a sweat and Kalea was nearly on her knees. She sank down onto the grass, wiping her brow with the sleeve of her shirt. "I think that's enough." Kai sat down beside her. "I don't want to kill you."

She flopped onto her back and groaned. "I am going to hurt tomorrow. All over."

Kai grinned. "I'll rub it better if you want."

Propping herself up on her elbows, she met his smile with her own. "I wonder what Leith will say to that."

Kai looked over his shoulder at the cool inviting water. "Leith said you couldn't swim; he didn't tell me."

Kalea raised an eyebrow at him. "Go on then, I won't peek."

"I should hope not." Kai walked down to the water's edge and began to strip off.

Kalea lay back and shut her eyes feeling the sun warm her body. Very soon, she could hear Kai splashing in the water. "Is it cold?" she called.

"It's not hot," he answered. Kalea smiled to herself. Men were such babies. Laying there in the sun, it was easy to drift off and she nearly did but suddenly she heard hoof beats. Leaping to her feet, she grabbed her sword at the same time calling "Kai! Visitors." She need not have worried for it was Leith. Kai seeing that plunged back into the water.

Leith took in the scene in a jiffy. "Trying to defend his virtue lass? I wouldn't bother, he lost that a long time ago."

Kalea grinned in response. "We haven't broken any rules. You said I couldn't swim and I haven't. And I haven't peeked either."

Leith roared with laughter. "Don't want too either. You might be disappointed." There was some splashing and Leith grabbed her by the shoulders and turned her away from the river.

"I hope you're not doubting my manhood Leith. Especially in front of my future bride," Kai said grinning as he towelled himself off with his shirt. He could see Kalea's shoulders shaking with mirth as she stood with her back to him.

"Bride?" queried Leith. "I said you could court her; I didn't say you could marry her." And when he saw Kai's crestfallen face, he relented and peered at Kai's genitals and nodded. "You won't be disappointed there lass, that's if I let him marry you."

Kai hastily pulled on his trousers and grinned at Leith. Kalea was used to this sort of talk from her brothers and wasn't bothered at all. Leith turned her round so that she could see Kai. He wanted to see her reaction. Kai was pulling on his boots, still naked from the waist up and hair damp from the water. Even Leith had to admit, he was a fine figure of a man. As Kai stood up beaming at Kalea, Leith heard her breath catch in her throat. That would do, the response he had been expecting. If she hadn't been roused by the sight of her man at his best, she had chosen incorrectly. Leith was pleased. "Right lass," he said giving her a hearty thwack of the backside. "In you go and don't be too long about it."

"I don't suppose I can watch," Kai said wistfully. "After all, you are here to keep me under control."

"Quite right, you can't." Leith slapped him on the back. "Now come here Kai. What's all this talk of marriage?" He was pleased to see Kai blush and looked over his shoulder to see Kalea walking into the water. They sat down with their backs to the water.

Kalea saved him from having to answer Leith's question by yelling. "Kai! You lied. It's freezing!" she dived in.

Kai laughed and yelled back. "I didn't want you to think, I was frightened by a little cold water." He turned his attention back to Leith and taking a deep breath, he said, "I was going to ask but thought you might think it too soon."

Leith met his eye. "Can you make her happy? Can she make you happy?"

"I have never felt so happy as when I am with her," Kai answered seriously.

"You hardly know her," Leith said solemnly.

"You don't know her much better than me, and you love her," Kai came back.

Leith was a little shocked. It wasn't until Kai said it, he realised that he was right. So, he had a few weeks on Kai, but it wasn't that long and, in that time, he had come to love Kalea, as a daughter. "Mayhap you're right Kai," he admitted. "I don't want Kalea hurt. If you are sure and only if you're sure, I give you my permission to ask. She's lived with one grumpy old man; she doesn't need to live with another."

"I'd never hurt her," Kai said earnestly.

Leith nodded and continued. "I make one condition, you ask her when, and only when, we return from East Anglia." Kai nodded his agreement and the two men shook hands. "We leave the day after tomorrow."

Kai was surprised. Arthur normally didn't make these types of decisions without Kai being there. But then he supposed, that he had been too busy with Kalea. As if sensing his surprise, Leith added. "Arthur, Lud and I have been talking all morning." Kai nodded. "Anyway, how did my girl do with her axe training?" Leith asked.

Kai grinned. "She's good," Leith answered with a grin of his own. "I must admit, she took me by surprise a few times. She's quick and can see an opening if ones there." There was a sparkle in Leith's eye. Was it pride, Kai wondered? "You have taught her well. If she had the strength of a man, she would make a decent warrior." Yes, it was pride. The old man's face lit up. The conversation ended abruptly as they heard splashing and guessed that Kalea was coming out.

"Don't you dare look," Leith growled at Kai. Then called to Kalea. "Did you bring anything to dry yourself on girl?"

"Err! No," she replied.

"Use my shirt," Kai offered gallantly. Then added, "You look far better than me in a wet shirt, but I'd rather keep that pleasure for myself."

That made Leith smile, "Are you sure Kai?"

"I'm sure."

"Thank you. I'll rinse it out when I'm finished."

"No need." Kai was thinking that it would smell of her, and he quite liked the thought of that.

"Kai tells me you did well at practice," Leith told her.

"Kai is too kind," Kalea grumbled. "I was awful. I either ended up flat on my face or sword less."

Both men laughed and Kai answered. "Don't be too hard on yourself. Towards the end you were doing well. You did very well hang onto your sword when I tried to disarm you at the end."

"It hurt my wrist like hell," she grumbled, secretly pleased that he had thought well of her.

"You'll hurt tomorrow," Leith added. "And you've only got a day to get over it before we leave for the east."

"Is Arthur going to rally the chiefs there?" she seemed unsurprised that they would be leaving so soon.

"That he is. It won't be an easy job."

"Is Kalea going?" Kai asked.

"Of course," Answered Leith. "Where I go, she goes."

"But she'll be travelling with a war band," Kai worried.

"I won't hold you up if that's what you're worried about," Kalea answered with a touch of annoyance.

"It wasn't that at all." Wanting to turn around so that he could see her. "It's just that there are a lot of men and it's a dangerous journey."

Leith patted Kai on the knee. "Don't you worry about Kalea. The journeys not a problem. She has done it before with just me as company and survived. This time, she has two protectors and a war band. No harm will befall her." Kai wasn't convinced. "Now lad, there's your trouble. This is not some mild maiden you have here and she'll fight beside you, not hide behind you." Kalea was flattered and when Leith added. "Are you ready yet? You're taking an age."

She responded brightly. "Ready for anything." They turned to find her smiling broadly at them. "My favourite two men. What could be closer to bliss?" Both faces lit up with silly grins.

When they arrived back at the village, they could see that plans were well underway for their departure. People were rushing backwards and forwards gathering supplies for the war band and in the paddock, the horses were being checked for fitness. The trio made sure their own horses were well looked after before making their way back to the drinking hall. Arthur was pouring over some plans on the table and looked up when they came in. "Kai, Leith I need your advice." The two men abandoned her and left Kalea standing alone. For a while, she watched the three heads bent over the map and Leith pointing to various spots and then without a word she left.

Making her way through the village, she came to the house of Ellen, the wise woman. Knocking politely, she waited for permission to enter. Ellen greeted her.

"I had thought I'd see you," she stated. "No sooner had word gone through the village that Arthur was heading East with the warband, I thought Kalea will be down for some healing herbs."

Kalea smiled. "You are indeed wise mother," she said respectfully.

"I have started to prepare, but I will need your help to gather sufficient."

"I will gladly help. I will just tell Leith where I am. He worries you know."

The wise woman smiled. "And well he might be with a girl as pretty as you. Hurry back and we will make a start straight away."

Kalea obediently did as she was told. The men had hardly moved since she had left. She waited for a moment and when they still had not noticed her spoke. "Excuse me." They looked up startled at being disturbed. "If you need me, I am with Ellen." They nodded as one and Kalea turned briskly about and left.

Kalea was exhausted. Ellen had taken her out gathering herbs and they had been gone hours. They had scoured the fields and woods collecting different types. Some Kalea knew but many Ellen had to explain how to prepare them and use them and what they were best to treat. Ellen was determined that Kalea was not going to leave the village without being prepared for anything. As well as the usual cures that Kalea might need, headaches, wounds, fever, stomach disorders, Ellen had made sure that there was a supply of reviving herbs and even one for making sure a man's seed did not grow in a woman.

Kalea had no idea what she might need that for with Leith around. Nevertheless, she was an eager pupil. If she didn't understand, she questioned. What would happen if you mixed certain herbs and roots? Would it matter if you ate them raw rather than boiled them? There was no way that she could know everything, but she learnt enough, she hoped, to keep them healthy. They had been so busy that they had forgotten lunch and it was sunset when at last they finally returned to the village. Ellen had forged quite a liking for the young woman, who was keen and polite, she felt quite sorry for her as they plodded wearily home.

"Come in Kalea, I will get us something to eat," she said as they arrived at her home.

Kalea lowered the pack she was carrying. "Thank you but no mother. I must return to see Leith. Thank you for teaching so much today."

Ellen smiled. "Perhaps when you return from Anglia, you might consider becoming my apprentice."

"I would be honoured." Kalea smiled. "Goodnight, Ellen."

"Good night child," Ellen said leaning forward to kiss the girl on the forehead. Kalea dragged herself back to the drinking hall. As she entered, the four men turned to look at her. They were surprised at her weariness.

"Kalea, are you alright?" asked Leith. She smiled wearily at him.

"Just tired. Would you mind helping me with my boot?"

"I will," Kai answered. Kalea smiled gratefully and sank down onto the bench. Kai pulled her boots off and she sighed with relief.

"Come and have some food," Kai coaxed still on his knees before her.

"Can't. Too tired. Must sleep." She leant forward and kissed him on the lips much to his and the others amazement. Then without a further word, she shambled off behind the screen.

"Don't you go to sleep dressed," Leith called.

"Alright," came a sleepy reply. Then all was quiet.

"She gone to sleep dressed," Leith commented. They all laughed but quietly.

The next morning, everyone was up bar Kalea. The four of them were still discussing plans when they heard a mad scrabbling from behind Kalea's screens. They looked at the screens bemused and suddenly Kalea exploded out.

"Has anyone seen my boots?" Her hair was everywhere and her clothes creased from sleeping in them. The men couldn't help grinning.

"There over there where you left them," Kai stated.

"Thanks." She rushed over and started to pull them on.

"Don't you even say good morning now?" Leith asked watching her struggling to get the boots on.

"Sorry. Good morning, everyone," she said stamping her feet that were stubbornly not wanting to go back in her boots. "I promised Ellen, I would help her this morning. You could have woken me instead of leaving me sleeping half the morning away. I'll see you later." She was trying to tame her hair whilst heading for the door.

"Hold it right there, young lady." Leith's voice was stern. "You're not going anywhere until you have eaten something. You missed a meal last night and you're not going to miss another." Leith's voice had halted her in her tracks. She turned, mouth open to protest but one look at his face changed her mind and she came back and sat down. "And before you even think about it, you will not bolt your food. You will sit here like a civilised person and eat nicely." Kalea glowered at him. "Now, don't you be insolent," he warned. Kalea poured herself a beaker of milk and tore of some bread. It wasn't until she started to chew, she realised how hungry she was. Then it was really an effort not to bolt her food. She grinned at Leith.

"So, why is it you are always right?" she asked. He rewarded her with a smile.

"When you have lived as long as I have, you will know."

"Would you like to tell us what you have been doing?" Arthur asked as much to keep her at the table as curiosity.

Kalea really would rather eat than talk and was already helping herself to some honeyed oat cakes. "You have a very good wise woman." Kalea desperately tried to talk in between mouthfuls so as not to spray the crumbs around. She poured herself some more milk. She really was hungry. "I have been gathering cures and learning and very interesting it is too."

"Can you cure the boil on my bum?" Leith teased.

"Well, I could if you wanted me to." Kalea had a milk moustache which made her look quite comical. "But I would rather not. I have no wish to look at your hairy backside, thank you." They all laughed. "Can I go now?"

"After you have wiped your mouth clean," Leith explained patiently.

Kalea hastily cuffed her mouth on her sleeve and stood smiling. "I'll see you later," she said and almost casually, walked to the door. Leith called after her, "Not so late this time." There was no response but they heard her thunder down the steps. Just as well, or she would have heard them all laugh. "Kai, are you really sure about this?" Leith asked.

Kai's eyes twinkled as he answered. "Oh yes. Life would never be boring."

Kalea apologised for being late, but Ellen didn't seem to mind. The two bent their heads low and spent the day preparing leaves and roots for Kalea's newly acquired healing chest. They had finished just before lunch and Kalea said to Ellen that she would like to go for a swim. Much to her surprise, the wise woman said she would come too. This pleased Kalea, had never swum with another woman before and she didn't want to disturb Leith who would only grumble. Ellen knew of an even better spot to swim in. At this point, the water was deep and wide. The two women stripped off unselfconsciously and jumped in. For a while, the age difference didn't matter and they were just two girls having fun. As they sat drying themselves in the sun Ellen said. "I haven't had so much fun for a long time."

Kalea returned the feeling. "I know, I am always being guarded by Leith and he gets bored if I am too long. Anyway, it's not much fun swimming on your own."

Ellen grinned at her. "I doubt if I will have you as a partner for long. When you return, I expect Kai will want to swim with you." She was amused to see the girl blush.

"I don't think it's swimming Kai wants to do." Kalea grinned. "And anyway, Leith will make sure that that I won't go 'swimming' with Kai, no matter what I want." Ellen giggled.

"Well, Kalea, if you ever need any help with women's things, don't be frightened to ask. And I will help you no matter what others will say."

Kalea hugged the woman. "Thank you have been more kind than I could have hoped for."

"It is nothing child."

Kalea returned to the drinking hall after had eaten with Ellen. The whole village was buzzing with activity and the hall was little different. As she came in, Kai looked up and came towards her with a big smile. Without thinking, he gave her a huge bear hug and breathed deeply. She smelt so good. His hug was returned.

"You haven't been swimming alone, have you?" he asked.

"No," Kalea answered still holding him close. "I went with Ellen."

"Ellen? I didn't know she liked swimming."

"Perhaps, you never took the time to ask." Kalea looked up into his blue eyes and desperately wanted him to kiss her. But it was not to be as Lud interrupted them.

"When you two have quite finished."

"Later," whispered Kai.

"Yes please," she returned. Kai went back to the table and Kalea went to pack her things. It didn't take long and she even managed to take a nap despite the noise in the hall. When she awoke, nothing much had changed and it wasn't until much later, that Kai and Kalea managed to escape together. Even then, they had very little chance of being alone. The village was teeming with people. Some doing tasks for Arthur's trip and others just out to find out the latest gossip in the late afternoon sun. The two would be lovers walked hand in hand out of the village.

"I'm not sure that I am happy with you coming along," Kai mused thoughtfully. "It will be dangerous."

"You mean, more dangerous than making the journey with just an old man?"

Kai laughed. "Well, yes actually. You see the two of you were more able to slip by unobtrusively, whilst a warband of fifteen, will not be so easy to hide. We will actually be making ourselves a target." This had not occurred to Kalea, who assumed that the sheer size of Arthur's warband would make the fiercest warrior quake at the knees.

"You need not worry about me," she said bravely. "As long as I am with you, I will be fine."

"I hope so." He took her into his arms and kissed her. Kalea was getting used to his kisses and welcomed them. In fact, she looked forward to his gentle but urgent touch. A mere kiss was enough to send the fire racing through her body and she felt scorched when the kiss finally ended. They held each other tightly, neither wanting to let go. Another kiss, more demanding that the first and met with equal ferocity. Kalea's body was shaking with her need for him and it took a great deal of will power for Kai to stop. He wanted to meet her needs and fulfil his own. He murmured her name into her soft mouth and she responded with an equally muffled. "I know we must stop." Reluctantly, they released each other and returned to the hall.

Chapter 3
An Eastern Alliance

The next morning, dawned bright. The weather still held and the warband assembled on the edge of the village. There were a great many bleary faces and Kalea looked tired although she felt quite bright. She sat astride her war horse with a pack horse beside her. The pack contained all the herbs and cures that she and Ellen had picked. Kalea sincerely hoped that she would not be called to use any of them. Despite the early hour, the village was full of busy people turning out to see Arthur on his way. The atmosphere was light hearted; although many of the warband would rather spend more time with their loved ones. The horses milled about, eager to be off and Kalea watched many a tearful farewell. Leith sat quietly by her side. He was aware of the talk round the village. Strangers were always good for gossip and they had caused quite a stir, what with them leading the war band off again so quickly. Of course, Kalea was the biggest curiosity, especially as eyes were quick to see her attachment to Kai. There was a great deal of speculation and not a little jealousy when they saw her riding with the men. Leith smiled to himself; he like to see them stirred up a bit. With the last instructions given to Lud, Arthur wheeled his horse round and rode off as a brisk pace. The rest followed after.

Arthur pushed them hard. The pace was fast and furious. His full intention was to get to the East Anglian village with a chief names Alfred. His plan was clear in his mind. Alfred had the largest, most defensible village on the coast and he would assemble the rest of the chiefs there. He had no wish to tarry too long, his position in the South was volatile and he wanted to be back as soon as he could so that he could re-enforce the other half of his men. If they pushed hard, they could be at the village within 4-5 days. Another couple was as long as he wanted to spend there before pushing back as soon as possible. He glanced over his shoulder at Kalea who was talking to Leith. He had made it clear to Leith, he would not be held up by the girl and if she started to slow them down, he would leave her behind. Leith had seemed unconcerned, but Arthur wondered at her stamina. She caught him looking at her and gave a bright smile, he returned it and looked forward again and sighed. Kai looked at him and raised an eyebrow and Arthur shook his head and pushed on.

As the afternoon wore on, Kai dropped back to see how Kalea was faring. They had not stopped since leaving. Lunch had been eaten on horseback and the only stops had been to water the horses. He was surprised to find her in fine fettle. With a smile, she informed him she had seen worse. Leith gave him, an 'I told you so', look which prompted a smile from Kai. The pace, which they travelled, was beginning to drop as the horses grew weary. Finally, Arthur decided it was time to stop. The sun was sinking in the sky and the horses were beginning to plod. As usual in these things, human needs came a poor second to the needs of the horses. So, before the weary riders could take a rest, the horses had to be watered and seen too. Arthur found Kalea humming as she rubbed down her two horses.

"How are you?" he asked. She looked round startled. She had been too engrossed in her work to hear him approach.

Kalea gave him a smile. "I'm fine. How are you?"

Leith was right, the girl was exceptional. "A bit stiff," he answered truthfully. "I could do with a rubdown too." He expected her to blush but instead she laughed.

"Well, stand in line. I've got Leith's horse to do and then he said he could do with backside being massaged. Too soft, that's your trouble."

"You cheeky puppy!" Arthur made to cuff her but she ducked nimbly out of the way laughing.

Kai appeared from nowhere, his face smiled but his eyes were suspicious and he looked shrewdly at Arthur.

"What's going on here?"

Kalea still giggling, rushed to hide behind him. "He was going to beat me."

Arthur roared. "Kai, you are going to have your hands full with this one. She throws insults at me and then tells you, that I was going to thrash her. Which I was not!"

"What on earth did you say?" Kai asked mystified. He could feel Kalea giggling against him.

"She said I was soft."

Even Kai had to laugh. "I think perhaps you deserve a thrashing," he said grasping her wrist. She wriggled like a fish and Kai let her go not wanting to hurt her and she fled still laughing back to the camp.

The two men, still laughing shook their heads. Poor Leith, who had just sat his weary bones down, leapt up and drew his sword as Kalea rushed to hide behind him. He was mystified and annoyed when Arthur and Kai came striding along behind her.

He sighed heavily. "Oh, it's you two, is it?" He put his blade away. "What have you been doing to her?" he asked suspiciously.

Arthur met his eye and spoke gravely. "I think you best ask Kalea." Leith turned and looked at her. She was doing her best to look innocent. Without further ado, he seized her by the wrist and dragged her out of the camp leaving the two men feeling very alarmed. Kalea was alarmed too. Of all the reactions she had expected this was not one of them. When they were out of earshot, he rounded on her.

His voice was grim and fierce. "This is not the place for games," he spat. "This is a warband. You," he growled poking an accusing finger at her chest and nearly pushing her over, "are here under sufferance. There are too many men here for you to start acting the fool. We are not here to have a lark and it's time you realised it. This is not the behaviour I expect from you. Now, grow up!" Kalea was mortified. The harshness of his voice left no doubt that she had seriously stepped out of line. She blushed from embarrassment and hung her head so he could not see how dangerously close to tears she was. "If I catch you acting the idiot again, I will tan your arse. Now, don't you go grizzling on me!" He warned. "You just get back there, sort the horses out and come straight back to me. Do you understand?" She nodded miserably. With that he gave her a push and she stumbled backwards. The straightening up, held her head high, walked briskly back to the horses.

Kai and Arthur had stood and watched the exchange. Whilst they could not hear what was being said, the intent was plain to see. When Leith began to use the threatening finger, Kai went to intervene but was held back by Arthur. "Don't Kai. It will make it worse." Kai was torn, he did not like to see Kalea cower in front of Leith, but at the same time Arthur was right. The last thing he wanted to do, was antagonise and already angry Leith. At that moment, Kalea stormed off and Arthur kept a tight hold of his friend's sleeve. She would not appreciate company until she had had time to compose herself. Their attention reverted to

Leith who was returning to camp, his face like thunder and it was clear to everyone that he was in a vile temper. He glowered at the two men and Arthur and Kai met his eye, not wishing to give the impression that they were in anyway worried.

"What are you looking at?" Leith growled.

"I'm really not sure," Arthur replied coolly. "A bad-tempered old bear?" Kai did well to hide his grin and clapping Arthur on the back, they turned and made for a space at the fire. They could hear Leith's muttered cursing as they sat down with their backs to Leith and exchanged a conspiratorial smile.

Kalea brushed the horses till they shone. Tears rolled down her cheeks despite her best effort to hold them back. Leith had never spoken to her like that before and she couldn't have felt any worse it he had spanked her. It wasn't only because her pride was hurt; it was because, she knew, he was right. She shouldn't have acted so frivolously even though at the time, it had seemed to be harmless. Now that she had regained control of her emotions, she walked slowly back to the camp. She had no real wish to return; she felt that everyone would see her shame. Walking into the camp, she carefully ignored Arthur and Kai and went and sat submissively next to Leith.

Leith was still angry. Every line of his body showed that. He didn't even glance at her as he handed her some bread. She thanked him and took and began to munch. It was dry and refused to leave her mouth, she almost gagged on it. Leith had no intention of relenting. If her father had taught her more lessons in respect, this would not have happened. Leith knew he was being harsh, but his anger was still boiling. It was not all her fault, not many women travelled with a war band and those that did, were normally of high birth and being escorted. However, the sooner she learnt that when travelling, regardless of how big the war band, it was a serious business and foolish pranks could at the best, bring discord amongst the men.

Others amongst the band had noticed Leith's temper and skilfully avoided even talking to him, although talk amongst themselves continued unabated. Many of them cast a wary eye at the grizzled old warrior who sat with the pretty girl who was actually a picture of misery. Darkness fell and Leith rose and without a word motioned for Kalea to follow. Just outside the campfire circle, he threw down his sleeping blanket. "Bed down there," he said gruffly. Then turning he called "Kai, a word." Kai who had been keeping a discreet distance rose and came over with an open smile.

"Is everything alright?" he asked looking at Kalea who was laying out her blanket next to Leith's.

Leith nodded. "Would you sleep on the other side of the girl?" he asked. "If she sleeps between us, there is less chance of anything happening to her."

"Of course," Kai said seriously, feeling quite honoured that Leith had asked him.

"No funny business now young Kai," Leith warned his voice almost a grumble.

Kai grinned. "I wouldn't dare, I have no wish to be gelded. I have further use of that equipment." Much to Kai's surprise Leith smiled. "I'll get my blanket." With that he left. Kalea was already wrapped in his blanket feigning sleep. It wasn't difficult, she was very tired and the telling off had seemed to burn off any energy she had left. It wasn't long before Leith lay down beside her and she was just drifting off on a smooth wave, when she felt Kai take up the other side. Before she knew it, she was fast asleep.

Leith woke early the next morning. *Kalea was right,* he thought, he was getting too old to be sleeping on the hard ground. He sat up and rubbed his face, turning to Kalea, he was surprised to see that in her sleep she had wrapped herself around Kai. Well, there wasn't a lot that could be done about it. Kai lay on his back, one arm outstretched and the other under his head and Kalea had her head on his chest with one leg thrown across him. Leith grinned. At least that would cheer Kai up. He rose and made his way through the slumbering men to the river. He washed his face and went to see to the horses.

Meanwhile, Kai woke. He smiled sleepily to himself and was just about to shake himself awake, when he became aware of the weight on his chest. Looking down, he saw the sleeping Kalea. His smile became bigger and he bought his arms round her so that he could enjoy holding her close. This bought a response from Kalea who snuggled even closer. There was nothing left to do, but enjoy the moment. He settled back down but this was enough to stir her and she came awake. It took her a minute or two to realise that she was cuddled up to Kai and she was in no great hurry to move. His great heart pounded smoothly in her ear and the warmth of his body in the cool morning was comforting. The fact that his arms were tight around her made her feel safer than she had for a long time and she wanted to stay there forever but she knew that soon the war band would be on the move again.

"Are you awake?" Kai asked softly. Reluctant to spoil the moment, Kalea nodded against his chest. In response, he hugged her closer and she returned it. After a while, she stirred herself and sat up, Kai lay smiling up at her. "That was a pleasant way to wake up." He grinned.

"I had just thought the same." She wriggled around and bent to kiss him. The kiss was brief but sweet. "I don't know," Kalea grumbled. "Why do I want to kiss you all the time?"

"Because I want to kiss you back, all the time," Kai answered sitting up and picking a piece of grass out of her hair. Quietly, they got and began to fold up the blankets. Noticing Leith had already gone, they went down to the river to get a drink. By the time they got back, the camp was roused and making ready to go. Leith appeared leading their horses. Kalea looked at him warily but Leith smiled.

"Good morning you two. Have a nice surprise when you woke up Kai?" he asked.

Kai beamed at him. "Good morning to you Leith. And yes. I had a lovely surprise thank you." Kalea looked abashed but not worried.

"Breakfast in the saddle, is it?" she queried taking her horse from him. He nodded as Kai boosted her into the saddle. She took the packhorse from Leith and tied the reigns to her saddle. The two men, were more reluctant to get back in the saddle and Kai went off to find Arthur, leaving Kalea and Leith alone.

"Are you still angry with me?" she asked feeling awkward.

Leith grinned in reply. "No, I am not but you did rile me."

"Well, you left me in no doubt of that."

"I was fuming," Leith admitted. "If it hadn't been that Arthur and Kai were watching, I would have tanned your hide."

The horse's mane suddenly became very interesting to Kalea. She didn't look up when she apologised. "I am sorry. I just wanted a bit of fun but I see I was wrong."

Leith patted her thigh. "Not to worry lass. Just make sure it doesn't happen at an important moment. I expect too much of you sometimes. I'll get us some bread." And as if that was the end of the matter, he strode off. Kalea sighed. Men were funny animals and she wasn't sure that she would ever really understand them. It wasn't long before Leith returned and handed her a chunk of bread. It was boring fare but Kalea knew it would be a long time before she got another chunk, and began to chew it. As she munched, she watched the warband prepare to leave. It was impressive that they were ready in such a short time. Arthur rode over to her.

"Good morning, Kalea. I trust you are well?"

"Good morning to you. I am fine, thank you. And you?"

He nodded and grinned. "Enjoy your breakfast." He went to turn but not before he took in her grimace and he led the band off.

Leith mounted up just as Kai rode up. He too, was eating a chunk of bread. "It's not the same without honey," he stated and Kalea agreed.

Once again, Arthur set a fast pace and the warband moved speedily and quietly through the countryside. From time to time, Kai dropped back for a word and Leith occasionally roused himself from an almost trance like to talk to her, but generally, they rode in silence. At one stage, Kalea dozed in the saddle until Leith gave her a nudge. And so, the journey continued, the days blurred together and Kalea was convinced that her backside would never be the same again. By the fourth day, they had reached East Anglia. Already, they had seen evidence of the raiders. Arthur had sent a few scouts ahead to request that the Chieftains meet at Alfred's village. The few villages they passed through, they did not stop at, other than for Arthur to have a quick word to request their attendance at Alfred's village. The chieftains were surprised to see Arthur, but quick to offer their hospitality, but Arthur wouldn't stop long. He was anxious to push on. A couple of chieftains accompanied the warband. Arthur's face grew grimmer as he saw the devastation that the raiders had caused. What did surprise him, was the people's resilience in the face of the enemy.

It was late in the afternoon when the attack came. They were passing through some heavily wooded land and it was Leith who noticed how quiet it was. He looked at Kalea and tapped his eyes, then his ears. Kalea strained to hear something but could hear nothing and by the time she realised she could not hear one bird singing, the raiders were upon them. The warband was well trained and responded well to the threat. Leith was between them and Kalea had time to free her sword. However, as an ambush, it had been well timed. The raiders smashed through the middle of them, effectively dividing them into two groups. Kalea lay about him with her blade but all was confusion. Horses were cannoning into one another and the warhorse she rode was biting and kicking with the best of them. Kalea blocked a blow from an axe, she looked desperately round to see if she could see Leith but he had become lost in the melee. A kick from a horse caught her thigh and the pain made her head ring, but she couldn't afford to lose consciousness.

Leith looked round trying to see Kalea. The battle fever was upon him and he was swinging his mighty sword with lethal intent. Another Saxon replaced the one he had just felled and his attention was once again focussed on the battle.

The raiders outnumbered them. Arthur fought on grimly. To his left Kai was swinging his battle-axe and clearing a swathe before him. He saw Kai look up and turned to see what had drawn his attention. It was Kalea. Even as he watched he saw that she was being overwhelmed by attackers. Spurring his horse forward, he battled towards her. He was nearly on top of her when he saw her get tipped from the saddle. With a last desperate lunge, he was at her side. Sliding from the saddle, he cleared a path to her and at last stood by her side. "Kalea!" he shouted urgently, "back-to-back." Without further command, she backed against him and as he took the men to the front and sides, she fought the ones to the rear. It wasn't long before Kai too had reached her and swinging his mighty axe cleared all the raiders from around them. Arthur grinned at him and he answered in kind. Kai couldn't take Kalea behind him, he needed space to swing his axe, but he needn't have worried, Kalea grabbed a loose horse as it passed and although it nearly took her off her feet, she managed to slow it enough. "Arthur!" she shouted fighting to control the plunging beast. Arthur turned and leapt into the saddle, leaning down he pulled her up behind him. The pair of them then joined the battle. Leith appeared out of nowhere and they began to fight to re-join the other half of the warband.

The battle seemed to last forever and Kalea thought it would never end. As fast as they slew the Saxons, more appeared but as suddenly as it had begun, it was over and the raiders had either fled or were dead. Kalea slumped wearily against Arthur's back. For a while, all was quiet except for the blowing of the horses and the stamping of shod feet. They looked round to survey the carnage. And carnage, it surely was. Bodies lay everywhere. Kalea slid from the back of the horse and bent over the body of one of Arthur's warriors. An axe had virtually sliced him in two. There was nothing to be done for this one. She looked up and met Leith's eye. "The pack horse would be good right now." He nodded and rode away to find the horse. Arthur and Kai, both joined her on the ground. She acknowledged them. "See who needs healing," she told them as she moved on to the next, trying to find Arthur's warriors amongst the dead Saxons.

"Here's one!" Kai called and she hurried over to him. Dropping to her knees, she looked at the young man before touching him. He had a deep cut that had opened his cheek and a few teeth had gone. The force of the blow had knocked the man out, which was just as well. Kalea examined him, this seemed to be the only wound and he would live. "I need my kit," she said to Kai. Arthur had gone to take stock of his men. Kai nodded and strode off. A voice called for help and Kalea turned from the first man and went to the next. Bending over him, she saw that he had taken an axe blow to the thigh. Blood was gushing. Quickly, she whipped off her belt and tied it tightly just above the cut. Only then did she examine the wound. It was nasty and she would need to be very careful about how she sewed this one.

"How is it?" the man groaned between gritted teeth. Kalea smiled reassuringly.

"I think you will be fine. Lay still. As soon as I can get a needle and thread, I'll have you sown up in a trice." Almost, as if Leith had heard her, he appeared out of the trees leading three horses, one of which was the pack horse. Seeing her on her knees beside a man, he leapt down and passed her the chest full of healing herbs. She began to work, pressing some leaves into the man's mouth and telling him to chew. At the same time, she cleaned the wound the best she could and taking a needle and thread from the box and began to sew up the gash. Before long, he was patched up as best as she could and she moved onto the next casualty. The wounds varied. Some no more than a scratch that required a stitch or two, some more serious. Kalea moved on. Ointment on one, stitches for another. Pain killing potions for still others.

Arthur and Kai had done as much as they could do and now came back to find Kalea moving amongst the wounded. Arthur had dispatched his able-bodied men to round up the loose horses and equipment they had lost. Walking amongst his warriors, he pleased to see most of them had survived. Only two dead. Grievous enough, but considering how outnumbered, surprisingly few. As he talked to his men, he noted how their wounds had been attended too and for the first time since they had left the village, he was pleased Kalea was along. One or two of his men might have been lost, if they had to carry to the next village before being treated. However, this threw his plans into disarray. He would have to stay longer than he hoped or leave his men to recuperate at Alfred's village. Six wounded, but only two badly, the Saxon dead were many.

Arthur had made them pay and it might in fact buy the East Anglian villages some time while the Saxons re-grouped and he hoped that they might think that there was a well-trained warband patrolling the fen lands. His men were returning in high spirits. This always happened when they had survived a battle. They had returned with the loose horses and some more that the dead Saxons no longer needed. The dead had been buried and Arthur saw that Kalea was now treating the minor injuries.

Leith was doing his best to help Kalea. There was a new respect in his voice as he watched her deal efficiently with the gore. He had to hold down the man whose leg had been badly sliced and also the lad whose face would never be pretty again. Now, they had progressed to smaller wounds. Kalea treated each one carefully not wishing them to get infected. Arthur suddenly appeared at her shoulder.

"Kalea," his voice was respectful. "Can we move the men? There is too much death here for us to stay." She looked up and met his eyes.

"Yes," she answered. "Rube's leg is the worst. But I think if we take it steady, he should hold out." Arthur nodded and turned. With a gesture, his men helped the wounded mount and then mounted themselves. Kai helped Kalea to her feet and led her to her horse, which one of the men had bought back. Leith loaded the medicine case back onto the packhorse and they started off.

"Are you alright?" Arthur asked her.

"Yes. Thanks to you," she responded. "I wouldn't have been, if you hadn't come to my aid."

"You would have been fine," he spoke reassuringly. "Kai was already on his way. I was just closer."

"Nevertheless, thank you."

She was splattered with blood. None of her own and her face was pale but she was still lovely. He grinned. "It's nothing." He rode forward so that he wouldn't have to hear her protests.

"Are you really?" Leith's gruff voice came from beside her.

"Really what?"

"Alright?"

She smiled that lovely smile of hers and answered. "Of course, I am. The only blood on me is not mine. How on earth do you keep your head in battle? I've never been so frightened in my life and so much is happening, how do you know you won't slice someone you know?"

Leith laughed. "Instinct. You did well girl."

Kalea didn't answer, just sighed.

The sun was setting when they at last made camp. Arthur had put as much distance between the battlefield and a campsite as he dared. They were all very glad to stop. For once, Leith took Kalea's horse as she took her medicine chest down and began to tend the wounded again. Checking their wounds and applying more balms and giving pain killing herbs. It wasn't until she had finished that she sat down next to Kai at the fireside. It was only then she saw the blood on his shirt. She had wondered why he was giving her such a wide berth and now she knew. He considered his wound too trivial to brother her with.

"What's this?" she said kneeling to take a look at his arm.

Kai gave his best grin, "Why, it's nothing little one."

"There is no disgrace losing an arm in battle Kai my love. However, losing one for not taking care of a wound is inexcusable."

Leith overheard this encounter. "Get your shirt off Kai. She's desperate to take a look at that broad chest of yours and you'll learn Son, that it's quicker to let her get her way, than to argue. Because she gets her way one way or the other." The men round laughed and Kai grinning, gave in gracefully and pulled his shirt over his head. Kalea laid her hands on the wound and they felt cool and cleansing. Then getting her medicine kit again, she soother ointment onto it, and wrapped it in clean linen. Once she was sure that she had done all she could for him, she ran her hands over his bare arms. Even in a situation like this, Kai had the power to excite her and she felt her body beginning to glow. She chewed her bottom lip as she busied herself helping him on with his shirt. Kai was also feeling aroused. Now, he wanted to feel her soft hands on his body, not just his arms. Their eyes met and an unspoken message passed between them, they both smiled and turned their attention back to their companions. Leith watching smiled to himself. They had it bad for one another and he was pleased. At least, the feelings weren't going one way. Kalea was tired and had to force herself to eat. It had been a tough day. She was not a skilled wise woman and she had had to deal with some difficult wounds, she just hoped she had helped and not hindered.

Kai looked at her weary face and speaking kindly, he said, "Do you wish to sleep?" She nodded. He stood and helping her to her feet, he picked up his and her blanket. She was soon fast asleep. For a while, Kai listened to the talk around the fire. It was largely about the ambush. Men were comparing stories and looking at the wounded. Arthur was lost in thought watching the flames dance and Kai wondered what he was thinking. His friend was a deep man and it was hard to know which way his thoughts would turn next. Was he thinking of the ambush, strategy, what he was going to say to Alfred or was he thinking of Kalea? Kai wouldn't have been surprised if he were. It wasn't often that he beat Arthur to a woman and he knew that Arthur had wanted her. What did surprise him, was that Arthur had backed off. It had been known for them to virtually come to blows over a girl but in this instance Arthur had stepped back. But Kai was suspicious, was this a new tactic? He wasn't worried, he trusted both Kalea and Arthur and Kai wasn't about to give either of them any excuse to betray him. He grinned and lay down on his blanket. Almost immediately, Kalea moved against him. For the first time, he was grateful that others were with them. He felt the need to hold her and to love her, and if it hadn't been for Leith and the others, he most probably would have.

When Leith eventually laid his blanket down, the two youngsters were asleep in one another's arms. Leith sighed. He would be glad to see them married. At least he wouldn't have to worry about Kalea's virtue. Not only that, he would like to see her settled. Kai was a good man and Leith had no reservations about entrusting Kalea to his care. For a while, he couldn't sleep and he lay watching the stars through the night sky. The camp became quieter as one by one the men slept. As always, when he survived a battle. Leith played the scene and over and over in his head. It was a way of analysing his moves and how they could be improved upon. Today, had been different. His heart had been pounding so frantically, he thought it would burst from his chest. His fear had not been for himself but for the girl. The first attack had been so intense that he hadn't realised he had been separated from Kalea until it was too late. On turning, he had seen her beset by Saxons. He had known only too well, what they wanted her for. They had no intention of killing her, well, not straight away. He had tried to reach her and then see seen her dragged from her horse. Where Arthur had come from, he didn't know, but he was extremely grateful to the young king. Even more so when he saw him slide from his horse to be at her side. Kai hadn't been far behind him and the pair soon cleared the Saxons from Kalea. Leith loved her dearly but even he had to admit that he was surprised at the feelings she evoked in these young men. He wished he had found someone like her when he way young, and with that thought swirling through his mind, sleep stole in like a thief and swept him away.

The next morning, the camp broke early. Arthur was eager to get to Alfred's village. Leith had to rouse Kalea and Kai who were both fast asleep. When at last everyone was ready, they set off at a brisk pace.

"You're going soft Kai. Sleeping in so late," Arthur commented sourly as they led the warband away. Leith, who as ever seemed to have an ear for everyone's conversation, chipped in.

"Wouldn't you if you had this wench warming your bones at night?"

Kai laughed brightly. No one could spoil he mood. Leith was right. There was nothing quite like having a woman snuggled against you in the morning.

"Long may it continue." He smiled back at Kalea who returned it with interest.

Arthur shook his head with a wry smile. The old warrior had a way of hitting the nail squarely on the head.

It was lunchtime when a very tired band of warriors arrived at Alfred's village. Alfred was waiting to welcome them. Arthur's scouts had arrived a day ahead, despite having to call into villages to request the attendance of the elders at the meeting. Some had already arrived so that the village was brimming with people eager to see the young king from the South that they heard so much about. Alfred stepped forward. "Welcome Arthur, it is good to see you again." Arthur slid from his horse and greeted Alfred heartily.

"My men met some of your raiders on the road and we have need of your wise woman." Without being told one of Alfred's men disappeared into the crowd.

"Come Arthur, I have had my hall made ready for you. You must eat and rest before we talk." Men came forward to collect the horses form the men and there was much groaning and laughing as the war band gladly handed over their mounts. As a lad took her horse, Kalea spoke gently to him. "Excuse me. But I would like to bathe. Is there a river or a lake where I may swim?"

The young man looked stunned at this slim young woman dressed in men's clothes. Leith stepped up beside her. "Stop acting like a fish son, and tell the girl what she wants to know."

The lad looked even more startled when he saw Leith. "My lady there is a small lake just outside the village." He pointed in that direction.

"Thank you," she answered.

"I suppose there is no point asking you, if I could possibly have a drink before we go is there?" Leith asked. Kalea just grinned. "Well, there's no harm in asking," Leith continued with a sigh. "Here Kai!" he called. Both Kai and Arthur turned round. "Kalea here wants to pretty herself up. We'll catch up with you later."

Arthur nodded and Kai called back. "I'll go if you want Leith. I'm sure you could do with some ale."

Leith chuckled. "Away with you lad. I'll have your hide off."

Kai laughed and followed Arthur.

Leith and Kalea grabbed their packs and headed for the lake. They were both in high spirits, relieved to have arrived safely. It wasn't long before they found the small lake and it looked beautiful in the sunshine. Leith sourced a suitable place and Kalea eagerly stripped off and threw herself in.

"This is wonderful!" she called. "I can't remember a time when I have been so dirty." Leith was going through her clothes.

"I think you are going to need some new clothes Kalea. These are beyond repair." Both shirt and trousers were covered in dry blood. "The best that can be done for these is burn them."

"Are yours much better?" she called.

He looked down at his blood-splattered jerkin. "Not really," he stated flatly.

"It's just as well I bought a few coins then," Kalea commented as she slipped from the water and began to dry herself. "I'm done."

Leith turned and saw that she had put her best dress on. He smiled. "You certainly look a lot better." As soon as she turned her back, he stripped off and plunged in himself. Kalea was right. Despite the fact that the water was cold, damn cold, to be truthful, it made him feel so much better. His weariness, temporarily left him and he felt invigorated. He emerged shaking himself like a dog.

"You know, as much as I hate to admit it, I can't help liking young Kai," he commented rubbing herself dry. Although he couldn't see her face, he guessed she was smiling. "I think you made a wise choice there Kalea."

"Why thank you Leith."

"And when you two wed, I hope you won't be too busy making babies to remember to give me a meal round your fire."

"Leith!" she squeaked indignantly.

Leith roared with laughter. "Don't you pretend to be shocked. I've seen the way you two look at each other. You can hardly keep your hands off each other and it only goes to show what a good man Kai is that he doesn't take you here and now. The gods know, you would be more than willing."

"Leith!" Kalea turned round catching the old warrior naked. "How dare you!"

"The truth girl, the truth!!" He hurriedly pulled on his trousers.

"So, you are right. When I get old, will I always be right?"

"I doubt it." While he had been washing, she had combed her hair and plaited it into a long braid that hung down her back. "Come on, get your gear, they will be wondering where we are." They walked in quiet companionship back towards the village. It was a while before Leith spoke again. "How many Saxons did you kill?"

Kalea shrugged. "At least one. When I was with Arthur, I took one through the throat. Maybe more. Toothpick was working very hard when I was mounted. But if I wounded or killed, I don't know. I was slashing like a mad woman."

Leith nodded. He suspected that she had inflicted a lot of damage as well as protecting herself. "Kalea, I just want to say, you did well in the battle and even better with the wounded."

Kalea flushed with pleasure at the compliment. "Not as well as a wise woman," she answered modestly.

"Perhaps not. But then a wise woman wouldn't have been able to take down a warrior and keep up with a warband."

"Thank you, Leith." Kalea glowed with pleasure from the old warrior. "I did sustain a wound in battle."

Leith was aghast. "You never said anything."

Kalea grinned, "I will show you now, before we get back," she said beginning to pull up her skirts. Leith eye widened in surprise. There on her thigh was a huge hoof shaped bruise.

Leith chortled. "I bet that hurt."

"Yes, it did. But I was too busy at the time to worry about it."

When they arrived at the hall, they found that they were not the only ones who had taken advantage of the time to clean up. Kai and Arthur both looked freshly scrubbed and were sitting at the table with Alfred. Other men were coming and going and a wise woman was treating the wounded.

Arthur looked up and saw them enter. "Alfred, you know Leith of course?" Leith came forward and shook hands with Alfred who nodded and smiled.

"Everyone in these parts knows of Leith," he spoke. "Welcome. Come join us. I am sorry to hear the news of your village."

Arthur then looked passed Leith to Kalea. She looked a vision, smiling sweetly, clean and neat in her dress. "This," he said nodding to her, "is Kalea. She is Ren's daughter, Leith's constant companion and has also acted as a wise woman on our journey."

Alfred turned his attention to the young girl who stood proudly behind Leith. He motioned for her to come forward, which she did. "Welcome Kalea. Your father was a good friend and I am sorry to hear of his loss. I hear that you have inherited your father's bravery. Please be seated and have some food."

Kalea came and sat down next to Leith who patted her knee reassuringly. Kai leaned over and filled her beaker with ale and Arthur offered her some meat and bread which she accepted gratefully. She did little to contribute to the conversation, but was happy to sit in the safety of the hall and listen. She intrigued Alfred. It was obvious that both men were clearly taken with her, yet she made no effort to encourage either. Arthur had already told him that she had been extremely brave and useful during the battle and afterwards tending to the wounded and yet, she did not look strong enough. Still the best flowers, bloomed in the face of adversity. "Kalea, if you wish to rest, I have arranged for some blankets to be hung so you have some privacy."

Kalea looked over her shoulder and smiled. "I see that Kai has already told you that Leith likes to keep me close."

Alfred grinned. "I can understand why." He looked knowingly at the two men on either side of him.

"I am most grateful," Kalea answered respectfully. "I will take a rest if you will excuse me?"

"But of course," Alfred responded.

Kalea rose. "Sweet dreams," Leith said as she disappeared.

Kalea lay down on the makeshift cot, which seemed like it was made of feathers. With a sigh of utter contentment, she shut her eyes. She listened to the buzz of conversation. Occasionally, she heard her name mention but before too long she slept. She had no idea how long she had slept. But for a while she lay there listening to the men talking. Sitting up, she rebraided her hair and stepped out behind her screens. The men, almost as one, turned towards her. She smiled shyly and Leith patted the seat beside him.

"Feeling better?" he asked.

"Much. Thank you."

"How's the bruise?"

"That has not changed much."

"What bruise?" Kai asked.

"She took a kick from one of the horses. It really is quite something," Leith chortled.

"Can I see?"

"It is in a place that it would not be maidenly to show in front of so many men," Kalea responded demurely.

"Leith got to see," Kai complained.

Leith howled with laughter. "Yes. But I'm not going to ask to kiss it better. Oh Kalea! You do make me laugh." Then added, "Tomorrow, the last of the chieftains will come and Arthur will talk to them. Don't mention your bruise."

Kalea laughed too. "Are they not all here yet?"

"No, it seems that some are reluctant to leave their villages. While others are keen to come."

Kai interrupted them. "Excuse me Leith. I wondered if I might take Kalea walking."

Leith eyed Kai with interest. He was becoming fonder of the lad by the minute. "Yes, you may."

Kai offered Kalea his hand which she took, and together they left the hall. Alfred watched Arthur as they left. His look, while guarded, left little doubt that he disapproved of the girl's choice in men. While it was obvious that Leith had already decided that Kalea had made quite a catch. He himself, had taken a liking to Kai. Whereas Arthur was more thoughtful and sombre, Kai was quick to laugh and had a ready sense of humour. He raised an eyebrow thoughtfully. Tomorrow would see just how clever this young king was. Alfred thought that later on he would seek out Leith's view on Arthur. After all, Leith was a fen man and would have their best interests at heart.

Kai and Kalea stepped outside the hall into the dusk.

"I had not realised that I had slept so long." Kalea took in the last rays of sunset.

Beside her, Kai took a deep breath. "It was not that long. An hour or two and goodness knows, you deserved the rest."

"You are a kind soul Kai."

"Not a bit." He took her hand and led her through the village. "I was very proud of you. The way you kept pace with the warband and coped with being in the company of so many men. Not many women would have coped so well."

"I am sure many women would."

"I doubt that very much. You didn't complain once and kept up easily."

"I was bought up with men," Kalea responded modestly.

"And have turned out to be a very resourceful young woman." They had reached an area of woodland that ran close to the village and Kai quick to spot an opportunity ducked into the trees dragging Kalea after him. "Alone at last." His lips close to hers. "What torture, sleeping so close and not being able to touch you or kiss you. It wasn't very kind of Leith."

Kalea's lips touched his and she smiled. "I am sure that wasn't his intention. He just felt safer knowing you were there." She was silenced by his kiss and it was most welcome. His tongue met with hers and she felt herself melting against him. She held him close, her hands in his hair, holding his head close to hers. Her heart was racing and her body was filled with anticipation. Kai kept his lips against her when the kiss ended; he could not bear to be parted with her. He wanted to crush her to him and never let her go. "Kalea," he murmured his voice gruff with passion. "I love you."

Kalea's racing heart missed a beat. "I love you too," she spoke against his lips. "So very much." The next kiss was even deeper and demanding and was met with equal passion. Kai was aware that he was in danger of losing control. His erection throbbed painfully and it didn't help that Kalea was pressing herself against him. He knew, she would offer no resistance at all if he was to press the moment. She, herself was past the point of no return. He groaned pulling away from her. "The sooner I wed you, the better," he growled.

Kalea was breathless, her eyes dark with desire. "Was that a proposal Kai?" her voice was low. She wanted to step into his arms again and follow this through to its conclusion, but she knew it wasn't fair on him. After all, he was the one exercising control, not she. There was nothing she wanted more than for him to touch her in places that ached for his touch. She watched him gulp, fighting for control. Even now, she dared not move or else she would end up begging him. Finally, after a long moment, he smiled.

"Of course, that was a proposal. But you must not tell Leith I have asked, for I have broken my word. I promised him that I would not ask you until we were safely home." Kalea said nothing and stood looking at this man that she adored.

"Well?" Kai asked uncomfortably. "Are you not going to give me an answer? Or are you going to make me wait until we get home?"

"Kai, you know my answer. My whole-body answers you with every kiss. I will do anything; go anywhere to be with you. Yes, I will marry you." Kai took her hands in his and kissed them.

"I want to kiss you, but I dare not," he said gruffly. "But hopefully, it won't be long before it won't matter and we can do as we want." He led her out of the trees. "I hope Arthur sorts this out quickly." He added as they walked back through the village. Kalea said nothing, she was glowing with happiness. Who could have believed that after such a short time, she could be this happy? She wished her family could be here to see it.

That evening Alfred had prepared some entertainment for his many guests. He also introduced Kalea to his wise woman, Rachel. As wise women go, Rachel was scary. Not just to Kalea, but also to all those who knew her. Nobody could be sure how old she was, but she seemed to have looked old forever. She drew Kalea aside and praised her for her work on the wounded but Kalea was uncomfortable with the woman, she seemed to be looking into Kalea's very soul, searching for something. As a result, when the wise woman asked Kalea to visit her, she politely refused and she sensed the woman didn't like it. During the evening, Alfred announced. "Our wise woman, Rachel, interprets dreams Arthur. Why don't you tell her one of yours and see what she makes of it?"

Arthur looked abashed. "I'm not sure my dreams are to be shared in mixed company." This was greeted with much laughter.

"How about Kalea?" the wise woman asked. "Tell me your dreams precious."

Kalea frowned perplexed. "Do you know, I can't remember a single one since we left the village?" The hall went quiet. Kalea looked round suddenly aware of the silence. Eager to break it, she hurried on. "But before that I used to dream of a horse. A wild horse that was the most beautiful horse I had ever seen."

"And what colour was this horse?" the wise woman asked again.

"He was a grey. Dapple." Kalea warmed to this theme. Her eyes glazed as in her mind's eye she once again saw the stallion.

"Did you ride him?"

"Perhaps, I can't remember. But I used to watch him gallop through the waves."

"So, what does this mean Rachel?" Alfred asked.

Rachel smiled a crone's smile. "A horse in a maiden's dream often means a man. One she would like to ride." She watched Kalea blush red as her seemingly innocent dream was interpreted like this. "But it can also mean that she is strong and reckless and seeking adventure."

"That's more like our Kalea!" Leith laughed. Everyone joined in and then many began to ask Rachel to interpret their dreams. Kalea leaned close to Leith. "I do not like her."

"It's because she is old. There is nothing to fear from her. I have met her before. She is certainly strange but there is no harm in her," Leith answered. Kalea was unconvinced. However, she held her tongue and said no more. Rachel wasn't so easily diverted. She turned back to Kalea. "I see great things for you girl. Not a wise woman but you could be a king maker." Kalea did well to hide her surprise. Rachel laughed and unable to bait the girl further, turned her attention back to the men. Kalea sat quietly beside Leith. She was uneasy. There was no way she could bear a king, or could she? Beneath lowered lashes, she glanced across to Arthur and then dropped her gaze back to her beaker when she saw he was looking at her. No, the old woman was just trying to stir up trouble for whatever reason. Why would she lie with Arthur? Her heart was set on Kai. Her curiosity was roused and she wanted to ask Rachel how? But she dared not. Glancing at Kai, she decided, she had no need to know. The only reason she would lie with Arthur was if Kai was dead, and this was something she didn't even want to contemplate. For a moment, panic rose in her and she nearly fled, but she was not her father's daughter for nothing. She held fast. There was no way she would let the old witch scare her from the room.

Kai glanced up and looked at Kalea's beautiful thoughtful face and could not wait to take her home. Leaning across and taking her hand, he nodded in the direction of the door and with a smile, she rose and followed him. Once outside he turned to her. "So, what do you think of Alfred's wise woman?"

"I don't like her much. I don't think she likes me either," she stated flatly.

Kai smiled. "She most probably thinks that Alfred wants you as his new wise woman."

"She wouldn't, would she?" Kalea was horrified. "There is no way I know enough to be a wise woman."

Kai laughed at her. "You are too modest. And what do you think of her prediction? Are you going to leave me for Arthur?"

"Not this side of heaven," Kalea answered without hesitation.

"So, Alfred's wise woman isn't so wise. In fact, she is wrong." Kai was relieved. He was shaken at how his confidence waivered in these matters.

"Not necessarily."

"So, you are leaving me for Arthur," Kai said shocked.

"No. I am not." She reached up and took his face in her hands and pulled him down close to her so that he could look into her eyes. "What do you see in these eyes?"

"A beautiful woman," Kai spoke quietly.

"No, you do not. You see my love for you. She was right. If I didn't love you as much as I do, I could be Arthur's woman and bear his child. So, she was right, I could be a kingmaker. But I choose not to be, because I love you." He kissed her, which was exactly what she wanted him to do. Holding him tight she knew for sure she had made the right decision.

The following morning, the whole village was bussing with gossip about the leaders turning up for the meeting with Arthur. There were comparing them on who was the strongest, the wisest, bravest and most eligible. New people were turning up in preparation for the meeting were eager to see who was arriving. Arthur had taken Leith and Kai off to discuss his plans with them away from prying eyes and ears, so, Kalea was left with nothing particular to do. She had no one to talk too. Arthur's warband were busy flirting with the local girls and anyway, she didn't know any that well anyway. She wandered through the village and spotting a friendly looking woman, she asked her where she could buy some clothes. The woman was happy to help in exchange for some gossip which Kalea gave her. Soon, Kalea had new shirt and trousers and happily wandered down to the paddock to see the horses. She leaned on the fence and watched the horses milling around. The warhorse she had acquired when Leith and she had left their home, came over and nuzzled her hand and she stroked his velvet nose. A cool wind had risen and while the day way bright and sunny, she knew that wet weather was on the way. Without thinking, she looked to the north east. Her own village, or what was left of it, was no more than a day's hard ride from here. And yet, being so close, she did not feel at home. The fen lands stretched out flat and true. Land that was so familiar and yet she knew no one. This was not uncommon; people in general, did not travel far. They had no need to. Simon's village had been the closest to her home and yet until she had visited with Leith, she had never met Simon or any of the others. The warriors sometimes travelled and women only if a marriage had been arranged for them.

She sighed. Such a short time and so much had changed. She had travelled further than she had ever dreamed. Lost everything and found something more precious than everything she had lost. But for some reason, today she felt sad. Being so close to where she had been born, stirred in her a longing to see her family. Even her mother who had been dead for so long. Tears sprang unbidden to her eyes and she buried her face against the horse's mane in an effort to subdue them. What she wanted to do was to saddle up and ride wildly across the countryside as she had done when she was younger. But she couldn't do it. Not now. The countryside was full of raiders and it was too dangerous. If she did and returned unharmed, she would face Leith's wrath. She had no wish to do that again.

Kalea returned to the drinking hall. Food had been prepared for the visitors and she took some fruit and went to lay down quietly. With little to do, she fell to sleep and did not hear the men come in to start the meeting. Leith came and peered round the screens and smiled when he saw her asleep. He and Kai had been looking for her and here she was safe and sound all the time. Kai looked at him and he nodded with a grin. Kai returned it. All was well.

All the leaders sat round the table and at first little was said of the situation, they exchanged pleasantries and gossip and broke bread together. Then at last they began to address the problem of the raiders. Arthur put forward suggestions and the leaders argued. Putting up countless barriers as to why they couldn't be implemented. The conversation went round and round with no one giving or gaining any ground.

Kalea woke and lay for a while, listening to the comments. Every now and then, she recognised Arthur's voice and Kai and Leith, but the rest were just voices. Quietly, so as not to disturb them, she slid from her cot and edged her way round the wall until she got to the door. As she exited, women started to appear with plates of food. Kalea was surprised that she had slept so long but she offered to help and her offer was accepted and she was soon carrying in platters of food. She leant over Kai shoulder and blew in his ear as she placed a pile of meat in front of him. He turned quickly, and then realised it was his woman and grinned. She winked at him as she rushed off to fetch yet more food. At last, it was finished and the women sat together in the kitchens and ate themselves. Kalea along with them. And for the first time ever, she enjoyed mixing with the women.

When she left them, she went and sat on the hall steps unwilling to draw attention to herself by entering the hall. Listening to the voices inside, and she had the feeling that this was not going well. She was not in the least surprised. The talking began again. Once again, Arthur tried to persuade the leaders to give ground and compromise to part with some of their warriors to form a warband to fight the raiders. None of the leaders gave ground. They did not want to part with one of their men. They needed each and everyone. Round and round they went and it grew late.

Kalea could tell that Arthur's patience was wearing thin. She peeked through the door and the set of his jaw said it all. Finally, he growled. "Look, you have come here today and most you have bought is two men each. You bought no more because you would not leave your people unprotected. Look round you. The size that just these few, make a warband that would be enough to drive every Saxon from the land." But there was no bending them. He took a good look at the stubborn set of their faces and leapt to his feet. Slamming his beaker down on the table, he shouted. "I have had enough of you!" and he stormed out the hall nearly knocking Kalea over.

The room filled with angry voices. Kalea fled and ran after the storming war leader. He was striding so fast that she had to run to catch him.

"Arthur," she shouted.

He stopped and turned. His face dark with anger. "Kalea! What are you doing here?"

She caught up her breath coming fast. "Running after you!" she grinned at him but failed to diffuse his mood.

"Your kinsmen are impossible!" he growled walking off. Kalea scuttled after him. "They will not listen. Do they not care what happens to their people? What's the point of being stubborn if it means your people die?"

Kalea grabbed his arm and he swung round to face her. "Arthur. It is hard for them. Each one of them sees themselves as you do. A warlord in command of his own land and people. They haven't as much as you and it is not just the Saxons they worry about. Each is concerned that while they are away, another warlord will take their precious piece of land away from them." Arthur looked down at his feet thoughtfully.'

"They are proud men. They like to think that they are capable of looking after their own people."

Arthur sighed. "Kalea walk with me for a while. I cannot go back in there when I feel like strangling them. Nothing can be achieved by that."

Together they walked through the night. Finally, Kalea spoke, "What if you suggested a summer village?" He looked at her quizzically. "What I mean is, the land around Alfred's village is large enough to take all the village or near on all the villages. Could you not suggest that during the summer when the raiders come, that they move all the villages here?" At Arthur's raised eyebrow. She rushed on to explain further. "Each village could build their own houses and paddocks, close but not too close. Then in the summer they could move all the people, animals and possessions here. You could say that in addition to the protection that this affords them, it would be a valuable time to trade and exchange ideas. Then when the raiders come, they would find empty villages and nothing to take and when they eventually turn up here, the warriors could unite, and drive them from the shores. If you stand by the paddocks, you can see for miles. They would not have to build an extension to Alfred's village but their own villages, but because you would be able to see them all, they would be able to send help without risking their own homes. Then in the winter, they could go home," she finished with a rush, shocked at her own boldness at suggesting such a wild idea.

Arthur looked at her. Her eyes were alight with excitement. "It's not a bad idea at all. That way, they would all maintain their own village structures while banding together. Not bad at all." He looked at her and badly wanted to kiss her. "Kalea you would have made me a good wife."

Kalea was glad it was dark and he could not see her blush. For a moment, he stood stock-still and stared at her and just when Kalea thought she could bear it no longer, he spoke, "Come on. Let's get back. I want to see what the stubborn old fools make of this one." He set off, striding out with purpose. With a sigh of relief, Kalea trotted after him. As they mounted the steps, he turned to her. Fearing he might kiss her, Kalea stepped back. And he might have, but instead he said "Thanks" and with that he went in. Kalea once again sat on the steps outside.

The conversation stopped when Arthur re-appeared and he strode to the table. Without sitting down, he began. "Right, I will waste no more time with you. I have matters of my own to deal with. I have made the journey, because one of your kinsmen thought that I might be able to help you. I can see now that he was optimistic and this is no easy task, he has set me. So, I have talked and so have you. We are no further forwards than we were this afternoon and it is now late. I have one last proposal to put before you. If at the end of this, we can reach no agreement, I shall be forced to leave you to sort out your own problems. I intend to be on the road with my men by tomorrow at midday."

Everyone was shocked to hear that including Kalea. It had the desired effect as they all listened carefully. Then Arthur began to lay out Kalea's idea. She smiled inwardly. At first, there was much dissention then almost as one, they began to come round. There were problems to iron out and some people were more flexible than others but suddenly a plan began to make shape. Kalea slipped in to take to her bed and as she did so, Arthur winked at her. It was a long time before sleep came.

The next morning, it was obvious that Arthur's prediction that they would be on the road by midday, would not come about. The men talked long into the night, and agreement had finally been reached. The leaders had accepted Arthur/Kalea's plan and now began the planning in earnest. Leith was in his element. He had fought with many of the leaders here and was eagerly catching up on the news from other villages. Arthur was up to his neck in practicalities and barely had time to look up. Kai managed to slip away and found Kalea with the horses.

"It looks like we will be leaving tomorrow morning," he stated.

"I thought Arthur was being a bit optimistic. Still nevertheless an agreement has been reached."

Kai put his arm around her shoulder eager to be close to her. "I had rather been looking forward to going home," he spoke wistfully.

Kalea laid her head against his chest. "Me, too."

The day passed slowly for Kalea. There was very little she could do. She went round and had a word with the wounded men she had treated to see how they were healing. But Rachel had done a good job and they were ready to move. At last, she went to the market place and with the last of her pennies she bought Leith a new shirt. After this, she packed away the medicine chest and the few belongings that she had bought and spent the rest of the day feeling very bored.

The evening finally came and Alfred had a feast prepared for all his guests to celebrate that at last East Anglia might become a safe place to stay. Leith was heavily in his cups and she spent the evening talking Kai. Knowing that they were going to make an early start in the morning, she turned in early but was unable to sleep because of the wild carousing going on.

Chapter 4
Return Journey

The day dawned grey. The rain that had been promised was a lot closer now but everyone was in high spirits. Arthur's men were all mounted and ready to go and now all that was left to do was to say goodbye. Kalea sat quietly with Leith waiting to lead off. It seemed that everyone had risen early to see the young warlord and his band off. Arthur was smiling broadly as he said his final farewell to Alfred and finally, they were on the road again. The journey back did not seem as sombre as the journey there had been. The men were chattering like magpies. Even the wounded were happy to be on their way home. The scouts that Arthur had used to bring the leaders together, were now used to range ahead and watch for raiders.

It was late afternoon when the rain that had been threatening arrived in a downpour. This finally managed to dampen spirits and the men were miserable and wet. The scouts had picked a fairly sheltered spot for the night but the rain was so heavy that there was little chance of getting a fire lit. As a result, most of them slept sitting up with their blankets over their heads. Kalea hated it. She was wet through and her clothes clung to her. Even huddled together under the blankets with Kai and Leith she did not feel warm and every now and then shivered. Kai put his arm around her but he was cold and wet too, so it did very little to help.

Not much sleep was had and the band rose early. The morning was grey and the rain still fell. Getting back in the saddle, Kalea thought that she had never felt so miserable. They set off at a fair pace. Kai suspected this was to get them warm more than anything else. By midday, they had covered a lot of land, the rain had stopped and the sun was once again trying to break through. Not long after, the sun did break through and its warmth was very welcome. The horses as well as the men, started to steam as they dried off and it made Kalea smile as they cooked dry in the heat. Blankets were hastily unrolled and hung over the rear of the horses to dry them out. The sun was setting and it was late before they finally stopped for the day. Spirits were rising again and now that they were dry. Kalea's skin itched where her clothes had dried on her and she wanted nothing more than to take them off, but that was not an option. Soon, they had a good size campfire going and they all sat round eating their provisions.

"Thank goodness the rain has stopped," Kalea commented to Leith.

"The ground is still damp," he answered grumbling to himself. "You're right. I'm getting too old for this."

"I'm getting too old for this too," Kalea responded but she was really too tired to think straight and as soon as Leith laid out his blanket, hers was beside it and she was asleep.

The days blurred into one another as they headed home as fast as they could. Fortunately, there was no more rain and it made it more pleasant. At last, Kalea recognised the countryside round Arthur's village and the men started letting out wild whoops. Arthur turned round to Leith and Kalea. "It is a tradition with my men that we ride in fast, so be warned. When I say the word, they will go hell for leather home and if you are in the way, they will knock you flying." Leith and Kalea grinned at him. Arthur looked past them at his men and with a wild smile yelled. "Home!" It was met with wild yells, everyone ploughed forward including Kalea and Leith. They entered the village at break neck speed and everywhere was laughter and confusion as the horses excited by the gallop milled around. Kalea was caught up in the excitement of the moment and was laughing at the exhilaration of careering into the village.

Their approach was not unknown to the village. The watchtowers at the perimeter had warned the villagers of Arthur's return. As a result, everyone had turned out to see them. Loved ones rushed out to see their men return and there were many tears for Arthur's two men who had not returned. Concern over the wounded came next, and Kalea saw Ellen rush forward to take control of the worst one. But there was also lots of happy faces at seeing most had returned unharmed. Lud of course, was at the thick of it, and Leith looked up to see Arthur looking very puzzled in deed and he wondered what was going on. By the time the horses had been sorted out and everyone had returned to their homes, it was getting late. Leith looked at Kalea as she finished rubbing down her horse.

"I suppose you would like to go for a swim despite the lateness of the day?" he enquired.

He was rewarded with a smile. "I'd love to go for a swim if you wouldn't mind. I just can't wait to get these clothes off." Leith didn't blame her.

"Come on lass. I could do with a wash myself and there is bound to be a big feast tonight so you had better look your best."

It wasn't long before Kalea was in the water, with her clothes on. Taking them off, only when they were soaked through, then stripping off, she gave herself a scrub. The water was cold but welcomingly refreshing. Living in the same set of clothes for days was not pleasant, she decided, especially when the closest you could get to water was a drink from the canteen. She dressed and waited for Leith who made a good deal of fuss about how cold the water was. While he was dressing, he suddenly said, "Kai is going to ask you to marry him."

Kalea was glad he couldn't see her face. "Is he?" she returned innocently. "How is it that you know before I do?"

"Because he asked my permission." Leith smiled to himself. "Will you accept him?"

"Do you really need to ask?" Kalea teased.

"Yes, I do. I would not have the boy make a fool of himself if you are going to refuse him."

Kalea turned her face full of delight. "Of course, I will marry him. How soon do you think we can wed?"

"Grief woman!" Leith spluttered exasperated. "He hasn't asked you yet."

"But you told me he will so, I know he will."

Leith thought about it for a while. "Well, there is no reason why you can't be married soon. But I would think it would be best to wait a week so until the village settled down before you wind it up again for a marriage feast. Besides, you better find someone to make you a new dress. You can't go getting married in your trousers."

Kalea laughed she hadn't thought of that. "I will have to ask Ellen who makes the best dresses."

"Not," said Leith sternly, "until after Kai has asked. And don't let him know I warned you."

As they walked back to the village, Kalea smiled to herself. Poor Leith, he was trying desperately to do his best for her.

By the time they had arrived back at the drinking hall, the feast had already begun. There was music and the hall was full to overflowing with people. Leith wasn't at all perturbed by it and led Kalea up to Arthur's main table where Lud,

Kai and Arthur were already eating. They looked up and seeing them moved to make room at the table. Once again Kalea found herself seated between Arthur and Kai. Her beaker was filled with mead and she was offered a bowl or rich stew. Kalea ate it hungrily. "This is better than dry bread," she said scraping the bowl clean.

Kai lent towards her and inhaled deeply. "You smell like summer meadows."

Kalea sniffed back. "And you smell like you could use a swim."

Throwing back his head, Kai howled with laughter. Well, my lady. You won't have to sleep next to this smelly hog tonight.

"Perhaps, it is just as well," she spoke.

"I promise that first thing tomorrow. I will take a bath."

"That doesn't really help me now." Kai wasn't sure if she was serious, he felt a bit offended and then he saw the twinkle in her eye.

"You are teasing me!" he laughed.

"Yes, I am." The atmosphere was one of great celebration. Arthur had every right to look pleased with himself. Kalea tugged on his sleeve to get his attention. He turned to her with a bright smile.

"What is it my little peace maker?" She smiled at the compliment.

"Where have all these people come from?" she asked leaning close so that he could hear her over the din.

"These," Arthur waved his hand at the men that Kalea had not seen before, "are the rest of my warband back from the south. It appears that shortly after we left, Mark of Cornwall decided he had had enough of fighting and took his warband home."

"Really?" she queried. "Why?"

Arthur shrugged. "I don't know. It's worrying in some respects but nevertheless, I am grateful for the respite. It gives my men time to come home and rest before Mark decides to have another try at taking my kingdom." Kalea looked thoughtful. Arthur tilted her face up to meet his eyes. "Now, don't you go concerning yourself with it?" Her eyes were beautiful, as dark as midnight. "We'll worry about it tomorrow. Tonight, we celebrate being home. And besides," he added, "with the war band all together again, there is nothing that I can't handle."

Kalea met his gaze. "I believe you are probably right."

"What are you doing with my woman?" Kai voice came loudly over her shoulder making her jump.

"Kai, my friend." Arthur was well in his cups. "Not a thing, though that isn't to say I wouldn't, given half a chance. It seems you have stolen the march on me here. I was merely, reassuring Kalea that with the warband together, there is nothing we cannot handle."

Kai laughed guarding his thoughts well. "That is quite right," he added and Kalea shrugged and sat back to enjoy the party. Arthur was well gone. As he tried to fill up his beaker, he managed to spill most of it on the table, so, Kalea stepped in and filled it for him. She was beginning to feel quite light headed herself. Leith was not better than Arthur and everyone seemed to be having a great time. Kai suddenly took her hand and leaning towards her said in her ear. "Come with me." Without hesitation, she rose and followed him through the partying people into the cool night. It was a relief to be away from the noise and the heat.

Without speaking, Kai led her away from the hall and together they made their way from the village and down by the river where all that could be heard was the gentle gurgle of the water. He took her in his arms and kissed her deeply. Totally intoxicated, not by the mead but by the smell of her, he desperately wanted to take her. Kalea was transported with joy and as his hands wandered to her breasts, she gasped with pleasure. She did not want him to stop but he did.

"Kalea," he murmured his voice gruff with passion "will you marry me and marry me soon?" he asked his lips still against hers.

The answer 'yes' was almost breathed into his mouth as he kissed her again. The kiss was more urgent and demanding but met with equal passion.

Kalea broke this time and holding his head close to hers said, "We must go back. I am lost." Kai smiled.

"At least you are honest. I can wait. But not long."

"How long?" teased Kalea.

"Till tomorrow," he said.

"But I need a new dress!" Kalea protested.

"You can wear a sack if you like." Kai laughed.

"Leith would never agree to that. You know him. He wants to see it done properly. How long does a new dress take to make I wonder?"

Kai shrugged. "No more than a week, I hope. I don't know that I can wait much longer." His manhood throbbed painfully. *Lack of use,* he thought, but dared say nothing to Kalea. "I think tomorrow, you best find the best seamstress you can."

Kalea laughed. "Do you think she can do it in a day?"

"Not my luck," Kai groaned.

With that they walked back through the village. They had been gone longer than they thought and as they returned, the met many of the warband returning to their homes. They all hailed Kai and gave him good natured catcalls when they saw he was with Kalea.

The hall had emptied considerably since they had left. Lud was nowhere to be seen and Kai assumed that he had gone home. Leith and Arthur had fallen asleep at the table. A few hardened campaigners sat chatting quietly in the corner but it wouldn't be long before they too either slept where they were or wandered off home. Kai led Kalea to her screened off section and kissed her chastely on the cheek.

"I will see you tomorrow."

"I hope so," Kalea whispered and stepped behind the blind. She heard Kai leave and undressing, climbed under the skins. Excitement made it hard to sleep and for a while she laid thinking of her good fortune before sleep stole in.

The following morning, Kalea was awake early. Dressing and stepping out from behind her screens, she found a scene of chaos. Leith and Arthur were still asleep at the table, and a few more people lay scattered about the floor. It was obvious that some women had been in and tried to clean but were reluctant to disturb Arthur. However, they had left out breakfast although Kalea doubted the two men would feel much like eating when they woke. Kalea felt starved and sitting on the other end of the bench, she poured herself some milk and dipped an oatcake in some honey. Once she had had her fill, she left the two men and stepped out into the bright sunshine. The village, not surprisingly, was quiet. Not many people were up and about. Only those with urgent chores had left their beds to do them. Kalea headed for Ellen's house, she went quietly so not to disturb anyone. At Ellen's door, she listened for signs of movement and was not disappointed, inside she could hear Ellen singing to herself. For a moment, Kalea stood and listened. Ellen had a sweet voice. Finally, when she feared she might be discovered eavesdropping, she knocked. Ellen opened the door and invited her in. She was very pleased to see Kalea and for a while they talked of the wounded and what she had done. Ellen was impressed with her handy work and said she was destined for great thinks. The two women sat down, ate cakes and drunk a brew that Ellen had made. Kalea felt very comfortable with her. Ellen was perhaps the closest female that she had known.

"Your stitch work was very neat. Where did you learn that skill?" Ellen asked.

"Horses."

"Horses?" Ellen looked aghast.

Kalea nodded. "When we had battles, the wise woman would treat the warriors, but no one bothered with the horses. Some of them picked up some nasty wounds and I loved them, so I sewed them up. I can't say I enjoy it, but I couldn't let them bleed."

Ellen laughed. "Well, your work on them has certainly benefitted our warriors. The stitches were very neat."

"Thank you." Kalea could contain herself no longer and burst out. "Ellen, Kai has asked me to marry him and I have accepted."

Ellen's face lit with obvious delight. "Congratulations!" she got up and kissed the girl. "There will be a few broken hearts in the village when the news gets out." She laughed. "Competition for Kai and Arthur is fierce."

Kalea grinned. "It won't cause trouble, will it?"

Ellen hugged her. "Well, if it does, it won't concern you. So, he finally asked. It was obvious that he was totally besotted with you from the first. When's the day? Have you decided yet?"

Kalea sighed. "That's the problem. I have to get a new dress and until that time, we'll have to wait."

"We'll have to make sure that it gets done quickly then, shan't we?" Ellen smiled. "What better time, than now. Come on, we will knock up Peter and his wife can show you any cloth she might have." Grabbing the girl by the arm she towed her out of the door and down between the houses. "I am a fair seamstress myself," she added. "We can have it done inside a week if we're lucky."

Kalea had never been so excited. Peter's wife Meg was only too pleased to show off her linens. Her weaving was the best in the village and she had bolts of cloth that she had dyed herself. Fortunately, for Kalea, there was a fine selection. Cloth of the palest green, a pretty blue and creamy buttermilk that was so pale that it was almost white. In the end, they settled for the cream and after Kalea had paid for the cloth, they hurried back to Ellen's house to examine their purchase.

Ellen was nearly as excited as Kalea. Almost at once she started to measure out the cloth and began to cut it into shape. The material was so soft, it was like a cloud. Meg had excelled herself, Once Ellen was sure of Kalea's measurements, she shooed her away so she could get on with the task. Kalea wanted to stay and watch but Ellen assured her that she would only get in the way.

Kalea looked up at the bright blue sky with not a cloud in sight and wondered if the day could get any more perfect. It could because as she looked down, Kai was striding towards her with a big grin on his face.

"Good morning my lady. Where have you been? I've been looking for you everywhere."

"I've been with Ellen," Kalea explained smiling at him and taking his arm to walk with him. "My bride dress is already being made."

Kai laughed. "You didn't waste much time."

"I didn't want to give you the chance to change your mind."

"As if I would," Kai said indignantly.

"Are they awake in the hall yet?"

The grin on Kai's face said it all. "Sort of. Arthur has taken to his bed and Leith has a sore head and is even worse tempered than usual. If that is possible."

"Oh yes. It certainly is. So, you didn't tell him that you had asked me?"

"I didn't even ask if he knew where you were. I didn't dare! I saw you weren't there and fled looking for a band of Saxons to fight single-handed." Kalea giggled. "I think we had better pick our moment and this morning, I think, it might be better to let sleeping dogs lie."

"Good point. So, what do we do while we're waiting?" Kalea asked.

"I have a few ideas but not ones I would share with a maiden," Kai said with a roguish grin.

"The sooner that dress is finished the better," Kalea replied thoughtfully.

They went to Kai's home, to visit Lud. He was in fine humour have consumed half the mead everyone else had. He thought someone ought to keep a clear head and as no one else was prepared to sacrifice, he nobly rose to the call. Kalea liked Lud. He was like Leith in a lot of ways and she trusted him. Lud liked Kalea too. He thought Kai was very lucky winning the girl. He admired her bravery and honesty. Granted she would win no prizes for being the most ladylike woman in the village, but she was beautiful and strong. A man could not ask for everything. The three of them did not venture back to the hall until very late in the afternoon. In fact, the evening meal was just being served.

The hall was a very different place this evening. For the most part, it had been cleaned and the only people in it were Leith and Arthur. Leith had recovered a lot from earlier on and was at least happy enough to greet them. Arthur, on the other hand, had not shaved and still looked extremely hung over. The three of them exchanged rueful smiles.

"So," said Kai sitting down next to Arthur, while Lud and Kalea sat with Leith, "are you feeling better Arthur?" Arthur passed Kai a scathing look; his eyes were still blood shot. "I guess from that the answer is no."

Kalea giggled and Arthur glared at her, which was enough to stop her. She looked down at her plate as Leith patted her on her knee.

"Have you been playing chaperone Lud?" he asked.

Lud did his best to look mystified. "Not at all. There turned up no more than a moment ago. Kalea looked at bit of a mess and she had grass stains on her dress."

Kalea did her best to hide her shocked face. Leith whipped round to give Kai a look of absolute vitriol. Kai gave an apologetic grin and shrugged.

"You did WHAT?" Leith leapt to his feet ominously in front of Kai. Lud threw back his head and roared with laughter and gripped Leith firmly by the arm.

"Do not harm the lad. I was teasing. They have been with me all day. Though why they wanted to spend time with me is beyond me. Unless of course, they didn't trust themselves to be alone." Kai was chuckling.

"My apologies Son," Leith gruffly announced to him. "You Lud, I will sort out later and you will be lucky if you don't lose another arm." There was much laughter at this. Except for Arthur, who sat morosely looking at the food he had no stomach for.

It was not a late evening. After yesterday's excesses, everyone was tired and Arthur barely said a word all evening. They retired early in the hopes that everyone would have a chance to recover.

The next morning when Kalea woke, she felt refreshed. In fact, she hadn't felt as good for a long time. She bounced out of bed and found that Arthur was already up eating breakfast.

"Good morning," she said, "you look a lot better today."

"I feel a lot better, thank you. Will you join me?"

"I'd love too." She sat down and helped herself to some food and drink.

"I suppose I'd better not ask you if you want to go and watch the deer with me," he stated. Kalea wiped her mouth and shook her head. Arthur sighed. "Kai tells me that he is going to ask you to marry him. Has he asked yet?" He hardly needed her reply as she smiled sunnily at him. "And I assume from that smile that you have accepted?"

"Yes, of course."

Arthur suddenly found the crumbs on his plate very interesting. "I told Kai that I thought it was too soon and he hardly knew you."

"And what did Kai say?" Kalea asked cautiously.

"He said it was long enough for him to know you were the right woman for him." He looked up and met her eye, she was beaming with delight. "So, when is the big day?"

Kalea shrugged. "When I have my bride's dress ready."

Arthur nodded. "Well, I wish you joy. Kai is a good man."

"Thank you."

Arthur finished his last mouthful and rose. "I'm off to watch the deer. I will see you later."

"Alright," Kalea answered. She watched him leave. Nothing could dampen her spirits but she wished there was something she could say to Arthur that would make thing better. But she knew there was nothing and anything she said would only make things worse. She sighed and resolved to go and find Ellen and see how the dress was progressing.

The days flashed by. Kalea's days were filled with dress fitting. It was under a week and the dress was nearing completion. Ellen had done a magnificent job and had worked diligently on it. Even drawing on help from other women who she considered had the neatest stitches. The dress was the most exquisite thing that Kalea had ever seen let alone owned. Ellen had sculpted it round Kalea's body so that it fitted tight to her body and then flared from her slim hips to swirl round her ankles. The neckline had been cut round and low, so that it showed off Kalea's fine neck and shoulders. The sleeves were long and close fitting, but the most amazing thing was the fine stitch work. Ellen and her friends had embroidered a network of fine leave and red rose buds on the bodice and sleeves. The overall effect was stunning. Ellen was now working out which flowers to use for Kalea's headdress.

Chapter 5
Fate Plays a Hand

At last, the day had been set. The day after tomorrow she and Kai would be wed. She could hardly contain herself. Leith was being as patient as he could be with her but even he was getting caught up in the wedding fever that was surging through the village. Kai and Lud had been to the house that originally had been for Leith and Kalea, but now was being made ready as a bridal bower. Kai had arranged for a larger sleeping platform to be made and the carpenter, as a gift to them both, had excelled himself and raised the platform higher, so that the small house had room underneath it. Kai and Ellen made sure that come the day, the new housewife would have everything she needed to run her home and at the end of the day, they were pleased with the result.

Leith was fed up with Kalea bounding around everywhere and, in the end, growled.

"For god's sake girl, keep still. I feel tired watching you. Would you like to go for a swim? At least that will keep you quiet for a while."

"Yes, please Leith," Kalea yelled and rushed off to get a cloth to dry herself with.

"While you're there. Change into your kit and I'll give you some sword practice. You might need it on your wedding night to keep Kai at bay," Leith said with a grin.

"Leith!" she shouted indignantly. However, she returned shortly dressed in her trousers and carrying her boy's sword. Leith grinned at her.

"We are just going to have to get you a better sword. Perhaps, I will make that my wedding gift to you."

"Aren't you supposed to give us something for the home?"

"Since when have I worried about what I am supposed to do?"

"Quite right too," Kalea agreed. After all, she normally had little regard for what she was supposed to do.

The rode out to the river. Both chatting happily on everything and nothing. When they arrived, Leith got down and began training Kalea with her sword. She had become proficient with the boy's sword. Training and using it in a real situation were different and she had had some experience of using it in combat. Now, Leith could train her on finer points of strokes and timing. Leith gave her a good work out before he allowed her to plunge into the cool water.

Leith sat on the bank enjoying the sunshine. Perhaps, she had burnt off some of that excess energy, he hoped. He felt contented. All in all, it had turned out all right. He had a new home and a new warband, fighting with the best leader in the whole country. Peace had settled and no matter how temporary, it was welcome. The summer was drawing to an end and the people could now concentrate on making ready for winter. In East Anglia, the winter would be even busier as they would be making new villages so that when the Saxons returned in the spring, they would be ready for them. Here, however, the only thing of import, was Kalea's marriage to Kai and Leith's only worry was that his new shirt would not be ready. He grinned. Life didn't get much better than this. In two days, Kalea would be Kai's worry and good luck to the boy. It didn't matter how many times Leith told himself this, he knew he would miss having her around all the time. They may not have been together that long, but they were very close and had been through a lot.

Kalea was enjoying swimming in the cool water. Occasionally she called to Leith and teased him, but he was in a good mood today and refused to rise to the bait. She grinned. Wait until he saw her in her bride's dress. He would be speechless and that in itself, would be an achievement.

From the darkness of the trees, the riders watched the pair by the water. No word was spoken, but it seemed that the time was nearing. The woman had just left the water and wrapped herself in a large piece of material to dry off and the man had shed his sword and his shirt. A nod from one was all it took, and the riders spurred forward.

Leith and Kalea weren't aware of the riders until they were upon them. Leith had just enough time to bend for his sword before a blow to head felled him. Kalea leapt back into the water, but was soon surrounded by horses and was jostled from one to another. One lent down to grab her, she fought free but another had already grabbed her by her hair. Soon, she had been flung face down in front of one of the riders. In desperation, she sank her teeth deep into his thigh before a blow put her lights out.

Kalea didn't know how long she had been unconscious, but woke in the same position. It was uncomfortable and the horse's movement hurt her stomach but for a moment she lay still trying to make sense of what was going on. Her head still rang with blow she had received and it made thinking difficult. Who were these riders? The brief glimpse she had had of them before they rode her down, could only confirm that they were not Saxons. So, who? It was no use. It made no sense. She tried to raise her head and groaned as her vision blurred and a throbbing began to beat in her temple.

"My Lord, the girl is awake," spoke the voice of the horse owner.

"Good. Stop and let her dress. We will make faster progress if she rides her own mount." Without further warning, the horse stopped and the rider tipped Kalea onto the ground where she landed on her backside. She quickly realised that she was only wrapped in her drying cloth and scrambled to pull it round her. Looking up she saw that rider who had thrown her down was an older man, not as old as Leith, but older than Arthur and Kai. As she glared at him, he threw her down her trousers, shirt and boots.

The one he had addressed as my lord rode over. "Get dressed girl and hurry." She glanced around at the men. "For god's sake, no false modesty. Get your clothes on," he spat impatiently. Kalea had no choice but to comply. As she dressed, she took careful note of those around her and her heart lifted when she saw Leith tied to a horse nearby. Once dressed, another man led over her horse and she got on. She noticed that he had tied her reigns to his saddle so that there could be no escape.

"Hold out your hands girl." The rider who had carried her on his horse, tied her wrist securely and then added with a voice laden with threat. "You behave and nothing will happen to you. Kick up and..." The implication was left unspoken but the intent was clear enough. Kalea said nothing and sat with her back straight.

They set off at a very fast pace. Kalea guessed that they wanted to put as much distance between them and Arthur as they could. The ringing in her head didn't ease. Twisting round in her saddle, she took a look at Leith. His face was grim and blood trickled into his good eye. When he saw her look, he shook his head and with his chin pointed to the front. Kalea turned back. In front were at least four riders and from a glance to the rear, another three or four. Her mind refused to function clearly as much as she tried, she could think of no reason why they would want to kidnap her and Leith. There was plenty of time to contemplate though as they pushed on.

"Arthur!" Kai called as he walked up the village smiling brightly. "Have you seen Kalea?"

Arthur grinned. "You haven't lost her already, have you? You are going to have trouble keeping track of her. But yes, I saw her not so long ago. Leith was taking her swimming because she kept fidgeting around."

Kai laughed. "That sounds like Kalea. Well, I won't go looking for them. I want to keep my wedding tackle. Thanks."

Arthur roared with laughter. "He certainly is formidable. At least you have Lud to sort him out for you."

"I very much doubt Lud would. He would most probably hold me down while Leith did his worse." With that, Kai joined Arthur watching as the blacksmith forged some new weapons.

Kalea wondered *how long they had been riding?* It seemed like hours and most probably was. The sun was low in the sky and she guessed it was late afternoon. The time seemed to go on interminably. The riders' round, spoke to each other very little and kept pushing on at a pace that was guaranteed to exhaust the horses. One of the men had thrust a piece of dry bread at her which she had refused to accept but apart from that, they ignored her and just dragged her on and on.

The sun was setting and Kai was becoming concerned and a little frustrated. He had looked everywhere and failed to find Kalea. He wasn't too concerned just yet because it would appear that she was with Leith, but he could not find hide or hair of either of them in the village. He had tried Ellen's the stables and Lud's but with no joy. He strode into the drinking hall to find Arthur chatting to Lud.

"Have you seen Kalea?" he demanded with a definite edge to his voice.

Arthur looked up and his smile left his face. "Haven't you found her yet?"

"I wouldn't be asking if I had," Kai snapped crossly. Arthur rose and he looked at Lud concerned.

"Has anyone seen Leith?" Arthur asked and all the men in the hall, shook their heads. "Well then, that's one good thing, at least you can guarantee that if we find one, we shall find the other. Has anyone seen them since they came back from the river?"

Kai sighed and shook his head. "I've been all over looking for them. Ellen wouldn't let me in because she doesn't want me to see Kalea's dress, but she says that she hasn't seen her all day and I can't see that she would lie."

Arthur picked up his sword. "Come on then, before we lose the light altogether. Let's go and check out the river. Do you know where she swims Kai? Or have we got to ride the length?"

"No. I know where." Kai was now very concerned. They couldn't possibly still be at the river but it was the last place they knew they had been and therefore, the only place to start.

The horses were confused being taken out so late, when normally they would have been bedding down. Kai led them down the river in the fast-fading light. They arrived at the place where Kai had seen them swimming dismounted. Almost immediately, it was clear that something was seriously amiss. Even in the dim light, Lud found Leith's sword straight away and a further search found Kalea's pack and her boy's sword. They looked at each other. There was very little light left and it was hard to ascertain what had happened her.

"We'll have to go back Kai," Arthur said gripping Kai's shoulder. He didn't need light to know that his friend's face would be filled with anguish. "We've lost the light. We'll come back at first light. I'll get some men and we'll find them. I promise." Kai looked out at the dark sky. He was overwhelmed with guilt not having acted sooner. What if Kalea had come to harm? Where was she?

They rode back to the village and waited in the hall for first light. Arthur watched his friend pace back and forth with concern.

"Kai, this isn't going to help. We need the light and when it come, we need you fresh."

"I know, I know," growled Kai with frustration. "Knowing that doesn't make it any easier to accept. I can't sleep when I don't know if she is safe."

Arthur met Lud's eye. Lud's face was grim, grimmer than he had seen it for some time. If Kai's heart was breaking, then so too was Lud's. Arthur sighed. He too felt guilty. If he hadn't been so flippant with Kai earlier, then Kai might of rode out to see where she was. It was going to be a long night and the prospects did not look good.

Meanwhile, Kalea and Leith were still riding. The horses were very tired and plodding but the leader of band forced them on. The night was bright and only thing that was keeping Kalea awake was anxiety at what was going to happen to her. Rape was a strong possibility but if that was their plan, why hadn't they done that and gone off? At last, a halt was called. Leith and her were dragged down from their horses and tied roughly to a tree. Water was poured down her throat and she was glad of it. One of the men sat next to her and tore off pieces of bread and thrust them into her mouth. She had little choice but to eat. At last, when they were convinced that their captives had had enough to eat to keep them alive, they left and went to sit round the fire. Kalea turned her head to look at Leith.

"Are you alright lass?" he asked quietly trying not be overheard by the men by the fire.

She nodded. "Are you?"

"Got a bit of headache but I have no doubt, I'll live."

"What do they want?"

Leith shrugged. "Don't know. Don't know who they are either."

Kalea fought back tears. "What are we going to do?"

"I'm open to suggestions," Leith whispered. "Don't cause trouble. Perhaps, if we behave, we might have a chance to escape."

"But the longer we leave it, the further from Kai we are." The desperation in her voice made Leith wince.

"At the moment, that's the best I can come up with. Now, try and get some sleep, this lord, whoever he is, is going to be pushing hard tomorrow if today is anything to go by."

Kalea rested her head on his shoulder. She thought her fear would keep her awake, but sleep was an escape from the fear, and she fell into a deep sleep.

The light had hardly begun to touch the sky, when Arthur woke, jolted from a bad dream in which all his friends had been killed. Sweat was on his brow and looking up saw that Lud had fallen asleep at the table and Kai had at last sat down. His friend's face was a picture of abject misery and Arthur's heart ached for him.

"Kai. Rouse some men," Arthur said forcefully. Kai leapt to his feet, eager to be doing something. "Six should do." Arthur scrubbed his face with his hands and then picking up a pitcher of water, poured it over his head. He shook himself like a dog. Lud had roused himself at hearing Arthur's command and now stood waiting for his own orders. "Lud!" Arthur walked over to him and laid a hand on his shoulder. "We will do our best."

"I just hope it's good enough," Lud commented sourly.

Arthur sighed. "I would give all I own to bring Kalea back here for him."

"I know and so would I. I'll go down and get the horses ready." And with that he was gone.

The morning star had not left the sky when Kalea was roughly shaken awake. She groaned as she was hauled to her feet. The long hours in the saddle had done nothing to improve the situation and she ached. Without ceremony, she was picked up and dumped on her horse. She looked round for Leith and saw the same fate had befallen him, she opened her mouth but Leith shook his head and she remained silent. Without further ado, they were off. The pace again was back breaking and Kalea was convinced that the horses would keel over with exhaustion. This was not the case. They were good horses and had been well cared for. Looking to the east, she could see the sun beginning to break the rim of the earth. Judging by that, they were travelling South.

Arthur, Kai, Lud and six of the warband rode down to the river. Kai was not to be spoken too. The men were now aware that Kalea was missing and as a one, they agreed not to say anything. Words would fail to convey how sorry they were and would actually add to Kai's misery. Dismounting away from the place they walked the final few yards and began to scour the area for some clue as to what had befallen Leith and Kalea. After about half an hour, they returned to compare their findings.

"Looks like they were surprised," Arthur commented dryly. "There is little sign of a fight."

One of the warriors stepped forward. "From what I can see there was at least six of them. They came out the trees," he said pointing in that direction. "I tracked back and found a place where they must have waited. They seem to have gone back the same way and judging by the tracks, they're heading west."

"The Welsh!" Lud spat.

"Not necessarily," Arthur added thoughtfully. "This could be a rouse. Ben," he spoke to the warrior who had just spoken. "Take one other and follow the tracks the best you can. Let me know what you find. Kai, Luke and I will range off to the south. The rest of you, scout round and we will meet at the tall rock at noon and discuss where we go from there." All the men swung into the saddle. Lud looked at Arthur.

"I suppose I get to stay in the village."

Arthur smiled. "You know me too well old man."

"Arthur, look after Kai."

"Don't I always?" Arthur grinned and Lud just met his eye sternly. "I will," Arthur said firmly and with that he wheeled his horse around and caught up with Kai and Luke.

They had been riding for hours. Kalea didn't know where she was and spent the time taking note of her captors. At least she was beginning to know, who was in command of this band. The man they called my Lord, was in his late thirties, she would have guessed. He was tall, slim and well built. He had a hawkish nose, wore a beard and had dark curly hair that hung to his shoulders. His second seemed to be the big bear of a man with a shock of red hair and a scar running from his hairline down to his jaw. Then there was the older man who threatened her yesterday. Two blonde lads, not much older than her and looking to be brothers. There were three others, but they were at the back and she hadn't managed to take much notice of them. Looking up at the sun, Kalea judged that it was nearly noon and they hadn't stop once. At last, they looked set for a break. They stopped by a river giving the horse's time to drink and filling the water bottles. A dry crust of bread was thrust into her hands and she gnawed on it distractedly.

Kai looked up at the tall stone. It was nearly noon and the three of them had ranged quite a way south with no success. As weary as he was, Kai was impatient to get on and find Kalea. Whoever had her, had a good half a day's ride on them and all the time it was lengthening. Kai was all set to take the warband west to Wales and have it out with the hill fort there, but Arthur was reticent. Kia didn't know why, but Arthur had a gut feeling that the riders turned south. Much as Kai would have liked to over ridden Arthur's command, Arthur's feelings were often right and it paid to wait and see. He wanted Kalea back and he wanted her now!

Kai was aware of how Luke and the others were watching. He knew that they thought that she could well be dead or raped. He shut his eyes against such a thought. There was no way she could be dead! The possibility that she could be raped was disturbing enough but he could and would live with it when he got her back.

Arthur watched him. He could almost hear his friend's thoughts whirling round his head. How Kai would cope should they find Kalea was another worry that Arthur wasn't prepared to face just yet. One thing at a time.

It wasn't long before the rest of his search party turned up. Ben was the one they wanted to hear from the most.

"I think you may be right Arthur," Ben said. "Although the tracks are still heading west, they are beginning to drop south. I reckon that sooner or later, I will find a river running south and they will take the horses down that to try and loose trackers."

"So," Arthur said grimly. "Kai, it is your call. Do we follow the tracks or try and intercept them on a direct route south?"

"I will go south," Kai said resolutely. Arthur nodded in agreement.

"Ben, go back to where you left the tracks and follow them. If they turn west, come back and find me." Ben nodded and rode off. "The rest of us will go south."

Kalea couldn't believe how hard they were riding. It was late afternoon and they hadn't stopped. The horses were plodding, lathered up with sweat and tired but they were still kept going. She kept opening her mouth to say something and then thought better of it. The sun was setting when they arrived at a copse of trees. As they rode in, a man came out to greet them. Now, Kalea understood. This Lord was a clever one, he had left a man here with provisions and fresh horses. She expected them to call a halt, but much to her surprised they did nothing of the sort, the swapped horses and once again went on their way at a faster speed than before. Kalea was exhausted by this time. In some ways, she wished that they would just kill her and get it over and done with. At least that way she could get some rest. The moon was up by the time they finally stopped and Kalea was relieved. Once again, she and Leith were tied to a tree while the others set up camp. Kalea was too tired to talk and just slumped against Leith and slept. She wasn't allowed to sleep long before she was woken with some food. "I don't want any," she said sleepily.

"You do as you told, if you know what is good for you." Growled the man in front of her. Reluctantly, she began to chew her stale bread. The men were a little more talkative tonight as if they sensed that they had ridden far enough to throw Arthur off the scent.

"Do you think Arthur even missed this pair?" asked one. The lord looked up, his hazel eyes glittering in the firelight.

"I think he knows damn well that they are missing," he remarked slowly. "Not many women are given a seasoned warrior as a body guard so I should think that she is someone well known to Arthur. But you have missed the whole point Max. What I wanted Arthur to know, is that I will not be bullied by him. I have come to his village and kidnapped two people from under his nose." He grinned wickedly in the firelight. "Arthur's people won't feel so safe now and

Arthur himself, will be wondering how we got past his watchtowers. For once, I caught him wrong footed."

"So, what are we going to do with them?"

The lord shrugged. "That is not important. We'll keep them for a while and see if Arthur comes looking. If he does, we shall see what he is prepared to give for them. Maybe we will exchange them, maybe we will kill them. I shall see how I feel."

Leith looked at Kalea who met his eye. The lord laughed. "I would love to see what is going on up there now. I bet he's chasing his tail. I expect Arthur to come looking. It will be quite amusing to see how much time he wastes looking for them."

At last, Kalea and Leith now knew why they had been taken. Spite. This warlord obviously suffered at Arthur's hands. Knowing Arthur, for good reason but this did not matter in the least to the Lord. The prospects did not look bright and Kalea couldn't believe that Arthur would waste much time looking for a girl and one-eyed warrior. Kai might. But without Arthur's warband what chance did he have against so many.

Arthur's band of men camped down for the night. They had been riding hard and were tired. Kai would have ridden until his horse dropped and then walked but Arthur had insisted that they rest. Kai looked haggard. So, far they had found no sign of the riders despite the fact that they had spread out to look. His gut told him they had gone south but he had many enemies and Mark Cornwall was but one. There were countless warlords in the south that would do something like this to spite Arthur. Watching the flames, he counted them. Who would be bold enough? Mark was chief suspect but there were others closer. Robert of Dorset and Martin were two others. Martin was smarting under a recent defeat and Arthur thought this was just the thing that he would enjoy doing. The biggest problem was rushing headlong into an ambush. Arthur was very aware that his search party was small. This could well be a plan, to lure him into a remote spot and kill them all. A clever trap indeed and one he mustn't fall into even for his friend. He looked across at Kai. They had been through so much together and this was another tragedy that he was sure their friendship would survive. However, it was hard for him to tell Kai that they must be cautious. It slowed them down when they continually had to watch for signs of danger. The fragile peace that held the country at the moment must not be jeopardised and they must tread carefully. After all, they were travelling through land that was no longer seen as Arthur's. He had no wish to offend a warlord and risk breaking that peace. The people need time to enjoy the end of the summer and make ready for the coming winter.

He sighed. There was no easy way through this and he found himself once again wishing Lud was here to offer counsel. He knew what Lud would say, that sacrifices had to be made to protect the people and if at the end of it all, it meant giving up someone or something you loved. So be it. Lord knows Arthur had made sacrifices over the years but each one got harder. And how to persuade Kai would be yet another problem.

The days blurred as the riders and their captives rode hard for home. Kalea couldn't even guess how many days they had been riding. Every now and then they picked up new horses and rode on. Kalea was so weary that she no longer cared about her fate. Arthur set a fast pace with his warband but this Lord out stripped even that and the planning that went into moving horses, picking up fresh ones and resting the tired ones before bringing it all together to start again, was more than clever.

Chapter 6
The South West

The longer they rode, the happier the men became. Kalea thought she had been in the saddle forever when at last they reached the summit of a rugged hill and there below in the valley was a large village. The men let out a loud cheer, which made Kalea jump and she began to take more note of the village below. This, she guessed was where they had been heading for all along. The riders set off at a cracking pace and were greeted noisily as they entered the village. There was a lot of back slapping and cheering. Women clinging to the leg of the men and looking curiously at the captives.

At the far end of the village stood a large imposing castle and within the outer walls were two large halls that stood apart. They were well built and ornate and Kalea guessed this was where they were heading. All at once she heard someone shout out welcome to Mark. Her head whipped round to look at the person they were addressing; it was the one they called Lord. Mark of Cornwall? She wondered. Kalea knew that Mark was Arthur's sworn enemy, but if this was indeed, Mark of Cornwall, he seemed to be well liked in his village. They arrived at one of the halls and Leith and Kalea were dragged down from the horses and bundled up the steps and into the hall. Food and drink were being laid out even as they came through the doors and there was much good-natured laughter and calling.

Leith and Kalea were stood in the middle and too the large part, ignored. Leith noted that Mark's warband was large and they all seemed to be here to greet his return. It wasn't until all the men were seated and eating that attention was turned to the captives.

"What have we got here then?" asked one. "A scrawny girl dressed as a boy and an old warrior who has seen better days."

Mark shrugged. "Two captives taken right from under Arthur's nose. And he's probably still trying to work out who too them." He laughed.

"Is the woman worth anything? Apart from a roll in the hay that is." There was much laughter at this and Kalea's chin went up.

"Don't know, don't much care." Mark shoved a piece of meat into his mouth. "She washes up all right."

"Yeah!" said one of the blonde lads who had been with the riders. "She'd been swimming in the river when we caught her. Not a bad body on her either." There was more laughter and eyes turned to Kalea. "Are you going to share her round?"

Kalea was horrified. So, here it was at last.

Mark pondered the question watching Kalea closely. "I shall see. When I have finished with her."

"Why did you keep the old man alive?" someone asked.

"Because all the time he was alive, she thought she might have some chance of escape. If he was dead, she would have been less co-operative," Mark said with a smile. The men nodded and smiled back. *He was a clever one,* Leith thought. Having eaten his fill, Mark turned his full attention to the captives. Turning to the man next to him, he said, "Have the girl taken to my room," then looking at Leith added casually, "and kill him."

Kalea couldn't believe it. A man rose and grabbed Leith while another made a grab for Kalea who dodged him.

"Wait," she spoke with more authority than she felt.

Mark turned to look at her with surprise. "And why should I wait?" he queried sarcastically.

"I want to make a bargain with you," Kalea said standing resolutely. Mark smirked and rose from his seat. He looked amused and approached her and circled her, taking a close look at her. Then standing so close, she could feel his breath.

"A bargain? I see nothing that you can bargain with girl. All that you have is the clothes you stand up in and what use are they to me?"

Inwardly, Kalea was shaking but she met his eye boldly. Leith's voice distracted her momentarily. "Kalea! Don't!"

"Silence!" Mark commanded. Then turning back to meet her eye. "You were about to say?"

Kalea looked into those hazel eyes that were so calculating and spoke boldly. "You are right, I have nothing but myself to bargain with. If you spare my warrior's life, then I will do as you bid me."

Mark made a dismissive motion and turned his back to her. "Well, that is no bargain at all. Why should I spare your man, when I can have you anyway?"

"Because," Kalea lifted her chin and answered coolly, "if you do not, I will fight you. And be assured I will do as much damage as I can, if he is harmed." Then with a bold look, that spoke of contempt. "Of course, if rape excites you, you may kill him."

Mark span on his heels his eyes wide with surprise and caught her look of contempt. He strode back to her and seized her by the jaw. He stared into her dark eyes and she remained unflinching. Then he laughed. "You're a brave young filly. I like that in a woman. And you," he turned to look at Leith, "are a lucky old man. Lock him up somewhere." Turning his attention to his serving women. "Scrub her up and take her to my room." Running a finger down Kalea's cheek he finished. "You had better be worth it girl." With that she was dragged away.

The women were rough as they manhandled Kalea out of the hall and to a small outbuilding off the kitchen. They took great delight in ripping her clothes from her so she stood naked. There was a good deal of prodding and poking as they waited for the water to be bought back. Then they doused Kalea with cold water and began lathering her down with some fatty, soapy solution. They were thorough if not gentle. Kalea did not protest, she knew it would be useless. Having washed her, they then dried her and combed her hair. The knots were pulled hard and it made tears spring to Kalea's eyes. When they finished, she was wrapped in a length of cloth and then dragged up the castle stairs to Mark's room. The door was shut behind her and she was left alone. Kalea thought she would cry. Naked she felt very vulnerable. A fire burned cheerfully in the hearth and she went and stood before it. She wasn't cold, but somehow it made her feel better. Looking round, she took in her surroundings. Mark obviously lived well. His bed was large and covered in furs and blankets. There were rugs on the floor and a table and chairs stood in the corner. Tired of standing, Kalea sank onto the rug by the fire to wait.

Waiting was a game that Mark played well. He sat with his men and drank and only when he was sure that Kalea had been waiting some time on her own, did he decide to go and see how she was faring.

Kalea was nervous. Having made the bargain, she was not sure that she could go through with it. Outwardly, she appeared calm but inwardly, she was terrified. She had no choice. If she didn't, she had not a doubt that Mark would give her to the warband. It was one or many. Not much of a choice.

Mark left the main hall and stopped by the well. Stripping off his shirt, he gave himself a dousing in water. This not only woke him up but also got most of the grime off him. Carrying his dirty shirt, he went to his rooms. It was quiet. No crying. He paused thinking for a while before entering. There she was waiting for him on the rug and she was beautiful. The women had done a good job of cleaning her and she had washed up a treat. The firelight caught in her dark eyes and hair gleamed. Casually, he threw his shirt down on a chair.

"So, my lady," his voice was deep and melodious, "who exactly are you?"

Kalea looked up at him shyly, his chest was broad and hairy and she made sure she held his eye. "My name is Kalea." Her voice was soft.

"Yes. So, now I have your name. But who are you?" His voice was even.

Kalea looked a little confused. "No one really." The look in his eye said that he didn't believe her. "I mean, I am not a warlord's daughter or anything like that. My father was a warrior."

"If you are no one of import, how is it that you have a warrior to protect you?"

"He is my guardian since my father's death." He clearly didn't believe her.

"Well, if you have no worth to Arthur, you better make sure of your worth to me." He looked at her coolly. "Come here girl."

Kalea took a deep breath and rose. She was shaking as she stopped before him and dropped the drying towel. Her mouth was dry and her breath was coming fast. He sat and looked her up and down, appraising her and noted her nervousness. Then he reached for her and pulled her to him, his lips came down on hers, harsh and demanding. For a second, but only a second, Kalea panicked, then she kissed him back. Warmth began to slowly build in her body. His hands roamed to her breast and stroked and tweaked her nipples. This intimacy had not been allowed and Kalea was overwhelmed by the sensations filling her body. Every inch of her skin had become sensitive to his touch. She gasped with pleasure and felt him smile against her mouth. Another kiss this time deeper and more demanding. Urged on by this new sensation, Kalea responded by pressing close to him. His hands were not idle touching her in sensitive places that she had not known were sensitive. Gently, he stroked her throat, her arms and her breasts and at each touch, her body demanded more. His lips left hers and with his tongue, he traced patterns over the skin on her throat. Transferring his kisses to neck, his hand travelled lightly over her flat belly and came to the triangle between her legs. With care he moved onwards. Kalea stood transfixed, her head thrown back, her heart pounding, her breath quickening. Without conscious thought she gave a moan of delight. Once again, he smiled. Without warning he stopped.

Letting her go, he sank back into the chair. Mark was surprised at her response. He had expected pleasure. But pleasure was always to be had from women. Whether you took them by force or not. However, he had not expected her to be so sensuous. The plan hadn't been to seduce her, but somewhere along the line, in that first kiss, his plans had changed. He regarded her with passion. As if she was suddenly aware that he no longer touched her, she met his eye. Mark smiled slowly; her eyes were glazed with passion. This was not going to be an ordeal for her and he was strangely pleased. He had gained a reputation over the years of being a skilled lover and he was adept in reading what a woman wanted. If she was aroused, he was doubly aroused. What he didn't understand was his desire for her was clear to her, and that aroused her more. His body throbbed for release and his erection was hard and pulsing. But it was not time. He wanted her to be ready. Watching her very closely he at last spoke.

"Help me with my boots." For a moment, she couldn't understand the command and then came forward to do his bidding.

Kalea's body was singing as she bent over to pull off his boots. What was he up to? She wondered. Why had he stopped? Her mind was in turmoil. Did he not find her attractive? She knew he did, she could see it in his face. In the end, she had to concede, she would have to wait and see. At last, the boots were off and she stood waiting further instruction. He sat looking at her thoughtfully.

"Come here." His voice was quiet and commanding. She did as she was told. "Closer." She was already close and was forced to step between his legs. As she did so, his hands closed on her breasts. Kalea wasn't sure what she should do, so she did nothing. Then sitting up straight, his tongue sought her nipples. Kalea gasped. He began, to suck and lick and Kalea no longer cared what he did. Then his kisses began a slow descent. As his tongue entered her moistness, she was absolutely transported and now was shaking not with fear, but with pleasure. Suddenly, he rose and took her in his arms. Her body trembled against him in its need. He kissed her fiercely and she was more aroused to taste herself in his mouth. Mark knew the battle was won as she clung to him pulling him closer, loving the feel of his skin against her breasts. Taking care not to hurt her, he backed her towards the bed and lowered then down on it. Even now, she was not worried about the act she was about to commit. There was no need for him to take time, but he would. Half the pleasure was teasing and this gave him true power over women. There was little need. Kalea was willing, even eager for his attention.

Kalea of course, knew nothing of this strategy. She welcomed him into her arms after he had shed the rest of his clothes. Even, his large throbbing member, did not frighten her. Already, she was aware that he had no intention now, of harming her and trusted to his skill to make sure she was pleasured. He guided himself, carefully, between her thighs and as he entered her, he kissed her deeply. Much to his surprise, his entry was not smooth, he met resistance. Taking his lips from her, he looked into her eyes, a question already in them.

"A virgin?"

She did not speak and answered with an almost imperceptible nod. An almost cruel smile curled her lips and he kissed her again. He pressed harder feeling the barrier tear under the pressure. Her eyes widened, but the pain was brief and over ridden by the pleasure as she felt him slide deep into her. Her insides felt like they were made of liquid and she gasped with delight. He adjusted her position, raising her knees to allow him deeper access to her. She needed no further encouragement.

Mark smiled, holding for a while inside her fiery smoothness. Then he began to move. Languid long strokes that made her back arch and push against him. This was a treat and he wanted to savour it. An innocent with such passion, the combination was just perfect.

Kalea was transported. Her whole body felt like it was about to erupt. It felt like she was climbing a mountain and the anticipation was almost too much to bear. She knew she was reaching the summit. Mark's movements were still rhythmic and smooth but sweat was beading on his forehead and she knew that he was riding the same wave. The wave broke and Kalea climaxed, the force of it causing her to spasm and gasp. Mark needed no more time and exploded in her, kissing her frenziedly as he lay spent on top of her.

"Well, my little flower," he spoke against her throat, "a maiden no longer."

He felt her smile. "Maybe not. But what a pleasure. If I had known it would be this good, I would not have been a maiden so long."

This time he smiled. Lifting his head, he looked into her eyes. "Ahhh, but who is to say that it is not down to my skill? Another might not have achieved what I have."

"Really?" Kalea was genuinely surprised. "You mean not all men love the same way?"

"You really are an innocent." He laughed rolling clear of her. "Some men are indeed skilled, but others are too intent on their own pleasure to worry about the needs of their women." To his surprised, she curled close to him, leaning her head on his chest.

"Well then, I am indeed fortunate," she said sleepily. And within moments she was asleep. This amused Mark. Women normally wanted to talk and be held. Still, he had to admit, the ride had been brutal and she had done well to keep up without complaining. Not much sleep and fear had made her weary and she had slipped into sleep, without as much as a murmur. As he lay holding her while she slept, he had to admit, she had struck a good bargain and there was no doubt in his mind that he had done very well out of it. He reluctantly admitted, that she was a good woman and with that thought in mind, he fell to sleep.

Arthur, Kai and the rest of the search party had ranged far to the south. They still hadn't found any traces of the riders. Ben had returned to tell Arthur that the tracks had faded away. This had not been received well. This meant whoever had taken Kalea was very clever and expected pursuit. They were into Dorset's land now and Arthur knew he would have to make a stop to pay respect and also enquiries. Kai was like a man possessed. Arthur couldn't believe that he could still function on so little sleep. His eyes were like two steel chips and his resolve to find Kalea did not waiver, but grew stronger. Arthur had no doubt that if he turned the search party and headed home, Kia would go on alone and search until he found her, or died in the attempt. He worried about him, knowing that pace was too slow for them to catch up with the riders. This was Kai, he knew and loved as a brother and while he readily admitted that he would have won Kalea if he could, he did not know if he would be willing to sacrifice his friendship for her.

Kai knew only too well what Arthur was thinking. His face looked to be carved from granite as he looked towards the village they were approaching. What he wanted to do was to ride round, go on and search further but he knew that diplomacy wouldn't let Arthur upset a warlord when he didn't have too. Kai knew, Arthur was right, the people didn't need any more battles but it didn't make it easier for him. Where was Kalea? Was she raped? Or worse dead? He didn't dare think on it. By the time they caught up, something would have happened if it hadn't already. He was exasperated and at the same time, resigned. He set his jaw and followed Arthur down to the village. They would be expected to socialise. Kai didn't feel much like it.

Mark woke to find Kalea entwined around him. Her head was nestled into his neck, a hand on his chest and a leg thrown across him. He stroked her glossy dark hair and smiled. Little had he known when he had stolen her, that she would be such a find. A virgin! What a rarity. And she was beautiful. Young, yes. Young enough to be his daughter but that mattered little. As for sharing her, he thought not. She stirred and murmured against his chest and nestled closer. Mark had not yet found a woman that he wanted to share his life with. There were enough bastards in the village for him to choose a successor and he really had felt no need. He had married when he was very young and both his wife and his first-born had not survived childbirth. After that, he took his pleasure where he chose.

At the moment, he had to admit he was captivated by her innocence. He decided he would keep her as his mistress until Arthur came and offered him something better, or until her charms wore thin. Then he would put her aside as he had so many others. Disentangling himself from her arms, he lent down and kissed her gently on the lips. She did not wake, so he progressed down to her throat and then onwards to her breasts. Kalea stirred but did not open her eyes so, he traced a pattern over her flat stomach and to the heart of her sex.

Kalea woke her body already warm and fluid. His curly head between her thighs was and exquisite sensation and she was more than ready for him. "Mark," she whispered. His tongue traced a trail over her stomach as he came up and kissed her deeply.

"Good morning my lady," he spoke quietly against her lips.

"Good morning my lord," she responded with a slow smile and drew him down to her.

Kissing her deeply, he slid into her deep velvety depth. Kalea had learned a little and drew her legs up to allow him deeper access. It was as wonderful as she remembered and she felt complete as he moved within her. This time she moved too, finding his rhythm and working with him. She was soon soaring and this time, knowing what was coming, reached for her orgasm, which was so mighty, she called out against his chest. Mark reached his release almost immediately, her response so great that it pushed his self-control over.

Supporting his weight on his elbows, he looked down into her flushed face. "You learn quickly little one."

"I have a good teacher." Kalea reached up and drew his head down so that she could kiss him. He allowed her to do so. Then he rolled clear and Kalea felt the loss and was shocked by the feeling. She moved closer to him and was rewarded when he drew her closer still.

"So, what shall we do with you?" Mark asked stroking her hair absent-mindedly.

"Whatever you want," Kalea answered. "My virtue is lost, so, what value I had is lost also."

He smiled not unkindly. "That was a good bargain you struck; however, you would have had a stronger bargain if you had told me, you were a virgin."

"And what good would telling you have done? Your men would have crowed and I thought it better not to be laughed at."

She of course, was right. And there may have been an auction for her maidenhead, although he would have claimed it as his right. At least she had earned her warrior his life and he hoped that he would be suitably grateful. A knock came on the door and young serving woman entered carrying a tray of food. She placed it on the table and as she was about to leave, Mark stopped her.

"Mary, this is Kalea and she is to be my woman for as long as it is my pleasure. Treat her well. Come back in an hour and scrub her up ready for me this evening." The woman looked at Kalea and nodded. Kalea grimaced. "And what is that face for?" Mark asked.

"Your women do a good job at washing but they are none to gentle. I think they are jealous."

Mark laughed. "Very astute Kalea. Now, come and east some breakfast." He rolled off the bed and began to pull on his trousers. Kalea lingered longer. "Come on girl, don't be shy. After what we have done, you have very little to be shy about."

Kalea pouted. "I know that. And I suspect you know me body better than I do, but I don't feel very comfortable about eating breakfast naked."

"What happened to your clothes then?"

"Your women didn't leave enough of them to salvage. They even took my boots."

Mark gave a rueful grin. Slipping his shirt over his head, he strode over to a large chest. Swinging the lid up, he delved in and began turning over garments. It didn't take him long before he came out with a delightful pale blue dress. He smiled triumphantly and threw it at her. "And don't ask who last owned it," he warned as she slipped it over her head. It wasn't too bad a fit. A tad short and a little tight across her breasts, but it only went to emphasis her figure. He nodded approving as she sat down at the table. "And tell the women, I want this one left in one piece." Kalea rewarded him with a smile and as he took a bite of his honey oatcake, he thought she was really quite exceptional.

Kalea in turn watched him while she ate. Mark was not handsome like Kai or Arthur but he was striking. His dark curly hair showed little signs of age. The nose was a little too long and hawkish and mouth was strong and sensuous. But his eyes were outstanding, maybe because his colouring was so dark; they were a pale hazel and beautiful. The lashes dark and long.

He looked up catching her studying him. "Do you like what you see?"

"I think I do," Kalea said coyly. "But I thought men weren't supposed to fish for compliments."

He laughed. "And what may I ask, do you know of men when you know so little of love?" he asked.

"I know lots about men," Kalea grinned in reply. "In my home, I was the only woman with three men. My father and two brothers and you do get to learn a bit when you are with them all the time."

"And where are your two brother now?" interested to know if her two brothers would be out looking for her. The smile left her face. Her face showed nothing. Not sadness, happiness or any other emotion he could think of. For some reason, he found that mildly disconcerting, although he did not know why.

At last, she sighed and shrugged. "Dead. Both dead. In fact, all of my people are dead. All bar Leith." She met his eye. "You see, I am not one of Arthur's people." She watched as an eyebrow rose in surprise. "I am from East Anglia. During the summer months, our villages are attacked by the Saxons and our only respite is the rough seas of winter. I lost my mother to Saxon raiders when I was about so high." She held her hand out just above the knee. "She died trying to protect my two brothers and me. My brothers were killed fighting the raiders over the last two years, which just left my father and me. My village was not large, and full of strong warriors, as yours is, and neighbouring villages had their own battles to fight." For a moment Kalea paused, then drawing a deep breath continued. "This year the Saxon raid have been worse than ever. Our village was already weak. Most of the warriors were already dead and the few left, were old, like my father and Leith or too young to fight. You as a warlord know, that young warriors are vulnerable. They are full of hot blood and make mistakes that can cost them their lives. When the last raid came, our village fell. All that remains are Leith and me."

"And how is it, that you two managed to survive when others couldn't?" he asked intrigued.

Kalea shrugged. "More out of luck than judgement. We were both left for dead. Leith took an axe blow to the side of his head and was knocked out."

"And you?" he encouraged when it was obvious that she did not wish to speak of it.

"I was knocked out too."

"What are you not telling me?" he queried.

Kalea smiled. "You my lord are too clever for your own good. Leith would like to tell this tale. He makes a big drama out of it and it is not. I killed a Saxon who was trying to rape me and as he fell, he knocked me over and I hit my head." She could tell by the look on his face that he was impressed and was looking at her in a new light.

"That was a very brave thing to do," he commented.

"No, it wasn't at all. I was fighting for my life. I didn't take a sword and do battle with him, there was a struggle and I stabbed him. Nothing clever or noble and he hadn't been such a great ox, I wouldn't have been knocked over. There!"

He grinned "Such modesty." And as she made a face at him, he pushed further. "So, how was it that you were in Arthur's village?"

"We went on to the next village and hearing that our village had been raised, it was decided that someone should go to Arthur and see if he could send help. As we were the outsiders, we were the obvious choice."

"He said that he was too busy fighting the Welsh and Mark of Cornwall, who I suspect is you." Mark laughed. "So, you see, the only reason that Arthur might come looking for us, if he feels that it would be an embarrassment to lose messengers. But of course, he could say that we had left the village and we must have met some sort of disaster on the way in which case, he won't bother."

"He will come looking." Mark smiled sardonically. "Arthur is many things but he is an honest man. He will not lie to save his skin."

This time Kalea looked at him disbelievingly. "For a scrawny girl who dresses like a boy and an old warrior who has seen better days?"

Mark laughed. "You have a ready wit, young Kalea, and you deserve the right to live." He rose from the table. "I have things to do. You will not leave this room unless you are escorted. Is that clear?"

Kalea nodded and then lifted up her skirts to show him her bare feet.

"I wouldn't get far with no boots."

Ginning he picked up his sword and left leaving Kalea sitting with remnants of breakfast. She sighed. Looking round at her surroundings, Kalea had little to do but to ponder her fate. She may be many things, but she was not stupid. *That's what you get for being too happy*, she thought. Her choices were few and bleak. Waiting for a chance to escape was one. First, she would need to plan how to get out of the castle. From what she had seen, it was well defended. Even the village was fortified with a high fence and a deep ditch surrounding it. Also, it was busy and people seemed to be around all the time. Even if she did escape, it was a long way back north to Arthur's village. She doubted she would survive on foot especially without Leith and she could not leave without him. And if she did make it back to Arthur's kingdom, what sort of welcome would be offered her? Kai would not want her now. How could he? She had given herself willingly.

There was of course a chance that Kai would come looking for her. But that didn't hold much comfort. Mark was fierce and strong and Arthur would not wish to risk an outbreak of war with winter so close and from what she could see of Mark's settlement, there was nothing of value that he needed so there could be no chance of an exchange. Even if there was something to exchange, what would Kalea do then? She was back to if Kai did not want her, where would she go and what would they do? The answer was of course was to go back to East Anglia and try and start a new life. That was a lot of ifs.

The last option was to remain here. There were many examples of people who had been captured living in peace in strange villages. Kai was a good example of that. She had no doubt that life with Mark would not be too unpleasant. So, he wasn't Kai, but he was strong and powerful. But that only lasted as long as he wanted her, it was what happened when he didn't that concerned her.

In the end, she concluded that she would just have to wait and see. There was no other way round it and to keep trying to seek a solution would just frustrate her. If there was a solution, it would present itself to her when it was good and ready. Life in the world was too unsettled. Threats from enemies all round and to survive to an old age was a bonus many didn't live to see. Kalea knew this, after all, she had seen her family and her village destroyed and she vowed she would do all she had to do to stay alive.

Mark bounded into the hall. It was clear to everyone there that he was in a good mood. Always a good thing.

"I take it the girl was good then?" Queried one of the men.

With a big smile, Mark said, "She was most…" He flung himself casually in her chair, pondering how best to answer. "Most enjoyable."

"So, we won't get a look in for a while," the man stated.

"I think not," Mark answered. He beckoned to his steward. "So, what have we got this morning?" he queried with a sigh.

"Some minor disputes for you to decide."

Mark rolled his eyes. "More whingers." He sighed. "Send the first one in."

Two serving women entered the room interrupted her frantic thoughts. One had come to clear the table, the other was Mary who beckoned to her to follow. Kalea rose meekly and followed her out. As they passed into a busy street, Kalea looked round interested and eager to see what was about. The girl gave her a push and Kalea lurched forward.

"Can I talk to you?" Kalea asked.

Mary looked at her hard. "If you want. I am not saying I will answer."

Kalea nodded her assent. "Are we in Cornwall?" Kalea asked innocently, although she already knew she was. The question made the girl burst out laughing.

"Don't you know?" Kalea shook her head. "Of course, you are. This kingdom belongs to Mark our king and as far as the eye can see." Kalea feigned surprise. "Have you not heard of Mark of Cornwall?"

Kalea nodded. "Yes, but only recently. And I had never seen him, and never knew where Cornwall was even." Kalea had achieved what she set out to do and drawn the girl into conversation. It was obvious, she was proud of where she lived and her king.

"Not very well informed in Arthur's kingdom, are you?" she queried. She spat Arthur's name as if it were venom.

"To be honest," Kalea answered "I'm not one of Arthur's people. I come from East Anglia. Have you heard of it?"

"Course I have," Mary retorted although Kalea thought she might be lying. "Is your king powerful?"

Kalea grinned. "We haven't got a king as such. We have a chieftain and compared to this great fortress, out village is tiny."

"How many people lived in your village?"

"I don't know. Not many." This made Mary laugh. "I was taking a message to Arthur when your king took me."

They had arrived back at the kitchen which had a room attached that served as a wash room. A large barrel was in the middle of the floor and it was full of water.

"Your bath awaits my lady," Mary said sarcastically and grinned. Kalea smiled back and went to the barrel. Mary came forward and took the dress that Kalea had shed. Kalea climbed into the barrel. The water was warm that was something. Mary was quick to notice the smear of blood on Kalea's thigh. "Were you a virgin?" she asked. Kalea looked down at the blood and then nodded. "I bet that pleased him. Don't get many of those round here," she said with a grin.

"What's he like Mary? I mean really?" Kalea asked as Mary scrubbed her down with a rough cloth.

"He's a good man. He's clever and strong and he's sees us alright. I've worked for him since I was little and my mum before me. He's got a temper, but if you treat him right, then he'll do right by you."

This didn't sound like an evil enemy to Kalea but she said nothing about that. "Be honest Mary. What do you think he'll do with me?"

Mary laughed. "I think you already know that." Kalea laughed too.

"You know what I mean."

Mary busied herself soaping Kalea's hair before answering. "If he likes you, he will keep you with him. If he doesn't, he will give you to the warband. If he likes you now and tires of you later, he will most likely give you a house in the village and leave you to it."

"Really?"

"That's what he has done in the past," Mary answered truthfully. "Don't give him a hard time, he is a good man." She watched Kalea as she thought about what she had just said.

Kalea realised that whatever bad blood there was between Arthur and Mark, it did not affect the fact that to their people, they were both fair and just rulers. "So, he treats his people well?"

"He is hard but fair," Mary answered rinsing Kalea's hair off and causing her to splutter. "What's Arthur's village like? Is it as big as this?"

Kalea knew that Mary was fishing for information and she was willing to give her some. "Yes, it is big. I don't know if it is as big as this. There were a lot of people. But as I said, my village was small and I couldn't believe that so many people could live in one place when I saw it."

Mary grinned. "Has Arthur got a big warband?"

"He seemed to have, but what do I know? I don't get to see all the war like things."

Mary indicated that she should step out which she did and then she slipped the dress back over Kalea's head. Whilst she had been bathing, people had been coming and going into the kitchen and back with food and clean clothing and Kalea was relieved to be dressed again.

Kalea lifted her skirts and pointed to her feet. "Is there any chance of me getting my boots back? I know they were old and battered. They were once my brother's and I would love to have them back."

Mary led her back to the hall and smiled at the girl. "I know where they are and will bring them to you."

"Thank you, Mary. And thank you for talking to me." Mary opened the door and let her into Mark's room.

Mary nodded with a smile. "I wish you luck," she said as she left.

Kalea went over and banked up the fire. It was not cold, but the flickering flames comforted her. She sat before them, watching the flames dance and let them entrance her. How long she stayed there, she could not say, but the door opening disturbed her. Leaping to her feet, she was surprised as Leith was led through the door. He had chains on his wrists and ankles but apart from what that, seemed unharmed. Kalea threw herself at him.

"Leith! Are you alright?" she asked giving him an enormous hug. She was surprised that he did not return it. He stood hard and unyielding. His face stony. The man who had led Leith in, grinned at her and withdrew. "What is it?" Kalea asked.

"You should not have done it," Leith growled. "You act no better than a whore."

Kalea stepped back, shocked by the venom in his voice.

"Leith, what are you saying?" she asked shakily.

"What do you think I'm saying? You leapt into his bed without thinking."

Kalea was stunned but even as he said it, her temper was rising. Stepping back even further she surveyed him with a hard stare. "Don't you dare stand judgement against me! Don't you dare!" She spat. He met her eye not giving an inch. "It's alright for you. The worst you can expect is a warrior's death. Is that what you were expecting?" He didn't acknowledge her. "I expected nothing that honourable. What difference does it make if I give myself willingly or not? He would have taken me one-way or the other. I did not want to be brutalised. Rape is not pleasant Leith. And then what could I expect? Certainly not death. If I didn't please him, I would have been given to the warband. I for one, would rather die but I am only a woman, I don't get offered an honourable death. I am not given a choice. I am not important enough." She stood there shaking with rage and full of indignation. "I had but one choice as I saw it. Whore for a king, or service his warband."

Leith did not flinch under this barrage and stood resolute. Finally, he sighed. He had not thought of it like that and he suddenly realised what she meant. "I'm sorry girl," he mumbled his shoulders sagged. "I did not see it as a woman does. I was too harsh." Kalea didn't move, she was still seething with anger. "May I sit?" he asked. Kalea couldn't trust her voice and nodded. Leith sank wearily onto the chair by the fire. "We are not having much luck, are we girl?"

Kalea drew a deep breath. "It could be worse." Leith shook his head almost in denial. "We're both alive." She looked into Leith's good eye and could see that he was tired and weary.

"I thought for a moment there, that we had made it. That luck had smiled on us. Now look."

It was unlike Leith to be so down so Kalea went and sat next to him and gave him a hug. "All is not lost Leith."

He turned to look at her, a sad smile on his face. "You're a good girl. But I fear now your marriage will not take place now."

Kalea met his smile with one equally sad. "Maybe our life in Arthur's village was not meant to be. I know what you fear, and believe me, I fear the same. Kai could never want me now and Arthur is too busy to search for long. See, I have considered the fates and I know that there is no turning back but what else was there for me to do? I have at least traded for your life." And she went on before he could say anything, "And I know perhaps you would rather that I hadn't, but to me, you are as valuable as Kai and I have lost one treasure, I cannot bear to lose another." For a while, they just hugged one another and Kalea did her best to hide her tears. "We do have a chance," she said at last. "I have spoken to one of the serving girls and she speaks highly of Mark. I know that Mark is Arthur's enemy, but he seems well thought of here. She said that when Mark tires of his lovers, he gives them houses in the village." She watched his face. "It won't happen overnight, if it does, then I will fear I will be fodder for the warband. But if I can hold him for a while, he might allow us a life in his village. It is not what we wanted, but may be in time, we can find our way back to Alfred. In time."

Leith gave a deep sigh. "I can't say I like it, but I see little choice in this."

"How are they treating you?" Kalea asked.

"Well, enough. They have me locked in a room, it is clean enough and has a bed and they make sure that I have enough to eat. But it doesn't make it any easier. I want to fight, but they won't give me a chance." He looked at her. "And you?"

"Mark has been kind enough," she answered noncommittally. Somehow, she felt she would be betraying Leith if she had told him that she enjoyed the sex act with Mark. After all, it was one thing being compliant but something totally different when she was being pleasured. Suddenly, the door burst open and Mark entered with two of his men. Seeing them sat at the fire he grinned.

"Ah Kalea, I see your little gift has arrived already."

Kalea bowed her head. "Thank you, my lord. It was most kind of you to let me see Leith."

Mark's smile broadened, pleased with her thanks. "I thought you might need a little company. If you can persuade the old man to behave himself, I might allow him a few more privileges." He gave Leith a shrewd stare. "However, by the look of the wily old rogue, I think that is most unlikely." Leith glared back. "You are fortunate old man, young Kalea prizes you most highly. You owe her your life." Mark allowed time for this observation to sink in. "She bargains well, but I didn't know what a prize she was. A virgin too! Wonderful! Yes, you are definitely worth her maidenhead."

Leith went to make a lunge forward but Kalea's firm grip on his arm stayed him. He made do with a growl, which made Mark laugh. "I have arranged for some food to be bought, but I have things to do." He strode past the pair and grabbed up some leather gloves and his cloak. As he returned, he leaned down and taking Kalea firmly by the chin, gave her a deep kiss, which she returned. "Yes, most definitely worth sparing your life." He looked from Kalea to Leith and saw the hatred burning in Leith's eye and with a laugh swept out.

"I'll kill him." Leith's voice was full of menace.

"You mustn't let him goad you," Kalea soothed. "He is looking for an excuse to kill you. Give him none."

"Easy to say."

"It is I who have to endure his embraces," Kalea said quietly.

"I don't know how you can bear it."

"With ease," she answered truthfully. "I value my life."

Mary came in carrying a tray of food. "The king says you're to eat," she said placing it on the table. Then from under her arm, she dropped Kalea's boots. Kalea grinned and Mary returned it. "You're lucky they aren't worth much, or someone would have had them. As it was, they were where we took them from you."

Kalea stamped them on. "My thanks Mary."

Mary grinned and left.

"So, she is the one you got the gossip from," Leith stated helping himself to some cheese and bread.

Kalea nodded. "At least they feed us well," she said tucking in.

They hadn't finished when the door opened and one of Mark's warrior's came in.

"Mark has decided you need some fresh air." His eyes narrowed as he looked at Leith. "Don't give me any trouble old man or I will kill the girl."

Leith looked at Kalea who grinned and shrugged. She was playing the game well. As she rose, she pulled Leith up and led him to the door with her arm through his. "Thank you," she said to the warrior as she led Leith passed him. Leith was tense beside her. "Leith do not worry. No harm will come to us."

They stepped into the sunshine. Kalea held her face to the sun. The strength was fading from it and this heralded the end of summer and the beginning of autumn. "The berries will ripen soon, if they aren't already," she said looking back the warrior guard for direction. He pointed with his chin and Kalea led Leith towards the village centre. The area around Mark's castle was relatively quiet but as soon as they approached the main centre, the route became more and more busy. Soon they were amongst a thronging crowd who looked at them curiously as they passed through, but did not attempt to harass them. Kalea guessed that was only because of their silent companion. She was aware that Leith was taking special note, a special interest in the layout of the village and she smiled. The village was well defended. Mark's stronghold would not be easy to attack.

Escape would be hard too. They entered the very centre of the village and the villagers had set up market stalls to trade their wares with one another and Kalea guessed, the small villages outside. Kalea was fascinated: she had never seen such a large trading area even in Arthur's village. Anything a person could need, could be bought here, from cooking pots and horses, to cloth and food. It seemed all too soon, when they were escorted back to the castle.

Leith was thoughtful, from the short circuit that they had done, it seemed that the village was thriving. The whole area was carefully laid out and a good deal of thought had gone into it. They entered Mark's living quarters and as soon as they crossed the threshold, their silent guard spoke.

"Leith," he said impatiently, "it is time for you to return to your own rooms." Leith looked at him and nodded. He knew better than to argue for naught. Kalea was right about one thing at least, and that was for the time being they were being treated well enough, and he had no wish to provoke confrontation until he had formulated a plan.

Kalea had no such reservations. "Please," she begged, "can't he stay a little longer?"

The guard grinned. "Sorry, I have my orders." He took Leith by the arm and led him away. The door closed and Kalea heard the lock being turned. She sighed and sank wearily down on the bed. Sleep came quickly, although it wasn't sought.

Leith sat down in his prison, which really wasn't too bad at all. The night had passed slowly for him as he could only think of Kalea and what was happening to her. She was a virgin no more but he was surprised how little this bothered her. Once again, the girl had stunned him with her strength and lack of fear. He now doubted that she had ever loved Kai, as she seemed to have put him behind her so easily. Why was she not more upset? He had not expected her to be so resolute and calm, he expected tears and tantrums. There was no doubting she was a strange one. However, he had to admit that he had been wrong attacking her for her actions but she had not been slow putting him in his place. Of course, it had taken him aback when she had turned on him but he had in truth given little thought to how it would be in a woman's shoes. In his defence, he had never had to, but now he thought about it, it must be hard to have one man force himself on you and to be used by a war band would be enough to break the strongest of women. He sighed. More times than he would like to remember he had seen women raped my Saxon marauders and the pitiful state they were left in was one that couldn't easily be forgotten. Very few recovered and some even took their own lives.

Nevertheless, he could not help feeling disappointed in her. She had sold herself and even though she had saved his life as a consequence, he somehow thought she was worth more. Kalea had betrayed Kai's love by agreeing so readily to be used as a cheap whore and even knowing that she had done so to save herself from Mark's warband, somehow it didn't sit easy with him.

Thinking of Kai made him uneasy. He liked the boy and he wondered how he was faring. There was no doubt in his mind that Kai would not give up on Kalea as easily as Kalea had given up on him. Knowing Kai, he would be beside himself with worry and impatient to find her again. But Leith doubted once he knew how Kalea had given herself over to Mark, he would want her for his own again. And Kalea was right, they didn't know how long it would be before they were found, or if they would be found at all.

Leith was sure that Arthur would mount a search party for them. After all, he himself had been quite taken by Kalea, but how long could afford the time and effort of his warriors was another thing. Arthur's fondness for Kai would ensure that it continued as long as possible, but there was only a certain amount of time that he could afford.

Arthur, Kai and the search party, had not come up completely empty at the village. Whilst, no one had seen Kalea and Leith with some riders, one warrior reported that he had seen on the neighbouring hilltop a lone rider with several horses heading south. Now, Arthur was certain that that Mark was behind this.

The party's spirits were low despite having been warmly welcomed. Arthur had strengthened his alliance with their chief if nothing else. Kai's brooding countenance was enough to put the dampers on the brightest mood. He had spent the evening scowling and it was obvious that he was eager to be off. Arthur glanced across at the hard set of Kai's jaw. He felt his friend's pain but didn't know how to ease it. Spurring his mount on, he set a fast pace for his men.

Kai kept an easy pace with Arthur. Despite the speed, he wanted to go faster. It didn't seem to help knowing the horses would drop, he wanted to gallop across the countryside. Arthur's two trackers kept scouting forward and found evidence of a lone horseman with lots of horses. It would seem that Arthur was indeed right. Kai's anger boiled inside him.

Mark unlocked his chamber door and stepped in. His servants had been in to lie out supper but he was surprised that Kalea wasn't waiting for him. Turning to the bed, he saw her sprawled out asleep. Raising an eyebrow, quizzically, he approached her. She really was quite beautiful. Her dark hair fanned out on the bed like a cloud, her skin was smooth and clear and her lashes dark and long brushed her cheeks. One hand lay curled gently inwards while the other lay on her flat stomach. Mark's smile was soft with none of its customary hardness. The girl was exhausted and well she might be. Truth was, he and his men were tired too. He decided not to disturb her and went to get himself something to eat.

Pouring himself some ale and spooning some stew into the bowl he sat down to eat while watching her sleep. She moaned, a sound of fear and then sat bolt upright, coming awake with a gasp. Mark had not been expecting that and jumped-up hand ready to grab his sword. Quickly, he went to her and took her in his arms.

"Are you alright?" he asked as she sat blinking away the dream.

For a moment, she didn't answer and just nodded, and then quietly she said, "A bad dream."

"Really? What did you dream about?"

Kalea shook her head. "It was nothing. Just a silly dream."

"Tell me," Mark prompted. Kalea looked at him and saw only concern and interest in his hazel eyes.

"At home, there was a band of wild horses. I dreamed of one of the ponies that I used to watch. It was misty and he had become separated from the herd and he was searching for them in the fen land. The mist was very thick and it was quiet, just the sound of his hooves on the mud. Suddenly, he stepped into a bog and sunk up to his haunches. He was struggling to get out and just kept sinking deeper. Then I woke." She shuddered. Mark hugged her close.

"And what do you think that means?" he queried as she sat back.

Kalea shrugged. "I knew a wise woman once who said that dreams about horses were sexual." Mark grinned at her and she grinned back. "But I never believed in dream reading and think it is a fancy. Besides, I can see very little sexual about a pony being drowned in a bog."

Mark laughed. "A practical view to be sure. Come and eat. It will chase the dream away." He took her hand and helped her up.

"You have already done that my lord," she said smiling shyly at him.

Soon they were seated at the table and Kalea helped herself to the sweet-smelling stew. Tasting it, she commented. "This is good."

137

"Why thank you my lady. I am sure my kitchen will be pleased to know that you find their cooking to your liking." He poured her some ale.

"Thank you for allowing me to see Leith today." He acknowledged her thanks with a nod.

"Did he receive you well? He seemed a little tense." Mark was fishing and Kalea took the bait carefully.

She laughed. "He is old and grouchy and he does not approve of me giving myself to you. Leith believes very strongly, that a woman should be wedded before she's bedded."

Mark nearly choked on his ale laughing. Kalea hastily rose and slapped him on the back, but it took a while for Mark to regain his composure in between laughing and spluttering.

"So, Leith would have me wed you, would he?"

"Well, I'm not sure about that, but I think he thought I was destined for better things," Kalea stated calmly.

"Better than marrying a king? Can it get any better?"

"I wouldn't have thought so. But I believe Leith would have taken great pleasure in making it as uncomfortable as possible for any suitors and you have deprived him of his fun."

"You are good for the soul as well as the heart," he chortled. "I can't remember the time I laughed so much." He offered her some blackberries, which she accepted. "Would you and Leith have stayed in Arthur's village?"

Kalea gave a shrug and licked blackberry juice from her fingers. "Leith has an old friend in Arthur's village."

"I guess that would be Lud," Mark added.

She nodded. "I guess he wanted to settle where he had a friend."

"And you?"

"My home is gone. I go where Leith goes. So, I guess, yes, we would have stayed."

"What did you do at home in your village? I had thought perhaps you could make some contribution to my homestead, while you're with me."

"You make it sound as if I am going somewhere. Am I?"

"That very much depends on you." Mark's voice had an edge to it that Kalea didn't like the sound of. A shiver ran through her. For a moment, Kalea could see why Mark was such a powerful enemy. His face told her nothing although she studied it carefully. She sensed there could be some danger in her answer if he didn't like it. It would pay to be diplomatic and she wasn't going to show how fearful she was.

"Depends on me doing what?" she replied with a knowing smile. She was surprised that her voice had a caressing, steady timbre. He shrugged giving her no further clue. Keeping her voice even, she continued. "What I do best, will be of no use to you."

"Don't be too sure," Mark replied with a sardonic grin, which she returned. "So, what did you do?"

"All manner of things really. I kept house for my father."

He nodded. "And?" he prompted.

"I'm very good with horses."

"Horses?"

"Yes. I used to gentle the wild ones and if someone had a horse with a problem, they bought it to me. I seemed to have a fair bit of success."

"Horses," he said thoughtfully and she nodded. "You are full of surprises. What else?"

"Isn't that enough?" she asked and seeing his face, could tell it wasn't. "I was training to be a wise woman."

"A wise woman? You are very diverse."

"Not really, horses get ill too," she explained. "I began to consult the wise woman to get cures for colic and draughts for worms. I became interested and she taught me what to use to stop a wound becoming infected and the ones to take away the pain. But to do these things, I have to be free to roam and that is something I am not."

He looked at her thoughtfully. "Not yet maybe. But perhaps later." The conversation was interrupted by Mary who had come to clear away the remnants of supper. Kalea sat quietly waiting instructions. Mark's eyes were on her and she felt his desire warming her. When at last the woman had left, she rose and came round the table to sit on his lap.

"It seems my lord that you have made a willing slave of me," she spoke quietly bent to kiss him. He received her kiss coolly. "Do you not want me?" she queried.

"Oh yes," he murmured against her lips. "I want you more than I should." He crushed her to him and felt her melt against him. Her hands were eagerly untying the laces of his shirt while his hands moved knowingly over her body. The hem of her dress was lifted and soon drawn over her head to be discarded with his shirt. Now, she sat astride him, her hot flesh pressed against his chest. Their kisses were getting more urgent and her hands moved to untie his trousers to release his manhood. At last, he was free and Kalea stroked and teased until he buried his head against her breasts. Then she rose and sank down on his hot shaft, sighing as he reached full length. Mark helped her set a rhythm and the two flowed together pressed tightly, like two well-fitting cogs. Hands moved stroking and teasing, kisses were hot and demanding. Mark revelled in his teaching. She moved smoothly and he watched her passion dark eyes as they made love. It was intoxicating and he was transported by her. Something past passion and lust, a oneness that he had not felt for some time. She flung her head back, her air sweeping her buttocks as her orgasm shook her. Mark was coming too, hot and hard. For a moment, he thought she meant to drain him dry as his orgasm seemed to go on and on. At last, they were both spent.

"A perfect match," he whispered against her breast as she cradled his head to her. Kalea said nothing, content just to hold him. For a long while, they sat entwined before he spoke again. "Come on girl, up. We can't sit like this all night." But before she could move, he stood carrying her easily with her legs still wrapped round him, he made his way to the bed. His progress was impaired by the fact that his trousers were sliding down his legs forcing him to waddle like a duck. Kalea started to giggle. "Are you laughing at me girl?" he asked grinning himself. He collapsed on top of her on the bed causing Kalea to laugh louder. By this time, Mark too laughing. He disentangled himself from her and rolled onto his back. Kalea still giggling, coiled herself round him.

Still smiling, he looked at the young woman beside him. He took her chin and raised her face to kiss her and his kiss was returned. A bond had formed between them and Mark was perplexed to find that he was fond of Kalea already. No, he did not love her but he felt strangely drawn. This woman would make a worthy partner for any man. He liked her ready wit and her strength of character. Compared to many fine well-reared women, she was ignorant. It was obvious she had no writing or reading skills and yet she was intelligent with a keen mind. And she was young, so young and beautiful. What she did not know she could be taught. And then he wondered why he was thinking like that? He had had many women in his time. Some cleverer, some more voluptuous and even more beautiful and yet this girl captivated him somehow. Why had she managed to escape marriage for so long? Her father couldn't have been that naïve as to think he could keep her forever.

Kalea was watching Mark and wondering what he was thinking. He had also captivated her. She found herself admiring him but was aware that it was most likely because she was his captive and had no choice in the matter. However, she could not take away from him the fact that he was clever, cunning and an obviously well-respected King. His people admired and liked him and she guessed that he had no shortage of lovers; she even suspected that half the children in the village, more likely belonged to him. Arthur has spoken of him as an enemy but one he respected. That had been evident in his tone. This was more than likely due to his skill in battle. Tonight, there was a softness in his eyes that had not been evident before. When they had been in the drinking hall, they had been hard and calculating and Kalea did not doubt that he could be ruthless and cruel. That he was a skilled seducer she would testify to that and she wondered if anyone could make her feel the way he did. Love didn't enter into the equation. Mark was no comparison to Kai. One dark, the other blonde, but Mark did not make her pulse race when he was close or her heart flutter. The attraction was purely physical. That said he was not unattractive and she considered herself very lucky.

They made love again before the evening grew old. It was the first time in a long while that Mark had not been in the drinking hall in the evening. His warriors missed him, but he did not think of them once. Only the dark almond-eyed woman who melted at his very touch.

The next morning when Mark woke Kalea was once again curled against him. He sighed. If he weren't careful, this woman would take over his life. Did he want that? He wasn't really sure he minded. His thoughts drifted to Arthur and wondered how close he was. A cruel smile played round his lips. Whilst Kalea wasn't convinced that Arthur would come for her, he was. It would take a while though he concluded. His warband had travelled swiftly and Arthur would have to scour the countryside for her. He nearly laughed out loud at the time Arthur was wasting. For a moment, he contemplated if she had been lying to him and that she had been destined to become Arthur's wife. But he quickly dismissed this. He had watched her carefully and felt he would have known if he had been lying. Kalea raised more questions than answers. Why would Arthur not want her as his woman? Suddenly, he became aware that she was watching him.

"Good morning my lady." He bent to kiss her and she welcomed him into her arms.

"Yes, I did," she whispered.

"Pardon?"

"You asked me yesterday, if I liked what I see? And the answer is yes, I do."

He smiled. They would have made love but a serving woman bringing in breakfast interrupted them. The woman smiled shyly at Mark and deposited breakfast on the table, when he had thanked her, she left. He puffed. The moment was lost.

"Madam, your breakfast awaits." Kalea pulled some skins round her, rose and watched Mark as he pulled on his trousers. Then bare chested, he joined her. Kalea was hungry and enjoyed her breakfast of milk, bread and honey. She was aware that he was watching her surreptitiously and wondered if her table manners were too abhorrent. Gulping down a mouthful, she looked at him.

"Do I eat like a dog?" she asked.

He burst out laughing. "No, no. I am sorry if I was staring a little a little too hard, but you really are a pretty thing."

This time Kalea laughed. "That's the first time I've been called a pretty thing. Normally, I am told that I'd make a fair lad given half a chance."

Mark laughed. "Where the men in your village blind?"

"No, but they had a healthy fear of my father."

He rose and pulled on his shirt and boots. She pulled on her dress and stamped on her boots. There was a look of disgust on Mark's face.

"What have you got on your feet?"

Kalea looked down at feet. "My boots." Mark grimaced. "They survived your women's scrubbing." Then seeing he was quite unmoved, defended them. "They are comfortable." He still looked unimpressed. "They were my brother's and..." she added. "It's better than bare feet."

"That is seriously debatable," he said dourly. "We'll do something about that later. Come on." He grabbed her by the hand and towed her towards the door. Grinning foolishly, she allowed herself to be led. They were soon out in the early morning air. The sky was blue and the sun was bright. Still dragging her behind him, Mark greeted those he met, whilst Kalea smiled brightly. Eventually they arrived at the stables. At the door, he stopped and turned to her.

"In here, is one of the meanest horses that has ever walked this Earth. His heart is as black as his coat. He will let no one touch him. Show me what you can do."

142

Kalea looked at him in amazement. "It will not happen in a day you know. I said I am good with horses; I do not do magic."

"No one's asking you to," Mark stated flatly. "You may take a long as you want."

"Alright," Kalea answered with a gulp. "Let me see him."

They entered the gloom of the stables and Kalea stood for a while allowing her eyes to adjust to the lack of light. In the furthest corner stood a stallion. As black as night, he was already aware of her and his ears were laid back and his teeth were bared. Kalea approached him slowly, talking in a singsong voice and being careful to stay just out of reach of the stallion's teeth. He was agitated and reared and plunged in his confined quarters. Kalea met his eye then sat down on the floor in front of him, still singing quietly to herself as much as him.

Mark watched from the door and when a groom went to enter, he stopped him. For a good while, the stallion stomped and threatened. Leaning as far over the door as he could trying to bite Kalea. She however, didn't acknowledge him and sat singing on and on. After a while, the stallion calmed a bit and stood stamping his feet and shaking his head. Still Kalea did not move, then bit by bit, the horse calmed down and started to be curious about this strange human who did not seem in the least bit interested in him. He leaned over the door of his stable to take a closer look. Kalea still sat singing. Mark was fascinated. As the stallion walked round the stable, his ears flicked forward and whilst his attention was diverted, Kalea edged closer. When the stallion next came to the door, although she was nearer, her posture and pose hadn't altered. Still singing to herself, she looked up and met the horse's eye. He returned her gaze and leaned over the door towards her. Cautiously, he reached towards her, Kalea didn't move. His nose almost touched her and he drew back. Kalea sat unmoving, still singing. Finally, the stallion tried again. Leaning as far as he could over the stable door, he snuffed her hair and face, his ears flicked back and forth. Finally, he could bear it no more and retreated into his stable. Kalea very quietly rose and still singing left him.

Mark was surprised at how much time had passed and was even more surprised when Kalea walked straight passed him.

"Well?" he asked catching her up. She massaged her backside.

"You could do this better than I," she stated with a grin.

"And madam, be assured, I would if we weren't in such a public place," he returned. "But what of the horse?"

"What of him? He will come round but I need to spend a lot of time with him. He is so handsome and will make an excellent war horse."

"Yes, well. I will believe it when I see it. When do you want to return?" Mark pondered sourly.

"After noon. I would like some trousers if I am to sit on a stable floor."

"And you were doing so well, acting like a girl."

Kalea grinned. "I would also like some tip bits. Apples and carrots will do. And to bring him on quickly, I will need to visit him at least daily."

Mark nodded. "Not a problem." He grinned at her thoughtful face. She was making plans to bring the horse round while still massaging her rear. Gripping her by the elbow, he steered her towards the market place.

"Where are we going?"

"You will see," he said mysteriously. They moved amongst the thronging people who were all eager to be about their business. As they saw Mark, they respectfully gave ground and greeted him. He in turn, acknowledged them smiling. At last, they arrived in front of the shoemaker. "Master William," Mark greeted him. William turned round to meet him with a small bow and a smile.

"My Liege, what can I do for you?" he asked respectfully. Mark smiled back.

"My young friend here, is short of footwear. I wonder could we prevail on you to make her some shoes. Two pairs, I think."

William looked down at Kalea's boots and frowned. "She is certainly in need of being shod. It shouldn't be too much of a problem. Take your boots off young lady."

Kalea who had never had a pair of shoes, let alone a pair made for her alone, looked non-plussed. Mark however, bent to assist and before long she was standing bare foot in the dusty streets. William took a piece of leather from his stall and laid it on the floor. "Please step on." Kalea did as she was told. Mark suppressed his laughter at her bemused face. William took a piece of chalk and drew round her feet. Then taking more leather, he wrapped it round the top of her foot making marks as he went. Kale was fascinated. "Right there you go," William said getting to his feet. "You can put your boots back on, if you must," he said with obvious disgust. Kalea hastily stomped her boots back on. William now turned his attention to Mark. "I presume, my liege, that you would like these as soon as possible?"

Mark nodded and smiled. "Bring them to me when they are ready. I shall see to it that you are well paid."

"You always do my lord," William said bowing.

With that Mark led her away.

"My goodness," Kalea remarked excitedly. "I have never had a pair of shoes, let alone made for me."

"I would never have guessed," Mark said with a sarcastic smile. "Ahh, I see our next stop. Good morning mistress," Mark addressed a stout matron who was selling cloth from her shop.

The woman bobbed a curtsey to him. "Good morning my Lord."

"My young friend has need of your services, I think." The woman came out from behind her stall and ran a critical eye over Kalea.

"She certainly does. This…" she said contemptuously, fingering Kalea's dress, "was certainly not made for this young lady. What have you in mind?"

Mark shrugged. "Unfortunately, dresses are not my area of expertise," he said respectfully. "I thought, I might leave the choice up to you."

The woman was obviously flattered by Mark's custom and bustled round with lengths of tape with which she measured Kalea around the bust, hips and her height. She stood looking thoughtfully at Kalea and then disappeared into her shop and returned with four bolts of cloth. She offered them to Mark to feel and he nodded the quality was good.

"Now, my suggestion is the green, the red and the cream," the woman said. "Her colouring being so dark will be complimented these colours."

Kalea was dumbfounded. Three new dresses at once. At home in village, she had two. Both old and both second-hand. One in better condition than the other, which was kept for best. It had never occurred to her that people could be so wealthy. Mark couldn't hide his smile as her eyes were a big as plates and her jaw was hanging open. He was in conversation with the shop owner, which gave Kalea a chance to recover from her shock. Suddenly, she felt very gauche and unworldly. In the village, everyone had known one another well and to a great extent, her tom boyishness had been overlooked and tolerated. They had not been long enough in Arthur's village for her to become used to large crowds of people or market trading. Mark had now finished bargaining with the shopkeeper and took her hand to steer her through the crowds.

"I had not realised you were so rich," she commented in awe of him now.

"Did you not? How do you think a king maintains his men and his kingdom?"

"I had never thought of it?" Kalea said. "Until recently, the word King meant no more than a very grand man and I had never seen one. Now, I have seen two, and lain with one." She marvelled at how far she had come in such a short time. "As for the distance I have travelled, if you had told me, I would go so far a year ago, I would have thought you drunk."

Mark laughed causing passers-by to stare. "But you must have had a market?" he queried.

Kalea shook her head. "No. Our village was too small. If you needed anything, you asked one another and if it was not to be had, some of the elders would take a cart and go to market once a month. I was never allowed to go with them."

Mark watched as she gazed around in wonder at what you can buy. She really was a child in a woman's body. "Now, if I was to say that you could have anything you wanted. What would you choose?" Her dark eyes met his.

"My Lord, you have been more than generous. I have never possessed so much in my life. So, I can't think of one thing that you could buy me." He nodded pleased with her response. "But if I could ask for anything at all, I would ask for a swim."

"A swim," Mark stated flatly clearly surprised by her request.

"Yes. You know a big area of water and doing what ducks do."

"I am not ignorant of what swimming is," Mark said his voice sounding hard although he was more bemused than angry.

"I am sorry," Kalea began hastily. "I did not mean to imply that you were in any way lacking. As your captive, you treat me very well. It's just that you did ask, and it is something I love doing." She did not let go of his hand afraid that she had angered him.

Mark found it difficult to feel angry with her for long in the face of such an innocent plea. "It's alright Kalea. I am not angry. I am used to women asking for more than that. I will see what I can do, but I will not promise. As you said, you are my captive and it would mean you being guarded while you swam. The question is, can my men be trusted with a naked woman. It is a lot to ask of them."

"You could come with me," she said eagerly.

"We shall see." They went back to the hall where once again food had been left for them. After they had eaten, Mark rose. Going to his chest, he rummaged in it and came out with a pair of trousers and a shirt. "Try these." He threw them over his shoulder. Kalea leapt to her feet and stripping off her dress pulled on the trousers and shirt. Mark watched amused. "Very fetching," he said as the trouser slipped to her hips.

"These are yours, aren't they? They are very fine. I've never had anything so soft."

He got a belt and bought it over. Hoiked the trousers up and fastened them in place. She grinned. "You are wonderful." Then she kissed him.

"Kalea. This just won't do," he said against her lips. "I have work to do. Someone will come for you and take you to the stables."

Kalea pouted. "As you wish my lord."

Mark left; she really was such a child.

Not long after, the door opened and a dour looking warrior entered. He didn't speak to her, but motioned for her to go out the door. Kalea didn't hesitate and stepped passed him. She knew where they were going and remembered the way to the stables. As they reached the stable door, her guard stepped forward and gave her an apple and two carrots.

"Thank you," Kalea said. "Could you cut them into pieces please? They won't last long if I have them like that."

The guard removed his knife and cut them into chunks. Kalea thanked him again and stepped into the gloom singing to herself again. The stallion's ears were back and his teeth were bared as he looked towards her, then he seemed to remember and he stepped back from his stable door. Kalea approached quietly, singing and sat herself in front of his stall. Hiding all but one chunk of carrot behind her, she sat still singing quietly. For a while, the stallion ignored her and then his curiosity got the best of him and he lent over the door to see her. Kalea had moved a lot closer and was prepared to be bitten, so she sat unmoving. His nose snuffed her hair and then her face. Kalea sang on, sitting relaxed and calm. His nose came to her hand and sniffed the carrot there. Kalea unfolded her hands to allow him access to the carrot. He threw his head up, wary of being grabbed but Kalea made no attempt to touch him and soon his head was back in her lap and he snatched the carrot and backed off. Kalea reached behind her and collected another tip bit. Soon, he was back. Wary, but getting bolder, he sniffed her face. Kalea did not stop singing but changed the one to be more soothing. He did not withdraw this time and then once again put his head into her lap to nuzzle her hand sniffing. This time Kalea lingered a little before opening her hands to allow him a piece of apple. As he munched it, this time Kalea lightly touched his nose. He flicked his head but did not withdraw.

147

Kalea smiled and sang on. She was parched and stiff but she would not move now she was beginning to win he trust. On and on it went. The same thing over and over and the stallion was getting bolder. Each time she touched him again and he became used to her gentle hand on his nose. Never did she try to grab him and he was beginning to like her touch. How long she sat there she did not know, but the stiffness was irrelevant compared to the horse.

When Mark came to fetch her, he found the guard transfixed by the door. When Mark tapped him, the man on his shoulder, he jumped and pointed to Kalea with his chin. Mark moved quietly around him and what he saw amazed him. Kalea was sitting crossed legged on the floor and the horse was dozing with his head in her lap. Mark could not hide his surprise and his jaw flapped open. For a moment, all was still and he took in the scene of the horse entranced by Kalea's soothing sounds. He was reluctant to break the moment and when he did, it was softly. Clearing his throat seemed as loud as a thunder crash and horse's head flew up narrowly missing Kalea's face. Kalea turned to look at him and nodded but did not stop her crooning. Slowly and as fluidly as she could, she rose, the horse was looking at Mark suspiciously, his ears flicking back and forth but Kalea ignored his signs of agitation and still murmuring as if to a frightened child, lent forward and stroked his face. For a moment, Mark thought the horse would either pull away or bite her but he surprised Mark, when he allowed her to stroke him. Moving with a languid grace, Kalea came quickly towards him, she allowed Mark to take her gently by the elbow and lead her from the gloom of the stable.

Once outside, she stretched like a cat. "I'm so stiff." She yawned.

"I have just the answer for that." Mark grinned. "I must admit madam, I am impressed that he hasn't taken your head off."

Kalea cocked her head on one side and looked at him quizzically. "Is that how you dispose of your captives? Give them to a fierce horse so that you don't have the trouble of disposing of them yourself?"

Mark laughed heartily. "I hadn't thought of that but it is a fine idea. However, the way you are progressing. I won't have a fierce horse to give them too. What is wrong with the brute anyway?"

Kalea smiled wryly. "He is frightened. A feeling, I know well. You have told me nothing of his origins, but it is obvious that is used to being free to as he wishes. He does not like it here. It smells strange, he is in the dark and nothing is as it should be. The noises are harsh and loud and people keep trying to make him do things that he does not want to do. He fears us and so he attacks us."

"Yet, he does not attack you," Mark stated.

"That is because I ask nothing of him. The noise I make is not harsh it is gentle. Even so, he is wary."

"He has been locked in there a long time," Mark mused. Kalea nodded.

"I will win him over and he will be the best war horse you ever owned."

"So, confident my lady?"

"Yes. We have much in common that horse and me. I too, have been allowed more freedom than was good for me and have had that freedom taken from me and yet, I have learned already, that bending my will to another is not such a bad thing. I have no doubt that I am lucky to have been treated so fairly by you, and now, this is something I will teach him."

The depth of her perception shocked him. For an uneducated girl, she had an uncommon grasp of things. "Well, Kalea, I shall look forward to my new war horse." He paused and looked her suggestively. "Especially if he is half the ride that you are."

Kalea exploded with laughter. "My Lord!" she exclaimed looking falsely shocked. "I had thought you were a man of breeding."

Grinning cheekily, he replied. "I had thought that was what we were talking about. Breeding." Causing her to giggle again. "Step this way." He gestured to the other end of the stable. Kalea still smiling at the banter led on and found two mounted horsemen holding to two tacked up horses. She felt a sudden stab of nerves. What did he have planned for her?

"Mount up my lady," Mark said leading her to her mount. Kalea reluctantly went forward and allowed herself to be boosted into the saddle. Her heart hammered painfully. "Now," he spoke threateningly. "Am I going to have to tie your mount to mine or can you be trusted not to ride off?"

Kalea's smile was not quite as bright as it normally was. "My lord, where would I go? I have no home to go to and all I know of Arthur's village is that it is north. I have no doubt that if I did run, you would capture me very quickly." He nodded accepting what she said. "Besides," she added feigning indifference "I really don't want to leave anyway."

Mark smiled to himself. Clever that was what she was. He swung lightly into the saddle and led off. Kalea caught him up and rode abreast with him. The Cornish countryside captivated her. It was beautiful in a rugged sort of way. East

Anglia was beautiful too but different. There were no tall hills and crags. A light wind lifted her hair and she felt a sudden urge to gallop.

"What are you thinking?" Mark asked watching the wind playing with her hair and seeing the faraway look in her eyes. She turned to meet his eye and gave him a playful smile.

"I was thinking what a beautiful land you have and I would like to gallop down the side of this hill."

Mark grinned. "Well go on then. Pull up on the top of the next brow." He pointed.

"Can I?" she asked surprised.

"I would not say if I did not mean it?" He smiled.

With an exuberant whoop of pleasure, Kalea sped off down the hill with Mark and his two men at arms, close on her heels. The wind made her eyes tear but it was exhilarating. Laughter bubbled up inside her and her mood passed to her mount and he kicked up his heels causing her to laugh more.

Mark riding close behind her could not help but smile at her laughter. Sometimes it took a moment like this to remind you of the enjoyment of the simple things in life. His life was often filled with plotting and planning and left little time for frivolous things. This young woman freed him from kingly restraint and allowed him to feel young again.

Kalea pulled up breathless half way up the next hill. She was still laughing when he came abreast with her, her horse was blowing with exertion.

"That was wonderful!" Kalea panted with feeling. "If I was to be struck down by lightening now, my life would be complete."

He grinned at her and for a moment, he came close to knowing how she had bewitched him where others had failed. "Come on." He led the way to the top of the hill. Kalea fell in behind him and as she crested the hill, he heard her gasp. Below them lay a perfect disc of water, shining silver in the sunlight.

"It's beautiful." Her voice was full of awe and catching Mark watching her, she smiled brightly. "What a perfect place."

"It's called Merlin's Mirror." Mark led the way down and at the bottom by the edge of the water he dismounted. "My lady wanted to swim?" he asked making a grand gesture towards the water.

"Yes, I do," Kalea responded sliding from the saddle and then much to Mark's amazement, she stood on tiptoes and kissed him. "You are too kind. Thank you."

"Now, don't throw yourself straight in," Mark warned and turned to his men. One threw him a bundle and the others grabbed the horses and then they both withdrew to a suitable distance. "Now, you may throw yourself in." Kalea needed no further encouragement and shed her shirt and trousers not at all embarrassed by her naked body. Grinning broadly, she pulled off her boots and waded in.

"Brrr. It's chilly. I must be going soft," she called. Mark sat down to watch her. Soon she was cutting through the water like a fish. For a moment, he thought that she was going to disappear over to the other side of the lake but then she turned and began to come back. "Why don't you join me?" she called.

Mark shook his head ruefully. "I don't think so."

"Why not?" Kalea stood like a mermaid with just her head and shoulders above the water. "Not afraid that I might duck you, are you?"

"I'm not afraid of a young pup like you," Mark commented indignantly.

"Well, why not then? I'll make it worth your while," she added with a grin. He laughed. She was irresistible and with that he began to shed his clothing. Kalea watched shaking with mirth at his haste. When he was finally naked, he stepped into the water. Grinning she had to admit that he made no fuss about the coolness of the lake which took great effort. As the water rose over his genitals, he allowed himself a small hiss. Kalea came forward to meet him and took his still warm body in her cool arms and pressing herself close to him. "You are indeed a brave man, my Lord." Her skin was goose pimpled and her nipples were hard and pressed against his chest. She pulled him deeper into the water.

"You had better make this worth my while." Mark's lips were hot against her cool cheek.

"Why do you doubt it?" she said kissing him deeply. He wasn't slow to respond and soon even in the cool of the water, their bodies were hot and ready. Sex in the water added a new dimension to their lovemaking. The cool water and their hot bodies, the lack of weight that made different positions comfortable and enjoyable. It wasn't long before they were both spent. Kalea clung to Mark and he crushed her to his chest.

"Well, you did not lie," he stated quietly.

"I don't lie well," Kalea added and then pushed him backwards so he went under. He came up spluttering and saw Kalea swimming a short way away, laughing. Wiping the water from his face, he sped after and caught her. She turned laughing in his arms.

"My Lord! You have caught me. I am yours to do as you want with."

"I thought I had already done that. Now come on, my young water nymph, it is time to return home."

Kalea did not protest but waded back to the shore. Mark had been thorough and the bundle that his men had thrown to him, contained drying cloth. The pair dried off and quickly dressed. Mark's two men at arms approached with the horses and Mark had a suspicious thought that *they had been watching*. He gave them a long hard stare and was rewarded with sheepish smiles. As he had thought, they had been watching. Still, there was nothing to be done about it, and he boosted Kalea into the saddle and mounting himself, led them home.

Kalea had been to the stable to see the horse, who now seemed pleased to see her. Surprisingly, Mark was already in his chamber rummaging in a chest. He produced another dress. This one elaborate and more exquisite that Kalea could imagine. She hastily put it on. This too, had been made for a smaller woman, but the fit though snug, was not overly tight. Kalea twirled round the room.

"How do you like it?" Mark asked.

"It's beautiful. I feel like a queen." Her face was alight with excitement.

"And you look like one too." Mark was thoughtful. "Tonight, we shall join my men in the feasting hall." Kalea frowned and looked worried. "There is nothing to worry about my dear. You are under my protection and all the time that you are, no harm will befall you."

"As you wish my lord."

He took her hand and led her to the feasting hall. The last time Kalea had been here, she had looked like a ragamuffin but tonight, she entered like a true lady. A hush fell over the hall as they entered as everyone was curious to see the woman that they had taken captive treated like a fine lady. Kalea, modestly, kept her eyes downcast and sat where she was led. Only when she was safely seated did she take a look around her. Conversation had resumed and she was able to observe most people without them being aware of it.

Mark was amused by her open curiosity. He offered her food and wine, which she accepted graciously. The food stopped half way to her mouth when she saw Leith seated with the warriors. His eyes met her and the look her gave her was unforgiving. Mark noticed her swallow nervously and then replace the food on her plate.

"You see my lady; I do indeed treat your man at arms well." Mark lent close to her ear so that he could be heard over the general conversation.

"My liege, I am very grateful," Kalea replied turning to meet his eye.

The evening wore on and Kalea spent most of the time listening to Mark talking with various men in his war band.

Leith watched Kalea from his seat. He was here on sufferance and they allowed him to join in the feast and talk, as long as he caused them no trouble. Tonight, he was quiet, Kalea had blossomed under Mark's attention and she looked like a true lady sitting on his right hand. It surprised him to see her so and it was obvious to all that saw them that Mark was mightily besotted with her and she enjoyed his attention. Leith wondered if she would have been so, married to Kai. It was hard to say. He felt sour although he knew he should be grateful that Mark was treating her so well. This was not the way it should be, he thought, as watched Kalea smiling brightly at Mark.

It was even more disconcerting, when Mark rose and took her hand to lead her back to his chamber. Kalea went willingly enough. Leith sighed. What to do? At this rate it looked as if they would never leave. Leith was none too happy with that thought.

The following morning, as they were eating their breakfast. Mark and Kalea were disturbed by a knock on the door.

"Come," called Mark looking up. The door opened and Mark's steward entered.

"I have two tradesmen here with some goods you ordered. Will you receive them my lord?"

"Send them in," Mark said gesturing with a lump of bread.

The man from the shoe stall and the matron from the material shop came in both carrying parcels.

"Alright. Let's see what you have got." Mark put down his bread and the woman stepped boldly forward. Putting her parcel on the chair, she produced a red dress, the likes of which Kalea had never seen before. Mark glanced at Kalea's face and saw the wonder in her eyes and smiled. "Do you want to inspect the work?" he asked Kalea.

Kalea turned to him. "I am sure the work is as exquisite as the dress." She rose feeling the fabric. "It is truly beautiful." The seamstress glowed with pleasure. "You must have worked so hard to finish it so quickly."

"Don't be too generous with your praises dear girl," Mark intervened quickly. "She will expect a generous tip."

"But my lord," the seamstress said with a low curtsy. "You have not seen the rest yet." With a flourish she produced the cream dress, which if possible was even more lovely. Kalea gasped with pleasure at the elaborate stitching that ran round the neck and cuffs in deep green. The woman gave the dress to Kalea and she held it up to herself and watched the soft swathes of cloth float round her feet. But the woman had only given her that, so she could produce the next dress of the palest green. This one was equally breath-taking, as stunning in its simplicity as the cream one was in its complexity. The woman had edged the neck and the cuffs with the cream and the contrast was wonderful.

Kalea whirled towards Mark. "There are magical. I can't believe that you ordered them for me."

Mark made a dismissive gesture. "So, you like them?"

"I love them," Kalea responded with feeling. "They really are too fine for me." The seamstress stepped back to let the shoemaker show his wares.

"If you would be seated my lady," he said. Kalea hastily sat, too overwhelmed to protest that she was not his lady. He opened his cloth bag and produce a pair of lady's slippers. As she was barefoot at the moment, he slipped them straight onto Kalea's feet. Kalea goggled at them like a fish. The leather was soft as cloth and they fitted her perfectly. "Would you like to try walking in them?"

Kalea obediently rose and twirled round the room. The smile on her face spoke for itself. "Why!" she exclaimed "They are so soft and comfortable, it is like having no shoes on at all."

The shoemaker smiled and then produced another stouter pair. Kalea sat quickly and tried these on. They fitted perfectly. Kalea grinned at Mark.

"You are pleased?" he asked.

"Oh yes! More than pleased." Kalea's voice was high with excitement.

Mark nodded. "You have done well," he said to the tradesmen. "I am pleased. Thank you for completing your task so quickly. See my steward, he will see that you are paid."

"Thank you, my liege." They said together and with a low bow followed the steward out.

"Thank you!" Kalea called after them. Mark grinned at her exuberance. The moment the door shut; she threw herself at him. "How can I ever thank you for what you have given me?" Mark laughed. "I will never want to go away if you treat me too well. And when you get fed up with me and cast me off, I will become a soured, withered shrew." This made Mark laugh louder but she silenced him with a kiss, her hands moving inside his shirt and across his chest. "Perhaps I can think of something you may like," she whispered against his lips.

The day was overcast and grey. Autumn was truly on the way. Kalea sat in the paddock and watched the black stallion cavorting round. She had named him Midnight for his black coat. The days had passed quickly. It had been over a week since she had been introduced to him and they had come a long way together. Watching him canter around the paddock enjoying his freedom took her back to when she had first started to groom him. Patiently, she had let him examine the brush, then when he was convinced, it would not hurt him, she had begun to brush. For a while, he had stood there shaking with fear but soon he began to enjoy the sensation. Now, he allowed her to groom him happily. Then she had introduced him to the halter. He had not liked that one bit, but she persevered and won him over. She clearly remembered the first time she had led him from the barn and the panic that him had rooted him to the ground in the yard. The day had been bright and he had stood trembling with fright at the bright light, the bustling people and strange smells. Kalea had stood singing to him and allowed him to stand there for a long time, before coaxing him on and into the paddock. Now the morning would find him hanging over the door looking for her. When he saw her, he would call a greeting. Then after he had allowed her to groom him, they would spend time in the paddock. He was still nervous and when she went to leave, he would be at her side in an instant. But his confidence was growing.

Kalea had done her best to find out where he had come from. The stable hands were of the impression that he had been caught running wild with the local herds. They called him devilish. Apparently, he had fought well and was so bad tempered, no one would go near him. They wondered if he had been washed up with a wreck as he was a magnificent beast and not the normal local wild horse.

The bright blue sky now belied its appearance and the sun produced little heat. The temperature was dropping but Kalea refused to give up her time with the horse.

Mark had produced a cloak for her. Today, there was no need for the cloak. Kalea strode back to the fence, smiled at her warrior nursemaid and grabbed the horse blanket she had left hanging there. Back in the middle of the paddock, she laid the blanket down and then flung herself on it. Rolling on her back, she stared at the autumn sky. It was the colour as Kia's eyes. But she wouldn't allow herself to think of Kia, it hurt too much. Neither would Midnight, he cantered up pulling up at the last minute and began to snuff at her face and hair causing her to giggle. Once he had checked that nothing was amiss, he began to graze.

Eyes on the sky, Kalea's mind began to wander. How long had it been since the Saxon's had destroyed her village? Two moons? Maybe three? She had lost track of time and so much had changed. In that short time, she had lost the last of her family, her home, made a friend of Leith, found a man to love and lost him and was now the plaything of a king. She had travelled more miles than she had known existed and seen things she never wished to see again. With a big sigh, she closed her eyes but not for long. Soon she was bumped by Midnight who had decided to lay on the blanket with her. Laughter bubbled out of her as she hastily adjusted her position so as not to get squashed. Soon he was flat out beside her and she rolled on her side and threw an arm around his neck.

"What do you say we just run away? Just you and me? Or shall we stay in our gilded cage?" She ran her hands over his muscled neck and he snorted. "Is that a, yes? We can't run, can we? They would hunt us down." And then she kissed him and lay close to the black glossy coat.

Mark arrived to see how Kalea work was doing and found her guard leaning on the paddock fence. He straightened as he saw Mark and with a subtle nod drew his attention to the scene beyond. A lesser man would have shown his surprise with more than a raised eyebrow. But Mark was no lesser man although he was amazed to see horse and girl curled up together in the paddock.

"How long have they been like that?"

The warrior shrugged with a rueful grin. "A while. You should have seen them earlier my lord. They were playing chase."

"Chase?" Mark was disbelieving.

"Never seen anything like it. She ran, he chased and then nudged her. Then he turned and ran off and she chased him." The warrior laughed. "It was really funny." He shot Mark an anxious look to see if he looked angry, but he just looked thoughtful.

Mark let out a piercing whistle. Girl and horse shot up, with the horse putting himself between her and the noise. So, Mark thought, he would protect her. Kalea seeing him ran a soothing hand over Midnight's flank and picked up the blanket. With not a word, the two approached slowly. Mark opened the gate and moved clear as they walked into the gloomy stable. Kalea filled trough with fresh water and patting him, left smiling to herself as she heard him stamping not wanting her to go.

"Well madam. It would appear that the horse loves you," Mark commented as they walked back.

"He's getting there," Kalea responded.

"And you?" he asked blandly.

"What do you mean by that?" Kalea asked wondering if he was trying to trick her in some way.

He didn't answer, just raised an eyebrow and escorted her a little roughly into the feasting hall. Leith was there with some of the warriors. Without uttering anything further he gave her a little push and turned and walked away.

Kalea looked over her shoulder at his retreating back, but he was already striding purposely out the hall door. She turned back and with her shoulders set went and sat opposite Leith.

"Who put a flea up his arse then?" Leith growled loud enough for all to hear.

Pouring herself a beaker of ale, Kalea shrugged. "Don't know."

"You haven't been letting your mouth run away with you? It wouldn't be the first time."

"No, I haven't," Kalea said bitterly. "Well, I don't think I have." Leith couldn't help but grin. "Don't laugh!" she scolded. "I am not one of those women who hangs around the powerful and the chieftains. I'm not clever enough to know what's going on, let alone start it," she ended grumpily.

Leith took pity on her and patted her hand. "Now, now girl. No need to get grumpy."

"I'm not!" Kalea bit back. Then grinned. "I guess I am. Well, he's so damn scary. He can be so kind and then he turns into a real…" Realising so many were very intently listening, she paused, "Damn scary thing." It wasn't just Leith who laughed. "I'd much rather deal with the bitey horse," which caused more guffawing. Lowering her voice, she whispered to Leith. "We've seen what he can do." She sighed. "How long have we been here anyway?"

Leith shrugged. In a growl, no louder than a whisper, he murmured, "Does he think Arthur is coming?" She gave an almost imperceptible nod.

"It's been a long time though," Kalea answered lowly. "It seems like a life time ago." She met his eye. "I'm not sure that I want them to come now."

"What do you mean? Of course, they need to come. I for one would rather spend my life in Arthur's war band."

"How do I live with this?" She made a small movement of her hand meant to encompass the whole place.

Leith harsh look told Kalea all she needed to know. Which was that whilst he had forgiven her, he still did not approve of her choice to give herself willingly to Mark. She dropped her gaze to her ale.

"I think I will go and wash the horse off me." With no further ado, she left feeling very unhappy. Not even Leith notice her slip the meat knife into her pocket.

As she passed down the door, she met Mary. The servant smiled at her.

"Mary. Can I have a pitcher of hot water please? I smell very horsey."

"Of course. I shall bring it up." With that Kalea went to wait for the water and carefully hid the meat knife. Mary turned up carrying a large jug of hot water and some drying cloths.

"Thank you so much Mary." She had already shed her jacket and with no self-consciousness, stripped off her shirt.

"Can I help?" Mary asked.

"Yes please." Mary set about soaping Kalea's back.

"Mary? Can I ask a big ask?"

"Take your trousers off," Mary commanded and Kalea obliged. "What is it you want?"

Kalea fidgeted and then turned to Mary. "I need the herbs that stop a man's seed from growing in me." Mary said nothing and continued to scrub Kalea's armpits. "I know it is a lot to ask and I have nothing to pay." Kalea rushed on worried that she had offended the woman.

Mary met her eye and nodded. "I will get it done." Much to Mary's surprise Kalea hugged her.

"Thank you so much." Kalea could have cried with gratitude. Mary helped slip the green dress over her head. Mary nodded and left and Kalea stood wondering what she was doing. She hoped she hadn't got Mary into trouble. The window in Mark's chamber overlooked the courtyard and Kalea found herself almost hypnotised watching the comings and goings of the people below. She envied the simplicity of their life. It had been like that with her before the Saxon raiders.

Kalea sighed. She was under no illusion how precarious her life with Mark was. So far, Mark had been generous and kind to her and his people seemed to appreciate his firm but fair hand. She was not fooled by his affection towards her. The tales she had heard of how he was intolerant of any misdemeanours, no matter how small. Large ones could result in death. Already she had witnessed a young man lose his hand for stealing. Something she would not like to witness often. Mark spent most of the day overseeing minor disputes and he would also ride out to make sure that the minor lords under him were behaving. Kalea knew that he was as fierce with these men and demanded, and got, total obedience. As well as receiving a percentage of the produce each of the small kingdoms produced, he also had first call on the lords' war bands. In addition, these men knew that one step out of place and they would be stripped of their land. Mark's war band was large enough to ensure total obedience. It seemed to Kalea that he spent most of his time plotting and scheming to keep his kingdom under his total control. And whilst the people in his large town, thought him a fair and just man, she suspected that outlying lords did not.

In all honesty, though, she could not complain. He treated her well and allowed her a degree of freedom. When he made love to her, he did so with a tenderness that left her breathless. But for how long? She wondered. A season? Two? How long before someone more interesting took his attention? It could even be shorter if Arthur turned up. What if after crowing over the victory of having stolen someone from under Arthur's nose, he had no further use for her? Her heart raced at the thought. Still, she had a weapon now, it was not a dagger, but would guarantee that she was not going to service the war band.

When Mark entered, it made her jump and she spun to meet him almost guiltily. She dropped a small curtsey.

"I'm sorry my Lord."

"Why are you sorry?" Mark threw down his jacket and took her in his arms. She melted into his arms. "What is wrong? Has someone upset you?"

Kalea took a deep breathe inhaling his musky smell. "Not at all, sire. I just miss my home."

"What with everything you have here?" She felt his voice rumble in his chest and she dare not look at him as she answered.

"You have spoilt me. But I am used to a small village. I knew everyone and everyone knew me. And, I know that my father was perhaps too easy with me, but I do miss him so. I am used to a much simpler life."

In answer, Mark tilted her head upwards and kissed her. "You are the sweetest, strangest woman I have known." His kiss grew more insistent and before long they were making love. Mark was tender and gentle and when they were both spent, held her against his chest.

With her head on his chest, Kalea listened to his heart slowing. "May I ask something?" He didn't need to answer, she felt him nod. "Why is it, that a man as handsome and powerful as you, are not married?" She felt him tense and then he sighed.

"I was once. She died with my child and I have never looked for another."

"Oh. I'm sorry," she whispered.

"Don't be. It was a long time ago."

Plucking up courage she quietly added. "Do you not need an heir?"

To her surprise, he chuckled. "Not short of them. One of them I think maybe older than you and is currently in my war band." Shocked. She lifted her head to look at him. The hazel eyes twinkled. "So, I wasn't married to his mother, but he is still my son. I will introduce you to him. You will see I produce handsome children," he added with a lazy smile.

"Could there be any doubt?" She smiled against his chest.

Kalea must have slept and was woken as Mark disentangled himself from her. She blinked blearily at him.

"Come on girl. We mustn't be late for supper." He began dressing.

"Is it that late?" She queried although she could see from the light drifting from the window that the sun was low in the sky. Reluctantly, she drew herself from the bed and splashed her face with the now cold water. He watched her naked body and smiled. There were certainly advantages to being a King. He watched her slip back into the green dress.

Without looking at him, Kalea spoke careful to keep her voice respectful. "Mark. Would it be possible for me to have some small coin?"

Watching her carefully, he replied, "And why would you need coin? Have you not got enough?"

She turned and met his eye. "Yes, my lord. You have been more than generous. But today, Mary was so kind and helped me wash and combed my hair and I would have liked to give her something for her trouble."

Mark laughed. "That is what she is. A servant to do your bidding. But if it would make you happy then yes you may have some coins." And without even thinking about it, picked up a purse and threw it to her.

Kalea caught it. It was heavy. "This is too much. I've never seen so much coin."

"Then you best spend it wisely." He smiled.

Putting the purse down, she came and hugged him. "Thank you."

"Welcome. Now let's eat. I've built up quite an appetite with you, young lady."

Kalea laughed and took his arm as he escorted her to the feasting hall.

Half way through the meal, Mark suddenly called. "Alan! A word." A young warrior stood up and sauntered confidently over the Mark. Kalea was agog. He had the same dark curly hair, hawkish nose and devilish eyebrows of his father. His eyes were brown rather than hazel and even the lazy, careless way he walked was the same.

"Father," he said with a small bow.

Mark smiled at him broadly. "Kalea, this is my son Alan. Alan, of course you have seen Kalea." Alan gave her a small bow. "Is he not a handsome chap?" Mark queried.

Kalea aware that she was staring, smiled at her own embarrassment. "Goodness!" she exclaimed. "You certainly can't deny he's yours." Both men laughed. "You even sound the same!"

"Is there anything else you'd like to compare?" Alan quipped.

Blushing furiously, Kalea spoke boldly. "Definitely your father's son."

Both men laughed and Mark waved Alan away. With a small bow and a wry grin, he turned and made his way back to the war band.

"Goodness!" Kalea said again. "Two peas in a pod."

Smiling Mark teased. "Do you think him handsome?"

"Why yes!" Kalea flirted. "But he lacks a certain something…"

"And what's that?"

"He's not you," she finished with a grin. Mark threw back his head and laughed. The harvest was in, everything was moving as smoothly as it should, it had been a good day. Now was the fun of hunting to bring in the meat for winter.

Chapter 7
Visitors

Midnight had allowed Kalea to sit on him. He wasn't exactly happy, but he was getting used to it as Kalea leaned over and cuddled his neck. He snorted and then began to walk forward. He didn't realise this was what was wanted of him. Kalea sat very still and allowed him to go where he wanted.

Suddenly, there was a commotion at the fence. Midnight turned to watch as a messenger rushed up to the warrior who had been set to guard Kalea. The guard looked up.

"Kalea! Come quickly! Mark has ordered you in. Now!" he shouted.

Kalea slid from Midnight's back and began to walk towards the fence.

"Move girl!" The urgency in his voice made her run. Midnight followed and in a trice was back in his stable. The guard grabbed Kalea by the collar and began towing her back to the castle, none to gently. Kalea stumbled along beside him.

"What's going on?" she asked.

"Don't know. Just told it was urgent."

As they virtually fell through the door, they were met by Mary and another girl. They grabbed Kalea and dragged her into the bathing room. Without further ado, they stripped her off and helped her into the barrel.

"Mary. What on earth is happening?"

"We have been told to bathe you and make sure you look your best."

"Why?"

Mary shrugged and helped Kalea out and wrapped her in the drying cloths. Then she was rushed up to Mark's chamber. A guard stood outside and he opened the door to let them in. Kalea looked at him wide eyed. Once inside Mary quickly slipped the red dress over her head.

"Mary, do you really not know what's going on?"

Mary met her eye. They had an understanding now. "No. I don't. One of the messengers rushed in and Mark then issued the orders." She liked the girl and been providing her with the herbs she requested and Kalea had managed to pay her very well. The coin was very welcome but she would have done it for nothing. She combed through Kalea's hair until it was smooth and glossy.

"I have to go. I am to help in the kitchen."

"So do I just wait here?"

"I would guess so. I wish you luck." Mary went to leave.

Kalea somehow felt she might need it.

Mark smiled. So, Arthur was coming, was he? The kitchen was bustling preparing a lavish feast and the hall was being tidied. He lounged in his chair in the hall feeling very satisfied. It had taken Arthur rather longer than he had expected, but nevertheless, it had gone as he had planned.

The word had been bought that Arthur was coming with six warriors. That told him a lot. Enough to put up resistance, but not enough to threaten Mark with his war band. Mark stroked his beard thoughtfully. He was questing. He had no evidence but he had his suspicions that Mark had what he was looking for. Of course, he was right. "Well, well, well Arthur." He was smiling. "I have you racing around the countryside wasting your time. Excellent!"

Meanwhile, Arthur and Kai had met up with the escort of warriors sent by Mark. They were led into the courtyard where their horses were taken and they were led into the feasting hall. Mark was sitting talking to a warrior and as they both turned to see the newcomers, it was obvious, this lad was his son. Arthur gave an almost imperceptible bow.

Mark raised a quizzical eyebrow, "Arthur! What are you doing in my kingdom?" as if he didn't know. "You are a long way from home."

Arthur approached him with Kai at his side. "I apologise for the intrusion Mark." Arthur met his eye calmly. "I am seeking your help in a matter."

Mark was enjoying this. "And why should I help you? We are not exactly friends."

Arthur met his eye. "No. We are not. But in the past, we have found it beneficial to us both to assist one another," he answered levelly.

Mark made a 'maybe' motion. "So, how may I 'assist' you?"

From his confident, arrogant manner, Arthur was certain that he was right. "Two people have disappeared from my village and I am seeking them."

"Careless of you to lose them in the first place," Mark replied with a slow grin. "And what are they to you?"

Arthur smarted. Yes, he was definitely playing a game with them. "Actually, they were visitors. Messengers from East Anglia and therefore, under my protection."

"Well, you didn't do a good job then." *Oh yes*, thought Mark, *this is going very well*. An angry tick was twitching in Arthur's jaw. But the young pup had good control.

"No, I didn't," Arthur conceded. "That is why, I felt it was my duty to ensure that they were safe and well."

"And who are they? Two warriors? Merchants?"

He was being played and Arthur didn't like it one bit but he had no choice but to play along. "An old warrior and his ward," he replied levelly with no trace of anger in his voice.

"Aaahh!" Mark's pleasure was evident. "I think I might be able to help you. A slip of a girl who dresses as a boy and an old warrior who has seen better days?"

Kai tensed and Arthur placed a hand on his arm to restrain him. "Those are exactly whom I am seeking. Are they well?"

"Well, you can see for yourself," he nodded to one of the warband and he rose as he had previously instructed leaving Mark watching Arthur with a sardonic grin. "I would have thought," he added once again trying to goad the young king, "that with winter approaching, you would have better things to do, than gad round the country."

"My kingdom is in safe hands," replied Arthur refusing to rise. A moment later the warrior returned and escorted Kalea into the hall. Kai gasped as he watched Kalea rock at the sight of them. Her face was pale but she looked lovely in a dress as bright as blood. Arthur's grip on Kai's arm tightened. Quickly regaining her composure, Kalea joined Mark.

"Sit," he commanded and dutifully she sat beside him. She could not take her eyes from Kai and he was the same. "As you can see. She is well. Does she not look lovely?" Kai made to move forward but Arthur restrained him. With a slight movement, Ben stepped forward and stood on Kai's right to help restrain him if necessary. Mark threw back his head and laughed. "Oh, I see." His voice was quiet and cruel. His eyes glinted wickedly. "Was she to have been yours Kai?" Kai growled and Mark laughed again. "You should thank me boy! I have broken your mare and she now is an excellent ride." Now it did take Arthur and Ben to restrain Kai.

There was a crash as Kalea's chair went over and she turned ready to flee. All attention was now directed at her. The hall went deadly quiet. Mark's hand flashed out and caught her wrist. "I did not say you could leave." His tone brooked no argument but with a twist of her wrist that shocked him, she broke free and strode towards the door. "Come back," Mark ordered.

"I will not!" Kalea answered defiantly.

"Stop her." The man who had bought her in, blocked the door. "I said, come back!" His voice was harsh. He was not angry. This could work out even better.

Kalea was shaking with anger. "No!" She stared at the warrior's chest. She would not look into the room.

"Madam," Mark was calm but his tone dripped venom, "you forget it is not just your life you gamble with."

"Kalea! No!" Came a gruff call from the back of the hall.

This was the first time that Arthur became aware of Leith's presence. But all eyes were on the back of the slim girl who dared to defy a king.

"Leith! I have no choice," she answered.

"She's a clever girl." Grinned Mark meeting Kai's eye. There was absolutely no doubt that Kai would have killed him given half a chance. Casually he lounged back in his chair, throwing a leg over the arm demonstrating how cool and relaxed he was.

The rage burned hot in her and holding her head high she returned slowly and deliberately to Mark's side. Bending down, she righted the chair and made to sit but Mark's signal stopped her.

"Now girl," he began cruelly, "tell them all who and what you are," he commanded.

"No."

Mark laughed but there was no mirth in the sound. "You are a feisty filly! Have you forgotten already what I reminded you of not moments ago?"

Kalea took a deep breath and fixed her eyes on a point at the back of the hall. She would look at no one. Especially not Kai. The anguish in his face broke her heart. Lifting her chin and squaring her shoulders she spoke in ringing tones. "I am Kalea, daughter of the warrior Ren." She took another deep breath and a single tear slipped down her cheek. Unnoticed to most, but not to Arthur and Kai. "I am a captive here and the King's whore."

"You may now leave." Mark smiled cruelly.

Kalea turned on her heel and lifted her chin even higher and walked with as much dignity as she could muster from the room. She was not going to give him the pleasure of seeing her run.

Leith at the back of the hall, had been held in check by the war band and he could have cried and cheered for the girl. Without thinking he began to bang his ale cup on the table. A sign usually reserved for a brave deed done by the warrior clan. To his surprise, others joined him and the hall was filled with drumming.

As she approached the door, the guard opened it for her and quietly spoke, "That was well done lady." Once outside, Kalea fled. Running up the stairs to Mark's chamber, tears flowing.

Back in the hall, Arthur and Mark still stood eyes locked. Mark had a smug smile on his face his eyes still glittered cruelly. Arthur on the other hand looked hard but calm and collected.

Mark raised a dismissive hand. "Now that the pleasantries are over, perhaps I can offer you, my hospitality. Some food and a place to lay your head tonight. After all, you have come a long way and will need to rest before you ride off tomorrow. Empty handed." He emphasised and gestured Arthur to the chair where Kalea had been seated. "The rest of your men, are welcome to join Leith."

Arthur bit his tongue. "That is most kind and we would be grateful." He took the seat and watched as Mark's son led his companions to the end of the hall, where the war band had made room for them. Kai looked bleak and Arthur felt for him.

With a nod, the serving women began to bring in a bounty of food and ale.

Arthur refused to be drawn by the events that had just unfolded. He began eating hungrily. "Your food is good Mark," he remarked in between mouthfuls.

Mark was impressed and raised an eyebrow at him. "The land has produced well this year. We will not starve this winter. I am looking forward to the hunting to bring in the meat."

"That is always the fun part," Arthur agreed. "Would you consider a trade for the girl and Leith?" he asked almost casually.

"You have nothing I want," Mark replied with a smile, "and certainly nothing I need." Arthur shrugged. "You do not seem overly bothered by that."

"I'm not," he answered.

"And yet you travelled all this way," Mark stated.

"I did it for Kai. They are of no consequence to me."

Not the answer Mark wanted to hear. "And what of Kai?"

Arthur smiled inwardly. Now, he was playing the game and shrugged nonchalantly. "He'll get over it. Name me a man who has never had his heart broken by a pretty girl."

"True," Mark said thoughtfully.

"He'll be sore for a while." Arthur was warming to the task. "But there will be other pretty girls who will smile at him and help him forget." He smirked and met Mark's eye. "Besides, he might not be wanting your cast offs."

That took Mark by surprise and he laughed heartily. "You may be right. I've said this before. In other circumstances, I would have liked you as friend."

"I too, think we would get on well." Arthur grinned inwardly thinking, *I don't think so. You are a sly, cunning bastard.*

At the other end of the hall, Kai sat down heavily on the bench next to Leith.

"I'm sorry lad," Leith growled with heartfelt sympathy. "I didn't do a good job protecting her."

Kai met his eye, his face grim. "You are hardly to blame Leith."

"And neither is she. I don't like it but she is doing what she thinks is best."

"Like bedding Mark." Kai spat bitterly and took a deep draft of the mead he had just been poured.

They were aware that Mark's warband were listening and would no doubt report back every word to Mark. Sighing deeply Leith turned to look at this heartbroken, angry man. "It was her best option. Him or the warband." Kai turned to meet his eye. "No. I didn't agree either. It took her, to point out that her choices were those two. Better one man than many. You don't have to like it, I don't, but that's the way it is." Kai didn't look convinced.

"She did well," Ben commented. Eager to break the tension between Kai and Leith. "It was bravely done."

"That it was," Leith agreed. "She's not lacking in bravery." He glanced a Kai and Kai was watching him.

"So, tell me old man," Kai asked scathingly. "How was it that you got taken without a fight?"

Leith didn't get a chance to answer as one of Mark's warband, laughed. "I can tell you that. We were far too good for him." That was greeted by cheering from the rest of warband. While Arthur's companions remained stony faced. "No offense old man but we weren't particular who we took." Leith said nothing but frowned into his ale. "When we arrived, there was the girl not a stitch on. Good body on her, I'll say that!" he gloated. Leith laid a hand on Kai arm, but it wasn't needed. Kai remained unmoved and took a deep drink of his mead. "And the old boy, was sat sunning himself. Not a care in the world. Thinking all was well and we just launched out of the trees. They didn't stand a chance. Especially after Jack gave Leith a whack on the head with his sword hilt. Down he went." Leith was unmoving as the war band took great delight in his humiliation. "The girl was harder to catch. She was as slippery as an eel. Who put her lights out?" he asked. A young lad shouted it was he. "It was young Eric."

"So, there you have it," Leith growled. "And here we are."

"Do they treat you well?" Ben asked eager to be away from that subject now.

"They don't treat me badly," Leith conceded. "Warriors tend to look after one another and they would have given me a good death if they had been ordered." The war band banged their ale mugs on the table in appreciation of the recognition that Leith had given them. "They treat me better than they would have Kalea." This was met with a lot of howling from the war band.

Eric yelled out. "I would've been gentle with her Leith."

Much to everyone's surprise, Kai gave a bark of laughter. "I'm sure she will be very grateful." And with a sad smile. "I hope she'll be very happy."

A new respect from the companions and the war band saw them drumming the table causing Mark to look up from the far end of the hall.

Leith patted him on the shoulder and Kai gave him a sad smile. "It wasn't meant to be Leith. It was good while it lasted."

Leith looked down; he didn't want anyone to see the tear in his eye.

Kalea slammed through the door beside herself in a total rage. She slammed the door so hard, the guard on the other side flinched. She screamed in total frustration and stormed round the room kicking, hitting and throwing anything she could lay her hands on. The crashing grew so loud that the guard opened the door to see what was happening and quickly shut it again as a very well-aimed goblet smashed against the door frame. The red mist had descended and her control was totally lost. She heaved over the table as if it was not more than a scrap of kindling, sending the bowl of apples crashing to the floor. The apples rolled off amongst the broken pottery. Next went the copper wash bowl complete with water.

The room already reeked of the flagon of wine she had dashed to the floor and now consumed with fury, she stamped on the apples filling the room with the rich smell of cider. As she kicked an apple across the floor, she noticed the small fruit knife, skid across the flags after it. All at once, the storm within her condensed to something as hard as ice. She bent and slipped the small knife up her sleeve and then straightening up, she went and stood looking out on the courtyard. Clarity came. No, she would not throw herself out the window, or maybe she would, but she would kill him first. She stood still amongst the chaos she had created and waited.

Mark was bored. He had achieved what he had set out to do, humiliate Arthur. The victory was very sweet. Even sweeter, knowing that he had stolen Kalea from Kai. He was glad he had been patient. He was not prepared to admit, even to himself, that he had been unnecessarily cruel to the girl. It had all played out very well. However, there was only so much crowing you could do without appearing to be totally callus, although he was. His eyes swept the hall, everyone seemed to be having a good time.

All this carousing, could be tedious, he decided. His mind turned to Kalea. She would, of course be angry and he admitted rightly so. This could add some extra spice to their lovemaking. With a cruel grin, he turned to Arthur. "If you will excuse me, I have a certain little filly that needs servicing."

Arthur grinned and nodded. "I will join the war band." Mark got up and once outside the door, rubbed his hands together in glee.

This should be fun, he thought and with a definite spring in his step mounted the stairs to his chamber. The guard he had left outside the door was slow to move.

"I think I should warn you sire; she has been throwing things around in there."

Mark grinned. "Little wild cat. I do like a feisty woman."

With that he swung the door open. The pungent smell of wine and apples hit him and with no sign that anything was amiss, he took his jacket off and threw it on the bed, which was the only thing that escaped Kalea's wrath. Kalea was stood motionless by the fire. Making a point of taking in the destruction her temper had caused, he turned to look at her. "It seems my lady has had a temper tantrum." Kalea said nothing, but it was plain that the fire still burned in her eyes. "That went very well, I think. And you played your part admirably." Kalea did not move. "Come here girl. Your anger excites me." Still, she did not move. "I said come here." His voice hard and cold. Kalea came towards him, the smile of victory on his lips did not help her temper.

Just as he was about to put his arms round her, her hand lashed out and only Mark's warrior reactions saved him from serious damage. His head jerked back as he felt something sharp on his throat. She came at him again. The paring knife flashing tearing shirt and the flesh of his arm, he caught her wrists bringing her close to him. "I see you have teeth," he hissed squeezing her wrists cruelly. She met his eye defiantly and refused to release the knife. Mark squeezed harder, hearing the bones creaking and watching as her face showed the pain she was feeling and eventually with a cry, the knife clattered to the floor. Still, she fought, trying to kick and bite. Mark was a strong man and all her efforts had little effect on him. His temper was rising now and he forced her to the bed. Despite her best efforts, he turned her round and threw her face down.

"Now, madam," he said through gritted teeth, holding her down with one hand while lifting her skirts with the other. "It seems, I will have to teach you a lesson on obedience." Freeing himself from his trousers, he entered her roughly, taking pleasure in her cry of pain. She stopped struggling and lay compliant. It was soon over. It was only then, that Mark realised how much he was bleeding. The skirts of her dress were splattered with blood. "I would suggest that you re-think your attitude," he growled as he re-adjusted his clothing. "You would do well to remember that while you are here, you are mine to do as I please." The front of his shirt was ripped and covered in blood. Picking up his jacket, he fastened it to the top. "I want this mess cleared up by the time I return and I expect you to welcome me like you should." Kalea had curled into a foetal position and wept.

Mark stormed out. Slamming the door behind him. He looked at the guard whose face remained impassive. Then swept down the corridor. On his way, he met Mary, who took one look at his face and sank into a low curtsey.

"Mary!" he growled. "Send someone to get Essie. I will wait for her in the receiving chamber. And while you're at it. Send up some wine to Kalea. She has spilt hers and made a mess."

Mary fled to do his bidding. Why would he need Essie, the wise woman? She wondered. Having sent a messenger down to find Essie, she poured a flagon of wine and picked up some cloths to go and clean the spillage in Mark's chamber.

Kalea was destroyed. She was sore and bruised. Her wrists didn't want to work properly. She wept bitterly and then tried to get up. Her legs wobbled as she began to clear up the devastation that she had wrought. Using the copper wash bowl, she began to put the wreckage in it and that is when she cut her finger on a sharp piece of pottery. She looked at the blood welling from the pad of her finger then taking the shard, she picked up the chair that she had thrown over and sat in it.

"I am done," she muttered to herself and with no further thought plunged the shard into her wrists sawing as she did so. The blood began to gush. She watched it with fascination. Then passed the shard to the other hand which was already slick with blood.

Mark undid his jacket and inspected his wounds. He wrinkled his nose in disgust. There was certainly a lot of blood. He had not expected that of her. The door opened and Mark was quick to pull his jacket round him. A servant showed in Essie. "You took your time woman," Mark spat at her.

Essie was elderly and she certainly wasn't afraid of Mark. She had delivered him as a babe and no babe she delivered frightened her. "Sire, my legs are old and do not carry me as fast as they used to. Perhaps, if you are in a hurry, it would be best to send a horse." She knew better than to ask what had occurred, she would draw her own conclusions.

Mark shook his head and gritted his teeth in impatience and frustration. "Well, you're here now. Come on woman."

Essie took her time and by the time she had got there, Mark had stripped off his jacket and blood-stained shirt. Essie peered closely at the wounds. "You were lucky."

"What do you mean lucky? I don't feel very lucky," he spluttered incredulously.

"A little higher, and you would have had little need for my services." She let that sink in. Mark grimaced and hissed as she prodded the wound. "Someone made a fair job at cutting your throat," she commented.

"Ow!" Mark yelped.

"Don't take on so. You've had worse."

"But I've forgotten those," he said through gritted teeth.

"I expect you deserved it," she said getting out a needle and thread. "I need to stitch the one at your throat, as it cuts further down, it is shallow and will soon stop bleeding."

"What do you mean I deserved it?" Mark asked rolling his eyes as she threaded the needle.

"You must have upset someone to get this," she said as she began to put a couple of stitches in the wound closest to his throat.

"Does anyone deserve to get their throat cut?" he groaned.

"Stop whining," she instructed. "It's done. The rest can be bandaged. You'll live. You will have the scar to prove it."

"To go with all the others," he muttered bitterly.

"Do they still live?" Essie queried as she worked on the wound on his chest.

"Does who still live?"

"The person who tried to cut your throat," Essie stated calmly.

"Yes," he spat.

"But not for much longer, I think. Lastly the arm. Shame to spoil such a fine shirt."

"What about me?" he whinged.

"You'll live."

"Sometimes Essie, you are a real crone."

Essie chuckled.

Mary opened the door and took in the scene at a glance. "Kalea! Don't!" she cried as Kalea plunged the piece of pottery into her other wrist. Dropping the flagon of wine, she sprinted across the room, snatching the pottery from the girl's hand and throwing it across the room. "No. No. No," she said as she saw the ever-growing puddle of blood. The rags she had bought up to clean up, were quickly torn into strips and she used them to bandage Kalea's torn wrists. "Kalea, no you must not do this. You are strong," she spoke soothingly as you would to a sick child. "Kalea, listen to me. Be strong." The girl was muttering something and when Mary lent close, she could hear the words I'm done. "No, you're not done. Not for a long while yet." She hoped it was true.

Leaving her, she went back to the door and opened it to the warrior outside. "Bran!" she said urgently. "I need you to help me."

Bran looked incredulous. "I'm not a servant," he said belligerently.

"I know. But Kalea is sick. I need help and I cannot leave her." Bran raised an eyebrow. Mary threw the door open. The smell hit him first, the hot, coppery smell of fresh blood, with wine and apples was almost overpowering. He covered his nose with his sleeve and then saw Kalea, slumped on the chair surrounded by blood. She looked broken.

"What do you need?"

"Essie is with Mark. Can you get someone to fetch her when she has finished? Also, I need some help with Kalea and this mess. Some hot water and rags and some extra help."

Bran didn't argue, and although he didn't run, set off at a great pace. Mary shut the door and returned to Kalea. She was unmoving, just muttering to herself and for the first time, Mary was angry with Mark. He had broken her and she was so sweet.

At last, the door opened and two of Mary's friends came in carrying buckets of water and rags. Mary shot a warning look at them and wordlessly, the three of them began to clean up. One of them went to get fresh water and came back with an empty one too to put all the broken pieces in. The clean water was for Kalea. Mary and her friend, stripped off the torn, bloody dress and began to wash her down. Kalea stood unresisting. The evidence of the fight was clear to see. Bruises were forming on her thighs and buttocks and a smear of blood on her legs gave credence to a rape. The girls' eyes met but they carried on with their task and then led the unresisting girl to the bed and put her on it. Covering her with some skins, they continued with the task of cleaning when the door opened again.

Essie left Mark getting his jacket on as usual, she had been paid handsomely and was now looking forward to sitting quietly in front of her fire. As she closed the door, one of the servants came up to her.

"Essie, someone else has need of your skills."

Essie sighed. The fire would have to wait a little longer. She followed the girl as she led the way to Mark's chamber. *Stairs! I'm getting too old for this.* A warrior stood guard and nodded to Essie as she swung the door open.

Mark stood. The stitches pulled and he sighed in resignation. He would have to go back to the hall and put on a brave face. He didn't really want to see Kalea just yet either in case she was still in a fury. Squaring his shoulders, he entered the hall, doing his best to look relaxed. He saw that Arthur had indeed moved down to sit with his party and Mark's warband. Even worse, he thought as he went to join them.

As Mark entered the hall, Arthur looked up. He was pleased to see that Mark looked decidedly rattled. He nudged Leith. He hoped Kalea had given him the hard time he deserved. Arthur moved up so Mark could sit beside him. "And how was your filly?" he asked innocently.

"A handful," Mark replied levelly.

Kai laughed. "You're lucky she didn't have toothpick." Arthur aimed a kick at him but Kai took no notice.

"Toothpick?" Mark queried.

"Oh Mark!" Kai had had way too much to drink and was going to take this opportunity to goad Mark. "Your education is sadly lacking. Did Kalea not tell you about toothpick?"

Leith, grabbed his arm. "That's enough, Kai."

"Leith! We can't possibly leave Mark ignorant of yet another of Kalea's skills." Despite Arthur's glare, he carried on. "Toothpick is Leith's name for Kalea's sword."

"Sword?" Mark queried. *The girl can do enough damage with a fruit knife, let alone a sword*, he thought.

"Well," Kai confessed. "It's only a boys' sword but she is mighty nifty with it. Leith here had been teaching the finer points of sword play." Kai smiled mightily.

Leith sighed but couldn't begrudge the boy wanting to get one over on Mark.

"She would have run you through or gelded you." Kai took a big swig of mead and nearly fell over backwards. "Or knowing Kalea, both." There was a lot of chuckling and questions were thrown at Kai and Leith about Kalea fighting abilities, which Kai answered with relish and Leith with no enthusiasm.

"Essie! Thank God you're here." Mary leapt to her feet.

The tang of blood still hung in the air despite the window being open and the attempt to clean up. So, Mark had his throat cut in his own chamber. "Mary, what is amiss?"

"It's Kalea. She has opened her wrists."

Essie hissed and moved to the bed to see the slim girl that she had been supplying herbs too. Her eyes were open but not seeing and she was muttering. "What is she saying?" Essie asked.

"All she will say is 'I'm done'."

"You're not done yet." Essie lent down and said firmly to the girl. "The gods haven't finished with you yet." Kalea met her eye. Nodding, Essie got a small bottle from her case and lifted the girl's head and poured a few drops down her throat. Then she picked up a wrist. The blood was already soaking through Mary's bandages. "Bad business this. I'm going to need your help with this Mary." Getting the needle and thread out of her bag again, she passed it to her "Thread that for me, my eyes are not what they were." Mary handed it back to her. "Right. Now. When we undo this, it's going to gush." Mary looked a little pale. Essie placed a tourniquet above the wound and pulled it tight. "What I need you to do, is mop the blood so I can see what I am doing. Ready?" Mary nodded. Essie undid the bandage and it did indeed gush and Mary mopped as fast as she could until the flow slowed. Then Essie stepped in with her needle. It wasn't long before it was stitched and rebandaged. The other wrist, was not as bad. Mary had stepped in before she had managed to saw at the wound, so there was not so much to be done and the blood flow was slower. Essie stood up and rubbed her back, turning to the other girl who had been stood watching, "Be a good girl and go and get Essie a draft of mead and some food. I think I need it." She sat down in one of the chairs. "She must not be left unattended Mary. I have given her some poppy juice so she should sleep 'til morning. I hope that the sleep will help heal her mind and I've a mind to keep her under for a few days." Mary nodded. "Do you know what happened here?"

Mary sat on the chair opposite her, although, she would never have dared if Mark had been there. She shook her head. "I expect we will find out from the gossip from the hall. All I know is that the king came storming down and asked for you and told me to take up some wine for Kalea, said she had spilt hers. When I get up here, the room is a mess and Kalea was sitting where you are with blood everywhere. Bran said, that's the guard that she came up from the hall in a temper and started throwing things about."

Pondering, Essie thought so the trouble began in the hall. "I have a mind to stay here, 'til the rascal comes back." Mary grinned at hearing Mark called a rascal. "You go now girl and see what gossip you can pick up. I will stay with her until I have spoken to the King. I expect he will send for you to be her nursemaid." The door opened and Mary's friend came in with a tray for Essie. "Thank you, my dear. May as well have my supper here while I wait for the King." The two girls left together. Leaving Essie, eating and thinking hard about the poor lass she had just treated.

At last, the hall was emptying. Some were already asleep where they sat, including Kai. Mark sighed. It had been a long evening where he had been forced to play the jovial host. The party had given him a sound ribbing about his sexual exploits with the girl, mostly the drink talking and he had endured, but he had surely had enough now. He rose, nodding to Arthur and retreated he shut the door to the hall with relief and hesitated. That girl! Mark thought, had rattled him. He was not used to it. He wanted to go to bed but he didn't want another

175

confrontation. He wasn't frightened of her; he just had no energy to take her down again. He plodded up the stairs and found that Bran was still on guard.

"Shouldn't you have been relieved by now?"

Bran shuffled his feet. "I said I'd do extra. The lady Kalea is ill."

"Ill? How?" Bran wasn't going to get drawn into this, and shrugged. "Go off now. I'll take care of it." Bran wandered off but Mark saw him glance over his shoulder at him strangely. He wondered what that was all about. Flinging open the door, he found the candles lit, the fire burning bright and Essie sitting comfortably in front of the fire.

"Good god crone! Are you still here? I need to go to my bed."

Essie eyes were as hard as flint. "You will have to find a different bed tonight."

"Why? What's wrong with the girl?" He was tired, he was injured and he was mortally put out.

"She tried to kill herself."

That shocked him. He was now wide awake and went to the bed and looked at the pale woman, asleep with her wrists bandaged. "Kalea!" he gently stroked her face and she didn't move. "Will she live?"

It was Essie's turn to shrug. "Maybe. She has lost a lot of blood and if it wasn't for Mary, she would be gone." To her surprise, Mark looked devastated. "I fear more for her mind, which is a hard thing to fix."

"What can we do?" he asked looking down at the slumbering girl.

More like, what can I do? Essie thought. "I have given her poppy juice which should make her sleep to morning. I have a mind to give her more, but we need to get her drinking to make up for the blood she lost. She must not be left alone; we do not know if she will try again. I will leave now and come back in the morning."

"Essie, don't leave. I'll have a room made ready for you. It's late."

"As you wish. I hope you haven't broken this girl, Mark. Mary speaks most highly of her."

"I hope I haven't broken her too." With that he left. Essie had never heard him admit that he had done something wrong. So, maybe Mary was right, she was a bit special.

Mark had slept very poorly. He had thrown some furs on the floor by the bed and stayed there. Kalea hadn't moved. He rose and put on a fresh shirt catching his stitches as he did so. Swearing profusely, he tucked it in when a knock came on the door and Mary entered carrying some breakfast and some hot water.

"I am having breakfast in the hall."

"This is for Essie. She is coming." Mark noticed her tone was surly. He was unused to this treatment from her.

He looked down, momentarily non-plussed before saying. "Mary, I would like you to stay with Kalea. When Essie is here, go down to the kitchen and tell them you are relieved of duties there and that they will need to bring you food." She did no more than nod and left.

"This is all going to shit," he growled. Now, he had to go down and put on a show for Arthur and see him off. Pulling on his boots, he waited for Essie. Almost as if summoned by his thoughts, Essie came in. "How is she?" she asked taking in the skins on the floor. So, she thought he cares enough to sleep near her.

Washing his face, he turned to her. "She's asleep. I don't think she's moved."

Essie nodded. "I'll give her some more when she wakes but not until she's had some water."

"I really want her to live Essie." His voice almost pleading. "I lost my temper. I shouldn't have. It was not her fault."

Never before had he admitted he was wrong. Shocked as she was, Essie replied levelly. "You should have thought of that before you harmed her."

The whole world was against him this morning. Mark was almost sulking as he slammed out.

Mark shut the chamber door. There was a new guard on duty this morning and he nodded to him as he went down to the hall. He was shaken, he hadn't felt like this for a long time. Not since he lost of wife and child in childbed. Now, he must act as a King should. He had fought battles, lost men and countless women had come and gone. This girl could not be allowed to make him falter from his course. Squaring his shoulders and putting on a bright smile, Mark bounded in to the hall as if this was the best day of his life. Inwardly, he was seething. He hated Arthur, Kai, Essie and Kalea. He joined Arthur at the table.

"Have you collected the provisions I had made ready?"

Arthur nodded, "My thanks Mark. You look a little peaky this morning, is everything all right?"

"No. I think I drank too much last night." *You bastard*, he thought, *why don't you just fuck off!*

Arthur sensed that all was not well with Mark. But for Kalea's sake he would not push his luck. Mark rose and spoke to Alan. "Take six and escort the young pup to our borders. I would not have him get lost and come wandering back."

Alan grinned, nodded and then went to choose his men.

The search party finished breakfast and they said their goodbyes to Leith with reluctance. Arthur approached Mark. "I thank you for your hospitality. You have treated us well."

Mark's smile didn't reach his eyes. "You are welcome. I hope to see you again soon."

I bet, thought Arthur. "Perhaps, I might say goodbye to Kalea."

It took all Mark's control not stab him. "I'm sorry. The lady is indisposed today."

"Too much nightly action, I expect." Arthur smiled, thinking, *I hope you haven't hurt her.*

Then almost at once they were gone.

As they clattered out of the courtyard chatting happily to Alan and his men, Mark allowed his mask to slip. Turning to his steward, who flinched under Mark's thunderous face he growled. "Cancel the whingers. I will see no one today. In fact, cancel everything today. I will not leave the castle." His Steward nodded and hastily withdrew. The warband did not have to be mind readers to know their king was not to be trifled with today and were quiet. "Col!" Mark barked. His big red headed second stepped forward but said nothing. "Take some men and patrol, make sure everything is as it should be." Col nodded and the warband scurried out of the hall, unwilling to remain with Mark when he was in such a foul mood.

Once the hall was empty, Mark threw himself down in his chair. He could pinpoint the moment; it had all gone wrong. It was when, he hadn't let Kalea go. She had defied him and he would not be seen as a King who could be defied by anyone. If only he had let her storm out rather than stopping her, this wouldn't have happened, he brooded and, in all likelihood, he could have just laughed at her temper tantrum. But spite and hatred, had made him cruel and unkind. He rubbed his forehead. "Shit!" he spat.

A mistake. Yes. He had made them before and recovered. He hoped to God he could do it again.

It was a huge effort to wake up. Struggling, Kalea sat up. She felt groggy and confused. Suddenly, Essie was there.

"Hello Kalea, how are you feeling?"

"Awful," she croaked, her head was banging, she felt weak and she hurt in places that she didn't remember why they did so.

Essie passed her a beaker of water. "Drink. You need to drink lots." Kalea did as she was told and found she was thirsty. "Do you know who I am?"

"Are you Essie, the wise woman? I think I remember you from…" her brows furrowed, when was it?

"Last evening," Essie supplied kindly. "Do you remember what happened?"

Kalea looked down at her bandaged wrists, but she could not hide her misery. She nodded.

Essie sat on the bed and took the girl in her arms. "I know my lovely. It was a terrible thing but it will pass, like everything," she soothed the girl as she would a child. "It is good that you remember. It shows that your mind is strong."

"You said the gods had further use for me," Kalea whispered.

"And I am sure they do," Essie said kindly. "It is important for you to rest and regain your strength. Now, I will get you some more poppy juice."

"I don't want to sleep anymore Essie."

"Are you sure? Poppy juice will let you sleep without dreams." Kalea nodded. "Then I will get you something to help with the pain." She stirred some potion into a beaker of water and handed it to Kalea. "Drink it down. I will need to look at your wounds and it will not be painless." Kalea did as instructed and leaned back, exhausted by the effort.

"You will be weak my lovely," Essie reassured her. "You lost a lot of blood and it will take a while for you to remake it. Where do you hurt most?"

"It would be easier to tell you where it doesn't hurt," Kalea said weakly.

Essie smiled. She would be alright, this one. She was strong and even now, had a sense of humour. "Let's start at the top and work down to your toes."

"My head aches," Kalea began. "The back of my neck aches." Knowing this was caused by Mark holding her down. "My wrists hurt and between my legs."

"The herbs should take away most of the pain from all of those. I will look at your wrists when the herbs start working." Kalea nodded and her eyes closed. Essie sat watching and after a while, picked up one of Kalea's wrists. Kalea's eyes opened. "I had thought you asleep."

"No. Just resting."

"Is the pain better now?" The girl nodded and Essie undid the bandage. This was the worse one. The bleeding had stopped but Essie thought that she should

179

put a poultice on this one as the skin looked red and angry. She wanted no infection or it would carry this one away. She went to her bag and came back with a pot of goo which she smeared on the wound. The girl hissed as Essie rebound it. The other one wasn't so bad but was badly bruised and a little misshapen, this was the one that did the damage to Mark she concluded and she just bathed it and rebound that one too. "You very nearly did what you set out to do," Essie remarked drily. "If Mary hadn't come in and you had done the same with this one as you did on the other, there would have been no saving you. You were lucky."

"Was I?" Kalea returned. Looking at Kalea's face, Essie could see that she wasn't convinced.

"Yes," Essie said positively. Then looking the girl deep in the eye. "Mark was wrong to hurt you so, but he is a king and oft forgets what it is like to be a mortal. Every day, he has the power of life and death and he has to make tough choices. Because, he must show no weakness, he can sometimes be cruel without thinking."

"You like him."

Essie grinned. "I delivered him and he was a sunny child. The weight of the kingdom has changed him much. I am sure that the child I once knew is in there somewhere." She was rewarded by a smile. "I know, it is hard to imagine him as anything other than he is."

Sitting alone, thinking, had done Mark some good. He felt calmer, now what he had admitted to himself, that he himself was at fault. Almost, resigned. He decided, it was time to see if Kalea still clung to life. He hoped to God she did.

Opening the door quietly, Mark stepped in. Seeing Essie, he nodded. "How is she?" She indicated the bed and he looked to see Kalea sitting up watching him warily. "Thank God!" striding towards the bed, he hesitated to go to her and instead perched on the end. "I'm glad to see you awake." His voice was gentle and warm. She did not acknowledge him. "Madam, I did you a great disservice," he admitted not looking at her. "I am a fool and there is no greater fool than a king." He looked at her and she returned his gaze, her face showing nothing, her eyes-only wariness. Not looking away, he continued. "I allowed my petty need for vengeance to use you as a weapon. It was cruel and unnecessary." She still said nothing. "I come to ask your forgiveness. No. Beg your forgiveness. I am sorry that I hurt you, I am a fool." He humbled himself before her. Behind him, Essie could not hide her shock. She had never thought to see the day.

For a while, the room was quiet and Mark began to fear that she would not speak to him. Finally, Kalea spoke. "I would ask one thing."

"It is yours, if I can give it," Mark replied without hesitation.

"Will you promise that you will never give me to your warband." Mark's heart lurched. This is why she had thought to take her life, the fear of whoring for the warband. She continued. "Promise me, that you would give me a quick death rather than that."

He moved up the bed and took her hand gently. "I give you my oath as King of Cornwall, that my warband will never have you. I promise with my heart, that my warband will never have you. I will not promise you death, Kalea, I will promise you a life."

Essie grinned. He loved her and he didn't even know it himself yet.

"Then, I will forgive you, if you can forgive me."

He lent forward and kissed her cheek. "I deserved it. There is nothing to forgive."

And peace once again reigned in Mark's castle.

Alan, rode up to Kai. They were riding at a steady pace. There was no need to hurry now. They would camp over night near the border and then they would go their separate ways.

Kai looked at Alan quizzically. "Go on. What do you want to say?"

Alan smiled ruefully. "Kalea was going to be your woman?"

Kai looked ahead before replying. "Kalea was going to be my wife."

Alan was silent for a moment. "I'm sorry."

"Don't be," Kai responded, "at least, I now know that she is safe. And your father," as Alan looked at him. "There is no doubt that he is your father. But your father seems to be caring for her well. Kalea is one of those sweet women who come rarely into your life and deserves to be treated well. I admit, I would have had her for myself." He shrugged. "I had to know, that she was alive and I can rest a little easier knowing she is well cared for. She is a good woman."

Alan looked thoughtfully at Kai. "I will promise you, that the warband will never have her."

"It is of no concern to me now," Kai said with a trace of bitterness. "At the time, I last saw her, she was well."

"You are a good man, Kai."

"Am I? We shall see. I will have to go back to womanising." He grinned at Alan. "I am beginning to think this thing between my legs is only good for pissing with."

Alan laughed.

Arthur hearing this, wondered what his friend was really feeling.

Mark left the hall early that night. Mary was watching Kalea, but she was asleep. Mark dismissed Mary and after she left, stripped off and climbed into bed with Kalea. Feeling him, get in, she tensed.

"I will not harm you," he whispered. "I just want to hold you." And he pulled her back into his lap. Kalea snuggled back and he held her close to him. "I'm so glad I didn't lose you." Then he slept.

Mark woke still holding Kalea close. As he rose, she woke. Turning sleepily towards him. "Mark?"

Smiling, he turned. "Good morning my lady. Shall I serve you breakfast in bed?"

"Yes. Please." Kalea watched his naked body as he went to fetch her some food. Piling her plate with oatcakes that he liberally spread with honey, he filled a beaker with milk and came back with his best swagger. Kalea was hard pushed not to laugh. This surprised her. She thought that she would hate him, but she didn't. The evidence of her attack on him were evident, and she realised that her aim had been true, if he hadn't had the well-honed skills of a warrior and been so fast, she would have slit his throat from ear to ear. As it was, the cut to his throat, had but nicked him deeply, then shallowed out to a slash that crossed his collar bone. He had taken the bandage that had criss-crossed his chest but the one on his arm was a little deeper and that he still wore. She sighed. He was just a man after all. Handing her the plate and the beaker, he returned to get some for himself.

Slipping back into the bed he began to eat before speaking. "Thank you, for not turning me away last night."

This was not a king, but a man, confessing his need. Kalea, still pale and needing recovery time, smiled and said, "The comfort of your arms was welcome."

Mark was strangely pleased. Grateful for these kind words. Perhaps she could forgive him. "I will not burden you with my company this day. I have things to do. I will send Mary to you."

"My thanks." She drank her milk and watched him dress. She noted that he made sure his wounds were well hidden. Then he came over and kissed her tenderly on the lips before he left.

The warband found him to be in better humour today and for that they were grateful. There were many theories about what had galled him yesterday. Blaming it first on Arthur and then Kalea.

Leith hearing them, hoped Kalea was alright but was told that Mark had left strict instructions that she was not to be disturbed.

That evening, Mark ate in the hall alone. It was not unnoticed. Once he had finished eating, he left with barely a word to his warriors.

Taking a flagon of wine, he returned to his chamber. Mary rose from the seat by the fire as he entered. He gave her a smile and then waved her away. She went reluctantly and Mark guessed that she felt protective. Seating himself in the chair she had vacated, he poured a glass of wine and looked to his bed, where Kalea slept.

Shortly after, he undressed and went to Kalea. She moved sleepily over to allow him in. Taking her into his arms, he held her close. She was such a little thing. "Good night my sweet heart," he whispered.

The days passed. Mark healed, Kalea got stronger. On the fourth day, Essie decided that Kalea was strong enough to take a walk. Mark had cossetted her, and offered his arm to support her. Naturally enough, he took her to the stables. As she entered the stable, the stallion saw her and neighed excitedly. She laughed; Mark was pleased to hear her laughter again.

"Have you missed me?" she said walking towards him, holding out some apple that Mark had given her for him. He threw his head up and down in excitement. She offered him the apple which he snaffled up and then putting his head over her shoulder, pulled her towards him. Still laughing, she put her arms around his neck cuddling him. The horse was so gentle with her, almost sensing her vulnerability. Opening the door, she picked up his halter. "Would you like to come out in the sunshine for a bit?" He obediently dropped his head into the halter and then even without being led, followed her out into the yard. Mark moved clear, wary of the big beast. She led him to the paddock and she opened the gate for him and he went through, but surprisingly, didn't canter off but stood looking at her. "You want me to come?" She went through the gate and he started to nudge her. "I can't run. Shall I get on?"

"I don't think you should," Mark worried.

"I'll be fine." She started climbing the fence. Mark rushed to assist. Midnight edged closer to enable her to scramble on. Once she sat forward and stroked his neck, he began to move forward. "What a good boy you are," she murmured then sat up straight. Calmly, he took her for a tour of the paddock, then he began to trot. Mark's heart came up in his mouth, but Kalea sat firm and entwined her hands in his mane. Then he broke into a canter and Mark heard her laughter bubble up inside her and suddenly, the pair were having a grand time. Mark smiled. It was lovely to see her happy. They moved as one and it was a joy to watch. He was playing with her. Who would have thought that this animal which held the stable hands in fear, loved this young woman? This was not going to be his new warhorse; this was going to be Kalea's new warhorse. At last, Midnight came back to the gate and Kalea slid from his back. Patting him and praising him. Mark opened the gate and Kalea walked through with Midnight following behind like a dog. Then she put him back in the stable and the pair stood head-to-head, the horse blowing softly on her. With a last pat, she came back and took Mark's arm.

"That's was wonderful," she announced. He looked down at her sparkling eyes and flushed cheeks.

"It seems to have done you some good." Smiling at him, she nodded. "Do you feel up to going to the market place?"

"Yes. I think I can manage."

He led her through the market and watched her looking about. "Look! Blackberries! Autumn is really here."

"Would you like some, my lady?"

"Yes. Please." Fishing in his purse, he tossed a coin to the shopkeeper who passed Kalea a small woven basket. Taking it, she kissed him on the cheek and then popped one into her mouth. "They are delicious. Would you like one?"

"May I?"

Kalea popped one into his mouth. Before they had finished them, they arrived at the stall of the shoemaker's stall. "William," Mark called. The man came over.

"My Liege. What can I do for you today?"

"I think my lady could do with a new pair of riding boots." Kalea stood agog.

"I still have the young lady's measurements but I will need to have to measure the length of her leg and round her calf. If you don't mind?" Mark gestured to Kalea and William went to his knees in front of her. "Would you take your boots off?" she did as he asked and allowed him to measure her calf and the length from ankle to knee. "All done. Thank you, my lady." Kalea stomped her boots back on. "I shall get to work on them."

"Thank you, William." Mark took her hand and threaded it through his arm. "Now, madam. I am taking you back for a rest." She lent her head against his shoulder.

"I am ready for one now."

The moment, Mark was certain that Kalea was safely abed, he went back down to the hall to look for Leith.

Leith was eating with the rest of his warriors. As Mark approached, the warriors watched to see who he was looking for. He came and sat opposite Leith studying him. Leith refused to acknowledge him.

For a while, they sat there as such, neither speaking. Finally, Leith looked up and glared at him.

"You don't like me much, do you?" Mark stated calmly.

"No. You're wrong. I don't like you at all," Leith stated flatly.

The warband were silent, listening to this exchange.

"That's fair enough," Mark answered. "I've come to talk to you about Kalea."

"How is she? I haven't seen her for a long while." Leith met his eye steadily.

"She has not been well. But she is getting better. You will be able to see her soon."

"When?"

"As soon as she is able." Mark sighed. "I would like to know more about her. What can you tell me?"

"Why?" Leith demanded.

Mark studied him thoughtfully. "Because she is special and I have a mind to keep her."

Could this fierce, ruthless king have fallen for her? Leith wondered. "That she is," he agreed. "What do you want to know?"

Mark shrugged. "Whatever you know."

"She is the most irritating, frustrating woman child, I have ever met," he began, watching Mark carefully. "She is strong willed, stubborn and argumentative. But she is also, sweet, caring, strong, resourceful and has a joy about her. She is quick to laugh and slow to anger. Brave beyond normal women." Mark nodded encouraging him to continue. "She plays down that she

185

spitted that Saxon, but if you'd seen the size of him, she was brave to take him on."

"How is it that someone as exceptional as she, did not marry?"

Leith grinned sourly. *She would have, if you hadn't stolen her*, he thought. "Kalea was a wild child. More interest in horses, than people. She says they are far less complicated. When most girls were learning the craft of how to be a good wife, and flirting with the lads. Kalea was learning how to gentle a horse and deliver foals. Of course, lads were interested, but Kalea wasn't and her father wasn't helpful at all. There were none good enough for his girl."

"Kai said she had skill with a sword?"

"Kai shouldn't have spoken of it."

"There is no shame in it," Mark said evenly.

Leith shrugged. "For a maiden, she wasn't very maidenly. Horses, swimming and sword play. Not exactly what every man wants for a wife."

Grinning Mark replied. "No. Agreed. But that is what makes her so special."

"Kalea traded for a boys' sword." Leith continued watching Mark. The man was in love with her although perhaps he didn't know it himself yet. In some ways he was glad, it meant Kalea was safer. "It wasn't much of a sword, but it can take and deliver a blow. She wanted to know how to defend herself. I called it toothpick to irritate her, but she took the teasing well. To please her, I started teaching her some sword skills."

"And?"

"She's works hard and she is not half bad. If she had a man's strength, she would make a decent warrior. Not great but decent. But she is fast and agile. Yes. She has bloodied her sword. No. She wasn't frightened in a fight and gave a good account of herself. Then treated the wounded."

Mark was stunned. This girl was indeed exceptional and he couldn't believe that she could achieve so much. "I would keep her with me. You have been kept under constant watch and a warrior of your stature does not deserve it. You, are a respected warrior. Arthur speaks highly of you. I would not care to keep you caged any longer, so I offer you a place in the warband. Leith, she is very fond of you and I think you know, that you are staying here for a good while at least. For her sake, I make you this offer." Leith said nothing and continued to stare at Mark. "I would offer you freedom, but I think you wouldn't leave without Kalea."

"You're right." No emotion showed on Mark's face as he met Leith's stare. "You're fond of her, aren't you?" It was more of a statement than a question.

Mark nodded. "I admit, I am. She is an exceptional woman."

"She is," Leith agreed.

"All that I require from you, is that you give me a warrior's oath that you will not bear arms against me."

"Will you give me your oath that no harm will befall Kalea and that she will not be given to the warband when your need for her is over? It is her greatest fear."

Conditions. Mark had not expected that. He had already promised this to Kalea. The old warrior was a wily old fox. "In front of witnesses, I, Mark, King of Cornwall, do swear, that I shall never give her over to the warband." The warband were shocked, there were some groans, but the fox had been out foxed.

"Then, I, Leith of the warrior clan, do give you my oath, that while I am in your warband, I will not raise arms against you."

He really is clever, Mark thought. Even conditions in his oath. But it would do. Mark nodded. "Then Leith, welcome to the warband." There were cheers. They had come to like the old man or at least respect him. When the cheering and back slapping had quietened down, Mark spoke. "Col! See that our new warrior has what he needs." And with that he rose and left.

They made a good pair, Mark concluded. The girl who dressed like a boy and a one-eyed old warrior who had seen better days. He grinned. Who'd have thought that the two of them, would manage to negotiate such a fair deal with a man who was far from fair.

The hall that evening was in high spirits. Leith was taking some good-natured ribbing about how he had managed to deprive them of a fine prize. The old warrior took it all with a smile. He had a sword strapped to his thigh and a dagger in his belt. He was with his own kind. Not Arthur's granted. But warriors were warriors and they weren't such a bad set of lads.

He looked to Mark who was smiling at the banter and acknowledged Leith with a nod which was returned. It wasn't what they had wanted, but he admitted, it might not be too bad after all.

Mark left the hall with a yawn. It wasn't late, but he was tired. It had been a trying few weeks. Not everything had turned out as he had planned. Including getting his throat cut, and his woman opening her wrists. It had rocked him on his heels and he wasn't used to that. Wearily, he plodded up to his chamber. It had been his sanctuary before Kalea had hit it like a storm and despite the fact that it was as it had been, he still opened the door with trepidation. The candles were lit and the fire blazed cheerfully. Everything was calm and as it should be. Looking over to the bed, he saw Kalea was asleep. Stripping off his clothes, he slid in beside her with a sigh. As he gathered her into his arms, she stirred and he shushed her, like you would a child.

Turning in his arms, she sleepily kissed his chest. Mark found that he almost didn't dare to breathe. Then she started kissing across the scars that she had caused. Then she came up, kissing his neck and his ears. Mark didn't dare move his breath caught in his throat. Then kissing his eyes, she finally arrived at his lips, flicking her tongue over his lips. He gasped. "Kalea," he whispered huskily. He was aroused and he was frightened of hurting her. "I…" she silenced him, kissing him deeply. The passion rose but Mark held himself in check and made sure that he made love to her in a way that was both tender and gentle. She however, was eager for him, urging him. At last, they both lay spent in each other's arms. "Welcome back my lady," he murmured. He felt her smile against his chest. "I hope this time, I met with your approval."

"Yes, my lord. You did."

"I didn't know if you were ready for me." His voice was low and husky. "I didn't want to rush you."

"I am ready now." Kalea had been aroused by the fact that Mark had freed her from fear of being given to his warband, in addition, he had forgiven her for trying to kill him as a result she felt warm and grateful to him. She was now prepared to work for his regard and his affection.

"I guessed that," he said sleepily. He was also grateful that she had forgiven him for forcing himself on her. Turning on his side, he drew her to him and within moments, he slept.

Kalea waited for her guard to take her to Midnight. She sat fidgeting. When at last the door opened, it was Leith who walked in. "Leith!" She squealed with delight and threw herself into his arms, he returned her hug with interest.

"You look mighty fine girl." The girl's eyes were sparkling with delight and her cheeks were flushed. "I have been entrusted to take you to the stables." She immediately slotted her arm through his. "I hear that you have not been well."

She didn't look at him, when she replied. "I'm alright now." Leith knew she was not telling him something, but they had time now.

They soon arrived and Kalea turned to him. "You will have to wait here for a bit. He has no liking of strangers." Leith raised his eyebrows at her and she disappeared in to the gloom and he heard a horse whickering at her. "Hello my handsome boy. Shall we go out today?" The answer was obviously yes as Kalea emerged being followed docilely by a huge black horse. As he backed off and Kalea walked past him, she said. "This is Midnight. Apparently, his heart is as black as his coat. Would you grab a saddle? I have a mind to try him with one today."

Leith grinned and wandered in to find a suitable saddle. By the time he returned, both Kalea and Midnight were in the paddock and he was like a lamb with her. Popping the saddle on the top rail of the fence, he climbed up to sit and watch. Kalea led him to the saddle so that he could examine it, which he did, thoroughly. Then, Kalea picked it up and put it on his back. He looked over his shoulder at her and then shook like a dog, spilling the saddle on the floor. Kalea bent down and picked it up and put it on his back again. Once again, the great horse shook himself and off it came again.

"Ornery beast," Leith commented.

"He's playing."

"Don't look like playing to me."

Kalea picked the saddle up and then threw it on the ground and stamped her foot. Midnight's ears flickered. Then picking it up again, she put it on his back. This time he stood still. Kalea grinned at Leith. She bent under him to grab the girth, and Midnight nudged her up the bottom sending her sprawling. Leith could swear that the big horse was smiling. Dusting herself off, Kalea rose grinning broadly. This time, she did not present her rear to him, and turned the other way. He looked over his shoulder at her and she grabbed the girth before he could think of something else to do. Cinching the girth was another matter. Midnight filled his chest with air and pushed out his stomach.

"He's a belligerent bugger."

Kalea still grinning, slapped him on the tummy and he let a big whoomph of air and Kalea yanked the girth tight. The horse turned his head, looking at her accusingly. Then before, he had any further time to think about it, she was on his back like a flash. Leaning forward, she put her arms round the big beast's neck. He started moving forward at a walk and Leith watched as Kalea sat up straight, then he was off, cantering in circles. Midnight thought he was doing as he wanted and Kalea's instructions were so subtle, that he had no idea, that she was controlling the situation. For a while, they romped round the paddock, Kalea's laughter floating over to Leith. Eventually, they walked up to the gate and Kalea slid to the floor and unsaddled Midnight. Putting the saddle on the top pole and grabbing the saddle blanket she called over her shoulder. "Come and join me Leith." Dropping off the fence, he followed her. When she reached the middle of the field, she spread the blanket and sat down. He flopped down beside her. He realised that this was so no one could hear them.

"Mark told me that you had agreed to join his warband."

Nodding, Leith turned to her, tapping the sword at his hip. "Yes. I guess, he got fed up feeding me and me doing nothing." Kalea laughed. "He made a very persuasive argument. But basically, he did it for you. It seems that he wants to keep you around for a while yet." He paused. "What was wrong with you girl? You obviously didn't want to talk about it in the castle."

Kalea sighed and then was rocked as Midnight laid down behind her. Leith couldn't believe it. Kalea grinned and then leaned back on him. "When Kai came," Leith noted it was not Arthur, it was Kai. "I was in such a fury."

"You had every right to be. You handled that well girl. Did you not hear, even the war band saluted you?"

"No. I didn't. I was in such a temper." She looked sheepish. "I am not proud of myself. I lost control. I threw things, I kicked things, I smashed things." And then admitted, "I had a tantrum." Leith grinned. "You're not surprised, are you?" Leith shook his head. "Any way, amongst the mess, there was a fruit knife and I nearly cut Mark's throat with it."

"You what?" he said incredulously.

"I nearly cut his throat."

He laughed. "Only nearly?"

Grinning, she answered. "I would have done it, if he hadn't been so damn fast."

"Did you hurt him?" Leith asked still laughing.

"Quite a bit actually." She pointed to her throat. "It went in here, but because he moved so fast, it shallowed out and went along his chest." She drew the line across her collarbone. Leith shook his head in disbelief. "And then we fought and I slashed his arm."

Leith was feeling alarmed. Mark was not one to let this behaviour go unpunished. "Did he hurt you?"

"Yes," she confessed. "He could have hurt me a lot more than he did. He contained me, by crushing my wrists." She wasn't about to tell him about the rape. "He could have beat me but he didn't and left to fetch his wise woman, Essie, to stitch him up." Looking down at her lap. "When he left, I...opened my wrists with a piece of pottery." Leith's heart lurched. "I thought, that I was sure my punishment would be the warband and I could not do it. On his way out, he told Mary to bring me some wine and help me clear up and Essie says, that if Mary hadn't caught me in time, I would have managed the job."

"Oh Kalea," Leith spoke softly. "My dear girl. I had no idea."

"Neither did Mark. Mary, is a dear girl and got Essie to come and see me after she had finished with Mark. To his credit, Mark was horrified and has done everything to ensure I recovered."

"Let me see," Leith commanded. Kalea rolled up her sleeves and extended her wrists. Leith hissed seeing the damage she had caused. "You will not have to worry again; Mark has given me an oath in front of the warband that he will not give you to the warband." Kalea grinned. "What?"

"He asked my forgiveness for treating me so poorly and the condition I gave him, was that he would promise not to give me to the warband. He gave me his oath as King of Cornwall." They both laughed.

"Do you love him?"

"No," Kalea said with no hesitation. "My heart calls only for Kai."

"Can you be happy?"

"Happy? No. Content? Perhaps. As I see it, we have no choice to make the most of what we have. I am content knowing that I won't be passed on to the warband. One man, not many. I can handle that. What about you?"

Leith shrugged. "I suppose, I could be content. Warriors generally, are fair. As long as he treats you fair."

"I know you won't believe me, Leith. But somewhere in there, there's a decent man hidden below." Leith grinned. "I know, I know, it's hard to believe. But every now and then, he is warm and gentle and I wonder, where that bit is hidden."

Leith laughed and shimmied over to lean against Midnight, who surprising, didn't seem at all bothered.

Mark riding in with his hunting party, wondered how the two were getting on. Throwing his reigns to a stable hand, he strode down to the paddock and had to smile as he saw the two of them, leaning against the great black horse talking and laughing. Turning on his heels, he left them too it. He felt good that he had done something good.

Autumn was no longer a question but a fact. The days if not damp and dismal, were bright and crispy. The time passed quickly and Kalea had been right, whilst it wasn't what they had wanted, they found that they were indeed content. Mark was perhaps, happier than he had been for a long time and he put that down to the fact that Kalea saw the joy in everything.

One morning when Leith collected her, she was surprised that they did not head for the stables.

"Where are we going?" she queried.

"I am to take you to the combat practice area. I think, Mark wants to show off his skill with a sword."

"Is he good?"

"Yes. As much as I hate to admit it," Leith begrudgingly conceded. "I'm hard pushed to hold him off."

Kalea grinned. "High praise indeed."

As they approached, the area was strangely quiet. They had expected to hear the clash of steel and good-natured calling. They looked at each other, and Leith moved Kalea so that he could draw his sword. When they arrived, Mark was on his own, going through practice moves with his mighty sword and came to a halt when he became aware of their presence.

"Good morning my lady." He gave Kalea a devilish smile.

"My Lord." Kalea bobbed a curtsey.

"I hear that you have a small skill with a sword." Kalea gave Leith an accusing stare and he shrugged. He moved with a grace that a younger man would have envied and picked up a boy's sword. "While, I have to question why I should want to give you a sharp pointy thing, I would see what you can do." Kalea laughed and blushed. Coming to her, he offered her the hilt on his arm in a noble gesture. Still blushing, she accepted it and he bowed low to her. "Shall we?" he gestured to the training area.

Leith sat down on one of the many benches at the perimeter and Kalea came over and offered him the sword while she removed her cloak and jacket. "This is of better quality than toothpick," he teased and was rewarded with a grin. "Now, don't kill him K. Remember he is the one that keeps us warm and fed."

He heard Mark laugh and Kalea took the sword. She tested the weight and gave it a few swings before turning to face Mark.

He bowed low. "When you are ready." Watching her as she limbered up. Suddenly, with no warning, she lunged at him, going for a high stroke, as Mark moved to block, she reversed her swing and came in low, forcing him to retreat a step to counter. His eyebrows rose. "Very good."

"Not that good K. You didn't press your advantage."

"Thank you, Leith," Mark said drily. Leith sat grinning happily.

"Go on K. Show him your moves."

"He knows my moves," Kalea replied with a cheeky smile at Mark and Leith laughed.

Mark was better prepared this time and had learned, that she actually did have a little skill with the sword. This time as she saw an opening, he jumped back, letting her momentum take her past him and giving her a thwack on the backside as she did. Leith howled with laughter as Kalea turned all indignant to Mark and then threw herself at him. The clash of steel rang out as the two blades met. Mark found that while he could indeed, handle her attacks, she was quick to see the smallest opening and quick enough to take advantage of it. She did make mistakes, but all young warriors did. Best here than in battle. Mark tried to disarm her and didn't succeed the first time and she managed to keep hold of the blade but the next time his blow was mighty and the vibration of blocking must have loosened her grip and with a swirl of his blade, Kalea's flew from her grip.

For a moment, she stood panting, shaking her wrist, then bowed low. "It seems my Lord, you have beaten me. I am here therefore at your mercy."

Leith applauded and Mark laughed. "Well done! You gave a good account of yourself."

Then Kalea did what Leith had seen her do before which was self-depreciating and guaranteed to make Mark laugh. "You are too kind. But…" At this point, she waggled her hands at him. "These are not going to stop you lopping my head off."

Mark bellowed with laughter. "Leith, you taught her well. If she can't disarm you with her sword, she can with her humour. Pick up your sword madam." Kalea picked up the sword. "Would you like to try again?" She gave no reply, but launched her attack. The big sword, parried the lighter one and she disengaged before he had a chance to disarm her and came in low. Mark sidestepped and with a glancing blow, deflected her blade. Very soon, Kalea was sweating hard and blowing harder. "I think, perhaps, we will stop there for today." Kalea nodded her agreement. Turning, Mark went and fetched a scabbard for her. "I have had the belt made longer," he said handing it to her. "That way, you can wear it at your hip, or if you prefer, over your back. Whichever you find easier."

Kalea now turned her attention back to the blade that he had given her. It was very fine, light but strong. "This is a most generous gift." She slid the blade into the scabbard. "Thank you."

"I was hoping it would win me a kiss." Kalea stepped willingly into his arms and they kissed deeply. Leith turned away, embarrassed at this shared intimacy. When they at last surfaced, he commented.

"You are a brave man indeed to arm her. For all the god's sake, do not upset her, she will geld you."

Mark laughed. "Now, shall we seek out some refreshment?" As they walked back to the hall, Mark with his arm about Kalea's shoulder he remarked. "The sword is called 'bee sting'." Leith roared with laughter and Mark continued with a wry smile. "Come now, Leith. It is a better name than 'toothpick'." Still chortling, Leith acknowledged he was right.

"Do you love him?" Leith asked as they walked arm in arm down to the stable.

"No," Kalea answered again without hesitation. Since Leith, had become her permanent body guard, he had asked her this often. "It is and always will be Kai," she answered firmly before continuing. "He treats me well Leith. He is kind and gentle and for that I am grateful."

"I did notice that he had mellowed since you cut his throat."

"Perhaps, that is it." Kalea giggled. "Somewhere in him, is a softer side."

"And you bring it out," Leith stated. "He loves you; you know that don't you?"

"Perhaps," Kalea said thoughtfully. "If he does, then I will make it my duty to ensure that I give him no call to hate me. He will never be as Kai was to me, but I will not have him hate me."

Midnight as usual, was pleased to see his friends. He now would wear full harness and still followed her about like a dog. Kalea had enlisted a stable hand to help her with him, the one she trusted most. Jack was a young lad and had a kind temperament. He was more than a little nervous, when she first introduced him to Midnight, but with her beside him, they had coaxed the horse to accept him and now Midnight allowed Jack to groom him and tack him up.

Once in the paddock, Kalea put the great black war horse through his paces. He really was getting very good. Leith had been helping by yelling, shouting and rattling his sword. At first, Midnight hadn't liked it one bit, rearing and plunging but now, he had become accustomed to this loud noise. Leith began the ritual. Waving his cloak and yelling, while Kalea rode Midnight straight at him at a gallop. At the last minute, the horse pulled up sharp and then almost contemptuously, reached out and gave Leith a shove with his nose, sending him sprawling on his backside. Kalea burst out laughing.

"Bloody bugger!" Leith grumbled getting to his feet and brushing himself off. The horse was as bad as the girl.

"Come on Leith," Kalea chided. "Give him his due. He could have run straight over you."

"He's still a bloody bugger," he grumbled giving the horse a rub on the nose.

"I think he is ready for Mark."

"I think your right," Leith agreed.

The next morning, Mark accompanied them down to the stable. He had heard much about the beast from the lads. Young Jack was proud to boast that Midnight would only allow him into his stable. The others when they tried, were threatened with bites and kicking.

Once again, Midnight followed Kalea out and into the paddock. This time she called for Mark to join her. Taking his hand in hers, she gently reached out to the horse and put Mark's hand on the velvety nose. His ears, flicked but he allowed the touch as Kalea encouraged him. Then drawing Mark to the saddle, she motioned for him to mount. Kalea soothed as Mark swung neatly up. Kalea came to Mark and laid a hand on his thigh. "I have taught him to respond to knee and weight. Be light on the reign, you will not need them much." He nodded to her, looking down into her excited face. Almost with no instruction, Midnight moved off. Mark shifted weight and Midnight went straight into a canter. He was well trained. As they galloped round the paddock, all three humans smiled. Then, Kalea motioned to Leith and the two of them began yelling, waving their swords and capes. Mark, hesitated for a moment, but only a moment and the big horse plunged forward unfazed by the noise. Mark was worried that he might run them down but at the last minute, he skidded to a halt and gave Kalea a hefty shove with his nose. With a whoosh of breath, Kalea landed on her backside and Leith laughed.

"I told you he was a bloody bugger."

Grinning Kalea got to her feet and rubbed Midnight's face. "So, how do you like your new warhorse my lord?"

"I think that like the woman who trained him, he is exceptional." Mark slid lightly from the saddle and patted the horse's neck. "However, he is not my warhorse." Kalea looked perplexed. "He is your warhorse. He loves you as much as you love him and I would not part you from him." Kalea threw herself at him and he lifted her and spun her round. Leith and Midnight watched with amusement.

Chapter 8
Wolves of Winter

Winter was upon them. It was bitterly cold and the snow was falling. In the castle, all was well. The yule log was in and sufficient food to last until spring, hopefully. Some travelling entertainers were welcomed and kept the hall in songs and stories. Winter was a good time of year for all, even the people of the village. The work for the year was done and all that was to be done, was keep warm and wait for spring.

Sitting at the top table with Kalea beside him, Mark couldn't help wonder how his life had changed so much in half a year. This young, beautiful woman had captivated him. He was loathe to admit it, even to himself, but he loved her. He watched her smiling at the entertainment. Was it that she seemed to be so happy always? He wondered. It had awoken in him the ability to see the joy in the little things. The sex between them, was hot and sensuous just thinking of it aroused him. He loved the way she held him to her. The way he felt so powerful and yet gentle with her.

Leith had fitted in well with the warband, taking the ribbing of being too old in good part. It had helped that he had put a few of them on their arses in the training square. *I maybe one-eyed,* he thought, *but I can still give theses puppies a run for their money.*

Kalea watching the hall with excitement, could not believe how far she had come either. She had learned so much about love making and was an eager and willing partner. More than willing to try what he asked of her, she could not believe what she had done both with him and to him. Just the thought made her body warm and her face flush. She did not love him, but she did desire him.

Sitting next to her, sipping mead, Mark glanced at her and saw that her colour was high. Running a finger over her thigh he whispered in her ear. "What are you thinking of my lady?"

"You," she murmured quietly. Her pupils were huge, and her already dark eyes looked black with her lust for him.

Mark took a sharp intake of breath. By the gods, she was gorgeous. "Perhaps, we should adjourn for a short while," he said with a slow smile, which was returned.

"What an excellent idea."

They almost, sneaked out although it didn't go unnoticed in the hall. No way was Mark going to take her to his chamber. There wasn't the time. Thrusting her through the door to the receiving room, he slammed it shut and leaning against it pulled her into his arms. As they kissed, Kalea released him from his trousers and then sank to her knees before him. "No, no, no, no," Mark growled as she took him into her mouth. "I will be too quick." Taking her by the elbows he drew her up. As he kissed her, he turned so that her back was against the door and then lifting her skirts, entered her. She was hot and ready. Mark did try and exercise some control but could not maintain it. He need not have worried as Kalea was right behind him, shuddering with the force of her own orgasm. "By the gods, woman. You are a temptress." He smiled against her lips. "I haven't been this lusty, since I was your age."

"I, so needed you," she whispered into his mouth.

"So, I see. I hope I lived up to expectations." They both stood still locked together against the door.

"More than." She smiled. He withdrew, leaving Kalea feeling somehow incomplete. Her skirts fell to the floor again.

Adjusting his clothing, he looked over his shoulder and gave her a devilish smile. Kalea laughed.

They slipped back into the hall and took their places. Consternation on his face, he watched as Kalea lifted her skirts at the back before she sat, arranging them around her. Raising an eyebrow, he looked at her and she giggled.

"My lord. I do not wish to ruin my dress and everyone will know what we have been up to if I have a wet patch on the back of my skirts."

"You cunning little minx." He laughed, took her hand and kissed it. "They will know anyway?"

"How?"

"How can they not? We are both looking very satisfied." She giggled. "You really are quite delightful."

"And you my lord, a quite desirable."

It was a true yule celebration. The women were invited into the hall as well as the warriors. Meat was being roasted. The yule log burned brightly and Kalea thought it was so big, it might still be burning in spring. The day dawned and Kalea and Mark were woken by Mary bringing in breakfast. Snuggled deep under the furs, they were warm and cosy and in no rush to leave. Mary had thrown more kindling on to the fire and smiled as she left.

"Stay there," Kalea ordered and then sprinted naked from the bed to grab some food and bring it back to him. He smiled. The smile she had come to know meant that he approved. Then pouring them each a beaker of milk, she climbed back in and snuggled her now cool body against his warm one.

"You my lady, are incorrigible."

"Whatever that means, I expect you are right." Kalea munched her oatcake and washed it down with milk. "It is still snowing. We never had so much snow in East Anglia. Although it did get very cold." Having finished eating and unwilling to get out again. Kalea took his plate and her own, and leaning out the bed placed the plates on the floor. Mark pounced on her.

"What a delightful sight. Stay where you are. I have a yule present for you." Kalea smiled.

"I am ready to receive it," she purred as she pushed back against him.

After, they lay together in the warm furs and Mark began to doze. Kalea stayed still not wishing to disturb him. Just when she thought he was asleep, he stirred.

"This won't do." He stretched. "Everyone will be bustling round and here we are, lazy pair." Giving her a light slap on the rump and causing her to squeal, he rose. As he dressed, he turned to look at her as she reclined provocatively on the furs. "You're insatiable." He grinned.

"I expect I'm that too." Kalea grinned. "You taught me all I know. You are firmly to blame."

He chuckled and went to his chest. From it, he produced a blood red dress. "Here you are my lady. I have you a special yule dress." Kalea scrambled out of bed to him.

This was beautiful. The material soft and embroidery of green holly leaves with golden vines. "Oh!" she exclaimed. "This is beautiful." She slipped it over her head and allowed him to lace her in. The look on his face told her, that he was pleased with the result. "This is so unfair. I have nothing to give you." She pouted.

Laughing, he kissed the big bottom lip. "Your company is enough, K."

She liked him calling her K. Leith had started it and now it became her pet name.

Hurriedly, she washed her face and brushed her hair until it shone. This was something Mark never tired of, watching her combing out the bed knots and smoothing the dark hair. Popping on her soft leather slippers, she stood up and twirled for him. Mark sighed. She was so lovely. It did worry him at how much he wanted her but to give her credit, she gave him no cause to worry that she would play him false.

Then together they went into the hall. Mark was not wrong. Everything was a bustle. The hall had been decorated with holly and mistletoe and everyone was in high excitement for the evening entertainment. Kalea suddenly saw Leith at the far end of the hall and letting go of Mark's arm went pitter pattering and skipping down the hall calling to Leith. Mark smiling, noted how all the men's eyes followed her. Leith caught her and swirled her round.

"Look at you!" he exclaimed. "My girl's all grown up." Giggling, she kissed his cheek. "K, you look like a vision." Kalea held out her skirts for him to inspect. He nodded in approval. "Are you enjoying it so far?"

"Yes. I like the decorations. It's not the weather to be out in, is it?"

"No. The snow's getting deep."

Mark joined them. "Leith." They clasped hands. "K seems quite excited."

"Our celebrations were a lot smaller and we had huts, not castles," Leith said. "She looks very beautiful in her new dress."

"Yes, she does," Mark agreed.

Kalea, looked embarrassed. Leith grinned. "She doesn't take compliments well." He nodded towards Kalea who was squirming a bit. "It is because she doesn't think she is worth it."

They were interrupted by a visitor; a druid bard had appeared at the castle doors despite the weather. His cloak had been taken from him and he came to Mark, who greeted him warmly. "Valim! You are welcome in this hall. What brings you out in this weather?"

Valim bowed low, "I have had urgent business to attend to and thought I might take shelter here for the Yule, if you will permit me."

"Of course, dear man. Please be seated." Mark indicated a seat at his table. Kalea looked on shyly. He was obviously a man of great importance. Mark sent for food and wine. "Let me introduce you to my lady, Kalea. Kalea this is Valim a wise druid and bard."

This gave Kalea an excuse to look at this druid. She had only seen one before, and that when she was a child. She had thought them all gone. It was hard to judge how old he was. His skin was lined and his long hair was grey and tied back in a tail, but his piercing blue eyes were those of a much younger man. He could be anywhere between 40 and 60.

Valim regarded the girl with great interest as she smiled at him. "I have heard some talk about you lady."

Kalea blushed and Mark laughed. "Sir, I hope what you hear is good."

"What is it you hear?" Mark asked, wondering what Valim had heard.

Not taking his eyes from Kalea, he answered. "I hear that Mark of Cornwall has a new spring Queen. That she is fae and has a way about her."

Kalea's eyes widened in surprise as Mark turned to her. "Are you fae, K? Have you indeed cast a spell on me?"

She gave her delightful throaty chuckle. "Indeed, I am not. No one has said that I am a changeling and I have never even tried to cast a spell. I have a way with horses and dogs, but that is no way magic and I am far too clumsy to be a fairy."

"You have indeed got a way about you." Valim studied her carefully and Kalea began to feel most uncomfortable. Mark laughed.

"Yes. She has. Although I don't think she is aware of quite how powerful her ways are."

"Tsk! My lord. You tease me."

"And yet," Valim said consideringly, "you stir strong emotions in people."

Kalea was taken aback. "Yes," she admitted. "You are right. But this is something that has happened since my home was raised by the Saxons. Do you think someone has put a spell on me?" she asked concerned.

Valim laughed exposing white even teeth. "No. Kalea, I don't think you are bewitched. I think maybe, something that was asleep within you, was awoken." He had fascinated her.

Leaning forward. "I don't feel any different," she confided. "Yet, I hadn't thought of what you said, but I somehow feel you are right."

"Of course, he's right," Mark interjected. "He is a wise and respected druid."

"May I ask a question?" Valim nodded and Kalea continued. "Is there still a Merlin of Britain?"

"What do you think?"

"I don't know. People in my village were always saying, 'by Merlin's beard' and such like and I have heard the stories of Merlin's magic. We have, or had an oak grove, and we were always respectful and left offerings in the circle, but I haven't seen any druids in it."

Valim smiled kindly. "Yes. We still have a Merlin, although both the Romans and the Christians would rather, we hadn't. Our Merlin, is young and called Accolon. A Welsh prince and a talented druid. Perhaps, you will meet him one day."

"I'm not sure I want to," Kalea confessed. "I find it all a bit scary."

"And yet you are brave woman." Mark watched the exchange with interest. He liked Valim a lot, but had little doubt that he would use people for his own means. "You would make a valuable priestess."

"Oh no," Kalea protested. "Please don't even consider it. I am happy with my life as it is." Silently adding, *I would not give my life to the gods.*

Valim smiled and Mark took her hand. "Have no fear, my sweetheart. I will not let him whisk you away from me." Mark met Valim's eye, his refusal in his eye and Valim nodded in agreement. "Would you stay in the hall with the warriors Valim? Or would you prefer your own room."

"I shall stay in the hall." Valim had no wish to be on his own. Gossip from the hall was far more interesting.

Mark opened the door to his chamber quietly. He had been unable to find Kalea in the chaos of the hall, and had thought this the only place she could be. He was right. Kalea was asleep on the bed. Bending over her, he kissed her smooth cheek. "My lady. The feast is about to start and they are waiting for us."

Kalea opened her eyes and smiled at him. Then sat up rubbing her eyes. "It was so noisy in the hall, I thought to escape for a bit," she explained. "I didn't mean to go to sleep."

Mark waved away her explanation. "It is of little consequence." He watched her as she splashed her face with water and then ran the comb through her hair. "K. Your hair is beautiful."

Kalea gave him a cheeky grin. "It is when it is groomed. It was not always so. I expect at times it looked like I had birds nesting in it." He grinned back. "I used to wear it in a tail or a braid mostly to keep it out the way."

He took her hand. "Come my lady. Let's see what feasts are awaiting us."

Kalea was amazed at how much had changed since she had last been there. The hall had been laid out differently, to allow a large empty area in the middle. More tables and benches had appeared to cope with the extra people. Sitting next to Mark, the serving people began bringing out large platters of steaming meat, hot bread, butter, vegetables and fruit. The noise was colossal, as people enjoyed copious amounts of ale, mead and wine. Valim stood and raised his staff, the hall fell silent, then the druid gave the Yule blessing and the noise erupted again.

Mary, suddenly turned up at the table and Kalea smiled at her ally. She bobbed a curtsey to Mark and then turned to Kalea. "I have a gift for you."

Kalea looked horrified. "Mary! You really shouldn't give me gifts. I have so much already and I have nothing to give in return."

With a smile, Mary bought her hand from behind her back and in it, was a crown that she had made of holly and mistletoe. "It is a small thing. When I saw your dress, I thought that you needed a crown."

Kalea rose and came round to give the girl a hug and a kiss. "It is so beautiful. Thank you so much Mary." Mary put it on the girl's head and with a small bow to Mark, returned to serving.

"My Yule Queen," Mark said smiling at her flushed face. Coming back to her seat, she lent to kiss his cheek. "What was that for?" he asked.

"Just because," Kalea answered.

The musicians, having already eaten their fill, struck up a tune and Mark took Kalea's hand. "My lady." At Kalea's alarmed look. "It is traditional for the King to start the dancing. You do dance?"

"Yes," Kalea confessed. "But not well." But allowed herself to be led onto the floor. A great cheer went up and he heard her lowly say. "Oh dear!"

However, she was not a poor dancer and was able to follow his lead with ease. Soon they were laughing as they spun across the floor. More dancers joined them. The joy on Kalea's face, spurred Mark to make moves that he would not otherwise have dared to make her laugh. As they made their way back to the table, Leith grabbed her hand and dragged her back onto the floor. Mark watched with amusement as the old warrior danced with a good deal more enthusiasm than skill. Leith blowing heavily tried to return Kalea to Mark, but was intercepted by Alan. Kalea was flushed with exertion and made a pretty partner. Watching the two youngsters, Mark raised an eyebrow at what he perceived as an inappropriate touch from his son who was obviously drawn to this lovely young woman. Rising, he cut in, and Alan bowed low, realising that he was being gently reminded, just whose woman she was. Mark managed to get Kalea back to her seat.

"What fun!" she exclaimed excitedly taking a big swallow of wine.

"You may be advised to drink the ale, if you are thirsty. Too much wine will give you a headache in the morning." He motioned over a serving woman, who gave Kalea a large beaker of ale. She was not at all bothered. Wine wasn't much to her liking anyway.

Kalea danced the night away. She danced with Mark, Leith and Mary. She even danced with the druid Valim who was a skilled dancer. Alan didn't ask again. Mark shared many things with his son, but not his women. It was late, and Kalea's feet hurt, but she was happy. The people in the hall were beginning to drift away, some had already passed out at their tables. Mark leant over and took her hand and Kalea was willing to leave. Still wearing her crown, they left.

Mark shut the door and took her into his arms. "My beautiful winter Queen." He kissed her passionately. With his lips against her, he breathed. "Do you think you could love me, just a little?"

Kalea was surprised to admit. She could and her answer was whispered. "I think, perhaps, I already do." His heart lurched as he went to kiss her again, but she pulled away and stepping back placed her crown on the table and then lifting her dress over her head, she replaced the crown. Standing naked before him, she could see his desire in his eyes. "As your Winter Queen," she spoke boldly. "Tonight, I will do with you as I please."

He gave her that slow smile and bowed low. "I will be as you wish my Queen."

She stepped forward and backed him against the base of the bed. "Sit." Obediently he did so, feeling more aroused by the moment. She bent and took his boots off. "Stand." He did so. She stripped him of his shirt and ran her hands over his chest. Then she unlaced his trousers and pulled them off. As she came up, she took him into her mouth. Mark hissed and bit his lip in an effort to control himself. Just when he thought he could stand it no longer, she stopped and stood up. With a none to gentle shove, she pushed him back on the bed and before he knew it, she was astride him. He held her hips as she ground into him. It wasn't long before he could control himself no longer and she still rode him and with a gasp, her orgasm shook her causing her to collapse against his chest. Neither said a word or moved until with great skill, Mark rolled her onto her back without disengaging.

Smiling down at her, he spoke with a voice full of warmth. "Well, my Queen, shall we continue? Or would you allow, your poor servant to take his rest?"

"If my poor servant is so tired, perhaps we should rest." She tried to sound imperious, but failed. "I am not so heartless as to drive you to exhaustion." She lent up and kissed the corner of his smiling mouth.

He moved to the side. "I am grateful." Fully content, he drew her into his arms.

She loved him a little. That would do. He thought as he drifted off to sleep.

It took longer for Kalea to sleep. She had shocked herself, admitting that she did indeed love Mark. Not the all-consuming love she felt for Kai. But it was nevertheless, love she felt for him. Snuggling back into his arms, sleep stole in and took her.

The celebrations rolled on for days. The castle was full of happy and hungover people. On the fourth day, they received a visitor. When the man was bought before Mark, the hall fell silent. The news this raggedy man was bringing, could not be good. No one went out in this weather unless they had no choice. The man took a knee in front of Mark, who acknowledged him.

"Who are you?" He waved the man to stand, which he did.

"My name is Martin, my liege." Mark waited for him to continue. "I come from a village beyond the forest yonder and we beg for your help."

"And how may I help you?"

"We are being attacked by wolves."

"Have you no axes?"

Martin bristled. "Yes. We have axes. But if we go to the forest to gather firewood, they still manage to take you. We have lost two men in the forest, another bringing cattle from the byre to be slaughtered and a woman and her child travelling from their home to the village hall where we are all sheltering. Even going to feed the animals is a risk."

Mark considered thoughtfully. "And yet you are here."

"I was the only one brave enough to seek help."

Mark nodded. "Then I will come. We will come on the morrow." Turning to his steward, he said, "Feed him and find him somewhere warm to sleep. Get some provisions from the store that we may take them with us."

Martin bowed low. "My thanks." And then followed the steward out.

"Alan!" Mark called. "Find me six that would leave their hearth. I will leave at first light."

"I would come," Kalea said.

"K. It is cold and the snow is deep."

"I would come," she repeated stubbornly. Leith watching smiled. Same old Kalea. "It's not as if you are going to battle or chasing about in the forest after the wolves," she added. "You will just go to see. I would be with you."

Mark looked at her harshly. "Then, madam, if you insist, you may come."

She nodded firmly and Mark looked to Leith, seeing him smiling, he rolled his eyes.

Valim, the druid took the exchange in and said nothing. She was indeed an interesting woman.

As soon as the light broke, the group were ready to leave. Leith and Col were amongst the six warriors chosen to go. Kalea with her cape wrapped tightly round her, sat astride Midnight, who was not at all sure he should be out in this weather and was skittish. Martin led them on what Leith laughingly called Doris, the carthorse.

The pace was slow as the horses struggled with the depth of the snow. It got easier when they reached the forest as the snow had not been able to settle so deeply. The forest was eerily quiet and all the men were on edge. There was no chatter the only sound being the creak of leather and hooves hitting the hard ground. Kalea had bee sting at her back and she was mighty glad of it. She peered nervously into the gloom for signs of movement.

It was nearly noon, when they emerged into the village on the edge of the forest. The village was devoid of movement. Everyone being sheltered in the hall. They dismounted and Martin called that he was back. The hall door opened and people could be seen crowding to the door.

"Take the horses to the cattle byre. We can't afford to lose any. Bring the packs."

"I will go with the horses," Kalea stated. "Midnight will not like others handling him."

Mark sighed. "Go with her Leith and you Eric."

They took the horses into the byre and once they were convinced, they were safe, secured the door and walked back to the hall. Kalea between the two men.

"The wolves must be desperate," Kalea stated.

"Indeed," Leith confirmed constantly watching for movement.

At last, they were safe inside. Mark had already been made welcome and the villagers were sharing their simple fare. The packs had contained meat, bread and vegetables and were very welcome. Cloaks had been shed and Mark listened to the troubles that had befallen this small village. Finally, he spoke.

"I have listened and I would aid you if I can. I will send my hunters into the woods to trap and kill the beasts." This was met with much gratitude. "I will not delay. Already the light is fading and I would be back at the castle before full dark."

There was much rushing around then. The villagers unused to having such a distinguished guest. Leith, Kalea and Eric went and fetched the horses. Before long, they were underway again. The pace was slightly faster without Doris the carthorse but not much. The forest was a lot darker than before and the band moved quietly, constantly on the lookout for danger.

The danger, when it came, was so fast, that at first all was chaos. Dark shapes poured out of the trees and attacked the horses. Midnight lunged; teeth bared at a wolf that threw itself at his neck. Bee sting was out and was lashing down at the wolf. The two pack horses cannoned into him as they bolted in panic. Kalea was nearly unseated as Midnight staggered. There seemed to be hundreds of dark shapes leaping and snapping. Midnight was doing what all great horses do, biting and kicking while Kalea laid about with bee sting. It was difficult to see what was going on in the low light. She had no idea where anyone was and was trying to fight her way back to where the heart of the action seemed to be.

She saw a horse rear spilling its rider off. As it bolted by her, she saw it was Mark's horse. Fear clogged her throat and she urged Midnight into the fray and saw Mark facing off two wolves. With a wild whoop and sweeping bee sting to both sides, they plunged forward, coming between Mark and one of the antagonists. Slashing down, she held out her other hand to Mark, who grasped it and swung up behind her. She felt him get tugged backwards, before one arm secured him around her waist.

"To me! To me!" he bellowed still lying about with his mighty sword. From the gloom, other horseman began to converge on Mark. Not really knowing, but hoping that they were all there. "We need to get out of the trees," he shouted. "Run! As fast as you can."

With that, Kalea turned Midnight and urged him forward. He needed no further encouragement and took off like the wind. It was the stuff of nightmares. Growls, shouts and horses screaming in terror as they thundered through the forest. Riders had to lean as far forward over their horses' neck as they dared, so that they would not get knocked off by low branches while still slashing madly at their pursuers. Suddenly, they broke free of the forest and even the deep snow did not stop the horses who were now in full flight. Night had fallen, while they had been fighting for their lives, and snow still fell. Mark turned to see how many of them had survived this onslaught. He was pleased enough to see all his company were with him. Even more relieved to see that the wolves had stopped at the forest edge. Wild laughter, bubbled up inside him.

"Leith?" Kalea flung over her shoulder, still urging Midnight on.

"Safe." Mark laughed in her ear. "They are all with us."

As the lights of the watchtowers came into sight, the riders allowed their mounts to slow. Despite the cold, the horses were hot and blowing. The rest caught up.

"Any one hurt?" Mark asked.

"I'm bitten," Came back Eric. But everyone else confirmed they were ok.

"That was exciting," Leith commented and they all laughed. It was like surviving a battle. The joy of still being alive bringing out a lot of banter. "There were loads of the buggers." General agreement.

"That was more than one pack," Mark pondered.

"Games short. Perhaps they combined to hunt." Col said.

"More than like." Came the general agreement.

At last, they clattered into the courtyard. Stable hands came forward to take the horses, Jack rushing up for Midnight. Alan came rushing down the castle steps.

"Thank the gods. We were about to send out a search party when your horse came home without a rider," he said with feeling.

"Treat him well, Jack," Kalea asked. "He has done well today." Jack nodded and with that, Kalea slid from the saddle into the waiting arms of Mark. As she did so, she buckled and Mark was hard pushed to catch her.

"My lady. Are you injured?" she could not answer, her head was swimming. Mark scooped her up. "Eric, take a horse and get Essie."

"A horse?" Eric queried.

"She is old. Her legs don't work so well and dragging her out of her warm bed, she will not appreciate having to walk." He nodded and was gone. Mark carried Kalea into the hall and laid her on one of the tables. With Leith's help, he took bee sting from her back and removed her cloak. It was immediately, obvious, what was wrong. Her left leg was streaming with blood. She had been bitten badly. "Hot water. Cloths," Mark ordered. Alan rushed off. He started taking off a boot, while Leith got the other one. Taking his knife from his belt, he started cutting her trouser leg off. The leg was absolutely drenched and Mark realised, that he too was covered in her blood. He hissed. It was a lot of blood. Alan returned with the cloths and water and Mark who immediately started to bathe the blood from the wound. Leith took a sharp intake of breath.

Valim appeared. "Apply pressure to it," he barked and Mark did as he was told and cast a glance at the druid as he began to mutter words under his breath.

It looked bad. Kalea stirred and tried to sit up.

"Oh no, my lady. You stay still," Mark ordered. She slumped back.

"I'm sorry," she murmured.

"What for?" Mark asked grimacing, as he revealed the extent of the damage. But Kalea had swooned.

"Looks bad," Leith stated and was rewarded with a black look from Mark that almost said 'you don't say'. "Is the flap of skin still attached?" he asked leaning over.

"It is. But not by much."

"Might have cauterise it," Col chipped in.

Mark sighed. He might well have to hit one of them, if they kept making unhelpful comments. "Where's Essie?" he growled. And as if summoned, Essie was coming through the door.

"I'm here," she grumbled. "Young Eric stuck me on a horse."

"You did say, last time, that if I needed you in a hurry, I should send a horse. So, I did. Get over here woman and work your magic."

"What happened here?" She asked drawing closer. Then cast a look at Valim as he stood muttering.

"A wolf took tried to eat her." She gave him a knowing look. "Not me woman."

"Are you doing this or is it me?" she asked Valim casting him a none too friendly look.

Valim bowed to her. "It is your skill, lady. I would not dream of interfering."

With a sage nod, Essie turned back to Kalea "That's nasty." Mark gritted his teeth with impatience.

"Can you help her?"

Looking at his worried face. "Don't know yet," she answered honestly. "She's a strong one, she's got a chance. I'll need more hot water." Alan scuttled off. Essie began to lift the flap of skin and peered inside. "I might be able to do something." She washed the wound again and ferreting around in her bag started to put some herbs underneath. Lifting Kalea's head and poured some poppy juice down her throat. "Swallow it down my girlie."

Kalea's eyes opened. "Hello Essie." Essie smiled. "Is Mark alright?"

Mark stepped forward, she was obviously in and out. "I'm here."

She smiled. "Oh Good." And the poppy juice put her under.

"Now, I can begin." She delved in her bag and found her needle and thread. Dipping the needle in the hot water she passed it to Mark. "Thread that for me," she ordered. Mark bit back a retort and did as he was asked. "This one seems intent on losing as much blood as she can." And she began to sew. There was quite a crowd watching her. As usual, Essie was quick and efficient. "There!" she said standing up, rubbing her back and admiring her handy work. "Right, let's get her up to her bed. I can finish off up there. But we need to get her trousers off and I don't think she would appreciate flashing her lady parts off down here." Mark made a face of complete exasperation and tenderly lifted Kalea off the table.

"Eric's been bit too!" Col called.

Essie turned. "He said nothing. Brave lad. You go ahead lad," she told Mark, I'll see to Eric and come up after.

Mark ground his teeth. "Leith, your assistance please." Leith loped through the crowd and opened the door. Mark followed him as he loped up the stairs and swung open the chamber door. Mark gently placed Kalea on the bed. "Give me a hand Leith." Kalea was a dead weight and it took the two of them to get her jacket and shirt off. There was a bite mark on her arm as well, but the jacket had saved her. In the end, they cut her trousers off and Mark laid her back down.

"You love her, don't you?" Leith stated.

"Yes," Mark answered truthfully and met Leith's eye. Leith nodded.

"She saved my life tonight," he said sinking on the side of the bed. "How she knew, in all the chaos that I had been unseated, I don't know. But the wolves would have had me if she hadn't come back for me."

"I told you, she was useful in a tight corner. She's a brave girl."

Mark nodded agreement and the door swung open as Essie arrived with Mary.

"Shirts off," she ordered. "Some nasty scrapes down stairs and I don't want you two going down with anything, if I can prevent it." Rolling his eyes at Leith, Mark did as he was told. "You too." She pointed at Leith. Knowing it was useless arguing Leith stripped off. They did indeed have some scrapes and scratches, and Essie put some of her magic cream on them. "You'll do. Off you go, while I work on the girl."

Mark shrugged his shirt back. "Will she live?"

Essie, shrugged. "Lot of ifs here. She has a chance." Mark's jaw clenched. "Now, off you go," she chided. "Nothing to be done by you here. I will know more later." Mark took a deep breath squared his shoulders and nodded. With a look at Leith, the two men left.

"She's a tough 'un, that wise woman," Leith stated.

Mark gave a snort of laughter. "An understatement."

"You let her get away with a lot. I had not thought to see it," Leith added.

"She delivered my mother of me and has fixed all my ills, small and large ever since. She still sees me as the small child. Frustrates the hell out of me. But she is the best wise woman to be had and she knows it."

"Women! Onery beasts. Reminds me why I never married one."

Mark gave a bark of laughter and slapped Leith on the back.

Back in the hall, there was much discussion and they all clamoured round Mark for his thoughts. Mark really wasn't in the mood for all this, but he knew his duty and waved them all down, then pouring himself a mug of wine took his seat.

"We have a problem gentleman. We need to kill this wolf pack." He watched their faces. "They have had a taste of human flesh and they like it. We are armed, trained warriors on warhorses yet they were unafraid. We were lucky. That could have ended very badly. It ended badly enough. Did the packhorses make it back?"

"One," Alan answered "and it was injured."

Mark took a deep breath. "We need to remove this threat. Kalea saved me tonight. If she hadn't come back for me, I would not be here now," he admitted. "If the lady survives, I would have her cape lined with the skins of those who dared threaten us." A cheer went up. "Tomorrow, the whole warband will ride. Arrange it." All except the six rushed to organise it.

Mark plodded wearily up the stairs. The adrenalin of battle was spent. The anger and worry had drained him. He had a new respect for Leith who had managed well despite his age.

Opening the door, he took in Essie seated in front of the fire dozing. He sighed and her eyes opened.

"Essie," he acknowledged. "I have had a room made up for you. How is she?"

"She is as she was. We will not know for a while. It is too early. The pain will be great. You know that pain, I have stitched up enough of your sword wounds." Mark looked down at his feet. "We have moved her to the edge of the bed, so that you may sleep with her if you wish."

He met her eye. "That was kind, thank you."

"I will go to my room now and let you rest. Is it the one I had before?" she queried. He nodded. "I will be back first thing to see how she is doing." She patted his arm as she left. "You are a good lad, Mark."

Mark grinned. He had not been called a lad for some time. He stripped off and climbed into bed. Funny. But it was strange. He normally, slept on the side that Kalea had been laid on. Looking at her in the low light, he whispered. "Don't leave me." And with that he slept. The sky was just getting light when he woke. Unsure what had disturbed him, he turned to look at Kalea. Sweat beaded her forehead and her eyes were open. "K. Are you alright?" Silly question, he knew she wasn't. She looked at him and gave a shake of her head.

"It really hurts."

"I'll get Essie." He leapt from bed and hastily pulled on his trousers. Without bothering with the rest. He ran up the corridor and knocked on Essie's door. Come on, he thought and she opened the door rubbing the sleep from her eyes. "Essie, Kalea is awake and in pain."

She turned to grab her bag and came out. Mark strode off and was surprised that she was not with him. With a sigh of exasperation, he turned back and gripping her elbow, propelled her down the corridor at a more suitable pace. He could hear her huffing and puffing in protest. Flinging open the door, Essie was shoved in.

"You could do with a little more patience," Essie grumbled, moving over to the bed. "Hello Kalea, I see you're in pain." Kalea nodded. "Well, you won't be soon." Getting out the poppy juice, she dripped some into her mouth. Within seconds, the girl's eyes glazed and Essie patted her hand. "Don't you worry dearie; Essie is right here." Kalea's eyelids drooped and Essie nodded with satisfaction. "There she should rest easy for a time." Mark had been finishing dressing and now stood ready for the day. "When you go down to the hall…" Essie began.

"I know, I know, get you some breakfast sent up," he growled.

"That would be nice. But I was going to ask for a bucket of clean snow and Mary."

"Snow?" Essie nodded but said nothing else. "I will." And with that he was gone.

Essie went back to the bed. Kalea was hot and they needed to cool her down or the infection would set in and burn through her.

Mary shared Essie's breakfast and then the two of them began their work. They bathed Kalea in snow to lower her temperature and then inspected the wound. Essie was happy to see, that the wound while angry did not look infected. Lathering a heavy layer of ointment on it, they rebound it.

"Will it heal?" Mary asked.

Essie shrugged. "Depends. The skin might die, if it does, we will have to cut the whole lot off and try to cauterise it. We will know, by the colour and the smell. I hope that it will knit and be healthy."

Mary looked quite green. "Poor Kalea. Did you know that she loves another?"

Essie was surprised. "One of the warband?"

Mary shook her head. "Back in Arthur's village, she loved the warrior, Kai. They were to be married two days after Mark snatched her."

Essie looked towards the bed. "Yet, Mark loves her."

"Do you think so? I had hoped that perhaps he would come to love her."

"He might not know it yet. But I think he does. He seems a lot softer."

Mary nodded. "Yes. It has been noticed by the servants."

It was late in the day when Mark and the warband returned. It had been a success but a price had been paid. Horses had been lost and men injured, two badly. Essie was going to be busy. Mark's face was grim. At least it was done, they would have to worry no more.

The bodies of the wolves were on the back of the horses and were off loaded in the courtyard. The men were happy to be home and piled into the hall. Mark strode into the castle, as he entered, he snapped orders at the servants. "Find Essie. Bring food and drink. We need hot water and cloths. Fill the barrel for me."

He stripped his cloak off. The wolves, had been fierce fighters and once again, it had been mayhem. The sheer numbers of warriors had overwhelmed the wolves, but they had not gone down without a savage fight. Valim was already treating the men when Essie came in with Mary. It was clear that there was a wary respect between the two. Essie regarded Valim as a poor second to her skills but she said nothing to antagonise the druid.

Leith had been one of a small group, left to cope with any thing that came up. He walked up to Mark. "How are you?" he asked. Mark shook his head.

"It was not easy. At least, I bought them all home. How is she?"

"Not good," Leith said. "Essie has kept her under with poppy juice. I have spoken to Essie and she says that if the skin knits, she will be fine and if the skin dies…"

"When I have washed and eaten, I will go to her." Leith nodded. "By all the gods, I'm cold," he complained rubbing his hands together. Leith handed him some warmed wine and Mark accepted gratefully warming his hands on the cup. He looked towards the great fire burning in the hearth, but couldn't see it for men huddled round seeking some warmth. Turning to his steward "Find some fresh clothes for me. Make sure you do not disturb the lady Kalea."

"We have some freshly laundered clothes, sir."

"My thanks. Have them taken to the bath room." The steward nodded and left. "I just hope they have enough hot water to warm me through," he commented to Leith.

Leith looked at this King. He looked tired and drawn. It was not an easy job sometimes, being a king. "You look like you could do with a few days' rest."

Mark slapped Leith on the shoulder with a rueful smile. "You are not wrong there. Do you think I will be allowed?"

"You're the King. You can do what you want."

"I do wish that was true," Mark commented. "Right, I'm off to see if the bath is prepared."

The water was steaming, but despite the fire in the hearth, the room was still chilly. Mark stripped off and then cursed mightily as he eased himself into the hot water, his body so cold, that the water felt boiling, although he knew that was not the case. At last, he began to thaw and feel warmer. As his body got warm, the water felt cooler. He began to soap himself off in earnest. Finally, with great haste, he got out, dried and got dressed, his flesh goose pimpled at the sudden change of temperature again. With his jacket done up to his throat, he came back into the hall.

Essie was finishing up her tasks. The poor woman looked tired too, Mark thought. Food and drink had been supplied in abundance and Mark realised just how hungry he was. He joined his warband instead of sitting apart and ate, like the rest of them, grateful he had returned home safely. Essie shooed Col out of the way, and came to sit by Mark.

"You have earned your keep today." Mark passed her some mead.

"I always earn my keep," Essie retorted grumpily. "Have you seen her yet?"

"No. I will go now. What do you think?" he asked.

Essie sighed. "Another week and we will know. So far, the skin is healthy. Don't let the druid see to her."

"Why?"

"I have a bad feeling about him," she confided as if that explained a lot.

Mark nodded. "If you will excuse me?" and rose and left.

He entered quietly and seated himself on the bed beside her. Her eyes opened when she felt his weight on the bed.

"Hello K. Are you feeling a little better?" Odds were, she was not. Her eyes were full of pain. "The pain is bad, isn't it? I will go and find Essie."

She took his hand. "Can I have a drink please?"

"This I can do immediately." He poured a beaker of water and lifting her gently, helped her drink it. "Better?" She answered with a little nod. "Now, I shall go and find poor Essie." And he left in a flurry to return a short time later with Essie, who had been virtually carried to improve her speed. She was not best impressed but still went to Kalea.

"Hello my lovely. I have some more poppy juice for you. Only a few drops. We must try and manage the pain now, not take it all away. I need to know, if you are improving." Kalea gratefully accepted the poppy juice.

"Thank you, Mother."

Essie smiled at her. "You're welcome child. We need to get you up and moving soon. So, prepare yourself." Kalea nodded, but already her eyelids were fluttering.

"Isn't that a little soon?" Mark asked quietly.

"Another day at most," Essie answered knowledgably. "We must get the blood pumping down to the wound and the only way to do that, is to get her moving. It will help keep that skin healthy." *I hope*, she thought to herself.

When Mark woke the next morning, he found that he slept late. The fire had been banked and breakfast was laid for him. He turned to Kalea and found her watching him. "Good morning my lady. Shall I fetch Essie?"

"Not yet." Her voice was scratchy from lack of use. He caressed her cheek.

"How about some water?" She nodded and watched as he got out of bed and poured her some water. "Shall I try to prop you up a bit? Do you feel up to it?" She nodded and he grabbed some more furs and put them on her and as he gently lifted her, pushed them behind her, so that she was half sitting. Then he gave her some water, her hands came up round his to hold the cup and his heart was suddenly filled with warmth. Replacing the beakers, his voice warm as a caress, he said. "I am pleased to have you with me." Then with a shiver, "I best get dressed, or I will freeze."

"Sit with me a while," she croaked but sounded stronger.

"It will be my pleasure," he said hurriedly pulled on some trousers and a shirt. Then he scrambled back on the bed, throwing a fur over him too. "It is colder than a witch's tit!" He was rewarded with a huff of laughter. "I love seeing you laugh. I am hoping that it won't be long before you are laughing all the time."

"You are a dear man."

"A dear man? Not quite what I hoped for. Handsome. Yes. Desirable. Yes. Dear? No." She grinned.

"Those too."

"How is the pain?"

"Bad, but better."

"I'll get Essie. I'm glad I can still share your bed, but I really, really want to hold you." Stomping on his boots, he was gone.

It wasn't long before he was back, with Essie.

"Hello, my girl. How is the pain?" Straight away seeing her eyes, she knew the pain was bad. "Not as bad as yesterday I see. You are tolerating it better." Delving in her bag, she retrieved a small bag of herbs, and the bottle of poppy juice. Mixing the herbs in some water, she turned to Kalea. "Open." Kalea opened her mouth and Essie dripped only one drop of poppy juice into her mouth. "Drink it down." Handing her the beaker, Kalea did as she was told, she emptied the beaker. "Good girl. Now, we are going to have a look at that leg. Be warned, it will not be pleasant."

Pulling back the furs, she began to undo the bandage. As the last piece came off, a foul stench filled the room.

Mark reeled back, "God's woman! What is that disgusting smell?" His hand covered his nose in an attempt to shield him from the stench, his nose wrinkling with disgust and he tried hard not to retch.

Essie smiled. "That is a good smell." He looked at her incredulously. "The poultice I put on, has been pulling out all the badness." She pulled back the leaves to reveal the foul-smelling pus below. Mark stepped back further and gagged as the smell intensified. Essie began to clean off the wound and peered at it. Taking the fouled cloth, and poultice she threw it into the fire. The smell grew even worse and Mark retreated to the window and threw it open taking in a huge lungful of frigid air. The air was so cold, it burned, but it was preferable to the smell in his chamber. "You never used to be so squeamish," Essie scolded.

"I'm older and wiser now." Essie looked at him. "Alright, older." She grinned.

"Come, look!" Reluctantly, he came to the bed and looked down on Kalea's awful wound. "See! The skin looks healthy. Only two stitches weep now." She began to put a new poultice on and rebandaged the leg.

"So, she will live?" Mark asked.

Essie nodded. "I think she will. This should be the last poultice she will need. She should begin to improve now."

The smell was beginning to dissipate. Mark looked at Kalea who was still in a swoon. He was rather glad she was, with that smell. He at last felt confident enough to uncover his nose. Essie, covered her with the furs. "There," she said. "She should sleep comfortably for a while. I think I could do with a sleep myself." She packed up her bag. "I will be in my room if you need me." She yawned, rubbed her back and left.

Mark shivered. It was cold in the room with the window open but Mark didn't want to close it just yet. Kicking off his boots, he climbed back into bed and snuggled under the furs. Within minutes, he was asleep.

He woke and found Kalea already watching him. Smiling sleepily, he raised himself on one elbow. "Feeling better?"

"Yes. I've been better. But I feel better than, I did earlier. Mark? Please can you pour me some water please? I've tried to reach, but I can't."

"This I can do." He threw back the furs and went to pour her some water which he handed to her. Much to his surprise, lunch had appeared. He had missed breakfast, something he was quite grateful for, but now he was ravenous. "Madam, can I interest you in a little something to eat? I have bread, cheese, butter and honey."

Kalea, nodded. "Can I have some honey please?"

"Of course," he said happily. "Some sweet for my sweet." Cutting off a small piece of bread and slathered it with butter and honey. Putting it on the plate, he bought it to her. She picked up her bread and nibbled at it. Cutting some bread and cheese for himself, he came and sat on the bed with her. "I'm going to get into trouble with Essie giving you bread and honey. I have no doubt, she has some witches brew for you," he commented gloomily.

"There's a funny smell in here," Kalea stated.

Mark laughed. "I would like to say that it was a misfunction of my bowels, but sadly, K, it was your leg."

Kalea was aghast. "Does that mean that my leg is rotting?"

Reaching out to take hand. "No. K. It isn't like that at all. Essie put a poultice on it and it has been drawing all the badness out and that was what smelt bad." She looked relieved. "Thank you for coming back for me." His voice was soft and gentle and Kalea looked embarrassed.

She searched for words to say, but none came so she just whispered. "You're welcome."

"It was very brave. And I have to say, that brute of yours, was superb." That earned him as smile. "Right! I suppose, I better go down to the hall and see what mayhem has happened in my absence." He leant over and kissed her cheek. "I'll report to Essie and would you like me to send Leith up?"

"Yes please." And with that he was gone. Kalea sank wearily back on the bed. She was far from right, yet.

Leith came in with Essie who was grumbling. "Bloody stairs will be the death of me." Leith looked at Kalea and rolled his eyes. "Mark tells me you are awake. How is the pain?"

"Bad," Kalea admitted as the wise woman came to the bed. Her voice was still husky from lack of use.

"Let me see what I can give you," Essie said delving into her magic bag. "I will give you some poppy juice later as it will help you sleep but we shall use it sparingly now." Stirring some herbs into a mug of water, she gave it to Kalea who drunk it down. "That should take the pain down. It's not as good a poppy juice, but let's see if we can keep you awake for a bit. Mark also tells me he gave you some bread and honey. What was he thinking? You have had nothing to eat and very little to drink for three days, and he gives you bread and honey," she grumbled. Kalea looked to Leith who had seated himself in front of the fire and he grinned.

218

"He was trying to be kind Essie," Kalea defended Mark.

"That's as maybe. But I'm surprised you weren't sick. You must be careful not to upset a tummy that has been empty for a long while," she grumbled. "Bloody men." Kalea grinned at her and Essie grinned back. "That is better. A smile. Definitely on the mend." She put a little pouch of herbs next to the beaker. "These are for supper. You can if you want, sprinkle them on your food, or drink them with water. Mary will be up shortly with some broth." Turning to Leith. "You make sure she eats it all." He nodded. "I think, I will go and have a lay down before supper. I shall come back later and give you a drop of poppy."

"Thank you, Essie."

"Tis alright girlie." She disappeared out the door.

Leith got up and sat at the end of the bed. "Tough as old boots that one. She will most probably be here long after the rest of us are gone."

"She's good at her craft though."

"How are you?"

"I've been better," Kalea remarked.

"Yes. I guess you have. There's a strange smell in here." He wrinkled his nose.

"Mark tells me it is the poultice Essie put on my leg drawing the badness out. That's why the window's open."

"I thought it was cold in here. Is that a good thing?"

"Mark says it's good."

"Don't smell good." Leith laughed.

"Thanks Leith. I haven't seen it yet. Is it bad?"

"Yes," he answered truthfully. "I thought it would have to cauterised, but Essie decided, she might be able to fix it. That was a bloody brave thing to do, K. Stupid, but brave going back for Mark."

"You know how it is, in all the chaos, you just do things." Leith nodded in agreement. "The wolves would have had him though." Kalea shrugged. "And that horse of yours did well, carry both of you at that pace."

"He did. He has a big heart. I nearly got unseated. The packhorses cannoned into him, crushed my leg and nearly knocked him over. How, he managed to stay upright, I don't know. I don't know, how I managed to stay on."

"You're a good horse woman. Better than most men."

Kalea looked down. Then the door opened and Mary beamed at Kalea.

"It is good to see you awake." She carried a tray with a bowl of broth on it. Being brave without Mark being there, she came and put the tray on Kalea's lap and patted her hand. Kalea smiled back at her.

"Have I really been asleep for three days?" Kalea asked.

"Yes!" Leith and Mary answered.

"Can you manage? Or would you like me to feed you?"

"I can manage thank you, Mary. But you can join us if you like."

"I have to get back. It is good to see you awake." Much to Kalea's delight, she gave her a kiss on the cheek before leaving.

"I see you have a friend." Leith smiled.

"She is lovely." Kalea lifted the spoon and took her first mouthful of real food for three days. It was delicious. "This is good."

"Not too fast. It will make you sick," Leith warned. Kalea slowed down. Fighting the urge to shovel it down. She was soon full. "You better eat that or Essie will have my hide as well as yours."

"I have eaten loads," Kalea moaned. "I can't eat another mouthful."

"Pass it over. For the sake of us both, I'll eat it." Kalea leant back and could feel her eyes drooping. "I see, I've worn you out. I'll take this down with me and leave you to rest."

"Thanks for coming Leith."

"I'll be back tomorrow." He picked up the tray and watched as she pulled the furs around her. "Sleep well."

Kalea was disturbed by Mary bringing in more food.

"More food already? I've just had lunch."

Mary laughed, "That was hours ago. The hall is just sitting down to supper." Kalea looked to the window, she must have been asleep hours, it was dark outside. Someone had been in and pulled the window too. Mary put the tray on her lap and Kalea groaned.

"That's a huge amount."

"Eat what you can. I won't tell Essie if you don't finish." Taking the pouch that Essie left, she emptied the contents into the beaker topped it up with water and handed it to Kalea who downed it. Then starting working her way through the broth. Mary sat on the end of the bed. "You are quite the talk of the castle. Mark is telling everyone that you saved his life."

"I couldn't leave him to the wolves," Kalea said in between mouthfuls.

"They say, that you were equal to any warrior in the company."

Kalea grinned and pushed her bowl away. "They talk a good story."

"So, what's the truth?" Mary asked taking the tray away. "Shall I eat this? No one will know."

"Please do. The truth Mary is that Mark's horse ploughed by me so I knew he's been unseated. So, I went back to see if I could find him and luckily, I did. I did use a sword, but I don't know how effective I was." She shrugged.

"I think I prefer their version," Mary said finishing the broth.

"What are they saying?"

"They say, that there were hundreds of wolves and they were attacking you all. That swords were drawn, the light was so low, that they couldn't see what was going on and then suddenly, the king was calling them to rally, and when they did, he was up behind you and you both were lying about you with your swords. Then you led them out into the fields at a flat-out gallop and no one could keep up with you."

"That does sound good. But I'm don't remember that. All I remember is that Mark told us to run for the fields and I just gave Midnight his head, and we ran. That doesn't sound so brave, does it?"

Mary smiled. "I bet it's somewhere in between. Essie will be in to give you some poppy later. Sleep well."

"Thank you, Mary."

The candles were lit and the fire had been banked when Mark entered the room with Essie. Kalea was awake.

Before Mark could open his mouth, Essie said, "Still awake? You obviously feel better. Have you been eating well?"

Kalea nodded. "I'm stuffed."

"You will be, your tummy shrinks when you don't eat. Your wound is beginning to heal well. Tomorrow, I think we should get you up. Not standing, but sitting in a chair." Kalea nodded. "Now, let's give you some poppy to make sure you have a good sleep. Open." Kalea opened her mouth and Essie dripped one drop onto her tongue. "Sleep well." And she turned to leave. As she passed Mark, she threw back at him. "You know where I am." And with that she was gone.

"The woman is a witch." Mark looked at Kalea. "Why, I put up with her, I don't know?"

"Yes, you do. She is the best wise woman you have and she is good at her craft," Kalea commented.

He sighed shrugging off his jacket. "Mayhap your right." Stripping off his clothes, he slid under the furs. "It is still bitterly cold." She ran a warm hand over his goose pimpled skin and he shivered. "Are you really feeling better?"

"I think I am. I've managed to stay awake for a bit and that is an improvement. I can't believe that I have slept for three days."

"Essie said it would be better for you. Would you like to lay flat now?"

She nodded and he helped her sit forward and removed the extra furs from behind her back. Snuffing the candle, he put an arm across her. "I wish I could hold you close."

"I wish you could too."

Mark was disturbed by Mary bringing in breakfast, much to his pleasure, Kalea had wrapped her arms round him and snuggled in behind him. He turned in her arms and found that she was already awake. "Good morning, that was lovely waking up in your arms." She smiled sleepily at him. "Breakfast has arrived. Let's sit you up and I will fetch you something." He lifted her gently and piled some furs behind her and then still naked trotted quickly over to the tray. "It looks like it's porridge for you." He took the honey and poured some in. "That should make it taste a bit better." He bought it over and Kalea began to eat. He bought a plate over for him and slipped under the furs to eat with her. Having finished he took her bowl and his plate and put them back on the tray. He was just pulling on his trousers, when Essie marched in. He hurriedly pulled his trousers round him. "Haven't you heard of knocking," he growled adjusting himself and tying his trousers up.

"I've seen it all before." She smiled.

"You may have, but I would rather you knocked," he grumbled pulling on his shirt.

She ignored him and went to Kalea. "You are certainly looking a lot better. Let's have a look at your leg."

Essie, peeled off the bandage. The smell was bad, but not as bad as it had been. Kalea wrinkled her nose in disgust. Mark kept by the window, breathing in the fresh air. Essie pulled off the poultice and the smell intensified.

"That is vile!" Kalea gagged.

"No. It is good." Essie nodded. "It is much improved on yesterday. Don't you think Mark?"

Mark had to admit, that while it was still foul, it wasn't as bad as it was yesterday, although, he was by the window. Essie washed the wound off and then moved to throw the dirty, soiled bandages in the fire. "Oh no you don't!" Mark pounced on Essie. "Give it here," he demanded snatching it from her and then he threw it out the window. "The smell lingered for hours," he complained. Essie just grinned at him.

"You are such a girl," Essie said. Pulling a face at her, Mark looked at Kalea who grinned, but couldn't blame him. "Look, girl!" she peered at the wound. "Very little pus today. One more day should do it. Come and have a look, Mark."

Not wishing to be seen as weak, Mark came over to the bed and found that now the offending bandages had been removed, it wasn't at all bad. He looked down at the wound which took up the side and most of the front of Kalea's thigh and was surprised to see that it was indeed healing well. The skin was knitting and while it looked a bit inflamed, most of the wound was healing well.

"That does look better."

"I think we can say, that you are out of the woods," Essie agreed. "You are healing well. Let's get you up."

Kalea piped up. "I would bathe. I smell bad and want to wash the sickness off."

"You can't get the wound wet," Essie stated.

Mark on the other hand, was already trying to find a solution. "How about we take Kalea down to the bathing room and she can hand wash, then Mary can wash her hair. If she lays on the bench with her head over the edge, her hair can be washed without getting the rest of her wet." Essie nodded. "I'll see to it." And then he left. By the time Essie had finished rebandaging, he was back. He took a blanket from the bed. "Now my lady, let's cover you up." He wrapped the blanket around her and lifted her off the bed. "Your bath awaits." He carried her with great care and set her down in the bathing room. Mary was waiting and with a smile began to wash Kalea down and using Mark's idea, washed her hair. As Kalea was dried off, Mark came in carrying a dress and what could best be described as a fur lined dressing robe. He very rarely wore it himself, although he had had it made for him so he could wander around his chamber before he dressed.

He waited while Mary, put on the dress and then wrapped the dressing robe round her. Mary had combed her hair but it was still wet and the room of course was wet. Not wishing her to chill, Mark swept her up in his arms and carried her into the hall. As they entered, a cheer went up. Mark smiled and placed her on a chair that he had had put by the fire.

The warband gathered round, each expressing how pleased they were to see her up. Kalea smiled wanly at them, overwhelmed by their response. Valim, was also keen to talk to her but Kalea was cautious of him. He had worried her with his talk of being a priestess. It was a long day and Kalea was glad when supper was over and Mark carried her back up to bed.

"Well done. You lasted well."

"I'm exhausted," Kalea groaned.

"I'm not at all surprised. Your strength will return," he said confidently. He helped her undress and slipped the furs over her. He started to strip off himself.

"Aren't you going back down to the hall?"

"No. I don't think so. I would much rather spend my time with you." Bringing the candle over to the bed, he set it down and snuggled under the furs with her.

"It's so nice to be able to move about a bit." Kalea wiggled over to him and put her head on his chest, careful to keep her leg out the way.

"It's nice to have you in my arms again," Mark murmured into her hair. She smelt so good. Mary had rubbed rose oil into her skin and her hair smelled of a lavender infusion. "You my dear, smell good enough to eat."

He felt her smile against his chest. "I think we might have to wait a bit longer for that."

He laughed. "You must be feeling better." He snuffed the candle out and lay holding her until she fell to sleep and was soon asleep himself.

Chapter 9
The Coming of Spring

At last, winter's grip weakened. The snow melted and was replaced by mud. Spirits were lifting. Mark was back to riding out to make sure his kingdom was running as it should be. Kalea was back on her feet and wearing her new wolf skin lined cloak. Her limp was barely noticeable. Leith became her constant companion and he was first to admit, that apart from the wolf incident, he had spent a comfortable winter. Perhaps the most comfortable winter ever. *I must be going soft*, he thought.

Valim and the minstrels had left as soon as the snow did. Kalea had found Valim interesting to talk to but Essie had made her uneasy feeling known which made Kalea wary.

Mark would come back from his countless journeys tired and muddy but Kalea lifted his spirits. She greeted him warmly, no matter how muddy he was, and her natural happiness often caused him to laugh, when he thought he couldn't. Love making had resumed and Mark found his willing partner more than able to soothe him. All in all, it was a happy time.

Forays out on horseback, found Mark doing things he hadn't done since he was a young prince. Racing Kalea and jumping obstacles which would cause Kalea to laugh almost hysterically, which in turn made Mark laugh. He had to admit, that trying to beat Midnight, was an almost impossible task and he had taken to cheating, which made Kalea laugh even more. She was an excellent horsewoman. Mark never tired of watching her effortless control of the huge beast.

The weather started to warm and Mark took her to Merlin's Mirror. "Are you brave enough to swim?" he enquired.

"Of course." She slid from the saddle.

Mark waved his two guards away and slid to the ground. "Off you go. You're definitely on your own. It's not warm enough for me." He watched appreciatively as she unself consciously stripped off.

"Not even if I promise to warm you."

"You are a tease. No. You can warm me in the furs later." She pouted and stepped into the water and hesitated. "Is it too cold my lady?" He grinned seeing her flesh goose pimple. She looked suggestively over her shoulder.

"It is a little chilly, I confess." She edged cautiously in. Mark's grin grew broader. Then suddenly, threw herself in and came up spluttering and shivering. "I think your choice was a wise one," she said between chattering teeth. "I shan't be long."

"Take as long as you want." Mark laughed watching her slice through the water. Taking out a large drying cloth from the pack he bought, he stood enjoying the sight of her fish like behaviour. It wasn't that long before she launched herself out of the water and straight at him. "Oh no you don't my little mermaid." Mark laughed and held the drying cloth out before him, capturing her in and winding it tightly round her. "I know your game." He pulled her close rubbing her vigorously. She giggled. Even soaking wet, she was beautiful. The dark almond eyes twinkling mischievously. He kissed her. She had given him more pleasure, more fun and more laughter than he could ever remember having. She made him feel young. Having giving her a brisk rub down, she hastily got dressed.

"Not quite warm enough yet," she commented. "Although it could be me going soft. You spoil me too much." She pulled her fur lined cloak around her and shivered.

Mark boosted her back into the saddle. "It is my pleasure to spoil you madam." He swung lightly back into the saddle. "Just as you pleasure me." He gave her a devilish smile.

Giggling, Kalea bought Midnight close to him. "I'm sure, I don't know what you mean my lord." He winked at her, which made her giggle more.

Arthur was in his hall with Kai, Lud and some of the warband. The rest were out scouting Arthur's kingdom to make sure everything was as it should be. Arthur had been out too, but had decided to have a rest when a new visitor was ushered into the hall.

"Valim!" Arthur called as the druid strode up to him. "You are welcome. Just in time for the Spring Celebrations. You can give us your blessings."

"Arthur," Valim acknowledged. "I will willingly give my blessings to your festival." He acknowledged Kai and Lud who greeted him warmly.

"We were just about to eat. Come join us and you can tell us the news from about the land." Arthur gestured to a seat between him and Lud and with a nod Valim joined them.

Druids as well as Christians were always made welcome in Arthur's Hall. The druids were welcome for their stories and healing powers and although Christianity had spread through the land, the old ways were still clung to by some and Arthur had no wish to enforce his or anyone else's view on any of his people.

The food came and was laid on the tables. "Where did you spend your winter, Valim? I hope you found a safe and warm spot. Winter has been harsh this year," Arthur commented.

Valim nodded cutting some meat for his platter. "I spent the winter with Mark of Cornwall."

Lud gave a bark of laughter. "I bet that was fun," he said sarcastically.

"Actually, it was, mostly. It had its moments," Valim answered steadily. "Mark is much changed. Generally, he is much better humoured."

The three men exchanged glances. "How so?" Kai asked.

"Mark has found himself a spring Queen. An extraordinary young woman." He noticed the look that the three men exchanged. "Do you know her?" Arthur made a dismissive gesture. "Her name is Kalea. Her eyes are as black as night and she has Mark bewitched."

"Really? I would think Mark a difficult man to enchant," Arthur commented.

"And yet she has," Valim stated. "The Yule celebrations were a real joy. Something I am not used to experiencing in Mark's Hall. The spring Queen, became the winter Queen and enthused the whole hall with her sense of joy and danced all night." Once again, he was not slow in noticing the exchanged looks. There was a story here that he was missing. Despite subtle questioning of Mark's warband, they had been closed lips about where Mark had found this young woman.

"It sounds like Mark has found a special woman," Lud replied sagely.

What are you not telling me? Valim wondered but nodded pouring some more wine. "She is indeed. Not the normal kind of poppet that Mark has around him. Mark had problems with wolves this winter."

Arthur nodded. "They were bold this year. A lack of game I suspect."

"The wolves in Cornwall had decided on easier game and had started taking people from one of Mark's villages," Valim stated watching the men carefully. "Mark decided to visit that village and see what he could do to aid them. He took a small party, including the girl and set off. On the way back, they were attacked by wolves."

"What? Armed men on horseback?" Kai queried.

Valim nodded. "During the exchange. Mark became unseated and his winter Queen turned her horse and came back to save him."

"Mad woman," Lud muttered.

"That's as may be," Valim stated. "But I doubt she had any wish to be given to his warband. Sadly, the girl was grievously wounded and it was touch and go if she would survive."

"How so?" Arthur asked.

"A wolf had decided to make a meal of her and tried to take a bite out of thigh."

"Did you not use your magic, Valim?" Kai asked.

"I did try and cast a spell before Mark's wise woman arrived. She has little regard for my 'hocus pocus' as she calls it and warned me off."

"Was it bad?" Arthur asked concerned for Kalea.

"Yes," Valim answered truthfully. He used both hands to indicate the size of the wound. "The skin was held on by very little. Between my spell and the wise woman's skill, the girl pulled through. She is strong and brave and I would have had her as a priestess, but Mark would not hear of it. You do seem very interested. Are you sure you do not know her?"

Arthur shrugged. "We have heard talk but of course we are interested in what happens in Cornwall. Mark's good humour, determines how many attacks we will have to face this year."

Valim knew when someone was evading his questions. But until these men had relaxed and drunken a good deal of wine, he would find out nothing further. So, he changed the subject and moved on to Dorset, where he had stayed after he left Mark's.

It became a routine. Kalea swam daily. Mark did not accompany her all the time and sent Leith as his proxy to ensure, that her two bodyguards did not get ideas above their station.

Leith and Kalea were happy. Though they would not admit it. Leith had fit in well with Mark's warband and they respected his age and his skill. Kalea made

Mark happy and everyone in the castle appreciated his lack of black moods and even when he wasn't in the best of humours, Kalea had the skill to cheer him.

The spring celebrations came round. The Christians called it Easter, but it still was a celebration of the earth reborn. A huge feast was held outside in the castle courtyard so that the people of the village could join in with the feasting and entertainment. A group of minstrels had arrived and were made welcome, providing news from other settlements and new songs and music. It was a time to relax and enjoy that they had survived another winter before the hard work of sowing and seeding for the next crops.

All the preparations were underway. Mark was enjoying the moment, with Kalea's excitement running high. Once again, Mark had commissioned a dress for the festival. This time there were no wolves to spoil the occasion.

One day, Kalea was missing. Mark asked with exasperation. He was going to have to put a lead on her if she kept managing to escape the castle. Col put him on her track and told him that Leith and Kalea had gone down to the stable. He wandered in and could see Leith leaning over a stable door. He was surprised to see that it was not Midnight's stall. Walking across to Leith, he was just about to ask where Kalea was, when he spotted her in the stable. Even more shocking was the fact that Kalea had her arm up to the shoulder in a mare.

"What on earth????"

"The mare is in foal and cannot deliver the baby. The stable hands didn't know what to do and Kalea heard them and is trying to help to save mare and foal."

Kalea's face was splattered with blood and it was pressed against the mare's backside. With a cry of triumph. "I've done it! I've pulled the head forward. Pass me some rope." Jack rushed in with the rope. "Put a slip knot on it," she instructed pulling her arm out and then taking the rope from Jack, put her arm back inside. "There! Done! Wait for the next contraction." As it came, she cried, "Pull!" Jack heaved and the foal slid out. Jack and Kalea exchanged a grin.

"Well done, my lady." His voice was full of awe as the pair of them rubbed the young colt with straw. It sneezed and then began to try and struggle to his feet. The mare turned and the two of them moved swiftly out the way so that she could begin to lick her new baby.

Mark looked at her in amazement. He looked at Leith. Leith grinned at him.

"Valuable skills has Kalea. But not skills best suited to a fine lady."

Mark shook his head in disbelief.

"May I ask what you are doing?"

Kalea spun and faced him looking exultant and guilty at the same time. "I had to help," she pleaded. "Please, don't be cross."

Mark grinned. "I am not cross at all. Just amazed. Look at the state of you."

She looked down as if suddenly aware of the fact that she was covered in blood. She looked up sheepishly.

"Your face is covered with horseshit and blood." Leith grinned. Jack rushed off and came back with a bucket of water and held it up so Kalea could hastily wash her face and hands. "That hasn't made it much better." The resigned look on Kalea's face made Mark laugh.

"Jack, send someone to the castle to get madam here, a clean shirt, a drying towel and plenty of soap. Then saddle up the beast, I am going to dunk her until she's clean." With a broad grin, Jack set about his tasks. A lad appeared holding a sack, bowing to Mark he handed it over. Very soon, Leith, Mark and Kalea were on their way to Merlin's Mirror.

"There you are my lady. Kindly get in and make yourself presentable." Leith turned his back as Kalea stripped off and threw herself in.

"Will you not join me?" she called.

"I think not." Mark smiled indulgently as he sat on the grass next to Leith.

"Can I have the soap?" Mark looked at Leith who grinned. *This is not going to end well,* he thought. Then grabbing the soap, he threw it to her. It took her a while to capture it as it kept trying to slip through her wet fingers. She pouted, causing the two men to chuckle. Vigorously, Kalea soaped herself off and then plunged back into the water.

"I thought you were in for a wetting." Leith grinned.

"So, did I," Mark chuckled.

"Coming out," Kalea yelled and before Leith could turn his back, she came wading out and began drying off. Mark watched appreciatively. "See anything you like?"

Before, Mark could answer, Leith leapt in. "Get your clothes on, you wanton hussy," he scolded. "I thought, I taught you better than that."

Much to Mark's amusement, Kalea looked suitable chastened and hurriedly dressed in clean clothes. Leith winked at him making him turn his back to hide his mirth. "I'm done."

Kalea was already scrambling into the saddle. Mark looked at Leith with a new respect. He could certainly put fear into her. Obviously at some stage in the past, he had given her a real talking too, something she didn't want to have again. "You certainly look a lot better now," he said.

"At least, I saved both mare and foal. Surely that's worth a bit of blood and snot," she bit back defensively.

"And for that I am grateful."

"Blood and snot? Charming talk for a young woman," Leith chided.

"Leave off Leith. You're a fine one to talk," she growled grumpily.

Leith and Mark exchanged a smile. "She's a stroppy baggage," Leith remarked.

"I heard that," Kalea spat back.

Mark threw back his head and laughed.

The day of the spring festival dawned. Mark presented Kalea with her new dress. It was exquisite. The palest green with embroidery of flowers and vines around the neckline, sleeves and hem.

"My lord! This is too beautiful," she said holding it up in front of her as he sat watching her obvious joy. "You are too generous and I have nothing to give to you."

"I do not give to receive." He smiled.

"I think I may have something you might like." With a suggestive smile, she sank to her knees between his legs. She was right, he did like.

Having put her new dress on and combed her hair till it shone, the couple went down into the courtyard where the celebration was already starting. Kalea greeted everyone gaily and Mark smiled indulgently. Mary came to them to present Kalea with a spring crown, which she put on. Mark's heart lurched painfully and he sighed. He had not foreseen how hard he would fall for this slip of a girl. Perhaps, he thought, he should marry her.

The afternoon drew on and the minstrels struck up a tune and the dancing began. Kalea danced with everyone who asked. Mark and Leith of course, but she also danced with Jack and the stable hands, Mary, people from the village, both men and women and the warband. It seemed her energy was endless and all the while she smiled and laughed. Mark watched with amusement as everyone seemed to like her.

She collapsed in her chair beside him pouring herself some ale and offering some to Mark. He put his hand over his cup. "Thank you, my lady. But I am drinking wine. Are you enjoying yourself?"

Eyes twinkling, she looked at him. "Do you really need to ask? I am having so much fun. And you, my lord?"

"Yes. I am. I enjoy watching people being so happy."

"Are you not happy?" she asked concerned.

Turning to her, he pulled her face close to his and kissed her deeply. "Oh yes," he murmured against her mouth. "I am very happy." And he kissed her again. He was pleased to see, that her eyes were dark with lust when he allowed her to breathe again. "I am glad I have that effect on you."

"Oh yes," she breathed. "You do."

The light began to fade. Torches were lit and the celebration continued to late into the night. People began to fade away. Some slept where they sat. The minstrels put away their instruments. They had certainly earned their money today, Mark thought, he would reward them handsomely. He took Kalea's hand and led her back into the castle. Despite having danced most of the day, Kalea was bright with excitement and even as he led her, was skipping a few dance steps. As he closed the chamber door, Kalea turned to him.

"Am I the spring Queen?"

With a slow knowing smile, Mark replied. "Of course, you are my lady. Are we going to repeat the moves of winter?"

He watched as she removed the crown to strip off her dress. When the crown was back on. "Will you be my Spring Knight?"

Admiring her body, he bowed low. "Of that, there can be no doubt."

"Oh good." She smiled pouncing on him.

Mark lay dozing with Kalea asleep in his arms. He rather enjoyed letting her take the lead in their lovemaking and he looked forward to meeting the summer Queen and seeing what delights, she had planned for him. It occurred to him, that Kalea had not quickened with child and he wondered why. She had been with him nearly half a year, and as yet showed no sign. He had spent more than enough seed for a babe to grow. Perhaps, she could not have a child, he pondered. It was of no significance; he had his heir and a spare. He did however, think that Kalea would produce beautiful babies and he would have liked to see one. With this thought in his head, he drifted off.

It was, perhaps, three weeks, when a group of minstrels turned up at Arthur's Hall. Entertainers were always a welcome distraction. These however, were different. The leader of the troupe requested an audience with Arthur and was led to him, where he sat with Kai and Lud.

"You are welcome here," Arthur said. "I hear you would speak to me."

The man bowed low. "I have a message from a friend in Cornwall."

Arthur raised an eyebrow and exchanged a look with Lud and Kai. "And the name of this friend?"

"Her name is Mary."

"I know no such person," Arthur stated. Suspicious.

"She is a servant in Mark's Hall," the leader stated theatrically. Enjoying telling his tale and feeling of some importance. "She gave me a message that she said would be of some interest to you."

"Well, go on." Arthur's face was unreadable.

"The girl is a friend to the Lady Kalea." He noticed the interest in the men's faces. "She says that the Lady Kalea swims daily at Merlin's Mirror. That she accompanied by her man, Leith and two others."

"And?" asked Kai.

"That is it," he said. "That was the message. She said you would be interested to know. I hope that is so?"

"Yes. That is so." Arthur reached across and offered the man a coin. "I thank you for your service."

The man bowed and went to join the rest of his troupe.

When he was sure, that they could not be heard. He turned smiling to Kai and Lud. "Well, that is interesting. Kai, how do you fancy a trip to Cornwall?"

Kai laughed, "I thought you would never ask."

"I shall stay here. Lud, if you fancy a jaunt, you can go as well if you want."

"That would be my pleasure." Lud grinned. He was oft, left at the castle while the two youngsters went off and caused mayhem. Mayhap, this time he could join in.

"Take six. Leave when you're ready."

"First light tomorrow?" Lud queried to Kai.

"That sounds like a plan." Kai grinned.

"I hope that we can play Mark at his own game." Arthur's smile didn't quite meet his eyes.

Chapter 10
Reversal of Fortunes

The days were warming. Mark was seeing to his kingdom. He was out visiting his minor lords. In days past, he would have stayed a few days and had his fun with the local women before returning home. But he had no interest now, he wanted to be back before nightfall to see Kalea. He had no wish to take her with him as yet, he didn't want them wondering about this woman. The decision to marry her had taken root now and he would introduce her as his wife. Then there could be no excuse for bad manners and lechery. Perhaps he would marry the Autumn Queen he mused with a smile.

Col and Alan had been planning raids for Dorset and of course, Arthur's borders. But he had little interest. I must be getting old, wanting to stay by the hearth with my woman. That made him chuckle. No. He was not too old yet for battle. There would be raids. He decided but he would be a little less reckless. He had better things to do these days.

Leith had given up asking Kalea if she loved Mark. Anyone with eyes in their head could see that if she didn't love him, she was at least very fond of him. It was also plain to see, that Mark loved her and he no longer went to pains to hide it. *Long may it continue*, he thought.

It had been a tough year for them, but they had come through it and whilst it was not exactly what they had planned, it was better than they could have hoped for. Leith was happy enough with Mark's warband. They weren't a bad lot of lads, he admitted. There were one or two he gave a wide berth to. These were hard men with a cruel streak. You always got one, who enjoyed inflicting pain just for the sake of it. He had thought Mark was one, but he had mellowed and Leith found himself quite liking the man although he was loathe to admit it.

Most of the time, he enjoyed being with his girl as he called her. Kalea had blossomed. She was certainly a lot more at home in her own skin. As she grew more confident in her womanly abilities, she had become less shy about acting as one. She still, got stroppy with Mark and him, but Mark now laughed at her rather than getting angry, just as he did. Things she did, were still not suitable for a girl, but like in the village, everyone got used to her striding around in her trousers, and although many of the men surreptitiously, took the opportunity to appraise her long legs and slim waist, no one commented. Neither did they when she went hurtling around the castle at a flat out run. She was still Kalea the tomboy, still quick to laugh and still fast with her little sword. Leith was mighty proud of her.

Kalea had indeed grown up but she was not about to let that stop her doing the things she enjoyed. She had a good idea now of what Mark would tolerate her doing. He gave her free reign in the stable, knowing that Jack thought highly of her talent with the horses and would allow no harm to come to her. Kalea had also asked if she might learn to shoot a bow. Mark had looked at her with a look she came to know, when he was appraising her. "Why?" he had asked and without hesitation, she had answered. "Because it is something I would like to learn." He had bought one of his archers to him and asked if he would teach Kalea his skill. The archer had been hard pushed to hide his smile but agreed. Now, both Mark and Leith watched her practice. She had a child's bow. She had not the strength to draw a hunters bow, let alone a long bow. Leith and Mark had made a great show of hiding behind their shields even when they were behind her, making her cross. But she was mastering it. She hit the target more often than not these days.

Kalea herself, was surprised at how happy she was. Her home in East Anglia, now seemed like it had happened in a different life. Thoughts of Kai, still made her heart flutter, but that also, seemed to be a life time ago. Time had passed and it had made the pain seem less. She could see no way back, so she moved forward determined to make Mark love her more. She had more now, that she had ever dreamed of even seeing, let alone owning. Sometimes she thought she must be dreaming and would wake up in her straw bed in East Anglia with her father snoring in the next bed. Every morning, she woke up in Mark's arms, in a soft bed, with good food. She wore dresses of the softest cloth and with the finest embroidery and felt most of the time that she was acting the fine lady although all she was, was the King's concubine.

Kai, Lud and the rest of the small band, watched the four riders approaching from the cover of a copse of trees. They were in no hurry and seemed to be chatting happily between themselves. Kalea was easy to single out as the light breeze lifted her hair. They were too far away to hear what was being said. One rider turned to the two others and shoed them away and as instructed, they pulled up and dismounted. Kalea along with the other rider rode on and dismounted by the water. The two left behind, were obviously trying to peek and there was much arm waving from the last man left with Kalea. They assumed it was Leith. Then Kalea disrobed and was in, cutting through the water like a knife. Leith sat down to watch. About an hour had passed when the Kalea emerged from the water and began drying herself. Before long, she was dressed and mounted and the two picked up the other two on their way back to the castle.

"Mary didn't lie," Lud stated.

"No," Kai agreed. "It has its problems. There is very little cover."

"We'll wait for them to get out of sight, and walk down to see the lay of the land."

Taking their water skins, that's what they did. Lud being the best tracker Arthur had. Took special note of the dips and slight hillocks. Kai knew from the slight smile and deep concentration on Lud's face, that he had thought of something.

Sitting in the trees and eating their provisions, Kai looked at him.

"Well? What have you thought of?"

"The green blankets." Kai waited. "Where the two guards, nursemaids stopped. There is a small dip near that scrub of bush, two or three of us could hide there covered by the blankets and take them out when they dismount. Kalea and I would assume, Leith, then ride on. We can afford no noise, but we don't want to kill them. We need a degree of luck." Kai and the rest of the group nodded. "It might be best to wait until Kalea is in the water, Leith sits and watches so he won't be paying attention to the other two. Just before the water's edge, is another indent, did you notice?" He didn't wait for a reply. "Kai and I will lay there and once we are sure that you have taken the other two down, we will take Leith and the girl. I'm hoping that once, Leith sees me, he won't put up any resistance, but we can't guarantee that. We don't want any killing. Just silencing. We'll tie them up and leave them here. So, we will do it tomorrow, if they return." They nodded and began their wait.

The day was perfect, Kalea decided. She had had a wonderful day yesterday. Mark had stayed at the castle and by the time, she had come back from swimming, he had sorted out the minor disputes that had arisen in the village and was free for the rest of the day. As a result, she had had a lovely day with him, culminating in heated session of lovemaking. Today, he had ridden off early to see one of the lords on the outlaying borders and would not be back until late.

The sky was blue and it was warm. Perfect for swimming. This afternoon, she had a lesson with Tom the archer, which she was looking forward to. She was in an excellent mood.

Leith, was enjoying this morning too. Kalea's mood was infectious and all four of them were chatting and laughing. As they reached the bottom of the valley, Kalea did what she always did, which was take off like the wind. Leith laughed at her sheer joy, and set off after her but had little chance of catching her.

Kalea reached the top of the hill and pulled up waiting for the others to catch up. She laughed as they came up to her, horses blowing. Midnight had hardly broken a sweat. The large stallion tossed his head proudly and together they set off down the hill.

"Right lads. That's close enough for you," Leith commanded.

"Oh, come on Leith!" Kalea laughed.

They always put up a protest although they knew that Leith wouldn't relent. "You know the rules. And no peeking!" Leith demanded.

"They must know by now," Kalea chided.

Leith laughed. "I feel the need to remind them." At the water's edge, they slid from the saddle and Leith turned his back, watching the two warriors chatting to each other. He shielded Kalea with his body and didn't turn until she had slipped into the water. Then he turned and sat down on the grass, watching Kalea dip below the water. As she resurfaced, he called. "Is it cold? I might fancy a dip myself?"

"It's not bad at all. Leith. Do you fish?"

"I'm a warrior. Not a fisherman," he replied indignantly.

She laughed. "It's a shame. There are some big fish in here."

"I think you are the biggest fish in there. What is it that you like so much about the water?"

"Don't know," she answered swimming off. "I just feel free."

He didn't know what alerted him, some small noise or just instinct. He looked over his shoulder, he could see the horses, but not the men. He began to feel uneasy. He stood up and turned to have a better look. Where were they? They couldn't both be having a piss. His hand went to the hilt of his sword.

"Kalea," he said softly. She hadn't heard him. "Kalea! Trouble!" He shouted his eyes not leaving the place where the warriors should be.

Kalea didn't need telling twice and was swimming full speed towards the shore. Leith drew his sword.

"Leith! Hold!" As if by magic, Lud and Kai appeared before him. Leith had already raised his sword and froze in place.

"Lud!" He smiled.

"We've come to take you home." Lud grinned hugging Leith as he sheathed his sword.

Kalea stood still up to her shoulders in the water. Her heart flip flopped at the sight of Kai. He stood firm and unmoving. His face hard and closed and yet he still held the power to stop her in her tracks. He went over to greet Leith his smile warm and bright and something in Kalea's heart froze a little. He turned to her, his face once again a mask.

"Get dressed Kalea and make it fast." There was absolutely no way, he was going to turn his back. Leith came between them, offering her a little privacy. Kalea said nothing but scrambled out of the water and dried herself roughly before dressing. "Come on. Hurry up," Kai growled. Kalea virtually ran to Midnight and Lud stepped forward to boost her into the saddle. He patted her knee and nodded. Leith mounted up behind her. While Kai and Lud doubled up on Leith's mount. The lads had already mounted up on the guard's horse. Grabbing Midnights bridle, they towed him forward. Midnight didn't like it much but had little choice. As they arrived, Kalea saw her to nursemaids trussed up on the ground. She met their eye so they could see she had no choice. Her face was unreadable. Then she was dragged away.

"It will be alright," Leith whispered.

"Will it?" she asked softly.

As they entered the trees, the rest of the horses were bought forward and everyone exchanged mounts. Kai would not look at Kalea and she would not look at him. They moved off at a fast pace to put as much distance between them and Merlin's Mirror as possible. Leith rode next to her.

Kalea felt sick. Her heart was breaking. Kai hated her. He couldn't even bear to look at her. She rode hard keeping her eyes firmly between Midnight's ears. The pace was gruelling, but Midnight was up to the job. Kalea, just kept up.

It was late when Kai called a halt. Kalea dismounted and saw to Midnight's needs before coming back to the camp where a fire had been set and they all sat around eating and chatting. Kalea was largely ignored. Quietly, she went on the perimeter on her own. She felt totally miserable. Leith came and sat next to her and handed her some food. He looked at her and could see how awful she felt. He knew she wouldn't cry, but tears were in her eyes.

She ate her meagre rations and with no further words, wrapped herself in her saddle blanket and closed her eyes. She felt totally bereft. The man she loved sat no more than a few feet away, but he hated her. The man who loved her and treated her well, was falling further behind. Even worse, was the fact that all the men around the fire, were cheerful at having Leith back with them.

Leith laid beside her. He was sure she was awake but she didn't open her eyes. *Poor Kalea,* he thought.

Mark was on his way back. The light was fading. He was tired. It had been a trying day. He began to doubt the wisdom of giving Harry control of this large portion of his realm. The man was mean spirited, he brooded, and he had not enjoyed his company at all.

Col rode up. "Mark what ails you?"

Mark made a dismissive gesture. "I'm doubting Harry's capabilities of ruling."

"Why?"

"I don't know." Mark shrugged. "He seems overly harsh."

Col threw back his head and laughed heartily, much to Mark's annoyance. "Yes. He is much like you used to be." Only the big red headed second would dare to say it.

Mark looked at Col, calculatingly. "Do you imply, that I am going soft?" Col didn't need to answer, his half-hidden snigger said it all. "So, you do." And grinned. "It's that blasted girl."

"And you wouldn't trade her." Col grinned. "And, I don't blame you. You're not soft, but you have mellowed. It is not a bad thing. You're still hard enough to do the things that need to be done."

Mark was concerned. "Do the warband think I'm soft?"

Col slapped him on the shoulder. "They do not," he reassured. "They quite enjoy not having to watch what dogs you kick in the morning."

Mark laughed this time. "I'm not that bad."

"Not now you aren't. But you were." Col grinned. "The youngsters used to find other places to be."

"I shall have to start kicking some dogs again."

"Please don't. The dogs are becoming almost friendly." Col laughed.

Still smiling they rode on into the gathering gloom until the welcome lights of the castle came into sight.

As they rode into the courtyard, Mark was surprised not to see Kalea. Handing over his horse and taking off his gloves, he marched into the hall, ordering food and drink. He took a quick look round the hall and couldn't see Kalea. "Kalea?" he queried of those there. There was a general shaking of heads. Mark felt the first twinge of unease. "Leith?" More shaking of heads.

"Where the fuck!?" He turned on his heel and marched out. Meeting Col coming in.

"Everything alright?" He asked seeing the black look on Mark's face.

"Not sure." And Mark sprinted up the stairs. Col face darkened. This could mean trouble.

Mark threw open the chamber door. The candles were lit and the fire crackled cheerfully, but no Kalea. "Shit!" He hurtled back down the stairs finding Col waiting for him. Mark marched back into the hall. "Have any of you seen Kalea today?" Everyone in the hall began fidgeting nervously but the general consensus, was no. He turned to Col. "Get the horses back." Col left. "We ride," he announced to the hall.

A lone voice called. "But it's dark."

Mark's voice was dark and full of threat. "Do you dare question me? I can see its dark you cretin. We ride. Fetch torches." He was back on the steps and was mounted before the others. He impatiently waited and then rode out as fast as he dared in the darkness. It wasn't long before they were within sight of Merlin's Mirror. The moon reflected on the water making it a perfect silver disc. As they rode down the hillside to the water's edge, they heard shouts and on investigation, found the two warriors trussed up. Mark swore profusely.

"What happened?" Col asked sliding from his horse and cutting their ropes.

Rubbing their wrists, they got up. One stepped forward. "Don't know. One minute, we are standing there. Next, we are trussed up and on our own."

Mark dismounted and looked at them. Then struck one, as he fell, he kicked him. "You fucking fools. Why are you even in the warband? I set you a simple task. Guard the girl. And you lose her? You morons." He was beside himself with rage. He turned and struck the other one. "You dumb shits!" He swung back up into the saddle.

"Welcome back sire." Col grinned at him. "What do you want to do?"

"It's too late to do anything." He turned and rode back to the castle.

The atmosphere in the hall was very subdued. Mark sat brooding with Col and Alan.

"It was that shit, Arthur," Mark spat.

"Of course, it was," Col confirmed. "At least you know she will not be harmed."

Mark took a deep draft of his wine.

"So, what are you going to do?" Alan asked.

"What do you think I should do?" Mark asked.

Both men exchanged glances, they knew whatever they said would be wrong. They would have to tread very carefully or there was a good chance Mark would explode into a violent rage.

Finally, Col sighed. "You have two choices, as I see it. You either, just ignore it and carry on with your life." The look on Mark's face said it all. He looked absolutely disgusted. "Or, you go and get her." Mark brooded. "I would say, that the first option holds little interest to you. Although, perhaps it would be the wisest option." Mark met his eye. "As I thought. So, we go and get her."

"Will Arthur let you have her?" Alan queried.

His father's face said it all. "Well, I didn't. So, I doubt he will." There was a menace in his voice. "Nevertheless, I will try."

"Why?" Alan asked.

Mark didn't answer for a long while. "It seems like the pup king, has out done me. I don't like that. I have no choice to play his game as he had to play mine. We will go. We won't hurry. I will have the girl and I will have his kingdom."

Kalea was awake early. Truth, was she had not slept much. She was tired. There was much cursing and she was on her feet and moving before she was even aware of it. She found one of the party, raising a whip to Midnight.

"Stop!" she ordered.

"Bloody beast bit me."

"He doesn't like anyone touching him but me!" She went to Midnight and calmed him. The man, backed off still holding his shoulder. The others alerted by the shouts; came to see what the commotion was about. They found Kalea saddling up Midnight.

"Let's get going," Kai said.

"I should have warned you," Leith said. "He only lets Kalea touch him and me. If he is in the mood."

"Get Kalea in the saddle and let's go," Kai barked his face impassive.

Kalea had had enough. "You can talk to me, you know. I'm right here."

Kai met her eye. "Get in the saddle and let's go."

"That's better," she said. Lud and Leith smiled at one another.

Mark had not slept much either. Just when everything had been going so well. His hatred for Arthur was growing at an outrageous rate. But he was not going to run off without a plan, which even now he was formulating. He had time; he knew Kalea would be safe.

They arrived in Arthur's village and rode to the castle. Arthur came out to meet them all smiles.

"I see it all went well." He grinned at Kai who grinned back.

"Talk to Lud. He came up with the plan."

"Kalea." Arthur nodded. She slipped from the saddle.

"I would see to my horse." Her voice was surly, and Arthur raised an eyebrow.

"I'll keep an eye on her. Good to see you again Arthur." Leith grinned.

The rest of the horses were taken by the stable lads and Kalea led Midnight, into a stall.

"You alright?" Leith asked.

"What do you think?" The anger in her voice almost tangible. Hanging up the tack and given Midnight some extra feed and water, she shut the door.

"Come on lass. We best be seen."

Leith sensed trouble. Her shoulders were squared and her jaw jutted. All signs that she was spoiling for a fight. She had tried to provoke Kai, but he refused to rise. Any reaction would have been better than none. Fighting Kai might have at least given her an indication, if he had any feeling left for her at all. She marched into the hall and stood before Arthur.

"Ah, Kalea. I have been told you ride a bad-tempered beast."

She met his eye. "He is not bad tempered with me."

"Are you well?" Arthur smiled.

"As well as can be expected when I have been dragged across the country, not once but twice in under a year." The venom dripped from her voice.

Arthur was taken aback by this vitriolic attack. "Well, if Mark..."

Kalea interrupted. "Don't you dare do 'he started it!' You are worse than children the pair of you. I would like to knock your heads together."

"Watch your tongue," Leith warned.

Kalea turned a look of utter contempt on him. "I will not. I have had enough of everyone telling me what or who I must be. You must not do this; you must do that. Act like this, it is not seemly. It seems of little consequence what I want. He!" she jutted her chin at Kai "can't even talk to me and I am done. Now if you will excuse me." She gave a low sarcastic bow. "I will go and find Ellen, who it seems is the only person who allows me to be me." With that she turned on her heels and stormed off.

"Kalea!" Leith called.

"Let her go," Arthur said with a wry grin. "She has got a point and she needs to cool her heels."

Lud laughed. "My God! The girl's got spirit. Tells it as it is. I think she has every right to be in a temper. And you didn't help Kai. Treating her so coolly."

"What am I expected to do?" Kai bit back. "Welcome her back with open arms after she has been mating with Mark? I think not."

Leith tried to intervene on Kalea behalf. "Kai lad. She had no choice and she might have welcomed you back if you had just asked."

"Have Mark's leavings," Kai sneered. Arthur was surprised by Kai's reaction. It would seem he loved her still.

"I am not too proud," Arthur said levelly. "Nor am I too jealous to understand."

Kai snorted. "You're welcome. I, however, will not."

"I might well do so if the way is clear." Arthur met Kai's eye. "She has a right to be angry. We have used her badly. She has become a tool for two kings and not by her choice. It cost nothing to be kind Kai," he admonished. "Although, I confess I wasn't expecting to take the brunt of her fury. Now sit-down Leith and tell all."

Leith joined Arthur, Kai and Lud. He was pleased to be here, but he wasn't pleased with Kalea. Uneasy, that perhaps, he had once again failed her.

Kalea arrived at Ellen's without even realising it. Knocking on the door and found Ellen out. Sitting down, with her back against the wall she sat down to wait. Ellen was sometime, but when she returned her face lit up. "Kalea, you are back." She pulled the girl up and embraced her. She knew all was not well and she looked into her eyes. "You look tired, dirty, hungry and if I am not mistaken, angry. I'm sure I can help with most of those. Let's go for a swim."

"I have nothing to change into. All I have is what I stand in."

"I can help there too." Ellen smiled kindly. "Come in a moment." She went in and rummaged about and bought out a dark green dress. "I was given this in payment for curing Mary. You won't know her. It is too long for me and I suspect too big for you. But it will suffice."

"You are so kind Ellen." Kalea began to feel quite tearful at the woman's generous spirit.

"Nonsense." Ellen picked up the dress and some soap. "Now let us away. Everything looks better when you're clean." They walked to the river. Kalea kicked off her boots and jumped in. "You're supposed to take your clothes off first." Ellen laughed.

"I have been in these for a week. I'm not the only thing that needs a wash," Kalea called as Ellen stripped off and joined her. Kalea stripped off the wet clothes and gave them a good rub before taking them to the side to lay out to dry. The two women soaped themselves down and Ellen did Kalea hair. "The soap smells really good."

"I put rose oil in it," Ellen explained. "Let's go back and we can have something to eat. I sense you haven't eaten in the hall."

Kalea grinned ruefully. Ellen had been right, feeling clean put a new look on things. "I'm afraid, I lost my temper and gave Arthur the sharp edge of my tongue."

Ellen chuckled. "I am sure he deserved it." She passed Kalea a cloth to dry herself and noticed the large scar on her leg. "That looks nasty. Let me look. What happened?"

Kalea looked down at it. It had healed well although the scar was still red. "A wolf took a bite out of me."

"Who ever worked on it, had great skill," Ellen commented. "It is such a large wound; I am surprised it has healed this well."

"That was Essie, Mark's wise woman. You'd like her. She is quite elderly and very bossy. Even Mark won't argue with her."

They laughed. "So, what did she do? Apart from stitch it?"

Kalea slipped the borrowed dress over her head and Ellen thought it suited her well. Too big on the hip and breast, but the right length. "I can't tell you much from the beginning," Kalea confessed. "Apparently, she kept me under for three days with poppy juice."

"That was a bold move. It is very strong," Ellen stated. The two women walked back talking herbs and cures.

Meanwhile, Leith began his tale. He wanted to ensure, that everyone, but mostly Kai, heard how clever Kalea had been.

"When we arrived in Mark's Hall, Mark promised the warband Kalea when he had finished with her and ordered my death. The only reason I had survived so long, was that Mark thought Kalea would do as she was told if I was still around." That raised a few eyebrows because here Leith was. "Kalea bartered her virginity, for my life although of course, Mark didn't know it then, but she told him she would be compliant in exchange for my life and for some reason, Mark agreed. Right or wrong, it was a bargain she stuck too. Later, she explained it was really no bargain at all. She had no choice; it was just the degree of violence that she would have to endure." Arthur nodded. Of course, she was right. Mark would have had her anyway. "They treated me well enough. Warrior code and all that. They would have given me a warrior's death. Kalea would not be that lucky." Leith turned his eye to Kai, who whilst making a great show of not listening, certainly was. "When you came, it was what he planned. He wanted you to be humbled and he used Kalea as his tool to humiliate you whilst of course, humiliating her."

"I wondered if he had harmed her," Arthur interrupted. "He was certainly rattled when he returned to the hall later."

"What I didn't know until much later is that Kalea tried to cut his throat."

Lud laughed. "What a woman!" He said with admiration.

"Yes. She is." Leith again looked to Kai. "Apparently, only his fast reactions saved him from serious damage. But she did open him for here to here." He indicated with a finger. Did he harm her? I expect a lot more than she lets on. But the despair of failing and being humiliated in front of Kai, undid her. "She expected that she had earned her place as the warbands plaything, and she opened her wrists." Now, all attention was on the old warrior. "Luck or lack of it, played a hand in it. Mark had summoned his wise woman to attend to his wound and had sent a servant to give wine to Kalea. The servant found Kalea attempting to open her second wrist."

"Is this servant, Mary?" Arthur asked.

"Yes." Leith was surprised.

"It was her who sent the message, telling us where you would be."

"I'll be blowed," Leith stated. "I knew Kalea had struck up a friendship with the girl. It was her who saved her and bound her wrists until the wise woman had finished with Mark and could be sent to Kalea."

"Did Mark know?" Leith shrugged. "No wonder he looked rattled."

"That was the turning point for Kalea and Mark. I have no idea, what happened or what was said, but I do know that Mark promised that he would never give her to the warband."

Arthur shot a look at Kai but he had reburied his head in his ale beaker. "Does Mark love her?"

Leith nodded. "I would say he does. Whatever, after that he seemed to mellow."

"That's food for thought," Arthur pondered.

Meanwhile, Kalea and Ellen sat and drank elderflower tea and ate bread and ham.

"I learned a lot about the art of love," Kalea stated causing Ellen to splutter.

"I expect you did. And?" Ellen grinned.

"I now know why everyone wants to do it," Ellen howled with laughter. "Mark may be many things, but one of them is being a skilled lover. He knows how to give a woman pleasure and can make your body sing like a harp string." Kalea grinned as Ellen giggled.

"Well, my girl. It was not all bad then."

"Far from it. He treated me well. Like a poppet. He liked to dress me well, feed me well and teach me all kinds of lover's tricks."

"You were fond of him?"

"Yes. Is that because, I had nowhere else left to go? Or just that I enjoyed his advances? I don't know myself."

"Kalea. What are those marks on your wrists?"

Kalea sighed. "That Ellen is another story."

"I am in no hurry. Tell me."

And Kalea did. Not the abridged version that Leith had given, but the full one. She told of her feelings, of her fears, and that Mark could have hurt her a lot more than he did. She at last unburdened her soul.

Leith had finished his story and Arthur excused himself. He had a lot to think about. Without conscious thought, he found his self at Ellen's door. He could hear the voices of the two women within. They sounded happy enough and he wondered if Kalea had regained her composure. He knocked and the door was opened by Ellen.

"I would speak to Kalea," he stated and she allowed him in. "Kalea. I would speak to you."

Kalea looked at him warily. "I have nothing more to say."

"But I have. Will you hear me out?" She exchanged a look with Ellen and then nodded. "Come walk with me."

Kalea rose and Arthur immediately noticed that she had bathed and had on a dress that became her well. He did not compliment her, he knew it would sound contrite and false, so he said nothing. Moving aside, he made way for her to exit and with a nod to Ellen, joined her. They began to walk slowly together and Arthur caught the scent of roses on her. Speaking low and for her ears only, he began to talk. "I have come to ask your forgiveness." Her dark eyes met his for a moment before once again she looked ahead. "You were right and I was wrong. I cannot ask you to excuse me for the first part as I had no hand in it." She went to speak but he silenced with a gesture. "I do however, claim that the responsibility for this second part is all mine." He looked her, but she would not meet his eye. "You are right. Mark and I are like children, eager to prove who is the cleverest, the most dangerous and who wields the most power. That is no excuse for treating you so badly. I am as much as fault as Mark and I would ask you to forgive me."

Kalea turned to face this earnest young king. "I think I can do that," she answered seriously. "I must explain or you will think me fickle." And she took his arm and Arthur felt something in his heart stir for this brave young woman. "You must understand, that I had thought that my life now belonged to Mark. I could see no way back to here. No way back to Kai. So, I had to make the best of what I had. Was I happy? I was not unhappy. Was I loved? I don't know. I was Mark's poppet and he treated me well. Then once again I am wrenched out of what I was coming to know and thrown back here. Kai can't even bear to look at me and yet I love him still." She turned to face him. "Do you see, why I am so angry?"

"I do. Mark will come for you."

"Will he? I think you over estimate my appeal to him. Girls like me are two a penny."

"Girls like you, Kalea are as rare as hen's teeth. He will come. I cannot speak for Kai, but he is a fool to allow you to escape him twice. When Mark comes, I promise you, that should you wish to return to Cornwall with him, I will not stop you. The choice, this time, will be yours."

"Thank you," she said quietly. Arthur hugged her, inhaling how fresh and clean she smelt.

"Now, that you have forgiven me a little, I have something to show you." And he led Kalea to the house that was to have been hers and Kai's although she did not know it, "This is your house. You may keep it for yourself, or you may share it with Leith. Leith, by the way, is feeling quite bruised by the way he feels he has failed you and says that he is quite happy to stay in the warrior's hall."

Kalea entered and was delighted by the size and how well equipped the house was. She turned to Arthur. "Are you sure this is all for me?"

"I am," he said and she stood on tiptoe and kissed his cheek.

"Thank you."

"I think you might find a few things in here you might remember." He gestured to a small pile on the table. Kalea went to examine it. There were her two dresses, her small purse and toothpick. She picked it up with a grin. "I've missed toothpick. Thank you again. You kept it all."

"I had always hoped you would return," Arthur said. "Your message to Leith?"

"He can stay where he is." Her voice was harsh. "I have no use for him now."

Arthur was taken aback by her venom. "I shall tell him so." And with a bow he left her in her own home. Kalea rushed back to Ellen's and dragged her to see her new home. On the way back, using coin from her purse, Kalea bought some provisions. She would not starve. The two women enjoyed the rest of the day together exploring every nook and cranny. Ellen noted Leith's absence but said nothing.

Arthur came back into the hall looking pleased with himself. And he had every right. He felt like he had done the right thing. As he walked in, Leith looked up.

"What did she say?" he asked hopefully.

"Sorry Leith, she says you are to stay here."

"She'll relent," Lud said slapping him on the back.

"This is Kalea we're talking about," Leith came back gloomily.

Arthur sat opposite him. "So, what did you do, that has earned you, her wrath?"

Leith looked up at him. "It is more what I didn't do. I didn't front Lud and Kai out and ask if she wanted to go. Even worse, I didn't try and intervene between her and Kai and try to make some peace. She still loves him, you know. And finally, I put my happiness and need to be back here, above her happiness," he finished morosely.

"That is almost as bad as my sin," Arthur commented. "She has forgiven me," Leith grunted. "Where is Kai?"

"He left shortly after you. He didn't say where he was going," Lud answered.

Arthur gave a small smile. He had no doubt that Kai had followed him and was glad he had not been over familiar with Kalea, although he doubted, she would have let him anyway.

A routine had developed for Kalea. She had noticed that a lean to had been added to the house at some stage. No doubt for wood storage, but it now housed Midnight. Being on the edge of the village, she had a large amount of meadowland behind the house and with the aid of long rope, she staked him out during the day and housed him in the lean to, at night. Her days were spent with Ellen, where she was fast developing her skills with herbs. Now, she was helping, people bought her small gifts too. Some eggs, or bread and one of the men had even built her a stable door for the lean to. She was content.

Chapter 11
The Toy of Kings

Life in the village was a bustle. Kalea enjoyed walking amongst the people. She often saw Kai and sometimes he was with women. He did not acknowledge her and while her heart ached, she was learning to live with it. Kalea had now helped deliver a baby, which made for great excitement and she knew now, that being a wise woman, was what she wanted to do, although, she was asked to the stables on one occasion to help with a dose of colic, which she was able to do easily. Leith stayed out of her way and that suited her. She could not forgive him so easily but for what she could not say. Alone in her house at night, she would oft think of Kai and Mark and what the future would hold for her, but it would be as it would be.

Arthur smiled. So, Mark had arrived. He had taken his time, but Arthur had no doubt that Mark knew that Kalea would be safe with him. A clatter in the court yard announced their arrival.

Mark strode into the hall. He knew how this was going to play out. It would be a rerun of how it had been when Arthur turned up at his hall. He hoped that the outcome would be different. The strategies he had devised had merit but it all hung on Kalea.

"Mark! You are a long way from home," Arthur greeted him standing up to clasp his hand and slap him on the back.

Mark ground his teeth. So, it began. "I have need of your assistance with a small thing."

"Come sit." Arthur indicated the chair next to him. Mark did so. "So how may I help you?"

Mark fought the urge to hit Arthur. "I believe you have something I am desirous of."

"Really? How so?"

"Come now Arthur. Let us not play games."

Arthur grinned. "You mean the girl who dresses as a boy and a one-eyed warrior who has seen better days. I know where you are coming from. Yes. They are here. Leith!" Leith stood up and gave a small bow.

Mark acknowledged him. "And Kalea?"

"She's around in the village somewhere. She has taken to helping the wise woman."

"I would speak to her." And between gritted teeth continued. "If that is possible."

"Of course. Lud. Would you go and get Kalea please?" Lud nodded and left. "While we wait, let me offer you some refreshment."

Kalea had had a particularly busy morning with Ellen. Dealing with the normal run of things. Bumps on heads, splinters, boils and upset tummies when Lud appeared at the door.

"Kalea. Arthur would have you up at the hall. Mark has arrived." She took a look at Ellen, she put down the poultice she was working on and wiped her hands and swept out after Lud. He noticed that she looked fine in her dark green dress and her hair braided to hang to her waist. "Are you ready?"

Kalea looked at him. "As ready as I ever will be."

Lud led her into the hall, where Arthur and Mark sat side by side. He had to admire her courage, her back was straight and her chin was up. She swept a low courtesy.

"My lords."

Mark's heart came up in his mouth. It was not unnoticed by Arthur.

"Kalea. Mark would like to talk to you," Arthur stated.

"Perhaps, I could speak to Kalea in private," Mark requested.

"I think not. She is under my protection; I would prefer that we kept this in a public place."

"I would not harm her," Mark almost purred.

"No. I think not," Arthur confirmed. The edge in his voice brooking no argument. "Whatever, you have to say, can be said in front of me."

Kalea remained unmoving. Mark shrugged. He knew that Arthur would not make this easy. "My lady, you look well."

"Thank you, my lord. I am," Kalea answered levelly.

"I confess, I have been missing you of late." He paused watching Kalea's face. She gave him no sign. "I expect you are wondering, why I am here." Kalea still said nothing. "I would have you come back to Cornwall with me as my wife and Queen. I would marry you here, before Arthur as witness, so you know my word is true."

Arthur was shocked but did well to hide it. He looked at Kai who showed absolutely no emotion at all.

"What do you say my lady?" Mark was careful not to show how much he wanted her to answer yes.

Kalea met his eye. "My Lord. That is a kind and generous offer. But I am used to a simpler life so my answer is no."

"Why?" he asked. "Do I not treat you well?" He hoped it didn't sound like he was begging.

"Indeed, you do. But I am content here. Thank you."

Mark did not take his eyes from her. "Are you married or promised already?"

"No. Sire. I am not."

"There, Mark, you have your answer. Kalea, you may go." Kalea gave a curtsey.

"Wait!" Mark ordered and she spun back to face him. "Perhaps, we can trade."

Arthur smiled. "You have nothing I want, and nothing I need."

"I have a proposition for you. I will promise you 3 whole years where I will not attack your kingdom. I will also put at your disposal, half my warband."

Kalea's heart sank. Arthur was stunned Mark was desperate, he stroked his chin thoughtfully while he gathered himself. "Well, Mark, that is a very interesting proposal. It certainly would be beneficial to my people, to not have to worry about fighting Cornwall." He went quiet as if he was pondering. "It is a very tempting proposition." He looked to Mark, but Mark as ever was unreadable. "Kalea. What do you say?"

"For your kingdom, if it is your will, I will go."

"That is very generous of you Kalea," Arthur commented. "But I will not ask you to do anything you do not want to do. I think you have done enough against your will." He looked at Mark. "What would be your preference?"

Kalea met his eye. "Sire. That is a generous offer from Mark. My preference is to remain here but I say again I am prepared to go if it would help you and your people."

"I am sorry Mark. As tempting as your offer is, the lady would like to remain. It seems you must leave empty handed."

Mark rose and almost languidly, moved with the grace of a predator, to Kalea. Her breath, caught in her throat. He walked round her, moving lithely, like a stalking animal. He lifted her hair, and sniffed. "You still smell good enough to eat." Both Arthur and Kai held their breath. What was he about? "Does not every woman dream of being a Queen?"

Kalea, resolve began to crack and she was quivering. This was not unnoticed by Mark or Arthur. She drew a breath. "Yes. I am sure that most girls dream of being a Queen, but that is what it is, a dream. It's for fine ladies, not girls who dress like boys." She was ashamed of the quiver in her voice and fought the urge to look down. Mark still had power over her. Arthur wasn't slow to notice.

Mark smiled. He knew the power he had over her. Even now, he knew he could have her if he wanted her, right here in front of Arthur. He was tempted but he would not humiliate her again. He leaned over and whispered in her ear. "Madam, I know you want me. Is there nothing I can do to persuade you to come home with me?" Her breath was ragged but she stood resolute.

"No, you cannot." Her voice was low and husky.

He walked in front of her, looking at her in the eye before leaning over to whisper in her other ear. His breath tickled her ear. "You would refuse a man who loves you, for a fool, who loves you no more, because of his jealousy of me."

She shivered. "I would."

"Are you sure?" He stepped back watching her. "My lady. I offer you a good life and my devotion."

"I am sure!" she said definitively.

Mark gave a devilish smile, stepped forward and kissed her deeply. Kalea did well not to respond but he felt her melt. Stepping back, he wickedly grinned.

"As you wish my lady." He bowed low to her. "You know where to find me, if you change your mind." Kalea curtsied and was eager to leave the hall, but Mark stopped her again. "Before you go, my beautiful girl, I have a gift for you." He turned and motioned one of his men forward who came forward with a large sack which he placed before her. Kalea looked at it suspiciously.

"Thank you, my lord."

"Lud, help Kalea with her gift." Lud stepped forward and hefted the sack. Kalea curtsied again, turned on her heel.

As they left the hall, Kalea exhaled. Lud grinned. "Well done, Kalea. You did well. Would you like to open this here?"

"Yes please."

Lud led her to a small room off the hall and shut the door behind them. He put the sack down and when she didn't immediately open it, he queried "Kalea?"

Kalea laughed. "I'm most probably being very silly. I somehow expect something nasty to be in it."

"Would he do that?"

Kalea stood back surveying the sack. "Mark is a very complex man. He can be exceedingly kind and gentle. He can also be unnecessarily cruel. You never know which Mark will appear." She brushed her dress down, "I guess, I will have to see." And with that, she grabbed the bottom of the sack and emptied it out on the floor. There was a clatter and she jumped back as if it was going to bite her. With a nervous giggle, "It's bee sting!" She leapt on the sword and drew it. "Mark had this made for me. It's a bit better than toothpick." She showed Lud the blade. He took it and examined it. It was a very fine quality blade for a boy's sword.

"He gave you a sword?" Kalea nodded but was distracted by poking the pile with the scabbard. Lud watched her, puzzled and amused. When she had spread it out on the floor, she put the scabbard down. "Well?" Lud asked.

"It's safe. I don't know what I expected," she confessed with an embarrassed smile. "A snake perhaps?" Then she laughed. "Lud, I am an idiot. Why would he want to kill me?"

Lud grinned. "The man loves you. It is obvious to anyone with eyes in their head."

Kalea sighed and sank in the middle of the pile on the floor. "These are the dresses he had made for me." She picked up the red and the two green dresses. Then she picked up her wolf lined cloak. "And my cloak."

"Are they wolf skins?" Lud asked.

"Yes."

"We had heard that you had problems with wolves."

"Had you?"

"Some minstrels who spent the Yule with Mark, told us of the tale."

"Mark said that he hoped the wolf who bit me, contributed to it," she said with a sad smile. Then she laughed. "Look! He has returned my old boots. These were my brothers and despite the fact that he had these ones made for me, he kept my old ones. That was kind." In addition, was the comb he had given her and another parcel. Wrapped in oil skin and tied with ribbon. Kalea fumbled with the knots and was stunned when she opened it and found the most beautiful dress she had seen. It was white and embroidered with gold thread. A wedding gown. She sat holding it.

"Lud, what am I doing?" She looked at him. "Do you think Kai will ever forgive me?"

"There is nothing for him to forgive. He is just too stubborn to see it."

She sighed. "I love him still. Does he talk of me?"

"No. But he watches you." She looked at him. "He follows you and tries to be where you are. Kai is a proud, stubborn man with a fierce temper. He does not take slights well."

"A temper?"

"I know you haven't seen it, but he has." He paused and then added as if to excuse Kai. "He has not been lucky in love." Kalea scoffed. "No. You misunderstand. Kai likes the women and the women like Kai. He has a bit of reputation as a womaniser. But finding a woman to love, is different. Kai has found two, and both have betrayed him, one nearly cost Arthur his village and the other, his friendship with Arthur."

"Then there is me. He sees that I have betrayed him too."

"But you didn't."

"But he sees it that way. I have just turned down an offer of marriage from a man who loves me, to stay and watch the man that I love from a distance. Am I a fool?"

"No, my lovely girl. You are no fool. At least here you can live your life as you want. Pack your things and we will take them to your house."

"Lud. Would you mind returning to the hall and thanking Mark on my behalf. He has been more than generous."

"Of course." Leaving a sad Kalea packing up her treasures. Dresses far too fine for life in a village and a wedding dress that would never be worn.

"You love her, don't you?" Arthur stated more than questioned.

"Yes. I do," Mark answered with a sad smile. "I had hoped…" He paused and looked at Arthur. "I had hoped that I had done enough to win her love. It seems I haven't."

"I am sorry." The sincerity in Arthur's voice was evident.

"Are you? I doubt it."

"If I hadn't had her taken, she would know doubt lived happily with you."

"Perhaps," Mark conceded sadly. "It is of little consequence now. I think I know her better than you do. Kalea tells me that she had not been long in your realm, before I took her."

Arthur nodded his agreement. "She had not been with us long. But she had already made a big impression."

Mark laughed. "That's Kalea. Headstrong, stubborn, at times down right belligerent and yet she is one of the most gentle, caring and joyous girls you could ever wish to meet. She is exquisite. Women of her ilk, come but once in a lifetime and sadly, I have been unable to win her. I have laughed more in my time with her, than I have in years. She sees the beauty in the simplest of things." Then Mark did something that Leith should have done. He defended her and sold her virtues to Kai. "Only a fool would refuse the love of that girl out of jealousy of me. After all, how many women have we had, that have had men before us and yet we are not shy to take them," he spoke to Arthur, but they both knew these comments were directed at Kai.

"This is true," Arthur added. Mark did truly love her. For only if you loved someone, would you sell her to the man she loved.

"Who is this paragon of whom you speak?" Kai growled with a grin. "I would meet her."

Mark turned his stare on Kai. His eyes full of threat. "Oh! You know her already and if it weren't for your foolish pride, she would be yours. For you are surely the reason, I lost her." His voice was deadly and cold.

Kai anger rising, bolted to his feet but Arthur restrained him. "Kai! Mark is a guest in my hall. You will treat him as such." Kai sank down into his seat. The hall had been a quiet as a grave, through this exchange but the tension was broken by Lud's return. Seeing him Mark called.

"Has my lady, Kalea changed her mind?"

"I fear Mark, she has not. But she has asked me to come to you and extend her heartfelt thanks for your gift. She says it is generous beyond measure."

Mark nodded. "Please tell Kalea, that I regret that I will not see her wearing them." Then taking a slug of his wine added. "It is even a bigger regret, that I will not see her taking them off." And he laughed. "Arthur my cup seems to be empty." Lud bowed and left.

Lud found Kalea waiting for him. He hefted the sack over his shoulder.

"Mark says that you are welcome and that he regrets not seeing you take them off."

Kalea laughed. "Sounds very much like him." They left the castle.

"Something strange going on in the hall," Lud stated matter-of-factly.

"How so?"

"Don't know. I suspect Mark is winding them all up." Lud grinned. "It is his greatest pleasure. I expect Kai or Arthur will tell me in due course." He looked at her. "Do you think you can ever forgive Leith? He is heartbroken."

"Is he?" Kalea said coolly. Then she sighed. "I am finding it difficult. The truth is Lud, he reminds me of all that has gone wrong. And I don't want that. He is not wholly to blame, my choices come in there too, but," she paused searching for the right words. "I need space."

She opened the door to her home. Grateful to be away from the politics of Kingship. Lud put the sack on the table.

"He is an old man, Kalea. He knows that he has got it wrong and it pains him. Just remember, for all that, he loves you."

To his surprise, Kalea hugged him. "Lud, you are a good man." And then he left.

When he arrived back at the hall, the atmosphere had lightened. Most likely because everyone had drunk far too much. Arthur acknowledged him and Mark raised his cup but slopped the wine. He looked at Kai, and recognised the look, the lad had had too much to drink and he had a face like thunder. Lud decided it was prudent to leave well alone and joined Leith who was sat with the rest of the warband.

"Lud," Leith acknowledged morosely.

"What has gone on here?" Lud asked.

"Mark nearly provoked a fight with Kai," Leith stated.

Lud filled a mug with ale. "How so? Kai is not quick to rise."

"Mark called Kai a fool for not claiming Kalea."

"Yes. That will do it." Lud grinned. "The boy is stubborn not recognising that Kalea still loves him. He will not appreciate Mark pointing that out to him."

"That's what I should have done. Taken him aside and told him."

"Do you honestly think that would have done any good? Kai won't be told; he has to find out himself."

"She turned down marriage to Mark. Does he need any further proof?"

"He will take his time; he will get there," Lud hoped.

Kalea alone in her home, sat with her head bowed. *I can live without men,* she thought. Here at least, she could live as she chose. No man to tell her what she must do. She stood up and as she did so, there was a knock on the door. It was Ellen. She came in and took Kalea in her arms.

"Are you alright?" Her concern obvious.

"Yes. I think I am."

"I heard that you were back."

Kalea smiled. "Doesn't take long for word to spread." She put the kettle on the fire for some rosehip tea.

"So, tell all." But before Kalea could begin, there was another knock on the door. Opening it, she found a man from the stable.

"Hello Kalea. Lud asked me to bring you this chest." He carried a rather large wooden chest.

"Hello John. That was kind of Lud. Would you put it there? It will do well as an extra seat."

He did as he was asked and with a smile left. The chest was battered but it was better than anything Kalea had. Ellen looked at her.

"Mark gave me some gifts," Kalea explained. "I will show you as we put them away. I fear, they are far too fine for the life I have chosen."

Ellen lifted the lid and whilst waiting for the kettle to boil, they began to pack the chest. As each item went in, Kalea told the story behind it. Ellen was so impressed with the quality of the dresses. Especially the wedding dress.

"This was being made before you came back," Ellen commented. "So much work, could not have been done in haste."

"I think you are right. I will never wear Mark's wedding dress or I should think, the others. Not the sort of clothes to be wandering around in."

"I don't know. The dresses will be wonderful at the festivals. Although I suspect there will be much jealousy."

"I have never cared much for what other people think," Kalea said with a grin.

Kalea made the tea and passed Ellen a mug. Kalea began to recount her time up at the Hall, Ellen was agog, both impressed and saddened by what she had endured. "Kalea. Do you not think you could be happy with Mark?"

"I know, I could be happy with him," Kalea confessed.

"Then do you think your decision is sound? Kai is being an idiot and there is no guarantee that you will win him back. I am alone of choice and it suits me. But as much as I love having you with me, I would not sacrifice your happiness for mine."

Kalea smiled and kissed her cheek. "Ellen, you are a kind and wonderful woman." She seated herself on the chest. "I think, perhaps, this is the time to take for me. I too, wish to be alone. Both Kai and Mark have power over my heart. If I go with Mark. I will be a bird in a gilded cage and as pleasant as that would be, I would still be caged. Here, I am of value to no one. I am free to be who I please."

Ellen nodded. Perhaps, she was right.

The night was drawing in. Kalea barred her door and enjoying the solitude, thought back on her day.

In the hall, there was much carousing. Leith had already passed out and a couple of the warband had dragged him to a berth at the hall edge. Kai had left. No one knew for where. Mark was bleary eyed but still watchful. He noticed Kai's departure and wondered if he had gone to make his peace with Kalea. Arthur was not as drunk as he made out to be and saw everything.

Kai returned still looking like a thunder storm and Mark smiled. *Young fool*, he thought, so, he still could not bring himself to bend. If he knew what delights he was missing, he might do so, and he gave a short bark of laughter. Arthur looked at him and with a dismissive gesture, Mark returned to his wine.

As usual, Kalea rose early and saw to Midnight's needs. She had just poured herself some nettle tea, when there was a knock on her door. Opening the door, she saw Mark standing before her and he gave a small bow.

"Mark! What are you doing here?"

"Why! I am looking for you. I came to say goodbye."

Kalea stood aside and allowed him to enter. She knew that this would not be her best idea, but she couldn't resist his roguish grin. Even knowing this, she turned to meet his eye.

"I had hoped that having slept on it, you may have changed your mind."

She gave him a sad smile. "You know I will not."

He stepped towards her and took her into his arms. "You are the most frustrating, wonderful woman, I have ever met." And then he kissed her. Without the eyes of the hall on her, Kalea kissed him back. Her hands running through his curly dark hair. His desire for her was evident as he crushed her to him. As always, Kalea melted. The heat from her body was not to be ignored. Pushing him back, so he fell to be seated on her new chest. Without further thought, she pulled her dress over her head as he released himself from his trousers.

With no further words, she straddled him and he gave a hiss of pleasure as he was engulfed by her hot warm body. His hands on her hips, he tried to set the pace, but she was having none of it and before long, she shook as she reached the height of her pleasure. This alone, was enough to take Mark's control from him and he buried her head in her breasts as he released his seed. "Come home with me," he murmured and immediately regretted it as she rose from him and pulled her dress over her head. "I could make you happy."

She smiled at him. "Yes. You could. But I will stay here."

Adjusting himself, he stood and took her in his arms. "You want me," he stated.

"I do," she admitted. "And I suspect that you may have spoiled other men for me. They would have a great deal to live up to."

He smiled at her warmly. "Still Kai?"

Meeting his eye, she answered truthfully. "Strangely, not completely anymore. I feel the need to find my own way."

"You live alone?" She nodded and he laughed. "You have found Leith cannot be trusted to keep the wolves from the door."

Smiling, she said. "You are right. Perhaps, that is why I don't want him round anymore."

"I should go. They will be waiting for me." Mark looked down into the dark almond eyes. "I love you; you know. If you change your mind, I will come for you."

Kalea hugged him. "I love you too. More than a little. Thank you, Mark."

They kissed. "I best go before we get distracted again." He smiled. She opened the door for him and he lent forward and whispered in her ear. "Be careful of a wet patch, or everyone will know what we have been up to." He kissed her cheek as she laughed and with that he was gone.

In the courtyard, all was confusion as Mark's party plus escort and horses milled around.

"Where's Mark?" Arthur asked.

"Don't know," Col answered. "He must be around here somewhere."

Leith stood chatting to both warbands as Kai, Lud and Arthur watched the preparations. "There he is!" came a call and all eyes turned to the gate as Mark sauntered through eating an apple.

"Where have you been?" asked Arthur.

"About," Mark answered evasively.

"Have you seen Kalea?" demanded Kai.

"That's for me to know and you to wonder." He gave a devilish grin. Lud put a restraining hand on Kai's shoulder. Mark threw his apple core away approaching Arthur with his hand extended. "Thank you for your hospitality."

"You are welcome. I am sorry that things didn't turn out as you wanted." Arthur was magnanimous in his victory.

Mark shrugged. "Kalea will not be diverted. Still, as you once said to me, there will be other pretty girls. Sadly, not the one I wanted. Should the way be clear, you should see if she is willing. She is delightful." With that he turned and swung into his saddle. "Arthur." Arthur nodded. "I ask one thing."

"Ask."

"Should Kalea change her mind, send someone for me and I will come for her."

Arthur nodded. "I will."

"I don't hold out much hope. But you never know."

Col rode up to Leith. "Farewell friend. I hope I don't meet you on the battlefield. It will give me little pleasure to kill you."

Leith laughed. "You can try."

Mark arrived. "That was a cany oath you gave me old man. I hope for all our sakes we don't have cause to see how it ends." Then with a wry smile and a wave, he turned to leave. As he rode passed, he called to Kai. "You really are quite the arsehole Kai." Then he laughed and led his party off.

Arthur couldn't help but smile, it did not go unnoticed.

Thus, the Kings pawn, was freed.

Chapter 12
Normality Resumed?

Kalea was enjoying her new found freedom and had settled into her new home and life. She still avoided Leith and spent most of her time with Ellen, learning the wise woman's way as well as swimming. Midnight had become her greatest joy and the village had got used to seeing this young woman dressed as a boy, riding through and then out through the gates. Kalea knew, it was frowned upon by some, but she had little care about it and once outside the village she would set her heels to Midnight and they would set off like the wind.

"Is that Kalea?" Lud asked Arthur and Kai as the great black beast galloped in the distance.

Arthur laughed. "I would guess yes. No one rides at such a break neck pace as that. I'm going to catch her," he urged his horse forward.

"You can try," Lud yelled after him.

"He's got no chance," Kai said with a grin and Lud was somehow happy that at last Kai's humour was resurfacing. "I don't think the devil himself, could catch that horse."

"He's a stunner," Lud confirmed. "John said he has asked Kalea if he can breed from him."

"What did she say?"

"She was happy enough to lend him out." Lud grinned. "We should get some fine foals from him. We might as well go back. Arthur will be ages. I doubt he will even find them."

Kai nodded and looked wistfully over his shoulder at where Kalea had disappeared. "She still hasn't forgiven Leith."

"No," Lud confirmed. "I feel sorry for him. But I can see no end to it." Kai looked as if he was about to speak and then shook his head. "Kai do you still care for Kalea?" Kai opened his mouth as if to answer, then shut it, and nodded. "Don't be too proud Kai. I know she cares for you still."

Kalea had given Midnight a good gallop and he was blowing. She had slowed to a canter as she turned for home. Much to her surprise, Arthur was riding towards her. She smiled. "Arthur!" she called as he rode up to her.

"I've been trying to catch you." Arthur grinned back. "He's a fast one."

Kalea laughed. "That he is. John has asked if he can breed from him."

"I had heard. We should have some descent horses in a few years' time. That's what I'm hoping. Mark told me that you tamed him."

"Yes. He needed a gentle hand. He'd been locked in the stable for a long time."

"Mark said he was vicious. That the stable hands were frightened of him."

Kalea laughed. "He still is with the wrong people. He was frightened himself and so attacked. Now, he knows I love him and he thinks he can protect me too."

"How are you?"

"I'm fine." Kalea smiled at him.

"Have you settled in?"

"Yes. I love my new home. It is a very generous gift. Thank you, Arthur."

He acknowledged her thanks. "Are you happy Kalea?"

He was fishing. She turned to look at him. "I am. I am enjoying my freedom."

"Freedom?"

"Yes." She grinned. "You have given it to me. I am free from having to be anything else than what I want to be."

"Do you regret your decision not to go back to Cornwall?"

"No." She hesitated. "Yes." She laughed at herself. "I am a woman and you men are very keen that we fit into certain roles. Those of us who don't are regarded with great suspicion. Because I am safe in your village, I can be alone and not fear anyone. I consider myself very lucky. I get up when I chose, go to bed when I chose, I eat when I'm hungry and can just please myself."

"You said yes as well," Arthur queried.

"Mark was offering me a good life. I know you and Mark are enemies, but he like you, is a good king to his people and he can be kind and generous. I don't regret not going back, but I do regret hurting him."

"Kalea, you are a lovely girl." She was embarrassed by his praise.

"Not so much."

Arthur smiled. His leg brushed hers as he rode close. "Yes. You are. I hear you are becoming a competent wise woman."

"Not yet. But I am trying." She laughed. "I like being able to help people."

"I hear you have been helping out in the stables too."

"Sick horses were where I got the urge to be a wise woman. I have a way with horses. I was thinking of getting a dog too."

This time Arthur laughed. "Are you going to fill your home with animals?"

"Might do. But see, this is what I mean. If I get fleas from laying down with the dogs, there is no one to moan at me."

They rode back to the village and Arthur found himself laughing a lot more than he usually did. Now, he understood what Mark meant. Kalea was good company.

Kalea prowess as a wise woman was growing and she too was earning a little coin as well as produce and she was surviving very well. Today, she was going to spend a little of her coin and buy some new, well, second-hand clothes. It was best not to ask to closely about where the clothes had come from, and Kalea would not wear them until she herself had laundered them herself. Smiling to herself she wandered through the market until she found what she was looking for. Sorting through the clothes, she found a light weight brown dress, it had faded in places, but the material was thin and Kalea was looking for something light for the summer. Already, she was assessing how she would take the sleeves out. That made her smile, the people of the village wouldn't approve of her having her naked arms on show, there was also a man's shirt that was in good condition. Having decided these were the two she wanted, she started to banter with the woman in charge. She knew that she would get them for a good price as she herself had given the woman some herbs for the pain she was having with her moon cycle and she had not asked for anything. Better still, it had obviously worked, as she was in good humour. Kalea was enjoying some banter and haggling with the woman and had just concluded her purchase when Leith arrived at her shoulder.

Putting her purchases over her arm, she turned to him.

"Kalea, I would talk to you." His voice was humble. She nodded to him and together, they walked through the bustling market. "I am sorry I failed you. I can see now, that I did." She said nothing but continued walking. "I judged you harshly. I should have asked you if you wanted to return here and even worse, I did nothing to help you mend the peace between you and Kai. I am sorry. I put my own wants before yours. Can you forgive me? Can we at least be friends?"

Kalea turned to look at him and he was relieved to see that she did not look angry. "I can forgive you; can you forgive me?"

"There is nothing to forgive."

"Yes. There is. I have been overly harsh. I was angry and I hurt. I didn't know what I wanted and how to get it. I want you to know, I do appreciate what you have done. I am grateful that you taught me to use a sword and I was glad of your advice and company. Now, I am finding alone is what makes me happy. We can be friends, but I can't allow you to live with me. I need some time." Leith nodded. She smiled at him and linked her arm through his. "We can be friends. Come, share some food with me. I promise you; I didn't cook the bread so it is edible." Leith laughed.

Kai was watching. He was glad to see that Kalea was bending. As he watched, his heart lurched, perhaps she would be ready for him too. He was ready to admit to himself, that he still wanted Kalea.

In fact, Leith spent the rest of the day with Kalea. He went down to the river with her and sat and watched as she washed her new purchases thoroughly after they had some bread and cheese. He had to admit, he wasn't much on the nettle tea. But he was pleased that she saw fit to share it with him and didn't moan. Occasionally, someone dropped in to ask advice or some herbs, which Kalea supplied. She got paid sometimes in eggs, and meat although she never asked for anything.

Whilst she was soaking her washing, she sorted out more leaves and moss and berries for her collection and Leith enjoyed being with her and seeing her busy at work. As usual, she was good company and made him laugh. When he left to return to hall, he was happier than he had been since leaving Cornwall.

Lud was ecstatic when Leith came in all smiles. Although he had not been invited to share Kalea's home, they were at least friends.

Kai was now included in Kalea's orbit, even though he hadn't sought her out. Kalea was now recognised as Ellen's apprentice and was treated well. They may not approve of her riding her big black horse in trousers, or walking around in a flimsy dress with no sleeves, but it was recognised that she was fast acquiring skills that they could use when Ellen was not available.

The brown flimsy dress with no sleeves, was being worn the first time she decided that Kai would no longer ignore her. Arthur and Kai had been standing chatting in the market when Kalea came along. Her long hair was loose for once and she was carrying a basket for her shopping.

"Good morning, Arthur, good morning, Kai." Both men turned towards her and both smiled at her sunny face.

"Good morning. How are you?" Arthur asked taking in the slim well-turned arms.

"Morning Kalea," Kai spoke to her for the first time. She rewarded him with a bright smile.

"I am well. And you two?" She made sure she included Kai in her statement not giving him the opportunity to ignore her.

"We are well," Kai answered and Arthur smiled. So, he was thawing.

"We are just looking to see if there is anything we need being sold today."

"Robert, over there," she said pointing with a long slim arm. "Is selling some beautiful leather work. The working is really fine."

"We shall go and inspect it," Arthur commented. Noting that Kalea was making no effort to flirt with them, treating them as just another friend met at the market.

"And what are you looking for?" Kai asked.

"Nothing exciting, I'm afraid. I off to the bread stall. I have a problem with bread."

"How so?" Kai grinned.

"Sadly, I can't cook it." They all laughed. "I can put together a meal of sorts, which Leith tells me is tasty. Although of course he could be lying." Arthur and Kai laughed again. "But my bread is a disaster. I don't know why. It turns out like biscuit."

"That in itself, can be tasty." Arthur grinned.

"This is not what Leith or Ellen tell me. So, I admit defeat and must buy some."

"You can't be good at everything." Kai smiled.

"But I should be able to make bread," she said with a wry smile. "everyone tells me how easy it is. I shall have to go, or they will sell out."

"You could always come to the hall," Arthur called as she wandered unhurriedly away.

"I think not," she responded.

The two men exchanged knowing smiles.

Returning to the hall, Kai hailed Leith.

"Kalea tells us that she cannot cook bread. Is that the truth? We met her in the market and she was off to buy some."

Leith laughed; his spirits lifted a little. So, Kai was talking to her now, that was a good thing. "Bless her! She hasn't quite got the hang of it but it's not as bad and Ellen and I would have her believe."

Arthur grinned. "She says it is like biscuits."

Leith chuckled. "It's Kalea. She forgets it and over does it. In her defence, she can roast a chicken and do a real tasty stew. I wouldn't stay, if she couldn't but now, I understand why her father always bought his bread."

The men laughed.

Now, when Kai saw Kalea they always exchanged pleasantries. There was no sign of romance but at least they spoke, Arthur noted. He was not unhappy, although he had thought that if the frost between them didn't thaw soon, he would go calling and see if Kalea was interested in more than a friendship. However, he noted, that Kalea was not interested in men at the moment. Perhaps as she had said, she was enjoying her freedom.

The summer was being problematic for the wise women, not just Ellen although she was seen as the one with the most skill. A fever had hit the village and no one seemed to escape it except the wise women, which was a conundrum as they were constantly in the presence of the sick. Kalea was helping to prepare large quantities of healing herbs to reduce temperatures and whilst Ellen did most of the home visits, Kalea dealt with the mundane and tried to keep the stocks supplied.

It was one such day that Lud burst through the door of Ellen's home causing Kalea to jump. Before she could admonish him, he blurted out.

"Where is Ellen? She is needed."

"She is birthing a baby Lud. What is it?"

His face was haggard and her heart sank. "Kai, has a fever."

"I will come," she said without hesitation, she wiped her hands on a cloth and began adding things to her chest. Then hoisting it up, she went to exit only to have Lud, take the chest off her. She nodded and shutting Ellen's door they left. Kalea was hard pushed to keep up with the pace and was forced to lift her skirts so she was almost running. Grabbing a lad by the collar, she gave him strict instructions. "Run down to Bridie's and tell Ellen that Kai is ill and I am at the castle." He nodded and ran off. As they entered the castle door, Kalea then addressed one of the servants despite Lud's impatience. "I need two buckets of the coldest water you can draw from the well. Plenty of clean cloth and a jug of hot water. Bring them to Kai's room." And with that, she ran up the stairs behind Lud and followed him into Kai's room.

"Kalea! He has been thrashing around and he is burning hot." For once, Arthur's face was open and she could see the worry etched there. She nodded to him.

"Ellen is birthing a babe. I will have to do. Open the window." Arthur did so. She went to Kai and laid a cool hand on his forehead; he was hot to the touch and drenched with sweat.

He opened his eyes. "Kalea." His voice was hoarse.

"I am here."

"Stay with me."

"Of that you can be sure," she answered and his eyes shut again. Drawing a deep breath, she turned to the other two men in the room. "Take his clothes off."

"All of them?" Arthur asked but Kalea's dark eyes said it all. He and Lud stripped him naked and were about to cover him when she spoke.

"No. Do not cover him. We need to get the heat out of him." The door opened and two servants came in with all that Kalea had asked for. "Thank you. I need these replenished every so often so the water is cold." They nodded and left. Mixing some potion with the hot water, Kalea went and sat on the edge of the bed and lifting Kai head tried to get him to drink it. "Kai. You must drink this. It will help you." His eyes opened again and he began to gulp before falling back on the bed. Kalea then set to, ripping the cloth and dipping it in the cold water, lay one piece on his forehead. With another, she started bathing him. His teeth began to chatter.

"He is chilling. Cover him, Kalea."

"No. It is the fever fighting to keep him hot. We must cool him."

"What can I do?" Arthur asked.

Kalea looked down at Kai. "There is not a lot you can do. If possible, I would like a chair with a back so that I can sit with him. Possibly a trivet to put on the fire, so I can steep some healing leaves. But other than that, it will be down to me and him. Ellen will come up later and check I am doing alright."

"Will he live?" Lud asked.

Looking at their worried faces, Kalea was tempted to lie but, in the end, she told the truth. "I don't know. He is strong and I am determined. If I can break the fever, he will live."

"But can you?" Lud demanded.

"I will, if I can. I can do no more than try. I will do my best Lud." He nodded. "Send someone to stand at the door and if I need anything, or anything changes, I will send for you." They hesitated. "There is nothing for you to do here. Go! Let me work."

They left and Kalea once again, bathed the sweat off Kai. Cooling his body. The door flew open and Arthur came in carrying a cumbersome chair. "Where would you like it?"

"Over here by the bed, so that I am close." He put the chair down. Putting another cool cloth on Kai's forehead.

"If the fever doesn't break in three days, Kai's in trouble."

"You know this how?"

"Judging on how it's going in the village."

"How many have we lost?"

"More than we'd like, but less than could have been."

"Save him Kalea."

She nodded and he left.

Kalea sat down in the chair next to Kai. "Don't you dare die on me. I won't allow it."

Over the next hours, Kalea wiped Kai down and gave him some more medicine to help with the temperature. When he thrashed, she held him down, soothing him. At one stage, he opened his eyes. "Kalea?"

Stroking his face with her cool hand. "I'm here." He reached up and took her hand.

"Stay with me."

"Always. Now, take a sip of this water." And she lifted his head and he drank. Putting the beaker down and found him still watching her, he reached a hand to her and she took his hand and sat in the chair next to him. Lud came up with some food for her. He looked at Kalea and she shook her head. He looked down at Kai, "Lud, can you get some more cold water sent up?"

"Would you like some hot water too?"

Kalea nodded and he left. Although her appetite seemed to have left her, she ate. She needed to keep her strength up. The door opened and Ellen arrived along with two servants with the cold water.

"How is he?" Ellen asked stepping forward to see for herself. She put her hand on his forehead and although his eyes didn't open, he called for Kalea.

"I'm here." Kai settled down again. "He's very hot."

"You are doing everything, I would do," Ellen said sitting wearily on the bed. "Well done. Go home and get some rest."

"No. I told him I would stay, and I will. Besides, it looks like your need is greater than mine. How did Bridie do?"

"Another boy. He was tricky. Breach. Round the wrong way. But we got there. Bridie will be very sore for a while. It has been busy of late. I shall be glad when this fever leaves the kingdom. I'm quite looking forward to treating toothache and headaches."

Kalea smiled. "Go home Ellen. I will take care of Kai."

"Are you sure?"

"Yes. You have got the hard job. I look after one, and you look after everyone else."

Ellen laughed and kissed her on the forehead. "Take care. I will pop in and see if you need anything." And she left.

Kalea kept up her work and as the day drew to a close, she kissed Kai's lips and then sat in the chair next to him. Arthur came in, holding a large blanket which he gave to her. He looked at Kai, but said nothing and left.

Kalea dozed in the chair. Waking up at intervals, to tend to Kai. She tenderly bathed him in cold water and made sure he had medicine regularly.

When Arthur, came up with breakfast, she was asleep in the chair holding Kai's hand. He put the tray down and gave her a gentle shake. She jumped, and then saw Arthur but before she said anything. Her hand went to Kai's sweaty forehead.

"No change." Her voice was flat and tired. "I had hoped to break the fever by now."

"You need to rest."

She smiled as she shook her head. "Not yet. I promised him, I'd stay and stay I will. Thank you for breakfast." She tore off a crust of bread and gnawed it distractedly. "At least you have good bread."

Arthur smiled. "I'll check in on you later. Do you still want the water?"

"Yes please. The heat of Kai's body has warmed the water."

Arthur nodded and was gone. Once again, Kalea began her routine. Bathing Kai and making sure he swallowed down the potions she was giving him.

Another day and night went by. Kalea was beginning to despair but still she kept up with her routine. Ellen came but had nothing further to offer. Arthur and

Lud visited often bringing food and solace but it was evident, that they too had their doubt if Kai would survive. Every now and then, in his fever induced sleep he called for her, and every time she would respond that she was still here for him.

It was the dark on the third night as Kalea once again settled down in the chair. The crisis was upon them. She had been diligent in making sure his body was cooled. Not allowing the fever to burn through him and as she drifted into an uneasy sleep, her thoughts turned over and over, if there was anything left she could try.

"Kalea."

She was jolted awake and immediately, came to him. "I am here." Her voice was soft and her cool hand went to his forehead. "It has gone." She smiled with relief. His brow was cool, the fever had broken. "Welcome back to the land of the living."

"I had thought, I dreamt it." Kai looked at her. "I thought I had dreamt that you were here." His voice was husky, his throat dry.

"No. You asked me to stay and here I am." She lifted his head and he drunk the medicine that she gave him willingly. Kalea couldn't stop smiling. Allowing him to sink back on to his bed, she covered him in furs.

He held out his hand to her and she took it. "I thought I dreamed of a goddess soothing me."

She smiled; the old Kai was back. "I am afraid, I am a poor goddess. I am crumpled and I smell."

"You are beautiful."

Her heart beat hard in her chest and for a moment, she forgot how tired she was. "You had me worried for a while."

"That was never my intention." He was already tiring.

"Rest now."

"Will you stay?"

"Of course."

He took her hand and almost immediately sank into sleep. Kalea sitting in her chair, smiled and a glimmer of hope flickered as she too, sank into a deep sleep.

Arthur entered the room and placed the breakfast tray on the small table. He glanced at Kalea who was curled up in the blanket fast asleep her hand still holding Kai's. Looking at Kai, he was amazed to see Kai watching him and as their eyes met, Kai smiled.

Unable to contain his joy Arthur shouted. "Kai!" Kalea bolted to her feet, looking confused and startled but Arthur was passed her and at Kai side. "It is good to see you awake. I am sorry Kalea."

"It's fine," she answered rubbing her face.

"When did this happen?" Arthur asked them both.

"The moon was high," Kalea responded. "Sometime in the night." She stretched yawning as she did so. "Is Lud in the hall? I will go and fetch him. Then if you don't mind, I will go for a swim. I smell really bad."

Arthur laughed. "No, you won't. I will get Lud and I will have a bath made for you while you eat your breakfast."

"I have no clean clothes," she stated.

"I am sure we can find you some." Turning back to Kai, his warmth evident he said. "It is good to have you back my friend."

"Can you get Kai some porridge from the kitchen?" Kalea asked. "And before you go, can you help me sit him up?"

"Of course." Arthur helped Kai sit up and Kalea stuffed the blanket behind him, so that he was supported, then with a laugh of pure pleasure Arthur left.

Kalea went to the tray and spread some honey on an oatcake and came back to sit on the edge of the bed. Still smiling, "Would you like to try a piece?" He nodded and she broke a piece with lots of honey off and popped it into his mouth. As he chewed her took her wrist and once the mouthful was finished, took each of her fingers into his mouth and licked the sweetness off. Kalea breath caught in her throat, and her body was flooded with a hot tingle. She gave a slow smile but the intimacy was broken and Lud burst into the room. Kalea leapt up guiltily and hastily moved aside as Lud rushed to Kai's side and gave him a huge bear hug.

"I am so pleased to see you lad." His broad smile being met by Kai's own. He turned his attention to Kalea. "I thank you." Kalea smiled back. "Your bath should be ready now."

Kalea popped the last of the oatcake into her mouth and washed it down with some milk. "Then if you will excuse me. Don't wear him out Lud. He is weak. He needs food and rest."

Lud nodded and as she went to leave. He called after her. "That was a job well done Kalea."

She turned and left. Fortunately, for Kalea, a servant was by the main door. She had no idea where the bath room was but he was eager to show her. Once inside, she sighed and stripping off, eased herself into the large bath of hot water. Arthur had been true to his word. There was a lump of sweet-smelling soap and shirt and trousers had been laid out for her. For a while, she lay enjoying the warmth of the water, but nearly dozed off and so, she set to scrubbing herself clean. At last, she felt clean enough, and stepped out to dry and dress. The shirt and trousers were obviously Arthur's and even with the trews laced tight, they still slid to her hips. She smiled and stomping her boots on, left, thanking the servants as she did so. They quickly relieved her of her dress and told her that they would return it when it was clean. She didn't argue and thanked them again.

Exiting the castle, Kalea drew in a huge breath. She had been in Kai's chamber for three days, and it was lovely to be in the fresh air again. The sun was high in the sky and there wasn't a cloud in sight. She was greeted by numerous people as she made her way home via Ellen's.

"Kalea! I have heard the news."

"Already?" Kalea queried yawning. "I had just come to tell you."

"Good news spreads fast. How is he?"

"He will be fine. Needs to build up his strength a bit. But the fever is gone. I thought we were in trouble there."

"Go home. Go to bed. You look like you need it."

"I shall have to see to Midnight first. I have left him tethered in the field for days."

"No. You don't. Leith has been down and looking after the beast. He is fine."

Kalea smiled. "Good old Leith. In that case, I will have a sleep." She yawned again, kissed Ellen on the cheek and left.

Back at home. Kalea barred the door. She wanted no one barging in. Taking off her boots, she climbed up onto the sleeping platform and was asleep almost before she laid down.

Ellen walked into Kai's chamber. Arthur was sitting on the bed chatting and moved out of the way so Ellen could have a look at Kai.

"How are you?" she said laying a hand on his forehead.

"Better. Thank you. Where's Kalea?"

Ellen laughed. "Asleep, I would think."

"She has sat with you for more than three days." Arthur grinned. "She has earned her rest."

"Three days?" Kai queried.

They both nodded. "Three days and three nights, she has sat in that chair. Despite the fact that we tried to send her away," Arthur quipped.

"I had not realised that it was so long," Kai pondered.

"Now. You just have to rest and get well. Don't try to go running off. I doubt your legs will support you. Take it slow," Ellen warned. "There is nothing for me to do here, so I will leave you in peace." As she went, she noticed Kalea's chest of cures. "Arthur, perhaps you could get this returned to Kalea. But do it tomorrow. I think, she has little use of it today."

"I will Ellen. And thank you."

"Don't thank me. Kalea did all the work." And she left.

Arthur looked at Kai. "She's seen you naked now. You have got no chance of wooing her. I'm in with a chance." They both laughed.

"Did she really sit all that time?"

"Yes. She bathed you. Gave you medicine and slept in that hard chair. While you languished on a soft bed and gave her nothing but trouble." Arthur grinned.

Kalea opened her eyes. It was still light. She climbed down and threw open the door and realised her mistake. It was early morning and she had slept right through. She washed her face in her bucket of water, which was now, neither fresh nor cold and looked round her. Her meagre supply of food, had gone off. A sniff saw the milk was sour, the bread and cheese hard. She decided to go up to the hall and share some food there. Stomping on her boots, and combing her hair, she went round to get Midnight, who was very excited to see her.

"Yes. I have missed you too. We are going to go for a long ride today but I have to get some food." As if to confirm that, her stomach growled hungrily. When was the last time, she ate? She wondered and concluded it was the one oat cake that she had shared with Kai yesterday morning. Saddling up, she swung into the saddle.

Riding through the village, she was greeted by people going about their business and before long, she rode into the castle courtyard. John, had just come out of the stable leading Arthur's horse. She smiled as she slid from the saddle and tethered Midnight to a post.

"Come and meet Midnight John. You will have to get used to him, if you want to put him to your mares."

John looked warily at the big beast and tied Arthur's horse up and approached cautiously. Kalea grinned. As he came closer, the stallion's ears went

274

back and he watched with great suspicion. Kalea motioned him next to her as she stroked the black velvet nose. Voice softened she spoke. "Midnight, this is John. He is a good man. Give me your hand John." Almost reluctantly, he did so and with Kalea's hand about his, she put it on the horse's neck. Still using her most soothing voice. "There's a good boy. You see, it is alright. I wouldn't let anyone harm you." Midnight's ears flicked forward and he turned to smell the man who now touched him. Kalea still stood close to John but removed her hand and John began to stroke the muscled neck. "See. All is well." Kalea soothed and John turned to grin at her. "He has accepted you now. As long as you are gentle, he will be gentle with you. No fast movements and definitely no slapping. I am going to see if I can scrounge some breakfast."

"I'm not sure you should leave just yet," John spoke lowly, not wishing to agitate the horse.

"You'll be fine. You are friends now." And she left before he could protest further. As she came into the hall, a cheer went up and she smiled broadly and bowed low. Arthur came over and hugged her.

"Good morning." Leith was also waiting to hug her and before long, she was enveloped in his bear hug. She laughed.

"I had wondered if I could share breakfast."

"Of course." Arthur motioned that she should sit next to him. She did so and at the sight of the food on the table, her tummy rumbled loudly.

"Please forgive my stomach, I have been neglecting it and it thinks my throat has been cut."

Arthur laughed. "Help yourself."

The only problem of eating when you're starving, is that it is hard to remember table manners. Kalea poured a beaker of milk and downed it in one, cuffing her milk moustache on the cuff of her shirt, then cutting of a piece of cheese, she munched it quickly and groaned with pleasure. Bread and butter followed. Leith and Arthur watched her with amusement.

"That was wonderful," she stated having eaten her fill. "I'll soon be able to fill your trousers out. I take it these are yours?" She pointed at her legs.

"Yes. They are." Arthur grinned.

"They fit well enough on the hip, but the waist is a little too large. I shall return them when I have laundered them."

"No hurry. You may keep them if you please."

"I might well do that. The shirt is particularly fine. Leith, thanks for looking after Midnight."

Leith smiled. "Least I could do while you were busy elsewhere. He wasn't best happy, but he tolerated me."

"I'm glad about that. I have just left him to make friends with John and I would hate to go out there and find that Midnight had taken his head off." The men laughed. "How is Kai?"

"Took your time to ask." Leith laughed.

"For this, I am sorry. I seem to have slept a whole day away and then, find that all my food has spoiled. So, I thought it would be best to eat something before I fainted away."

It was more an explanation, rather than an accusation but both men exchanged a guilty look. "He is much improved." Arthur hurried over the point.

"Now, I have eaten, I will see for myself. Thank you for breakfast." And she rose. Arthur came too.

The pair entered Kai's chamber to find him, wrapped in the blanket and sitting in a chair. His face lit up when he saw her.

"Well, look at you!" Kalea exclaimed. "You look much better." She came forward and placed a hand on his forehead checking the heat, as she withdrew, he caught it.

"I have yet to thank you, for saving my life." His voice was sweet and low.

Kalea beamed back. "It was a life worth saving." Lud moved over and she sat beside him on the bench. "I confess, I haven't been up long myself. Make sure you drink lots, not wine. And eat plenty," she instructed and Kai nodded seriously while Lud smiled. At last, they had made peace. "I can't stay long," she said getting up. "I have left Midnight with John making friends. I hope," she added. "But I best rescue him."

"Will you come back?" Kai sounded hopeful.

"I must give Midnight some exercise and it will give me a chance to blow the cobwebs away. If it is not too late. Yes. If it is, I will return tomorrow. Take care." And with that she was gone. Arthur shrugged and followed.

"What are you smiling at?" Kai asked.

"You and Kalea. She is going to make you work hard to win her back. Rightly so. Everything worth having is worth working for." Kai was not impressed.

Arthur walked down the steps of the castle with Kalea.

"May I ride with you?"

"Of course. If you want. But be warned, I will be riding hard."

"That does not frighten me." He laughed.

John was smiling running his hands over Midnight.

"See!" Kalea crowed. "I told you he was sweet."

"I don't know about that," John answered rubbing Midnight's nose. "One of the lads came over thinking he was a changed horse. He isn't. Nearly took the poor boys head off. He certainly is a stunner."

"Would you like me to stable him here? You could get better acquainted."

"Would you? I wouldn't let anybody else touch him."

"He wouldn't let anybody else touch him." Kalea grinned. "I'll leave him here when I return. I could do with a walk through the market that's if Arthur will lend me a few coins. I didn't pick any up on the way out."

"Of course." Arthur boosted her into the saddle. Then he swung into the saddle himself and the two horses walked side by side out the gate. "I see you and Kai have come to a peaceful arrangement."

"Yes. It's hard not to form a bond with someone when you are fighting for their life." Arthur nodded. "He will, however, find me a horse of a different colour."

"How so?"

"A lot has happened in a year. I have grown up some. I am no longer a wild child." She laughed. "I am now a wild woman."

He grinned. "Will you let him into your life again?"

"Are you fishing Arthur?"

"Perhaps."

She grinned. "I don't know yet. I am no longer needing a husband. I have a wise woman's ways. Perhaps, I will take a lover instead."

Arthur roared with laughter. "Madam, don't let Leith hear. He will be horrified."

With a wink, she retorted. "And he no longer holds me in his sway either."

Arthur chuckled. "Valim said that you would make a good priestess. Perhaps, he was right."

"Now, there is one I don't trust. Mark's wise woman said he was a bad 'un. I think she has his measure. I would not be a priestess to be told who to give my favours too. Even if it be Herne himself."

Arthur laughed again. They had reached the village gate. With no further ado, Kalea put her heels to Midnight and they were off at a flat-out gallop. Arthur set out to catch up, if he could. All he could hear was the thudding of hooves and Kalea's laughter bubbling out behind her.

At last, Kalea pulled Midnight up. He had enjoyed the flat-out race with Kalea leaning low over his neck. He had kicked up his heels, which had made her laugh harder at his exuberance.

She turned him to look for Arthur who was coming up fast. *But not fast enough*, she thought with a grin. "What took you so long?" she teased as he pulled up next to her.

Slapping his horse's neck, he conceded. "We were just not fast enough."

"I don't know that many are." Kalea grinned.

"Where did Mark get him?"

Kalea patted Midnight's neck. "Jack, in Mark's stable said, he was found running with the wild ponies. I should imagine, the ponies, will be much improved by running with him. But he is not local stock. Jack wondered if he had come from a ship wreck. No one really knows. He is a mystery."

"He'd make an excellent warhorse," Arthur commented as they turned for home.

"I trained him for Mark and he did let Mark ride him. Mark said that as the horse loved me above all others, I should have him."

"That was a generous gift."

"It was. He is certainly no lady's palfrey."

"You ride well."

"It is what I love doing. That and swimming. As Leith says, not the most sought-after traits in a woman."

"They are in a special woman."

"Are you flirting?" she asked semi-seriously.

"Maybe."

"Should I consider you as a lover?" she teased.

"Who's flirting now?"

Kalea laughed they had arrived back in the courtyard. Slipping to the ground, she stretched, Arthur would have thought before, that she was unaware of how gorgeous she looked. Now, he wasn't so sure. John came out of the stable and she handed him the reigns. "You've given him a good run, I see."

"We have had some fun," Kalea agreed. "Would you like me to rub him down?"

"No. I'll do it. But if I scream, come and save me," John teased.

"Count on it."

Arthur took her by the elbow. "Now, why do you want some coin?"

"I need to buy some food."

"No, you don't. We'll raid the kitchen."

She grinned. "What a good idea."

"Do you want to see Kai first?"

Kalea tilted her head to one side. "I don't think I do."

Arthur laughed. "You are a cruel mistress."

"That I am. Now, what delights do you think your kitchen holds?"

Kalea walked home with a basket full of good things to eat. She decided, she would share them with Ellen, if she was willing, of course. There was ham, cheese, bread, a portion of venison, a whole cooked chicken and some veg as well as fruit. More than enough for her for a few days. It had been a good day. Now, Kai was on the mend, she could relax. She had enjoyed her ride with Arthur and she had seen a different side of him today. She had considered him quite serious, but he had been fun. Humming and feeling very happy she arrived home.

Arthur walked into the hall smiling. He hadn't laughed so much for a long time. Especially not with a woman. He was not going to see Kai straight away, he wanted to settle down a bit first. No way, did he want Kai to see how happy Kalea had made him. But Leith noticed. Kai had better start working hard.

Lud came down to the hall and sat down opposite Leith.

"How's Kai?"

"Much improved," Lud said cheerfully. "He would be down here if he had the choice. I have just asked for a bath to be made for him so that he can get dressed. He is going to need help to get down here though. Have you seen Kalea?"

"Not since she came to share breakfast," Leith answered truthfully.

Lud grinned. "She's a strong one. You should have seen her with Kai this morning." Leith raised an eyebrow. "She's not going to forgive him that easily for treating her so coolly."

"Mark has changed her. He has given her a lot more confidence in who she is and what powers she has. Not a good thing. Kalea was always strong willed but Mark cossetted her and towards the end encouraged her to see that she was of value. I could never have seen her cutting me off as she did before Mark."

"I can see that." Lud nodded. "I think she has dug her toes in. She has been used as a major piece in the game and now she has taken herself out of it. She did it very well. I couldn't believe how well she handled the two kings when they had the power over her and she still spoke well."

"She is brave. I give her that."

"Kai has finally seen sense and wants her now. Do you think she will have him?"

"I can't say. I thought I knew her, but she is a different woman now."

Kai gained strength and was once again out and about. He sought out Kalea and she was careful to keep him at arm's length, which frustrated him. She also made sure; she did not discourage him.

There was a knock on Kalea door one morning. Opening it, she was surprised to see Kai.

"Good morning. Is everything alright?" she queried.

He gave her his best Kai smile. "Good morning. Nothing is wrong, I just came to talk. Can I come in?"

"No. I think not."

He was taken aback but wasn't so easily turned away. "Then perhaps, you would walk with me."

She rewarded him with a smile. "Yes. I will." And she stepped out closing the door behind her. Together, the strolled through the village.

"It seems of late; you have been avoiding me," Kai said carefully.

"Does it? I'm sorry. That is not the case. I have been busy with Ellen."

He nodded. "Does she keep you busy?"

"Wise women are always busy. If you are not treating people, you are out collecting various cures. Although it is quieter, since the fever left the village."

"Has it gone completely?"

"It seems so. You were one of the last."

"And the hardest to fix." He grinned.

She returned it. "But we did fix you. Others weren't so lucky."

Kalea fought the urge to link arms with him, but knew he would see this as an open invitation.

"I had hoped that you would agree to go riding with me, but have noticed you are not riding of late."

Kalea laughed. "I have no mount. Midnight is otherwise engaged servicing the mares."

Kai laughed with her. They had completed a circuit and were now close to Ellen's house. Ellen's door was open which implied she was in and treating.

"I will leave you here. I shall go and help Ellen."

He acknowledged her decision. "May I call again?"

"Yes. I would like that," she confessed.

"Then I will see you soon," he said as she ducked through Ellen's door.

When Ellen was sure that Kai had left, she turned to Kalea.

"Was that Kai, I saw you with?" Kalea grinned and nodded and the two women burst out laughing. "So, now he is pursuing you." Kalea nodded again and they both laughed again. "Do you feel the same about him?"

"Oh yes!" Kalea clapped her hands together in glee. "Why do you think we were walking? I didn't trust myself with him." They giggled again.

The next morning, Kalea was working with Ellen when Kai came through the door.

"Good morning, ladies. I wonder Ellen if, I might borrow Kalea?"

"If she is willing, yes." She looked at Kalea and winked.

"What is it, Kai?" Kalea asked.

"Come and see." He smiled.

She stepped outside and out and smiled with pleasure. Kai had bought two horses down from the stables. Impulsively, she hugged him. "What a treat! Ellen! Come look!" Ellen came out and saw that Kai was looking very pleased with himself. "It looks like I can go riding again."

"Make sure it's only the horse you're riding," Ellen warned with a wink. Kalea laughed.

"I will be good. Can I go and get changed?"

"Of course." They walked back to Kalea's house, smiling and chatting and Kai waited outside with the horses, while she changed. She was soon back and he boosted her into the saddle. Arthur was talking to the blacksmith as they rode passed and gave a wave, which was returned. He smiled to himself.

They reached the village gates. Kalea now turned her full attention to her mount. Kai had got her a dapple-grey mare and she was a sweet thing. She was eager to please and an easy ride. She turned to look at Kai, and with a wicked smile, she urged her forward and they were off at a gallop. Kalea laughing in exuberance. Kai soon closed the distance and the two raced forward neck to neck.

She looked across at Kai, who was grinning at her. Leaning over the mare's neck, she tried to urge her faster, but she was not Midnight who seem to be able to find more speed. The mare did try, but she had little more to give, and Kalea was content to ride abreast with Kai. They eventually, pulled up, the horses blowing while they grinned happily at each other.

"That was wonderful!" Kalea exclaimed. "Thank you so much, Kai."

"You are most welcome. It certainly was fun."

She patted the mare's neck. "Good girl. You were lucky I wasn't on Midnight. You'd have never have caught me."

"But it was fun running together," Kai said.

"It was," she admitted.

He suddenly looked serious. "Kalea. I have been an idiot." She met his gaze. "Do you think we could be as we were?"

"No. We can't. The innocent girl who survived the Saxon raid, is gone. I have learned so much since then." She saw the disappointment on his face. "I am a different woman now. I have been used. Mark used me against Arthur, Arthur used me against Mark and Leith used me to get back here. I no longer trust anyone except myself. Can you understand?" Kai did not nod, he watched her. He did understand. "I have a wise woman's ways. I've travelled half the country, twice." She paused. "I have learnt the importance of having women friends and they have taught me a lot about men." He was listening intently to her. "And I have known the love of a man." He didn't flinch. "We cannot be as we were, Kai. But that doesn't mean we can't be together as something else. Perhaps, something better."

"Do you still care for me?"

"Yes," she confessed. "I have always cared for you and always will. You know it too. When you had the fever, you asked me to stay, and I did. During that fever, I knew that you still cared too. This time it is different. I need to take time to find my way."

"I would wait, if you just tell me that I may be able to earn your love again."

Kalea's heart, ached for him. She leaned across, and touched his face. "Yes. I love you now. I just need to find a way to trust again." He caught her hand and pressed it to his lips.

"Mark said I was an arsehole."

Kalea's laughter exploded out of her. "That sounds like Mark. He does not suffer fools gladly. Why?"

"For letting my jealousy get in the way of claiming you."

"Well, you were a bit." She grinned and to her delight, he returned it.

"Did you turn down his proposal for me?"

"Yes and no," she answered truthfully. "I wanted to make my own choices. Here, I had a chance to live as I wanted. You had made it clear that I was of no interest to you. If I went with Mark, even as his wife, I would still be his captive. Do you understand?" He nodded. He was beginning to understand.

"Did he treat you well?"

"At first, not so much. Later yes. He gave me gifts, ensured I was safe and was kind and gentle."

"You care for him," he stated rather than asked.

"I came to care for him. Yes."

"Yet you turned down his offer of marriage."

"Yes. I have been honest with you Kai. Now be honest with me."

He had yet to release her hand and his blue eyes still held hers. "I love you. That is all I know. I have loved you since I met you. My jealousy, blinded me. I couldn't bear to think of you in the arms of another a man. I have no other defence."

She nodded, grinned and gave his hand a squeeze. "Now all is said. We can start fresh at the beginning."

Kai was relieved. At least, he had hope now.

They rode slowly back to the castle. The courtyard was not busy. Kai was off his horse and offering Kalea a hand down. She slid down into his arms and the closeness, offered an excuse for a kiss. It was taken. The kiss was light and brief, but was enough to ignite between them the flame that had been dying down to an ember. They walked together back to the stable, where a stable lad took the horses from them. John appeared.

"Kalea! Have you come to see Midnight? I am sure he would be pleased to see you."

They followed John to the paddock where Midnight held court with his herd of ten mares. Kai and Kalea lent of the fence and watched him as he grazed. Kalea let out a high-pitched halloo and Midnight's head came up and with a wicker of pleasure came cantering towards her, head and tail held high, showing off. Coming up to the fence, he leant over and using his head, pulled her close to him. She laughed and her arms went round him. Every time she tried to pull away, he pulled her back. The two men laughed heartily.

"He still won't let anyone touch him but me," John said. "He's managed to inflict a couple of injuries on the lads who walked too close."

"Kai, give me your hand." Kai didn't hesitate. Kalea took his hand and with hers wrapped round his, placed it on Midnight. "There's a good boy." Kalea voice was soft and soothing. "This is Kai. He is a good friend. Be nice to him." Midnight, regarded Kai suspiciously but allowed him to stroke him. Then he lent across and snuffed at Kai hair, causing Kai to laugh. Midnight's ear flickered but allowed Kai to continue, and when Kai tried to stop. He nudged him. They all grinned.

They finally managed to escape Midnight and Kai invited Kalea into the hall for some food. She refused.

"I must get back to Ellen."

"Then I shall walk you."

Kai bided his time, although it pained him to do so. He could not stay away. Making sure he saw Kalea at least once a day. They now walked hand in hand or arm in arm. Occasionally, they snatched a kiss but Kalea was careful not to let her passion ignite.

"You seem a lot happier of late," Arthur commented. "Could it be that you have rekindled your love for Kalea?"

Kai grinned. "I am trying. She is making me work hard."

Arthur laughed. "Is she much changed?"

"Yes and no," Kai admitted. "She is still fun and honest, but she is a lot more wary and cautious. She has little trust of anyone with the exception of Ellen and Midnight."

"Hardly surprising. Talking of which, Mark has been quiet this season. Perhaps he is nursing his wounded heart."

Kai smiled. "I can almost feel sorry for him. To have captured such a treasure and lost it must be quite a blow."

"Can you really?" Arthur asked with a wry grin.

Kai laughed. "Not really. His loss is my gain."

"If you behave yourself," Lud warned. "I'm beginning to wonder, if any man can hold that girl down. If the King of Cornwall with his considerable wealth and charm can't do it, what chance have you?"

"Just watch me," Kai said with determination.

Chapter 13
War with the Welsh

"Kai! Come and sit with me," Arthur called as supper was being served up.

"I'm eating with Kalea tonight." This was greeted with a lot of cat-calling. "I said I am eating with Kalea, not eating Kalea." He laughed. As more cat-calling broke out. "Sadly, I'm not alone, Leith and Ellen are there too."

"Someone's got to keep you in order," Leith said slapping him on the shoulder. "Come on lad. She will not be happy if we are late."

The two men walked down to Kalea's home, where she welcomed them in. There was a delicious smell. A chicken had been roasted and she had a pot of vegetables bubbling. Ellen was helping and had also lent some plates. Kalea had even gone out and bought some ale. Pouring Kai and Leith some ale, she went on to serve the meal with hunks of bread.

"This is good Kalea," Kai said chewing appreciatively.

"You'd say it was good, if it tasted like shit." Laughed Leith. "But he's right Kalea, this is very good." She handed out some bread, which Leith dipped into his vegetables. "You've been buying bread again."

"No. She hasn't," Ellen chipped in. "This is made with her own fair hands. At last, she has got it right."

Kalea laughed. "Took a lot of practice. But I got there in the end."

"You are definitely better with the healing ways," Ellen confirmed. "You don't seem to have any difficulty learning that."

So, the evening passed very pleasantly and all too soon it was time for them to leave.

"I'll walk Ellen home," Leith said chivalrously. "I won't be long. Don't be too long saying goodbye."

Kai laughed. "He's a rogue."

"That he is." She turned willingly into his arms and he kissed her deeply. Kalea knew immediately she was lost. She melted against him. Feeling his desire for her as he crushed her to him. Her hands pulled him closer and then…There was a cough. They parted reluctantly.

"Ellen said I shouldn't leave you two alone for long. She said you couldn't be trusted. That is obviously true," Leith said.

"I really don't know what you mean." Kalea smoothed her dress down and Kai laughed.

"Night Kalea," Leith called. He grabbed Kai by the arm and towed him away.

Smiling over his shoulder Kai called. "Night Kalea. The food was really good."

"Lock the door!" Leith added "and don't come out till morning. I shall make sure this puppy stays at home."

Kalea's laughter followed them.

A few days later, a scout came to the hall. He bought grave news. A Welsh raiding party had been hitting the borders. Villages were being burned and looted. Arthur started preparing the warband to leave at first light. Kai virtually ran down to Kalea's home. His frantic knocking was answered by Kalea.

"I am sorry to trouble you. But you need to know. The warband leaves at first light. The Welsh have risen." Kalea hesitated. Should she risk one moment with him? He kissed her and then stepped away. "I have to get back."

As he turned to go, she caught his wrist. "Kai. Be careful." He smiled and turned and kissed her again.

"I will."

The sky was just beginning to lighten and the warband were ready. Milling around in the courtyard waiting for Arthur to lead them out. Kai was mounted and ready to go. The women had come to see their men off. As he turned his horse, he saw Kalea. He smiled at her and she came and laid a hand on his thigh.

"My lady. You are up early. Have you come to see me off?"

She smiled up at him. "Yes. I have come to say goodbye."

He lent down to stroke her face. "Thank you."

She reached up to his face too. "Kai, come back safe."

"I intend to." He took her hand and kissed it.

Arthur rode up. "Kalea," he acknowledged. "Kai, are you ready?"

"Always." He turned back to Kalea. "My lady." And he turned his horse. With a sigh, she turned to find Leith and moved swiftly to him.

"Stay safe Leith."

"I'll do my best. I'll try to bring him back for you."

"Thank you." Kalea stood and watched until the warband were out of sight and now she knew what it felt like for the women when their men went off to war. They were all anxious, she turned and went home.

The battle with the Welsh, had been brutal, but Arthur had been successful. The Welsh had been defeated and he had chased them back across the border. His people were safe. He had lost men and there were some that were so badly wounded, they might not live. The men looked haggard and tired but they were in high spirits. The joy of surviving a battle where some of their friends had died. He looked across the fire at Leith. The old warrior had fought well and unlike the others, he was quiet. Kai, was smiling at the talk, but he was feeling subdued too. They all wanted to be home.

The warband had been sighted. Word spread through the village and excitement rose. Ellen was with Kalea when news reached them.

"There will be injuries. We need to be ready. Go to the gate Kalea. I will get someone to take all that we need up to the hall and I shall meet you there."

Kalea nodded and picking up her skirts ran for the village gates. There was already quite a crowd and she joined them.

A cheer went up when the warband came into sight. Everyone including, Kalea peering to see if their loved ones had returned. The warband seeing the gates, raced for home. The crowd parted and waited for them to ride in.

Kai saw her, standing by the gate with the other women and a huge grin split his face as he rode hell for leather towards her. She was also, smiling as she saw him and waved. Bringing his mount to a halt next to her, he offered her his hand.

"Come up!" he offered and Kalea needed no further invitations and seized his hand and was hoisted up in front of him. Kai's arms went round her and he held her in place. "Mmmm. You smell good."

Kalea giggled. Kai smelt of sweat, blood and dirt. "Are you hurt at all?" she asked.

"Not a scratch." He couldn't stop smiling. "Nothing a wash and a mug of mead won't cure." And he trotted into the castle courtyard with her in his arms. He lowered her to the ground and slid down after her, and before the whole warband kissed her passionately, a kiss that was returned in kind. She broke free.

"Leith?" turning she saw him coming towards her. She ran and hugged him. "Are you well?" He looked weary.

"Yes girlie, I am fine. And I have bought your lad back in one piece."

"I think I bought you back." Kai laughed. Arthur marched up smiling. Happy to be home.

"Do I get a hug? Everyone seems to be getting one bar me."

Kalea stepped forward and hugged him hard. "Thank you for bringing them home."

"You're welcome." He let her go, seeing Kai watching.

"I must go. Ellen will need me," she said watching the wounded being taken into the hall and with no further ado she was gone.

"Well," Kai pondered. "That was brief but pleasant."

The three men laughed. They marched into the hall and found the wise women were already busy about their tasks, Kalea included. As they went passed, they heard the young warrior she was tending ask. "Will I live?" He had taken a sword wound to the ribs and it did look nasty. Kalea had got his shirt off and was cleaning it.

"Oh yes," Kalea answered. "It may hurt like hell, but luckily, it has missed all the things that keep you alive." The lad sank back as Kalea got out a potion. She gave him and none to gentle nudge. "Are you swooning?" she asked but he was indeed. She put the stopper back on the bottle and got out her needle and thread. "That's alright then."

Kai had washed, changed and by the time he got back to the hall, the three wise women were working on the less hurt. Arthur had ordered up some food and drink and Kai poured himself a large beaker of mead. Arthur looked at him as he watched Kalea working.

"I'm surprised you two haven't declared yet," Arthur commented.

Kai laughed. "No. Kalea is managing to keep me at arm's length with the assistance of Ellen and Leith. My balls ache like you couldn't imagine."

Arthur laughed. The wise women finally cleaned their hands and came to the table. It amused Arthur to see, that Ellen put herself between Kai and Kalea.

"How are they?" he asked Ellen as he poured her some mead.

"Two I worry for. The rest will live."

Lud joined them. "Ladies, I have had some cots made up in the next room. I trust that you will be staying?"

Len, the other wise woman nodded. "A day or so at least," Ellen agreed.

"Kalea can share with me." Kai winked at Arthur as Ellen leapt straight in.

"No. She cannot. As the youngest and fittest, Kalea will do the night shift."

Kalea gave Arthur a pained expression which made him smile. He cut her some pork and handed it to her on the end of his knife and she took it.

"If that is the case, I will go to the stables now." They all looked at her as if they doubted her sanity. "Men aren't the only ones who get injured in battle." She picked up her healing bag, and left.

"That told us," Arthur said drily.

The stable was a hive of activity as lads rushed round seeing to horses. John, was overseeing them and turned to see her.

"Do you need some help?" she asked. His troubled face gave her the answer. "Which one has the greatest need?"

"Are you sure you can spare the time?" he asked.

"We have done the hard bit, and there are two wise women in the hall to cope with anything that may come up." He nodded and lead her to a stable where a great bay charger stood with his head hanging. Kalea entered and he lifted his head, it was an effort.

"Oh, my brave boy. What have they done to you?" She reached into her bag and unstoppered one of her pottery bottles and poured some on her palm. "Now, my sweet boy. Lick it up. It will make you feel better." The great tongue fell into her hand and licked it up. "There's a good boy. Now, let me see where they have hurt you." Running her hand down his body, she soon came to the problem. He had taken a sword blow on the rump. It was deep and raw. Kalea didn't know, how he had made it home. John, had already gone to tend to another and Kalea grabbed a lad, "I need some hot water." He nodded and scuttled off. Kalea wiped the worst of the gore from the wound by which time the water had arrived. Gently she bathed it and then sowed it closed. Removing a pot from her bag she smoothed it over the wound. He was feeling very poorly. She came round and stroked his face. "You should feel better now." Then she left to tend the next one.

It was late by the time Kalea got back to the hall and it was quiet. Ellen seeing her came over. "Have you finished down there?" Kalea nodded. She was feeling quite tired herself. "The two over there," she pointed, "are the worst. You may need to give them some pain relief." Kalea nodded again. "And the lad with the rib wound. You did well there." Kalea smiled. Ellen rubbed her face. "I am going to rest." Kalea nodded again as Ellen swept away.

She joined Arthur, Kai, Leith and Lud at the table. Leith poured her some ale.

"You look tuckered out."

"I am," she confessed.

"Did I lose any horses?" Arthur asked.

"One," Kalea answered. "I don't know how he made it back. The rest I have managed to patch up. There is a large bay, who's quite poorly. We may lose him yet. Though I hope not, he is a brave boy."

Arthur smiled at her. "Thank you for your service to my men and beasts."

"We do, what we can," Kalea acknowledged.

The men sat up late with her, but one by one they left. Kai offered to stay with her, but she waved him away. "You must rest also. I will be fine." He gave her a lingering kiss. "Kai."

"Yes."

"You smell much better."

He smiled and gave a little bow. "For my lady's pleasure. Good night."

"Good night." Kalea was alone in the hall at last. Well, not alone, but alone with the wounded. She made a round to make sure they were comfortable. Offering water and soothing words.

Kalea groaned with relief, when Arthur turned up the next morning.

"I am so pleased to see you," she admitted. "It is becoming harder by the minute to keep my eyes open."

Her eyes did look heavy. Arthur motioned her to sit and she sank wearily onto a bench. Even as she sat, her eyelids began to droop only to be dragged open again. Servants came in bringing more food, and she poured herself some milk. As she did Ellen appeared and Kalea was even more relieved. Ellen sat next to her. "How are they?"

"The two most grievous injured, are still with us. I have given pain relief to most. How, the boy that I treated, seems to be improving. Most of them do. I think we have the most of them."

"Good girl," Ellen said. "Now, off you go. And not to Kai's room."

"Too tired." Kalea dragged herself to her feet.

"Good job too." Ellen and Arthur grinned at one another.

"Kai tells me you are an exacting chaperone."

Ellen laughed. "It is not an easy job. I'm hoping to keep them apart, until Kai begs."

"You are a cruel mistress." Arthur laughed.

"She is worth waiting for," Ellen replied sagely. "I would like them to wait until Mid-Summer Celebrations. When Kai sees her then, he will be on his knees."

"Why?"

"Wait and see." Ellen began her breakfast before seeing to her charges.

Kalea woke. Judging by the light, it was late afternoon. She rose and washed her face with water from the pitcher that had been left. The water was cold but she didn't mind. She determined that she would not enter the hall until after she had seen the horses, knowing that if she did go into the hall, she would be distracted by the wounded. Slipping past the open door, she trotted down to the stable with her bag over her shoulder. Everything was calm today. John saw her and came forward.

"Kalea. You truly are a miracle worker. Come see."

The big bay's head was up a bit and when he saw her, he limped forward.

"How are you my brave boy?" she asked rubbing his soft nose. He dropped his tongue into her palm. "You want some more?" She opened her bag and dropped a few drops of pain killer on her palm. Immediately, he licked it off. "So, that is working." She stepped in and inspected the wound on his rump. Put some more cream on it and patted him gently as she left.

"You really are something else with horses," John stated. She smiled at the compliment and went to inspect the rest of her work.

"Am I in time for food?" Kalea asked as she walked into the hall. Almost at once, How, called for her and Kalea called back. "How! I need to eat. You will have to wait." She rolled her eyes at Lud who grinned. Leith ladled some stew into a bowl.

"You did well," he said with pride.

"So did you. I think yours was the only mount to return unscathed," she smiled picking up a spoon.

"I told you I was good," he said to Lud watching as the young woman tucked in with gusto.

"Arthur and Kai are visiting the rest of the warband in the village," Lud said to explain why they weren't here. "Ellen sent some of the wounded home to be nursed by their families."

"That was a good idea. They will feel happier at home and they will recover quicker."

"Not if they have half a dozen kids climbing all over them," Leith remarked sourly.

Kalea grinned.

Arthur walking through the village with Kai said. "Ellen is plotting something."

"She is?" Kai asked bemused. "What?"

"I have no idea. But she says that she intends to keep you and Kalea apart until the mid-summer celebrations."

Kai groaned. "That's ages away."

Arthur laughed. "No more than a few weeks."

"That's ages," Kai complained.

Chapter 14
The Summer Queen

Within a few days, the hall was back to normal. The wounded had been well enough to go home and for a while, the village was back to its normal pace. This wouldn't last long, as already plans for the summer celebrations were being drawn up.

Ellen and Kalea had been restocking their lotions and potions and were down by the river where they liked to swim. The two women were soon bathing in the cool water.

"Kalea. I want you to promise something," Ellen stated.

Kalea looked her warily. "Please don't ask something too difficult," she pleaded.

Ellen grinned. "It might be. I want you to promise that you will not give yourself to Kai before the summer celebrations."

"That is difficult." Kalea grinned. "Why?"

"I want you to bedazzle him in that green dress with the cream embroidery. I want to see him absolutely drooling."

The exploded laughing. "That seems a bit cruel. But I will do it. For you." Kalea laughed.

Kai was grumpy. It was absolutely impossible to steal a moment with Kalea. It seemed that even Arthur had joined in this conspiracy to keep them apart. They were never left alone for a moment. Even worse, was that everyone except him seemed to be enjoying it.

The days rolled by and the summer celebrations grew nearer. Some minstrels turned up with news from the South. Mark had sent a message for her, asking if she had got fed up living in squalor and was, she ready to come home. Kalea had laughed when she was told and told the performer that she was content here and on his return to the south, he was to tell Mark so. Ellen was keeping her on a very tight reign and she could tell that Kai was frustrated that he was not even allowed a kiss. He had tried the riding ploy, but Arthur had insisted on joining them and would not move from between them. Later when they were alone Kai cornered Arthur.

"What is your game?" he demanded.

"Sorry? I don't know what you mean?" Arthur answered innocently.

"Why are you keeping me from Kalea?" he growled.

Arthur laughed. "My friend. Be patient. Three days till mid-summer and I promise, all your obstacles will be removed."

"But why are they there in the first place?"

"Ask Ellen. I am but following instructions."

"Only because it suits you," Kai grumbled.

Arthur laughed.

At last, mid-summer arrived. Kai rolled down to Kalea's. Today, they are going to allow me to see her. He was disappointed, she wasn't in. Then he went to Ellen's. Neither of them was there either. He huffed and went back to the hall.

The courtyard was full of noise. Trestles and benches had been bought out. Enough for everyone. Children were running and playing. People were bringing things to the tables and everyone was dressed in their finest.

Arthur was overseeing the final preparations and saw Kai enter the courtyard.

"Have you seen Kalea?" he asked Arthur.

Arthur grinned. "Is she still eluding you?" and at Kai's scowl, he answered "No. Haven't seen her since yesterday. The celebrations will be starting soon, she will be here."

Arthur met Leith's eye and the old man chuckled causing Kai to give him a black look.

Down at the river, Ellen had given Kalea a good scrub and her skin was positively glowing. Back at Ellen's, Kalea was given some honeysuckle oil to rub into her skin, so not only did she smell good, but her skin was soft as velvet. Ellen had already put on her best blue dress and now slipped Kalea's pale green robe over her head. Lacing it tight at the sides so it showed off her breasts and slim hips. Laughing, Ellen brushed her hair till it shone. "You are going to have all the lads drooling," Ellen said with pleasure. "Kai is going to have to fight the hardest battle of his life to get past them."

Kalea giggled. "This is really quite mean. But I like it." She had even put on the shoes that she thought she would never wear again. But Ellen had one more surprise for her, lifting a cloth, she produced a crown of honeysuckle, much like the ones that Mary had made for her. This was slightly more delicate being made up of just a few strands woven together. Ellen placed it on Kalea's head.

"There! You look gorgeous. Now," she took Kalea's hand. "Let's go. I can't wait to see Kai's face."

The two women walked arm in arm through the village. The few people who were not already at the castle, couldn't take their eyes of the young woman dressed like a fine lady.

Kai was standing with Arthur, when he heard a murmur from the people by the gate, he looked to see what the disturbance was and his breath caught in his throat.

"By all the gods!" he whispered. Arthur turned to look and even he gulped. "She's a goddess. I knew it." His voice was low and husky. Handing Arthur his beaker, and without taking his eyes from her, he went to greet her. He bowed low. "My summer Queen." And he offered her his hand, which she took and gave him a curtsey.

"My lord." Ellen grinned. Kalea had him in her thrall. She had before but now he was captivated. She looked at Leith who was chortling with glee. He winked at her.

Kai lent down inhaling the beautiful scent. She was so fragrant. "Kalea, I am bewitched. You are absolutely...wonderful!" He bought her to Leith. "You knew, didn't you?"

Leith nodded and Ellen appeared at his elbow smiling broadly.

"I told you Kai that it would be worth waiting for." Lud smiled.

Kai smile said it all. "Well, you didn't lie." He couldn't take his eyes off her. He pulled out a chair for her and she sat and he sat beside her.

"Well, Kalea. You are the most beautiful thing here," Arthur said.

Kalea grinned. "I wash up well for a girl who dresses as a boy."

"I can't disagree there," Arthur agreed. Now, in the finery that were obviously given to her by Mark, he could now see why Mark was so desperate to keep her. She was beautiful without her finery, but with it, she was breath-taking. Arthur, raised his voice and the courtyard fell silent. "The Summer Queen has arrived. I now declare we can start our celebrations."

A cheer went up and the minstrels struck up a song and Arthur held out a hand to Kalea. "As the Summer Queen, it is our duty, to start the dancing. Sorry Kai."

"It's the only dance you're getting. And watch your hands."

Kalea rose and joined Arthur on the cleared area. "Kalea. You have outshone the brightest jewel," he said softly with a slow smile. "I am more jealous of Kai, than I have ever been."

Kalea being her normal self, refused to be drawn in a flirting match and laughed. "You are not trying to lead me a stray? Are you?"

"Sadly, I wouldn't dare when Kai, cannot take his eyes off you." He spun her round and lifted her high. Kalea matched him step for step but he didn't get to take her back, because, Kai came to take over.

Kalea smiled up at him. He put his hand on her waist and she felt herself warming. The desire was clear in his eyes and he smiled at her. "I am such a lucky man. Can you be mine?"

"Yes. I can."

They stopped to eat and drink.

"How long do you think they will last?" Ellen asked Leith.

"I don't even want to think of it," Leith said burying his head in his beaker.

"Don't grouch Leith. You were young once," Ellen teased. "Come dance with me." Leith knew better than to argue and did as he was told.

John came up to Kalea and asked for a dance. Kalea obliged but Kai couldn't keep his eyes off her. Kalea as usual was having a great time. Having been treated as the Winter Queen and the Spring Queen, she knew exactly how to behave. Women asked Kai to dance but he could not be asked. Arthur danced with all the women but he found, just like Kai that his eyes kept wandering to Kalea. The green dress suited her and bought out the darkness of her almond eyes. He didn't think he had ever seen something so perfect. Kai danced more than he ever done before. Kalea danced with Kai, Leith, Ellen and even Lud. The light faded and lamps were lit. The music played, everyone danced and drank. The children fell to sleep where they fell.

Kalea had had rather too much to drink, she was merry and Kai although he was laughing with all the rest, he continued to hold her hand, or touch her leg, or stroke her face. Eventually, he could bear it no longer and leaned across to whisper in her ear. "Shall we leave? I am desperate for a kiss."

Turning so her lips were almost on his, she whispered back. "If we dance, across the floor, we can slip out the gate."

Kai laughed. "They will notice. It will be like the light dims when you leave."

Kalea laughed back. "I didn't know you had a romantic soul, Kai." He kissed her lightly on his lips then stood and offered her his hand. Smiling she took it and he led her to the dance floor. For a while, they danced and then gradually, moved to the gates and then slipped out. Taking her hand, they ran. Both laughing as they did so.

Kai was right. Their leaving was noticed. Arthur rubbed his chin, thoughtfully. Ellen nudged Leith and Lud grinned to himself. He hoped they had fun. Though he could fail to see, how they wouldn't.

He noticed, that Ellen had taken quite a shine to Leith. Perhaps another new romance in the off. Poor Leith, Ellen would give him quite a run.

Once away from the light of the torches they kissed. The kisses getting more and more urgent. In the end, they were virtually dragging one another towards Kalea's home. At the door, she stopped him.

"Let me light a candle." She was breathless with desire. A light grew from within and Kai quickly stepped in and closed the door behind him.

Almost as soon as he turned, she was in his arms pressing herself against him. As he kissed her, his hands grabbed her bottom forcing her hips against his. His erection felt huge even to him and he moaned her name against his lips. She was fighting to get his shirt off and he let her go to help lift it over his head. He was grinning madly, as he emerged, Kalea stepped back and unlaced her dress and slipped it over her head whilst kicking off her shoes. She stood naked before him. "Oh!" he gulped before fighting to get his boots and trousers off. Kalea stepped into help but ended up hindering and causing them both to giggle. Finally, he was free. It was Kalea's turn to gulp. Yes, she had seen him naked, but she hadn't seen him aroused and his erection was huge. She grinned and came to him. The contact of skin against skin, sent pleasure rippling through her body. His hands were exploring her, and he was awash with sensuous pleasure, as her hands closed on him. Locked together, they moved back to the small cot that had been meant for Leith and fell back on it. For a split second, she was afraid, then he entered her. She gasped.

Kai stopped. "Am I hurting you?"

She smiled. "No. Far from it." She raised her legs allowing him to slip deeper into her. "Oh Kai," she whispered against his lips.

He gave himself a moment. Breathing heavily. His control was shaky and he throbbed inside her and felt her lift her hips for him. He was conscious of every movement, an exquisite ecstasy. As he began to move, he knew he wouldn't last long. Kalea writhed against him. Nipping his Adam's apple and seeking his lips, which was enough to send him over. Despite that his seed was already spilling, he still moved and suddenly Kalea was shuddering under him, her orgasm shaking not only her but him. Kai didn't think either one of them would stop. He collapsed on top of her, showering her face and neck with kisses.

"By the gods," he murmured into her hair. Panting, he raised himself on his elbows and smiled down at her. "That wasn't the romantic seduction I had planned. Far too fast and frantic."

Kalea reached up and smoothed his sweat soaked hair from his face. "It was perfect. I have waited far too long for you."

Kai could not stop himself touching her face, her neck, her arms. He felt like a thirsty man and he couldn't get his fill of her. Even now, he wanted her again. He withdrew from her, and Kalea felt strangely incomplete.

"Shall we go to bed?" he asked offering her his hand.

She took it and he pulled her into her arms. "Perhaps, we should bar the door this time."

Laughing, he turned and barred the door. Kalea went to the ladder and started to climb. Kai moving swiftly bit her bottom, causing her to shriek and scramble up faster. "Pass me the candle."

Kai passed it up and then climbed up after her. She had put the candle on a ledge and was laying provocatively on her side watching him. With a slow smile, he joined her and took her in his arms. For a while, they just held each other and then Kai began to explore her body. His hand reached down to her scarred thigh. "The wolf was a lucky one. From now, I am the only wolf that is going to bite you." His hands wandered further up and slid between her thighs. Kalea moved to allow him access. She was warm and moist, ready for him. "You are a temptress. I cannot resist you." He kissed her and she pulled him closer. This time, they took their time, exploring, teasing and finally Kai bought her to her conclusion well before his own and had her soaring again before he allowed his own release.

He pulled her into his arms. "I love you, Kalea." With her head buried against his chest, Kalea spoke.

"Kai, it is always been you, and it will always be you." And they slept in one another's arms.

Kai was dreaming about making love to Kalea, he fought to stay asleep but was dragged up by the throbbing in his loins. Opening his eyes, he found that he was not dreaming at all. Kalea was astride him moving with sensuous strokes. Smiling, no longer anywhere near sleep, he reached up to cup her breasts. Enjoying watching her, take control. He met her thrusts with his own, his hands dropping to her hips in an effort to control the pace. Kalea was having none of it and ground his erection deep inside her. Kai gritted his teeth, but could not stop himself spilling his seed, but she rode him still until shuddering, she collapsed onto his chest.

"By the gods, Kalea." His arms went round her and held her close.

She kissed him; her face flushed with pleasure. "Good morning," she whispered.

Rolling both of them on to their sides, he replied, "Yes, it is. A very good morning." He brushed her hair from her face. Even in the low light, she was beautiful. "So, when are you going to marry me?"

"Whenever you like."

"Now would be a good time."

She laughed. "With both of us naked?"

"I'm not adverse. But it will be hard to hide how much I desire you." He grinned. Her hand moved over his chest and she lay her head on it. "We shall declare today," he continued. "What's the betting, that Arthur makes us wait."

"It is no hardship to wait for a ceremony now," she said her lips against his chest. "We don't have to wait for anything else. The deed is done and now we can take our pleasure as we chose."

"I am grateful for that at least." She loved the feeling of his voice rumbling in his chest. "You will get a reputation of being a woman of loose morals."

"What do I care of what they think? All that matters is that you don't."

"You can be as loose as you like with me." Kai grinned. She disentangled herself from him.

"Let me see what I can offer you for breakfast. I need to keep your strength up."

"You will if you intend to use me as you have done." Kai laughed.

He followed her down the ladder and hunted down his trousers, where they had been cast in haste last night. He picked up Kalea's dress and shook it out laying it over her chest. "Are you wearing this today?" he asked. But Kalea shook her head.

"Not just yet." She had lit the fire and put on some water. "I need a swim before I put a dress that fine on." She handed him a plate with some bread and cheese and while he ate, she dipped into the chest and drew out her trousers and shirt, which she shrugged on. Then she joined him. Pouring out two beakers of tea.

"What is this?" he asked.

"A rosehip brew."

He took a sip. It wasn't too bad. "Do you not have ale in the morning?"

"Not normally. But if that is what you prefer, we will have to get some from the market."

He grinned. "I suppose I could get used to it." She slapped his arm.

Later, they walked down to the river. Hand in hand and chatting about nothing and everything. Once there, they both stripped off and Kai jumped in, splashing Kalea who shrieked and then dived in after. Soaping one another off, proved too much of a temptation and Kai was initiated to love making in water. A new experience for him, and he loved it and he decided there and then, that this was something he wanted to do again.

They lay in the summer sun drying off. Kalea thinking that this is how it should have been last year and Kai thinking that his life had never been better. Having dried, they dressed. Kalea putting the green dress back on and carrying her trousers and shirt back with her. They went via the market where a few stall owners had set up to provide for the village. Most had not bothered. Kai bought some ale, bread, honey, cheese and ham which they took back to the house.

"It's nearly noon. They will be laying out the tables for the celebrations. Shall we go up and tell Arthur our news?"

Kalea nodded. "He won't be at all surprised. I don't think anyone will."

"I suspect you are right." Kai grinned.

Lud was the first one to see the lovers enter the courtyard. They were arm in arm and he had never seen Kai look so happy. His eyes were constantly seeking Kalea's and any idiot could see that they had taken their relationship to a new level. He went to greet them.

"I see all is right in the world." He grinned at them.

"Yes. It certainly is Lud," Kai confirmed. "I have asked Kalea to be my wife and she has accepted."

"Congratulations to you both!" He enveloped them in a huge bear hug. "It's about time you two got together."

"I can guess." Arthur stood with a smile. "You have declared, at last Kai."

"I have."

"I need not ask what the answer was, your faces say it all." He came forward and gave Kai a hug and then kissed Kalea on the cheek. "Are you sure you can cope with him?"

Kalea laughed. "I am sure that I can make him toe the line."

"I don't know what you mean?" Kai protested. "What about me? How do I keep this wild child under control?"

"You will have to seek advice from Leith."

Leith who had been sleeping off the excesses of the night before, emerged from the hall. "What do you need my advice on?" he said, smiling at the young couple.

"Kai has declared," Arthur stated, "and he wants to know how to keep Kalea under control."

Leith grin grew broader, "Congratulations!" He slapped Kai on the back and then lifted Kalea clean off her feet and spun her round. "And you can't, Kai. You just have to go with the flow. Are you sure you can handle her?"

Kalea slapped him and he rubbed his arm.

"I don't know. But I'm going to enjoy trying," Kai answered with a rueful shrug. Kalea rolled her eyes in exasperation. They sat down to share the food that had been laid out.

Leith and Lud had gone off to arrange some more ale and mead. Then Ellen appeared and Kalea grinning, excused herself to go and talk to her friend. Arthur watched the slim woman virtually skip over to Ellen, then he turned to Kai.

"How are your balls?" He grinned.

Kai laughed. "Empty. The woman is insatiable."

Arthur laughed. *So, Mark had taught her well*, he thought, though he was too tactful to say so. "Worth waiting for?"

"Of that there is no doubt."

"Well, if you find you are having trouble keeping up…"

"Don't even think about it." Kai laughed.

Arthur was pleased for his friend, but he couldn't help feeling a little jealous that he had found someone before him.

"Well?" Ellen asked although the answer was written on Kalea's face. "And? Tell all."

"Kai has declared," Kalea said gleefully. Ellen hugged her.

"And?"

"Oh! Ellen! Do you really have to ask?"

"No. But I am." Kalea laughed.

"He's big."

"Bigger than Mark?" Kalea nodded.

"Not length perhaps, but girth."

"Is he skilled?"

"His touch is different but he knows what he is about. Yes. He is very skilled."

"That's why he is so popular with the girls." They giggled.

Arthur was watching. "I think you are being talked about."

Kai looked over to see the two women giggling together, he grinned. "I suspect you're right. I'm not sure, I'm happy with them laughing at me."

"Are you worried?"

"No. Not at all. I know where I am laying my head tonight." His eyes caressed Kalea even from this distance.

"Is she skilled?" Arthur asked.

Still grinning, Kai turned to Arthur. "As if I'm going to tell you that."

Arthur laughed. So, she was. "You are a lucky man, Kai."

"I know it," Kai replied. "Do I detect as little jealousy Arthur?"

"Maybe," Arthur conceded.

Kalea fanned herself with her hand. "Just thinking about it makes me quite hot and ready."

"I can see," Ellen said pointedly looking a Kalea's breasts. Kalea looked down and saw that her nipples were erect and she crossed her arms to hide them.

Ellen laughed. "He obviously fits well."

"Very." Kalea grinned. "I might well have to lure him away for a bit."

"I'm sure he won't mind. I have a gift for you. Hold out your hand." Kalea held out her hand as instructed and Ellen placed a small piece of cloth in her hand.

"What is this?" Kalea asked.

"This is a very useful thing. You place it within you. It stops a man's seed from leaking from you. Usually, I give it to woman who are having trouble keeping a man's seed inside them. But it can be used to keep lovemaking discreet."

Kalea grinned and added it to the small pouch she kept at her waist. "Very useful. Thank you."

Ellen nodded. "I had a wish to talk to you." Kalea waited. "I have developed an itch for Leith."

"Leith?" Kalea was incredulous.

"Don't look so shocked. Why not?"

Kalea shrugged and looked embarrassed. "I don't know. It's just," she thought carefully. "Leith is old and I always think of you as being the same age as me."

"But I am not. I am old enough to be your mother. And Leith is old enough to be your father." Kalea grinned. "What I suppose, I am asking. Is would you mind if I scratched that itch?"

Kalea's jaw dropped open. "I guess not." Then added. "If nothing else, it may cheer him up." The two women laughed.

Kalea returned to Kai and laid his hand on his thigh. The look in his eye said it all and he put his hand over hers. "We have got to stay until Arthur declares for us."

"I know. There will be a lot of broken hearts Kai. The women will hate me."

He grinned. "Do I care? I think not."

"What are you two plotting?" Arthur asked.

"I was saying that a lot of girls' hearts will be broken," Kalea announced. "It will be down to you to keep the girls happy Arthur."

"I think I can manage that." Arthur grinned. "Unless, Kai, you have some spare time on your hands."

"I have all the woman, I want, Arthur. But thank you for the offer."

Kalea watched Kai carefully, *you will not need any other women*, she thought, *I will make sure of that.* Her eyes went to Arthur and found him watching her, and she knew, he knew exactly what she was thinking, so she winked at him.

Arthur turned his back one to hide his smile and two to hide the effect that Kalea's lust dark eyes had on him.

The courtyard was filling and Arthur knew it would soon be time for him to restart the celebrations. As always, he was constantly watchful. Celebrations always ran for two days. It gave the chance for those who stood watch on one day, to join in on another. The Christians amongst them were quite happy to overlook the fact, that mid-summer, was truly a pagan celebration. But like many, they worked hard and enjoyed the festivals that allowed some escape from day-to-day existence.

Arthur drew his sword and with the pommel, bought it down on the table to bring the loud chattering to an end. Everyone in the courtyard fell silent to listen to their King speak.

"Today, is our last day of the mid-summer celebrations." His voice was ringing and not one person, even the children dared to speak. "Kai, adopted son of Lud, has declared his intention to make Kalea, adopted daughter of Leith, his wife. I have decided, that the first day of our Harvest celebrations, will be marked by their wedding. We wish them a long life of joy." Cheers went up and Kai taking Kalea's hand, stood and smiled. "So, let us conclude this celebration and look forward to the next," Arthur finished.

"You bastard." Kai laughed shaking Arthur's hand.

"Could I let you get off so easily?" Arthur grinned. "I thought, I'd give you a chance to change your mind."

"As if I would. Decisions like this are not taken lightly. Oh wait! You wouldn't know." Kai couldn't resist reminding Arthur of his single status.

Arthur grinned wickedly and held out a hand to Kalea. "My lady. As summer Queen, I insist that I have the first dance with you." He noticed Kai grit his teeth which added to his pleasure and he led Kalea onto the dance floor. Much to her consternation, he leant down and sniffed her. "You have the delightful aroma of sex, my lovely girl."

Kalea was no more, the naïve girl she had been and laughed. "I know. It is quite delicious, is it not?" she replied flirtatiously.

"It is indeed," Arthur agreed whirling her around. Bringing her back into his arms, he whispered in her ear. "Kai is a very lucky man."

"And I intend to remind him of it, often." She laughed.

Kai was very glad when Arthur returned her to him and went off looking for another willing dance partner.

"I told you, he would make us wait," Kai grumbled with a grin.

"Well, I am sure, I will find something that will wipe away the time. Something that will please you." And she ran her tongue over her lips.

"You are a very naughty girl," Kai growled.

"But you love me."

"That I do." He put his hand on her thigh. "I would die for you."

"Please don't do that. I love you better alive."

"Perhaps we should leave early."

"Perhaps we should leave late. Anticipation is known to increase the appetite."

"Is it Ellen who has been teaching you these things?" he asked his lips against her. "I shall have to have words."

As it was, they did indeed leave later than they wanted. The warband and many others, came to congratulate them. Leith took Kalea to one side and hugged her. "I am so happy for you my girlie. This is where we should have been."

Kalea hugged him back. "In some ways, perhaps, it was for the best. I for one, have learned a lot and not all bad."

"Mayhap you're right. I am just glad, that you and Kai are back together."

As, Kalea and Kai slipped away, Kalea noticed Ellen dancing with Leith and smiled. Poor Leith didn't know what was going to hit him. Their departure was cheered despite them trying to be discreet.

Kalea lit a candle and Kai barred the door and as he turned, she came into his arms.

"Well, wife to be. Shall we start in bed today?" he asked kissing her. She nodded and kicked her shoes off and then stripped off her dress. Kai was also hastily shedding his clothes and passed the candle to her before climbing up to join her. When his head cleared the sleeping platform, he found her on all fours. He needed no further invitation and slid into her causing her to gasp. Leaning over, he ran his hands over her smooth back and to her neck, sweeping her hair to one side.

"That was an invitation?" he whispered in her ear. Turning her head, she smiled and nodded. His hands cupped her breasts as he moved back and began to move. She had been right, the anticipation had indeed increased his appetite and no matter what restraint he may try, he knew it would not last long. That didn't matter as Kalea collapsed her arms gasping with pleasure and he allowed himself free reign. He ran his tongue up her spine and felt her shiver. "Now, my lady. Gently down." And the two lowered themselves to lay flat, Kai carefully inserting a hand under her hips so that he could flip them both onto their sides whilst still remaining joined together.

For a while, neither moved nor spoke. Enjoying the closeness. Finally, Kai began to shrink and Kalea tightened and was rewarded with a small thrust and felt Kai smile against her hair. "I saw you talking to Ellen. Arthur said you were discussing me," Kai said almost sleepily.

"Are you fishing?" Kalea grinned.

"Yes," Kai admitted.

"Ellen asked, if you were worth the wait and I said you were." Kai smiled. Almost word for word what Arthur had asked. "She then asked if you were skilled and I answered that you definitely knew what you were about, and were very skilled and she said that is why the women like you." Kai laughed. She had been a little more open than he had been, but the conversation had run the same.

"You were laughing," he commented.

"Are you feeling sensitive?" she queried. "You have no need to be. Ellen confessed that she had an itch for Leith."

"Leith?" Kai queried.

"That was exactly my reaction." Kalea giggled. "I know. I didn't believe it either. Anyway, she wanted to know if I had any objection to her scratching it. What could I say? But no."

They both laughed. "Poor Leith. At least, it might cheer him up," Kai stated.

"And that is exactly what I said." They both giggled. *Could this day get any better?* Thought Kai. I doubt it and it was his last thought before he drifted off with Kalea still seated in his lap.

The next morning when Kai awoke, he was alone and the smell of cooking came from below. Leaning his head over the sleeping platform, he smiled down at her. "Good morning. I smell something good."

Matching his smile with one of her own, she said. "Breakfast is ready my lord." He was surprised to see her already dressed and had soon shrugged on his trousers and shirt and then she then handed him a plate of eggs and bread.

"This is good," he commented as he ate his eggs. "What have you planned for today?"

"I will go and help Ellen today. I suspect that there will be a few ailments to deal with after two days of drinking. What about you?"

"I will go to the hall. I can't keep wearing my best shirt and I need to shave or a certain lady will be complaining that her flesh is being scraped from her body." Kalea giggled. "I also feel naked without my axe within reach. Can I bring some of my gear here?"

"Of course."

"I'll get Lud to help me."

"Do you think he'll mind?"

"No. He'll be pleased for me. I think."

"He might miss you, Kai."

Kai smiled. "He most probably be pleased by the fact that I've finally grown up. I'll walk you down to Ellen's."

Together, they left. As they approached Ellen's they spotted Leith kissing Ellen goodbye. They exchanged a knowing look and then Kai with his brightest smile hailed him. "Leith! You're up early. Are you going back to the hall? I'll walk with you."

Leith straightened up looking embarrassed. Kalea bit her lip trying to hide her mirth. Kai just grinned and Kalea tugged his sleeve. Leith strode away from Ellen and marched up to Kai ignoring Kalea altogether.

"Don't you dare say a word, lad," Leith growled.

Kai grinned over his shoulder at Kalea. "Would I dare?"

"Yes. You would, you bugger."

Kalea giggled as she shot into Ellen's where she bent double laughing. Ellen joined her. When Kalea finally, recovered, she wheezed, "And?"

Ellen winked. "He is mighty skilled. I might have to scratch that itch again."

Kalea howled with laughter. "I may never be able to look him in his eye again."

"I don't know about you, but I could do with a swim."

"Ellen! You do shock me," Kalea mocked indignantly.

Leith was still grumbling as they entered the hall, Kai could not stop grinning. Even better, when Leith stomped off, Arthur met Kai's eye but Kai just shook his head still grinning.

Arthur couldn't bear it and came over to Kai. "What's going on?"

"Come and help me pack some gear and I will tell you."

"Are you moving out?"

"I hadn't really thought about it." He shrugged. "I guess, I am really. There isn't really much competition is there? I mean stay and sleep alone or warm Kalea's furs. What would you do?" he asked cheekily.

"I'd stay here of course," Arthur said mock seriously.

"Of course, you would." Kai laughed. They entered Kai's room. "I'll be back every day. After all, Kalea has no use of a warrior during the day. She's off doing Kalea things."

Arthur laughed "And what's that supposed to mean?"

Kai looked a bit mystified. "This is Kalea. She doesn't really do what woman normally do like cooking, cleaning and sewing. She's off lancing boils, mopping snotty noses and fixing horses." Arthur nodded in agreement.

"So, you are telling me, you need to come back to get fed."

"No. She can cook well enough. Better than some, I've tasted but she's not going to hang round all day doing it." He grinned. "You won't believe what I have found out."

"No. I won't. But it has something to do with Leith. And you are going to enjoy telling me."

"You're right there." And Kai told him about Leith and Ellen.

Arthur's face had the same look as Kai's when Kalea had told him.

"Are you sure?"

Kai nodded. "Saw it with my own eyes. He was kissing Ellen when Kalea and I arrived."

"The old goat!" Arthur laughed.

"Who's an old goat?" Lud asked walking in. Both men laughed.

It was obvious to Leith, that Kai had let the cat out of the bag to Arthur and Lud. The men kept giving him knowing looks and smiling. In the end, he had to smile back. He had thought he was too old, to enjoy the charms of a woman and he had been pleasantly surprised when Ellen had invited him in when he had walked her home. Even more surprised when she had kissed him and one thing had led to another. It had been such a long time, he had wondered if he could remember how things were supposed to go, but it had all worked out very well and he was contemplating going to see if Ellen needed any company this evening. *She had not seemed disappointed*, he thought. Why should the youngsters have all the fun?

Arthur helped Kai take his gear down to Kalea's. Kai had shaved, washed and changed and left his best shirt to be laundered at the castle. Having deposited his chest, with some belonging, including his shaving gear, he saw Arthur looking contemplatively at the sleeping platform. He could guess what he was thinking. Arthur shook himself from his reverie.

"Let's go down to Ellen's. See if Kalea would be allowed to go riding with us tomorrow."

The two men arrived at Ellen's and could hear the two women's chatter, interspersed with a giggle or two. They sounded happy enough. As they entered, Kalea was bent over a child's knee giving the men a good look at her cleavage.

"Ladies," Arthur said and Kalea stood up. They watched as Kalea finished cleaning the wound and applied some ointment. The lad winced but didn't cry.

"You are going to be a very brave warrior." Kalea ruffled his hair and lifted him down. "Here." She offered him a jar of honey and the lad stuck his finger in it, then popping it into his mouth, rushed past Kai and Arthur.

"What can we do for you?" Ellen asked. She was aware of the scrutiny, both men were giving her and gave them her brightest smile.

The men also noticed that both the women had bathed and Kalea's braid was still wet from the water. "We have come to ask, if you might spare Kalea tomorrow morning to come riding with us?"

"I think I can manage on my own. That of course is if she wants to go." She looked at Kalea. "Of course, she does." She grinned.

Arthur smiled back. "Then we shall see her in the morning. Be good ladies."

Almost before they left, they heard the women giggle. "Told you," Kai stated.

"What are they like?" Ellen laughed. "Do they think I would have grown a horn out my forehead because I had slept with Leith."

Laughing still, Kalea answered. "They think that because you are older, you lose the urge to do such things." Then more seriously she added. "I think I had thought that too." And exploded into more giggles. "It's quite a relief to know that the urge is still there."

Chapter 15
More Trouble

The ride was not meant to be. Kai and Kalea were woken by frantic banging on her door; a voice called, "Kai! You are needed. The Welsh march on us."

Kai was down in a flash pulling on his clothes and Kalea wasn't far behind. He grabbed his mighty axe and then turned to face her. "Will you see me off?"

"You know I will." And he was gone. Kalea stomped on her boots and lifting her skirts ran as fast as she could to the stable. She whistled for Midnight. John appeared at her shoulder.

"You will not be allowed to ride with them."

"I know." She led Midnight in and saddled him up. The courtyard was already filled with horses and men. Arthur came out followed by Lud and Kai. As Kai appeared, he saw her with Midnight.

"Kalea. Now isn't the time to be foolhardy," he warned taking her into his arms and kissing her.

"I know," she whispered against his lips. "He is for you. If I can't be with you, then he must."

Kai looked at the big beast who was stamping his feet, picking up the urgency of both men and war horses. "Will he let me?"

"Yes." She turned to Midnight. "You must take care of him for me. I cannot come." She kissed the velvet nose. "Get on." Kai did so. "Move him with weight, you will have little need of the bit," she cautioned. Then she kissed Midnight's nose. "You be brave. He will have need of your skill." The horse blew at her, she went round and put a hand on Kai's thigh. "You come back to me you hear. My heart beats only for you."

He put his hand on her face. "As mine does for you."

Leith came lumbering through the gate with Ellen on his heels, hoping in all the confusion, he would be overlooked. Arthur smiled at him. "Good of you to

310

join us." Then as Leith threw himself into the saddle added. "We ride." Arthur pulled his horses head round and rode for the gates. They were moving far too fast for the women to keep up and all Kalea and Ellen could do was hug one another.

"Kalea!" Lud called. "Get changed, bring toothpick. If the Welsh get through, I will need every blade we can get." Kalea nodded picked up her skirts and ran.

"I know what I need to do," Ellen called loudly and began to move as fast as she could taking a couple of stable lads with her to carry her gear.

"John spread the word through the village. Gates to be kept closed at all times."

He nodded and was gone. Lud looked about. He had been left with the old and the very young. He had much to organise.

Kalea had bee sting at her back as she strode back towards the castle. A furtive movement caught her eye. Something about it wasn't right. She looked hastily round for aid, but there was none. Her heart beat ramped up and she drew bee sting. Moving as swiftly and as quietly as she could, she followed the fleeting movement. As she peeped cautiously round a house, there was nothing to see. Swiftly she moved on and there it was again. A dark shape moving furtively. Creeping forward she drew nearer. It was a warrior. Not one of Arthur's. He was moving to the fence round the rear end of the village and the intention was plain. He swung the large axe back, and as he did so, Kalea lunged taking him deep in the back and driving bee sting in up to the hilt. The axe fell from his nerveless hand, narrowly missing Kalea who was desperately trying to free bee sting. As he fell, he turned towards her and she saw his surprise at the young woman standing there. There was no way for Kalea to free bee sting now. So, she picked up the axe and ran.

As she got to the castle gates, Lud stood waiting for her. "We are breached. The Welsh are in the village. Shut the gates," she screamed.

Lud gave a yell and a handful of warriors appeared at his side. The gates were shut and she heard the bar fall as it was locked. She was now on the outside. "Where?" Lud demanded and still holding the axe, she ran back the way she had come. The body was still there and Lud turned it over and freed bee sting. "There will be others. Go! To Ellen. She has still not arrived at the castle." He handed her bee sting. Splitting the warriors, some old and some young. He set some to watch the fence where the Welsh warrior had fell, "There will be others on the other side waiting to be let in." He turned and strode off.

Kalea had reached Ellen's house and found her still inside with her aids. "Quickly!" Kalea shouted. "There are Welsh inside the walls." With that they hustled out and with Kalea as their only guard hurried to the castle where they were let in. Kalea was still in full battle flight and ran to the stables. "I need horses."

"There's not much left," John spat as he saddled up what he had left. Kalea was on the first one before the girth had been tightened. Grabbing the reigns of two more, she rode to the gate. They were opened and she set off like the wind dragging two more behind her. She rode until she found Lud and gave him the horses.

"I'll check the fence on the way to the gate," she called as she set off for the village gate. The warriors at the gate were fighting and she rode straight through the attackers slashing with bee sting and moving on before she had any idea if they had fallen. She used the horse as a weapon. Cannoning into warriors to knock them off balance and giving the defenders a chance to fight back. When she was sure that they were once again in control of the gate, she turned and belted off. Movement off to her right, sent her wheeling in that direction and she rode down another Welsh invader. She found Lud in a melee and drove her horse forward to cause as much chaos as she could. Suddenly, all went quiet and the defenders had held and repelled. Kalea was shaking with adrenalin as she pulled her blowing horse to a halt.

"Well done, Kalea. That could have been a lot worse, if you hadn't acted so swiftly," Lud said patting her on the back as he would a warrior and nearly knocking her from her mount. A shout went up from the gate and everyone immediately turned to face the new danger. Lud and Kalea ploughed forward, and found that the warband were returning. The Welsh were being routed and were fleeing from the village walls as the warband in full flight swept the perimeter and cleared what was left of the invaders.

The village gate was thrown open to allow them in. One of the first through the gate was Kai on Midnight and he swept through passing Lud and Kalea before even seeing them. Lud and Kalea exchanged a grin and rode in after them. They looked tired and battered. Both horses and men were dripping with blood, some theirs, but most not.

Arthur rode up to Lud. "What has been happening here?" he asked seeing both Lud and Kalea splattered with blood.

"Nothing we couldn't handle," Lud answered ruffling Kalea's hair. Kai was in the courtyard, dragging Midnight behind him and yelling for her. She rode up to him.

"Are you looking for me?" she asked sliding straight into his arms. He kissed her before he noticed her blood splattered clothing.

"Are you alright?"

"I'm fine. You?"

"Untouched. Midnight was brilliant." He patted the great horse. "What have you been doing?" He wiped a smear of blood from her cheek.

"Helping Lud." He took in her sword slung on her back and looked to Lud.

"I hope you haven't put her in any danger," he stated harshly.

"Didn't need to. She did that all by herself." Lud grinned. "She saved us is what she did."

"Hush now," Kalea shushed him. "I was just in the right place at the right time."

"I need to hear this," Arthur stated.

"What you been doing now?" Leith appeared at her shoulder.

"Leith!" She swung round and hugged him. "Are you unhurt?"

"Just a scratch. Ellen will sort it." Arthur grinned. "And you can keep your lips shut lad," Leith warned. Arthur raised his hands in surrender.

John came to take Midnight from Kai. "How are the horses?" Kalea asked.

"A couple in need of your skills." She went to follow, but Kai stopped her.

"They can wait."

"No. They can't," Kalea answered firmly.

Kai knew better than to argue. "I'll get you a bath made." She nodded and followed John into the stable.

Once the horses, were done, wounds sown, Midnight bedded down, Kalea wandered into the bath house. Laid out for her, were fresh clothes, shirt and trousers and as she stripped off and stepped into the large barrel, Kai came in and before she could say a word, stripped off and squeezed in with her. She giggled and ran her hands over his body to check that he was unharmed. He did the same to her. There was little room for too much intimacy and having scrubbed each other clean, the next problem was getting out, which caused much laughter.

Kalea was in no hurry to go to the hall. She had no wish to tend the wounded with Ellen and also hoped that Lud had not made her out to be a hero. Kai on the other hand had heard the story already, and was convinced that if Kalea hadn't been brave enough to check out the stranger, it could have resulted in many more deaths.

Together, they entered the hall and both Arthur and Lud rose to greet her. Kalea was already looking towards where the wise women were treating the wounded. She sighed and would have gone to help, but Kai grabbed her elbow and steered her towards Arthur's table.

"It seems I owe you a debt." Arthur smiled gravely and held out a chair for her. Kalea made a dismissive gesture and sat down, grateful that once again she was within the safety of the hall. "Madam, don't make light of your service. Lud says that you proved to be the best early warning, we could have had."

Kalea poured Kai and her a beaker of mead. "Lud is exaggerating. I just spotted something that wasn't quite right and dealt with it."

"Taking on a Welsh warrior armed with an axe," Kai stated proudly.

"I happen to have had some training of how to deal with an axe." Kalea smiled at him. "One of the best axemen in the kingdom gave me some useful tips. It wasn't that difficult. I was sneaky as a sneaky thing. He didn't have time to take one swing at me, before I skewered him."

"And did she skewer him." Lud laughed. "Bee sting was buried up to the hilt."

"Which was a stupid thing to do," Kalea retorted. "I couldn't get it back out."

"STOP!" Lud's voice boomed out and the hall fell silent. "Just stop trying to make out everything you have done, is of little consequence. You did me, no us, a great service today. Yes. You just so happened to spot a Welsh spy but you are the only woman in this village, who would have dealt with it. Yes. Perhaps you did make a mistake and get disarmed but you didn't let it stop you from warning me." Kalea had turned bright red and she dropped her gaze to her lap. Kai took her hand and gave it a squeeze. "Then you did not stay hidden safely within the castle walls, you mounted up and bought me horses so that I could be where I was needed. When you heard battle, you rode straight to the gate and used horse and sword to help turn the tide for our men. Then while I was in here, drinking and eating, you were out in the stable seeing to the injured horses. You are a brave young woman and all of us, owe the safety of our families to your quick thinking." He fell silent. Kalea did not look up.

Arthur began beating his beaker on the table and soon the whole hall was applauding her actions. Kai bent his head to hers so he could be heard over the din. "Lift your head my darling. Be proud. Not embarrassed. You did well." She met his eye and he smiled encouragingly at her. He nodded and she lifted her head. Then stood and hugged Lud to loud cheering. Then she sat back down.

"You don't like fuss, do you?" Arthur commented.

Kalea met his eye. "No."

"Is that the reason you refused Mark's offer of marriage?" Arthur looked at Kai. He had raised a ghost.

"No," Kalea repeated and then looked at Kai. "He is the reason I refused Mark. I had always hoped he would take me back."

Kai grinned. "I can be a bit thick at times, but I got there in the end."

"You are not thick, just proud and stubborn," Kalea defended him. "And I don't blame you at all." She reached out a hand for him which he took and pressed to his lips. A huge slab of pork sat on the table and Kalea tummy rumbled. "Excuse me! My tummy is reminding me, that I haven't had anything to eat since yesterday. I am hungry and thirsty." Arthur cut off a large slice for her, while Kai buttered some bread. Lud poured her mead and then all three sat and watched as she tried and failed not to bolt her food.

Having eaten her fill, Kalea began to feel very drowsy. The day had been overwhelming. She had not stopped all day and it was still early. Her eyes drooped and she leant against Kai's shoulder.

Looking down at her, he said quietly, "Why don't you go and lay down in my old room? Have a nap. You've earned it." She nodded and rose wearily.

"If you will excuse me." Arthur nodded and she wandered out. Within minutes of putting her head of the furs, she was asleep.

When she woke, the sun was going down. She stretched and rose. Leaving Kai's room, she went down the steps and paused at the hall door. Although she wanted to see Kai, she didn't really want to go back into the hall. She hesitated and was met by Lud who had been to the kitchen.

"Why are you lurking in the hall way?" he asked smiling at her.

"I don't know," she admitted.

"Come on." He threw an arm over her shoulder and led her back into the hall. She smiled sheepishly. Kai seeing her, smiled and then opened his arms to her and she went willingly and happily snuggled against him. She wasn't there long before Ellen came over.

"Kalea. Would you come and help us please?"

"I think she has done enough for today," Arthur said.

Kalea made a dismissive gesture. "It's alright Arthur. I will do what I can." And she got up and left.

"Poor girl." Arthur sighed. Kai nodded in agreement.

Lud grinned. "She is her own worst enemy. She can't possible say no to help someone. She did really well today, Leith. You taught her well."

Leith nodded. "That girl has more backbone than she has any right to."

"I'll not let her work all night," Kai growled.

"No. Don't." Leith agreed. "She has done her bit and deserves her rest."

Kalea was going round tending the wounded at the far end of the hall when Kai appeared at her elbow. "It is time for us to retire." She turned to look at Ellen. "Don't look at Ellen. It is our time now." Ellen nodded and Kalea allowed Kai to lead her away. Kai did wonder that if Ellen had argued, Kalea would have stayed, but she tucked her arm through his. On his way past the kitchen, Kai asked for some milk, bread and honey and after a tray was prepared, they left for the peace of Kai room. Seated on the bed, they shared a picnic and then after putting the tray on the floor, they climbed into bed naked. Kalea put her head on Kai's chest and listened to the steady beating of his heart.

"I love you." Her voice was quiet.

"I love you too. More than you can know," he answered. "I can't wait to have you as my wife."

She lifted her head and kissed him. They made love tenderly. Both aware of stresses of the day and when it was over, they lay in one another's arms.

"Midnight did you proud today," Kai said sleepily. "He was the best war horse on the field. His only problem, is he is like you. Reckless." He grinned. "No thought of how he might get hurt, just wanting to get the job done."

Kalea smiled. "I am not reckless," she protested. Then added. "Perhaps I am a little. More thoughtless. I do not think the process through, so it does not cross my mind that I might get hurt."

Kai gave a huff of laughter. "Mayhap your right." And with her arms tightly wrapped around him, he drifted off to sleep.

The morning dawned and Kai and Kalea slept on. By the time they surfaced, it was almost noon. Dressing, they went down to the hall to find that breakfast had passed and noon food was being laid out. Kalea ate quickly and then looking at Kai, said "I would go and help the wise women and then perhaps check the horses."

"Can you not sit still for a moment?" Kai asked.

"Of course, I can. But I feel guilty when others work and I do not."

"Do you see Leith and Lud working?" Kai nodded to where Lud and Leith were deep in conversation. "And Arthur no doubt, is still a bed."

As if summoned by his name, Arthur appeared at the hall door and Kai was right, he didn't look as if he had been up long either. Yawning, he came towards them.

"That was a hard day yesterday," he commented as he sat and poured himself some ale.

"Battle is never easy. I ache in my shoulders."

Arthur grinned cheekily. "Is that all that aches?"

"Behave," Kalea warned.

"My apologies." Arthur smiled sheepishly. "But it was tough."

"That's because, we were caught unaware," Lud interjected. "It should be asked how they managed to get so close before we got word." Arthur nodded. "That is twice, if you include Mark's raid when he captured Kalea. No offence Kalea."

"None taken."

Arthur rubbed his face. "We need to rethink this then. Our defences are not working as well as they should."

"Why did no one from the outer villages send word?" Lud asked. "I can understand why they managed to cross the border but why did no one see them?"

Arthur nodded sagely. Kalea stood up. "Excuse me please. I have no idea that anything I could say would be helpful."

"Stay," Arthur said. Kalea sat down again. "Sometimes, you have said things that bring forth good ideas."

Kalea looked down at her hands. She would far rather be with the horses.

"First off, we need to send out some men and see if any villages have been raided. We fought where we found the Welsh. We didn't go any further out," Kai stated.

"Just as well," Lud grumbled. "We could have been in trouble if they had breached the outer defences."

"Fire," Kalea said.

"What?" Arthur asked.

"Fire." And went on to explain. "If they had fired a village, the smoke would have been seen, and the warning would have been received sooner."

"See," Arthur stated. "That is a good idea. Perhaps, we should have fire beacons arranged for the villages so that they could warn other villages and if each village light their beacons, the warning would be seen sooner."

"Good idea." Kai nodded. "We have a plan then."

"So," Arthur stated. "Lud, give the order for groups to go out and arrange fire beacons." Then he added. "My head is not in the best place to deal with this."

"You pups need to go easier on the drink," Lud stated. The two men rolled their eyes and exchanged a long-suffering look. "I saw that. But what if there had been another raid?"

"We would have met the challenge," Arthur argued.

"Yes. But you would have been slower to react and chances are you would have been injured." No one but Lud would have dared to talk to Arthur so.

"I doubt it," Kai defended. Lud just looked at him.

"Now, may I go?" Kalea was uncomfortable with the disagreement and didn't want to get involved. Arthur just nodded and Kalea left hurriedly.

The three men watched her go. "She's a strange one," Lud pondered.

"Yes. She is. But utterly fascinating," Arthur stated.

Kai laughed. "And she's all mine."

"You lucky man." Arthur grinned.

Kalea virtually ran once she was outside the hall and was relieved to arrive at the stable. John greeted her happily.

"You did a good job," he said escorting her into the stable. "They are all still with us and looking cheerful."

Kalea laughed. "I didn't know horses could be cheerful."

He laughed too. "Well, I mean they don't look too sad."

Kalea found that John was right. The horses were looking cheerful. Not one of them looked unhappy or in pain. She grinned and John slapped her on the back, for a moment forgetting that she was a woman. He looked terribly embarrassed but Kalea wasn't at all bothered.

Kalea was in a great mood when she went back into the hall. She went straight to the wounded and was even more cheered by the fact that they were all recovering well. Turning back, she saw that Leith had joined the three men at the table and all of them were deep in conversation. So, she left them to it and went back to the stable to help out there.

Meanwhile, Arthur and his three closest advisors had organised small groups of the warband to range the country to ensure that warning beacons are arranged and set with a constant watch.

Arthur leaned back in his chair. For now, he had done all he could do. Later, he would visit the border villages himself but for now, he would stay here. "Kai, I don't much like you living so far from the castle."

Kai was surprised. "I am only sleeping away from the castle. I am here, every day." Lud looked at the two of them sensing a locking of horns.

Arthur's look was dark. "The fact is, it wasted precious moments, sending for you."

Kai scoffed. "Really?"

"Yes. Really."

Leith and Lud exchanged a look and saw a nerve in Kai's jaw, begin to twitch. A sure sign that his anger was rising. "You think you have the right to tell me where I can sleep?"

"I have the right to tell my warband chief where he should be. Although, I shouldn't have to tell him."

Leith stepped in. "Now stop squabbling like two street dogs. Arthur, you have no right to tell Kai where he lays his head. Do you impose that on any others of your warband?"

"No," Arthur conceded. "But Kai isn't just one of my warband. He is a leader of the warband."

"But you still have to wake your warriors who are at home with their wives," Lud added. "You only have the single men here in the barracks and the others would not stay here, when they can be at home with their families, which is why they fight with you." Arthur scowled fiercely. Not happy at being set upon by the two old warriors.

"So, now I have two old men telling me what I can and cannot do."

"You have two of your most trusted advisors telling you to be sensible," Lud concluded.

Kai his anger abated by the spirited defence of the two old warriors. "I don't know what you want me to do? At Samhain, I will marry Kalea and I won't be able to live at the castle then."

"Then perhaps, I should have a house built for you within the castle walls."

"That would work," Leith agreed. "Kai would have his own household and would be within reach."

Lud breathed a sigh of relief when Kai conceded. "Yes. Kalea might accept that. That could work. She could be close to her beloved horses."

"So, it is agreed. We will set it into action this very day." Arthur nodded.

Kai and Arthur set off, leaving Lud and Leith together. "Arthur's jealous," Leith stated.

Lud nodded. "He's hungover. He's angry that the Welsh got through his defences and came a lot closer than he liked. And he likes it not one bit, that his village was defended by an old man and a young woman. He'll have to get over it. He is jealous of Kalea, because she has taken Kai from him and jealous of Kai because he has Kalea." He sighed. "The sooner those two are wed the better."

Leith laughed. "I'm glad I'm not young anymore."

"You don't seem to be doing so badly." Lud grinned.

Kai met Ellen in the courtyard. "Have you seen Kalea?"

Ellen smiled kindly at him. "She is a handful. But no. I haven't seen her. I suspect, she is down with that horse of hers. I know I needn't tell you, but she is a good one that one."

Kai grinned back. "I know. I consider myself fortunate. I'll see if she is at the stables then." And with that he turned and marched off. Entering the stables, he found her cuddling the big black stallion and talking to John. "Ah! There you are."

Kalea turned and smiled at him. "There really are only two places I could be. At home or with the horses. I don't think it would be wise to be riding about today."

John smirked. "I wouldn't put that past you. You took that nag I gave you yesterday and made it work like a warhorse."

"And very well she did too," Kalea remarked. "Are we staying for food in the hall? I hope we are because I haven't been home to cook."

Kai laughed. "It seems I am not getting a very enthusiastic cook in my household."

"Nonsense," Kalea scolded. "I have just been busy elsewhere."

The men laughed.

Kai bowed low. "If the lady wishes, we shall partake of the food in the hall."

Kalea gave Midnight one last pat and joined Kai to walk back up to the hall.

"I have something which I need to speak to you about."

Kalea heard uncertainty in his voice. Not something she had heard often. "Speak plainly," she encouraged. "The worse that could happen is I will banish you from my bed tonight."

Kai gave a huff of laughter. "Arthur and I nearly came to blows today."

"Why?"

"He complained that I was too far away when he needed me for battle."

"He is jealous." Kalea grinned cheekily.

"Of that there is little doubt," Kai replied. "I said that I would not sleep back at the castle and he would have to get used to it." Kalea giggled.

"Oh dear!"

"Indeed. Then he suggested a compromise and said he would have a house built for us within the castle walls." Kalea stopped dead. "The idea does not please you?"

"Kai. I will go wherever you go. I am happy if it makes you happy. I don't mind at all and if that's what makes Arthur happy, then so be it."

Kai hugged her. "I love you. I would have said no."

"It matters not where I live as long as you are with me." She laughed. "I never thought I could be so silly."

"Not silly at all." He kissed her.

Then hand in hand they went into the hall.

Arthur watched them closely. Had Kai told her? If he had, she had accepted it well. He had compromised and already, workmen had set about clearing a space and working out dimensions. Was he keeping Kai close? Or was it Kalea? Now he would have both of them at hand. Whatever, a solution to the problem had been reached. It had been a tough couple of days. Sometimes, it was not an easy job taking care of his people. A King had to be more than a warrior and sadly the mantle could not be put down once it had been taken on.

Life resumed. Extra warning had been put into place and they worked. There were a few more Welsh raids but none managed to get anywhere close to Arthur's stronghold which stood in the middle of the kingdom. Mark of Cornwall had not raided once this season, or if he had, it had been blamed on the Welsh. Arthur suspected that he was at home nursing his wounded heart and had decided, that for Kalea's sake he would not raid. Or, more likely, he was having his own problems with the Welsh and the Irish. Whatever, dealing with one enemy, was more than enough to keep them occupied.

Chapter 16
Harvest Home – The Wedding

Harvest was upon them. Now, the people fought the weather in order to get the crops in before they were spoiled by rain or frost. Children were pressed into helping the adults collect nuts, berries and fruit from the trees.

Kalea and Ellen were equally busy, collecting herbs to see them through the long winter months as well as dealing with unwary people being stung or bitten by the wildlife and harvesting accidents. Autumn was a busy time of year before the long dark winter evenings when the people hoped they had done enough to see them through to spring.

The whole village was a hive of activity. The warriors had turned their skills to hunting and were bringing home, deer, boar in abundance. The local hunters were catching rabbits and such like, while the older men, fished. All the meat and fish had to be smoked and cured so that it would keep.

Of course, the wedding was the topic of conversation as Samhain, Harvest home was getting closer. The young couple had agreed that the ceremony was to be overseen by both the Christian priest, Peter and the young druid, Blaise. Thus, both religions would be appeased and they were eager not to offend anyone on a day of such importance to them. Both Blaise and Peter were happy with the arrangement, both being good friends, despite their differences.

The house that Arthur had had built for Kalea and Kai was nearing completion and he was well pleased with the result. Twice the size of Kalea's own home, it ran along the outer castle wall, built with stone as well as wood, it actually had two rooms, both with small fireplaces rather than pits. People Kalea had done a service too, either by tending to their ailments or to their animals, were eager to help and supply things and Arthur was surprised at how many of them there were. The thatch was going on and then it would be completed. All that remained was making it, furnishing it and with the help of the local tradesman and the castle servants, it was going to be easy to accomplish.

All in all, it was going to plan. The Welsh had had their noses bloodied too often now, and were content to stay on their side of the border and concentrate on preparing for winter. Arthur also suspected that the Irish Sea wolves, were at the door, seeking a last push before winter set in. Mark in Cornwall had given them some respite this year. For whatever reason, Arthur was grateful. If only he could get the warlords to come together, they could defeat the invaders easily. As it was, they were too busy testing each other.

This would be a problem to ponder on during the long winter months. With the harvest celebrations soon to be upon them, he had enough to deal with. Celebrations always bought their own challenges. Travelling traders came in to set up stalls in the market and the local traders did not like the competition and would often accuse the outsiders of short changing. The local people enjoyed having new wares to sample. Troupes of entertainers were turning up to ply their trade in the market place and often bought with them accusations of thievery. All complaints had to be seen to be dealt with fairly. Arthur relied heavily on Lud to handle most of these. This year, Lud had Leith to help him. As far as he could see, however, everyone was enjoying the preparations and there actually seemed less trouble than usual.

Kai was like a cat on hot coals. He had commissioned new clothing and now that they were done and he looked well in them, he was impatient for the day to arrive. Lud made sure he kept the young man busy, although he knew that Kai was of little mind to do anything now that he was ready. Leith teased him unmercifully, until Kai started retaliating by asking when Leith might ask Ellen to marry him and suddenly Leith went quiet. Lud found it all amusing.

Kalea and Ellen worked on the wedding dress. Kalea was delighted to find that Ellen had kept it and through the winter months, Ellen had embroidered it even more and the effect was magical. It was exquisite. Even the dress that Mark had had made for her, seemed less than this beautiful dress that had been made with love by Ellen. Ellen was proud. Not just of the dress, which she admitted she had excelled at, but of her protégé. Kalea had turned out to be a very apt student and was becoming a respected member of the village. People still frowned on her, when she rode through the village in trousers, but the majority had accepted that this was how she was and looked upon her fondly.

Kalea and Kai had escaped the hustle and bustle of the village and were riding round the watchtowers, seeing that everyone was alright and there were no problems. It was enjoyable away from the noise and talking to the men manning the towers without constant interruption. They were in no hurry to return and were happy to take their time enjoying the brightness of the day. All too soon the circuit was completed and they turned back to the village.

As they crested the hill, a rider came into view riding a rangy bay horse.

"Is that Valim?" Kai squinted to confirm his suspicions.

"It looks like it."

"Let's ride down and go in with him." Kai grinned.

"Let's not."

Kai was surprised that Kalea's voice was hard and flat. He had expected her to want to ride flat out to meet the druid. He turned to look at her, but her expression was closed. "Why not?"

Kalea did not take her eyes from the rider. "Essie, Mark's wise woman, says he's a bad one. She is very wise, and I tend to agree. Did you know he wanted me to be a priestess?"

"Yes," Kai answered watching her closely as she watched the rider intently. "He told us himself."

She turned to look at him. "Then you know why I do not trust him."

"Well," Kai grinned eager to lift her mood. "He has absolutely no chance now. You will be my wife and I certainly won't let Valim take you off."

She rewarded him with a smile. "He is a dangerous man, Kai. So much so, that Essie gave me something to protect against his magic."

"Really? I don't disbelieve you," he added hastily. "But what did she give you?"

Kalea reached to the pouch which she always carried on her belt and withdrew a small stone which she passed to Kai. He turned it over in his palm. It was an exceptionally good moon stone. Small, but the colours glowed bright. "She said that all the time I had the stone on me, charms and magic couldn't be worked on me." She grinned cheekily. "It didn't work with you."

He laughed and carefully handed it back. "How could anyone resist me?" he asked as she stowed it back in the pouch and gave him a playful slap. "Do you know how it is supposed to work?"

"It's supposed to evoke the protection of the moon goddess. The stone itself harness her power." With a grin, she continued, "Now, I don't know if that is true or not, but if Essie says it does, that is good enough for me."

"It is very beautiful. It was a generous gift."

"Indeed, it was. I owe Essie much," Kalea admitted. "And she suspected Valim of some trickery. She did not like his 'hocus pocus' much. Needless to say, I will keep away from him as much as possible."

"I can think of places to take you where he will not find you," Kai smirked and Kalea giggled.

Valim rode through the gates observing the frantic activity. He smiled. Life was hard for the most part and any excuse for a day of frivolity was welcomed. He was pleased to see that Arthur's village was thriving. People greeted him warmly, although they had their own druid, a senior member was always welcome and they met him with respect. Riding into the courtyard, he observed a new building and Arthur smiling overseeing the last of the thatching. Hearing hoofbeat, Arthur turned and his face lit up at seeing Valim.

"Valim! My old friend! Welcome!"

Valim slid from the saddle and enfolded Arthur in an embrace. "It is good to see you, Arthur. Your kingdom is looking good."

"It seems to be." Arthur slapped Valim on the back. "The preparations for Harvest home are nearly done. Come in and take some refreshment. You can tell me all the news from around the land." He led Valim into the hall and sent a servant off to get some food and drink. As they both took a seat, Arthur asked. "In which direction have you come?" Lud came into the hall and came over to join them. Greeting the druid warmly.

"I have come from Cornwall." Arthur raised an eyebrow.

"Again?"

"Yes." Valim nodded.

"And how is Mark?" Arthur asked.

"Mark is well but he misses Kalea. He tells me that his Winter Queen now resides in your court."

Arthur laughed. "Not quite. Kalea lives in the village but she chooses her own path now. She has become quite a notable wise woman." He noticed a strange light appear in Valim's eye.

"Mark seemed quite bruised about her loss," Valim stated. "He did say that should she wish to return now; he would come for her." They were interrupted by food and drink. Arthur poured Valim some mead.

As Valim drank his mead, Arthur looked at him shrewdly. "I fear that he will be disappointed yet again. As will you, if you had any plans for Kalea. She is to marry Kai as the start of our harvest celebrations."

Valim hid his surprise well. "Kai?" Arthur nodded. "Well, the lady wastes no time."

"Not strictly true. Kalea was to marry Kai before Mark stole her. So, they have found each other again." Arthur was quick to defend Kalea. "As you know, she is strong willed and she is much changed since she has returned from Cornwall."

"Imagine how strong her healing powers would be if she had a priestess's power," Valim pondered.

Arthur's eyes hardened. "Valim. You must understand, that Kalea does not want to be a priestess. She wants to be Kai's wife. You must not. I repeat, must not interfere."

Valim met his eye. "Arthur. I don't think you understand what potential she has. We need women to join and become priestesses. The goddess demands followers and there are few strong enough and with the skills to do what is needed. The few we have are either too old or too young to take the form of the goddess and do her work."

Arthur did not flinch under the scrutiny. "No. You don't understand. She is not yours to command. I will not allow you to spoil her life."

"How can her life be spoiled doing the will of the goddess?" Valim voice was hard and bitter.

Lud answered him. "She is doing the goddess's work. She is following her path at being a wife. Kai is a good man and I will not see him disappointed." Lud's voice held a warning.

Valim however, was not one to be cowed and met his eye with an equally flinty stare. Arthur could see that this could escalate into something quite nasty and stepped in hastily. "My dear friend. Let's not fall out. I do not want you as an enemy. I have enough enemies. I know, you have your heart set on taking Kalea. But you really must accept that the lady does not wish to go and I will not have her forced. We really can't jeopardise our friendship for the sake of one strong willed woman."

Valim sighed and nodded in defeat. "I agree. Although I think, she would be perhaps the most powerful priestess we will ever see."

At that moment, Kai came marching into the hall. "Valim! Good to see you." Despite the smile on his face, his eyes were hard. He greeted the druid warmly.

"It is good to see you too Kai." Valim smiled and Kai noticed that the smile did not reach the druid's eyes. "I hear you are to marry Kalea."

Kai's grin expanded. "That I am. I am glad you are going to be here to witness it."

"And where is the young woman?" Valim asked.

"Here and about," Kai answered noncommittally. He noticed the guarded look of both Lud and Arthur. "You know, Kalea. She goes where she will. But you will see her in her wedding finery. Lud. A word please." He turned Lud round and led him from the hall. "What is occurring?"

"Nothing," Lud answered his smile not reaching his eyes. "Where is Kalea?"

"Lud. I have known you and Arthur too long to know that you are hiding something. Kalea is hiding from Valim. Leith and Ellen are looking after her. They have agreed not to let her out of their sight. Valim will not catch her alone. Is he still after her to be a priestess? Is that it?" Lud nodded. "Kalea says that he is dangerous. But she is safe."

"Good work Kai." Lud gripped his shoulder. "So, you knew he was here."

Kai nodded. "Kalea and I saw him from the ridge. I remembered Valim saying he wanted her as a priestess so we thought it best to keep her out of sight for a while." He grinned at Lud. "No doubt he will try some trickery."

"I had always thought druids were respected and honest people," Lud commented wearily.

"So did I," Kai agreed. "So did Kalea. It seems that perhaps we should treat them with the same caution that we do war chiefs."

"It is a shame. But I think you are right. Valim says that there is a shortage of priestesses. The Christian god has claimed many followers, perhaps, that is the reason that not many want follow the old religions."

Kai shrugged and with his characteristic grin, "Who knows? The old gods, the Viking gods, the Christian gods? Are they all but one?"

"I really don't need you to be with me all the time," Kalea moaned as Leith escorted her to the market. "I am not afraid. Essie has given me a charm against druid magic."

"I know you are not afraid girlie," Leith grimaced. "But we want to keep things as sweet as we can. I know what you're like. You can't be trusted to keep your mouth shut. It is a celebration not a confrontation. We are just being cautious."

Kalea sighed. "Alright. I will accept that."

The days passed and Kai's strategy worked. Kalea was never left alone. Lud and Arthur also kept a close eye on her. Valim spent time with the young village druid Blaise but it didn't escape the chaperones notice, that on occasion, he could be seen ghosting through the village. It was clear that he was seeking Kalea.

One morning, whilst Kalea was working with Ellen, the young druid appeared at the door. He looked uncomfortable.

"Morning Blaise," Kalea greeted him. "Is everything alright?"

"Good morning." Blaise ducked through the doorway and looked at Ellen.

"If you think, I'm going anywhere young Blaise, you are mistaken," Ellen warned. He gave a brief nod.

"Go on. Out with it," Kalea cajoled. "You obviously have something to say. Did Valim send you?"

Blaise squirmed under the women's scrutiny. "The thing is..." he hesitated. Ellen and Kalea folded their arms. "Yes. He did," Blaise confessed. "He thinks you are avoiding him, Kalea."

"He's right," Kalea stated. "If he wants me to become a priestess, I'm afraid, I am not interested."

"The thing is," Blaise began again. "The goddess has few priestesses these days. They are either too old or too young. Kalea, you are so strong."

"Stop!" Ellen commanded. "She has made her feelings clear. Save your breath."

Blaise sighed. "I told Valim it was a waste of time. I'm sorry Kalea." He looked contrite. "I promised I'd try. Now, with any luck we can carry on as normal. If you will forgive me."

Kalea grinned at him. "There is nothing to forgive Blaise. All you need to know; is I love Kai and I am going to marry him. Nothing more, nothing less."

Blaise smiled. "Thank you. I will leave you now."

"Blaise. Tell Valim, that my choice is made." Kalea smiled at the poor druid. "I do not blame either of you, but I no longer dance to other people's tunes. I dance to my own music."

Blaise nodded and left.

Ellen grinned. "Well done."

"I am going to wear your wedding dress this time." Kalea laughed.

Two days to go and Kalea and Kai were in high spirits when they walked into the hall. Arthur grinned and beckoned them over. "I can see all is right in your world," he stated happily.

"Yes. It certainly is." Kai grinned handing Kalea to the table next to Arthur. She was in a fine mood too and patted his hand smiling.

"Are you ready?"

"More than," Kalea answered. She looked up and saw Valim who met her eye and came forward.

"Congratulations Kalea." She smiled happily at him. "It seems you have been avoiding me."

"My apologies." Kalea tried to sound as if she meant it. "But it is true. I have no wish to offend you by refusing your invitation. It seemed to be wise to stay clear."

Valim ducked his head in acknowledgement. "Let us let it be then," he conceded. "I have no wish to spoil the celebrations."

Kai rose and offered his hand which Valim shook warmly. "I am pleased it is settled," Kai spoke with feeling. Valim joined them at the table and no more was said on the subject. Before long, they were chatting and laughing happily.

After they had eaten, Arthur rose. "Now, come you two. I need to show you your new home." Kalea and Kai followed him out as he led them to the new house, he had had built for him. He threw open the door and motioned for them to go in.

Kalea couldn't believe her eyes. "This is for us?"

Arthur followed them in and unlocked the shuttered window allowing the light to spill in. "Yes," he answered simply. Kalea and Kai looked about them. As well as the fireplace, he had had a table and some chairs put in. Granted they were from the castle, but it was more than Kalea had in her home. The pots and pans needed were on a shelf along with a few provisions. He opened the door to the second room. Here there was a sleeping chamber with a large sleeping platform heaped with furs and underneath there was ample room for storage and a fireplace backed the one in the main room so warmth would be provided throughout. Kalea flung her arms round him.

"Arthur! Thank you. This is such a generous gift."

Kai also grinning broadly, gave Arthur a hug that nearly broke his ribs. "My friend. You have excelled yourself."

Arthur glowed in the praise and smiled broadly. "Now, I have both of you safe and sound within the castle walls."

"Yes, you have." Kai laughed. "We shall look forward to moving in after the wedding."

It was the day of the wedding. The day was perfect. The sky blue, the sun shining and the first chill of the morning was burning off. Kai was beside himself and Lud and Arthur couldn't help laughing at him. He had scrubbed himself until he nearly shone. He had put his new clothes on, then taken them off again, worried that they might get spoiled. Leith teased him unmercifully. Kai knew and laughed but inside his stomach was churning.

Arthur pressed a beaker of wine into his hand. "Drink this. It will calm your nerves."

Kai took a swig. "I am less worried when I go into battle," he confessed.

Lud laughed. "Yes. But you have been into battle many times. It is the first time you have been married."

Kai fidgeted. "Thanks for pointing that out."

Arthur slapped him on the back. "Would you like me to go and tell Kalea you have changed your mind?"

"No!" Kai said sharply. "By all the gods." They all laughed. "How much longer have I got to wait?"

"Nearly there," Lud soothed and Kai groaned.

Kalea had spent the night with Ellen and the women were down at the river bathing.

"How are you feeling?" Ellen asked as she soaped Kalea's hair.

"Excited." Kalea giggled. "I can't believe it's finally going to happen."

Ellen ducked her. "Come on then girl. It is time to get into that dress."

Ellen rubbed honeysuckle oil into Kalea's skin so her skin was soft and fragrant. Rubbing it behind her ears and between her thighs. All the time, the two women giggling.

Back in Ellen's home, Kalea stripped off and Ellen dropped the wedding dress over her head and then laced it tight to show off Kalea's curves. She stood back and put her hands on her hips. "Girl. You look gorgeous. Kai is a very lucky man. Now, get your shoes on. We are running late."

Kalea grinned and bent to put on her shoes, the ones that Mark had had made for her. Ellen shrugged on her best blue dress and combed through her hair. Then she set about Kalea's and brushed it till it shone.

"One final thing." Ellen turned and bought out the headdress that she had been working on for Kalea.

"Oh Ellen! It's beautiful!" Ellen had woven a crown of cornstalks, honeysuckle, poppies and red berries.

"It will be stunning with your dark hair." She popped it on Kalea's head. "Kai is going to be speechless."

"That will be a first." Kalea giggled.

Kai stood on the platform that had been constructed for the wedding. Blaise, the druid and Peter the priest stood in front of him and Arthur beside him.

"Has she changed her mind?" Kai worried.

"No. Of course not. She's making you wait on purpose." Arthur grinned squeezing his arm reassuringly. Kai turned to the castle gate. Leith and Lud stood in front but quite a crowd had already gathered and he couldn't see if she was coming.

"Stop fidgeting lad," Leith called. Kai grinned back and saw Valim join Lud and Leith at the front. "She'll be here."

The crowd went quiet and then a murmur spread amongst them and they started to shuffle. Kai froze. The crowd parted and Ellen appeared smiling broadly. As she stepped out in front of the crowd, she stood aside to reveal Kalea. Kai breath caught in his throat as did Arthur's. Then Kai smiled. "By the gods, Arthur. Can she get any more beautiful?"

Arthur swallowed hard. "I don't think it's possible." Kalea looked a vision in her pale cream dress with the beautiful embroidery and the golden corn headdress did indeed bring out the beauty of her dark hair and eyes. She walked with her natural grace to the platform and Kai lent down to offer his hand to help her up. She accepted smiling broadly. "My lady, you look wonderful."

Together, they stepped in front of Peter and Blaise and so the ceremony began. First, they were joined in front of the Christian God and then Blaise joined them in the old ways. So, they were doubly married. The two religious friends joined together at the end to say in unison. "Husband and wife." A huge cheer went up as Kai kissed Kalea and then the couple turned to face the gathered crowd beaming happily.

Kai raised his hand and the crowd fell silent. With his arm around Kalea's waist, he smiled happily at them. "Am I not the luckiest man in the kingdom? To have this wonderful woman as my wife?" A cheer went up.

Arthur stepped forward and once again the crowd went quiet. "People! My best friend and my brother has just found himself a wife and what a great way to start our harvest celebrations." Another cheer went up. "So, I would ask Valim to give us the Harvest blessing so that we can start our celebrations."

Valim stepped up onto the platform and raised his staff and bought it down on and intoned the blessing, his voice resonating with power. As he finished, the musicians started up a tune and everyone started chatting and moving to get some food.

Kai led Kalea to the top table and they sat in the place of honour. Kai leant over to her. "You are the most beautiful woman I have ever seen. Are you sure you're not a goddess?"

Kalea put her hand on his cheek. "I will be whatever you desire me to be. I love you my handsome man. Body and soul." He took her hand and kissed it.

"My heart is yours." His voice was low.

"As mine is yours."

"When you two have finished," Leith interrupted, "how 'bout a hug for your old friends." As the two turned to him, they found they had a little crowd in front of them beaming broadly. As well as Leith, there was of course, Ellen, Lud and John. They rose to hug each and every one of them.

"Well, girlie," Leith whispered to Kalea. "It turned out all right in the end."

"Indeed, it did," she confirmed. "I am the happiest girl ever!" she exclaimed kissing his cheek.

"I told you the right woman was there for you." Lud gave Kai a huge bear hug which would have broken lesser men's ribs. "I could not be prouder of you, Son."

"I would not be here but for your good instructions." Kai then added, "Well, mostly." Lud laughed.

Their excited conversation was bought to an abrupt end, when Arthur rapped his sword hilt on the table. Everyone fell silent and turned to face him. He smiled broadly. "I could not be happier than today," he announced. "The harvest is home and we have done well." The people nodded in agreement. "It is tradition that the King dances with the festival Queen for the first dance." He looked towards

Kai and Kalea. "But the right today, belongs to the Harvest Queen's husband. So, Kai, will you take our Harvest Queen to the floor?"

Kai grinned and offered Kalea his hand, which she took willingly. "It would be an honour." And with that led her to the floor. The musicians struck up a tune and Kai leaned down and kissed her briefly on the lips to much jeering and with a laugh, lifted her high into the air and spun her round. Then the dancing began. Soon the floor was full of people. As the music ended, Leith stepped in and Kai came back to sit with Arthur, his eyes still fixed on his beautiful bride. Arthur handed him some wine.

"My thanks."

"It does my heart good to see you so happy."

Kai turned to meet his eye. "Thank you. I can't believe I have been so lucky."

Arthur grinned. "You of all people deserve it, Brother." The music was ending. "But now, it is my turn to dance with the most beautiful woman on the dance floor." And slapping Kai on the back, he left.

Kai wasn't alone long as Ellen came and dragged him up to dance. "Ellen! The dress is wonderful," he told her.

"I was inspired when I made it," she replied modestly as Kai whisked around the floor.

Arthur's hand was on Kalea's waist. "Lady, you look radiant."

Kalea's laughed happily. "That is because I am so happy that I am almost overflowing."

"Everything is how you want it?" he asked.

"I couldn't wish for more," she answered as he swirled her round the dance floor.

Valim smiled as he watched the Harvest Queen dancing and laughing. The goddess looked favourable on this young woman. She was positively glowing with inner happiness. Thrice he had sought this woman for the gods and thrice he had been thwarted. Both men and women had rallied to protect her from him. He had used all of his druid arts, and they were not inconsiderable, and yet she evaded him still. The very goddess he sought to serve seemed to be aiding her daughter and not him.

He watched as Kalea danced with one man after another. Her joy infectious. Even Blaise, the young druid, seemed captivated. Was the story over? No. His druid sight told him that the gods still had use for this young woman. He must bide his time and wait until the time was ripe. Perhaps that had been his mistake up until now, he had tried to force the issue and it was not yet time for this woman, so blessed by the goddess, to rise up and be an all-seeing priestess. No. Not the end of the story. The end of a chapter. That was all.

Author's Note

Dear reader, thanks for joining me on my adventure into novel writing. I hope you enjoyed reading it as much as I enjoyed writing it.

I have loved books since I was a child and even spent many years working in a local library (bookworm heaven!).

I can't begin to guess how many books I have read over the years. How many authors I have followed and how many lives I have lived through great stories. These in one way or another, have inspired me to have a go myself.

Now, I have no idea how other authors write their stories, but for me, the story plays out like a film in my head and I am only there to transcribe the events that unfold. In that respect, I am surprised at some of the twists and turns the story takes. Kalea and co came to life and when I thought the story was going one way, my characters took off in a totally different direction. As for the hot sex, blame Kalea.

The Girl Who Dressed Like a Boy was originally, supposed to be a 'one off'. However, as I neared the end, Kalea was shouting that she had more to tell. So, this has become the first of a trilogy based on the three faces of the goddess. The maid, the mother and the crone.

I hope you will follow Kalea's journey to its conclusion.

One last thing, dear reader. We all picture our characters differently as the story unfolds. My curiosity is roused and I would like to know how you see my characters. If it was a film, who would you chose to play the main characters? Visit my website and leave me a message. It will be interesting to see, how close they are to how I imagine them.

CPSIA information can be obtained
at www.ICGtesting.com
Printed in the USA
BVHW052133170323
660681BV00008B/116